THE LAST SAFE HOUSE

A STORY OF THE UNDERGROUND RAILROAD

WRITTEN BY BARBARA GREENWOOD
ILLUSTRATED BY HEATHER COLLINS

KIDS CAN PRESS

For my children: Edward, Martha, Adrienne and Michael — great readers all.
BG

For my favorite designer, Blair.
HC

Kids Can Press acknowledges the financial support of the Ontario Arts Council, the Canada Council for the Arts and the Government of Canada, through the BPIDP, for our publishing activity.

Published in Canada by
Kids Can Press Ltd.
29 Birch Avenue
Toronto, ON M4V 1E2

Published in the U.S. by
Kids Can Press Ltd.
2250 Military Road
Tonawanda, NY 14150

www.kidscanpress.com

Edited by Valerie Wyatt
Designed by Blair Kerrigan / Glyphics
Music (pages 92–93) arranged by Matt Dewar

Printed and bound in China

CM 98 0 9 8 7 6 5 4 3 2
CM PA 98 0 9 8 7 6 5

Canadian Cataloguing in Publication Data

Greenwood, Barbara, [date]
The Last Safe House : a story of the underground railroad

Includes index.
ISBN 978-1-55074-507-8 (bound)
ISBN 978-1-55074-509-2 (pbk.)

1. Underground railroad — Juvenile literature. 2. Fugitive slaves — United States — Juvenile literature. 3. Fugitive slaves — Canada — Juvenile literature. 4. Underground railroad — Juvenile fiction. 5. Fugitive slaves — United States — Juvenile fiction. 6. Fugitive slaves — Canada — Juvenile fiction.
I. Collins, Heather. II. Title.

E450.G73 1998   j973.7'115   C98-930345-4

Kids Can Press is a Corus™ Entertainment company

Acknowledgments

This is a story of a family in St. Catharines, Canada West, in 1856, whose lives are changed when they are asked to help Eliza Jackson, a black girl escaping from slavery. Although the families are fictional, the background is fact, based on information from many reliable sources.

I am indebted to Daniel G. Hill's authoritative history of the life of escaped slaves in Canada, *The Freedom Seekers: Blacks in Early Canada* (The Book Society of Canada / Stoddart, 1981), and to a number of museums that house artifacts and collections pertaining to black history. The North American Black Historical Museum and Cultural Centre in Amherstburg, Ontario, was particularly useful. These, along with many other sources, helped me understand the realities of the Canadian portion of the Underground Railroad. Along with various social histories of the time, they also helped me envision Johanna's initial reaction to the arrival of Eliza Jackson and her subsequent growth in understanding.

In creating the background for my fictional Jackson family, I drew on many first-person accounts of escapes. Particularly useful was Benjamin Drew's *The Narratives of Fugitive Slaves in Canada,* published in 1856. William Still also recorded the stories of escaped slaves who passed through his safe house in Philadelphia. Many of these appear in Charles L. Blockson's *The Underground Railroad* (Prentice-Hall, 1987). Blockson's *The Hippocrene Guide to the Underground Railroad* (Hippocrene, 1994) provided detailed information on various escape routes.

A book of this nature needs a talented illustrator dedicated to historical accuracy. Many thanks to Heather Collins, not only for her painstaking attention to detail but also for the warmth and energy her art projects. And more thanks than I can express to two people who gave me constant encouragement and support through all the vicissitudes of such a large project: my husband and tireless researcher, Robert E. Greenwood, and my editor, Valerie Wyatt, who combines great creativity and sensitivity with her impressive editing skills.

CONTENTS

INTRODUCTION

This is the story of two families who meet in June of 1856.

The Jacksons are fleeing a life of slavery in the southern United States. The Reids live in St. Catharines, Canada West (now Ontario), a community that received hundreds of escaped slaves and helped them find new homes in Canada.

It is also a story of the Underground Railroad, a network of people who passed fugitive slaves in secret, by night, north to freedom. The routes the fleeing slaves used were kept such well-guarded secrets that even today we know only a fragment of the whole story.

The Underground Railroad began in the early 1800s and lasted until 1865. This book tells the fictional story of one family of fugitives and the true stories of many real people who fled to freedom or worked on the Underground Railroad.

Although the Reids and the Jacksons are made-up families, they are typical of many Canadians and Americans who put into action their belief that all people should live in freedom.

Mrs. Leah Jackson Eliza Jackson Ben Jackson

Johanna Reid | Mr. Reid | Mrs. Reid | Tom Reid

MIDNIGHT GUEST

Johanna woke with a start. She listened for the sound that had pierced her sleep. The house was silent except for the wind rustling the elms outside her window. She drew a shaky breath. A nightmare, that's all it was, a nightmare.

"No! No! Don't . . . Help!"

Johanna sat bolt upright. She *hadn't* imagined it. "Mother," she tried to call, but her voice was no more than a croak.

In the bedroom across the hall, a match flared and a candle sprang to light. "Mother!" Johanna tried again, but the light whisked past, throwing her mother's shadow briefly on the wall. The room went dark again and Johanna heard a new sound. Was it sobbing?

And then her father was striding down the hall. His presence made her brave. She slid out of bed and hurried after him. Light from the small candle outlined her father and brother, Tom, hovering at the sewing-room door. She crept nearer, and as she slipped between them, her father held out an arm and drew her close.

"Momma . . . Where's my momma?" The wail broke on a shuddery sob.

Johanna could see her mother bending over the cot that stood against one wall of the room. "What's going on?" she whispered.

Tom started to answer. "She's . . . "

"Go back to bed," her father interrupted quietly. "Your mother will deal with this."

Johanna craned around him. "But who's in there?" There was no answer, only her father's strong hand on the small of her back urging her along the hall. Tom had already disappeared into his room. Did he know what this was all about?

"Time enough in the morning for explanations." Her father's tone was sharper this time. "Go back to sleep."

Sleep? How can I possibly sleep? Johanna crawled into bed, shivering even though the June night was warm. There's nothing to be afraid of. Calm yourself. But when she closed her eyes questions crowded into her mind.

Why the secrecy? They often had guests, but she was always told about them, usually had to make up the bed and tidy the room. Mind you, now that she thought back, something odd *had* been going on. Quizzical looks, lifted eyebrows, half-finished sentences when she came across her parents talking together. And then, this afternoon, a wagon rattling to a brief stop beside her as she walked home from the store. The driver had leaned over. "Message for your pa," he'd said quietly. "Parcel arrives on the evening train." She'd assumed he meant a package from Toronto. Could the message have had another meaning? Tomorrow, she thought, first thing tomorrow I'll find out what's going on.

Johanna woke to kitchen sounds, her head aching from the broken sleep. With bright sunlight chasing away the night fears, she felt vaguely resentful. Tom knows, she decided, so why not me? I can keep a secret.

Dressed and with her bed made, Johanna stepped into the hall and glanced toward the sewing room. The door was ajar. All was silent. She tiptoed along the hall and sidled through the doorway. A small shape, completely covered by the quilt, was curled in the middle of the small bed. As Johanna turned to leave, she heard a sigh. The sleeping guest rolled over and the edge of the quilt flipped down. Johanna gasped. The face, still stained with tears, was black.

Who is she? A girl about my age, but . . . Johanna thought about her father's customers. Some, certainly, were black — escaped slaves who had fled to St. Catharines. Could this girl be one of them? But why was she in their house?

The girl's eyes opened, then widened in alarm. She scrambled to the head of the bed, pressing herself against the wall. In her arms she clutched a doll. My china doll! Johanna had to stop herself from snatching it away. As though reading her mind, the girl dropped the doll on the quilt and pressed herself harder against the wall.

Footsteps clattered up the stairs. Johanna turned to the door but her mother brushed past her. "It's all right, Eliza." Mrs. Reid's voice was soft and soothing, the voice she used to calm fretful babies. "There's nothing to be frightened of. It's just Johanna."

The girl swallowed and nodded as Mrs. Reid patted her hand. Then Mrs. Reid turned toward Johanna. "Eliza's had a bad scare," she said. "Come downstairs and I'll explain while we make breakfast." She stroked Eliza's head. "Now, don't you worry. Everything's all right. You rest and I'll bring you something to eat."

"She's a slave, isn't she?" Johanna asked abruptly when they were in the kitchen.

"Escaped slave," her mother corrected. "And not out of danger yet."

"But she's in Canada. They're free here. Orrin Brown told me he kissed the ground when he stepped off the ferry because he'd never be a slave again."

"Things have changed since Orrin arrived. Slave catchers are coming right across the border now, bold as brass. Why, just a few weeks back, you remember, they nabbed a fugitive down in Windsor. Dragged him onto the ferry in broad daylight. How people could just stand and watch . . . " As she spoke, Mrs. Reid stoked up the stove and set out a large frying pan. "Help me with breakfast, Johanna. Your father will be back any minute now."

By the time Johanna had fried ham slices, ladled out porridge and poured boiling water over tea leaves in the large brown pot, she had heard as much as Mrs. Reid knew of their guest's story — how Eliza escaped from a plantation with her mother and brother, how they traveled from one safe house to another, always heading north. Then their luck turned bad. One night tracking dogs picked up their trail and they had to separate. When they reached the next safe house, there was no sign of her brother, Ben. So Eliza and her mother had to go on without him. But that wasn't the worst of it. A few days later the slave catchers found them, caught Mrs. Jackson and nearly got Eliza, too.

"No wonder she's had nightmares, poor child," Mrs. Reid said.

"But how did she get *here*?"

"Abram Fuller brought her. Fetched her from the American side in a rowboat, after dark last night. He's brought so many slaves across the river lately that his house is being watched. So he brought her here."

Johanna turned this information over in her mind as she set the table. All very well for Mr. Fuller, she thought, but there'd been all sorts of whispering about town. Not everyone welcomed the escaped slaves flooding across the river. What if the girls at school found out? "Is she staying with us?"

"For a while. We'll keep her hidden until Mr. Fuller sends word about her family. Then we'll have to get her to a safer place."

Johanna turned away to hide the sudden relief she felt. Yes, let's keep her a secret. She can stay for a few nights — as long as no one finds out.

After breakfast, Mrs. Reid said, "Have a look through those dresses in the blanket box, Johanna. Eliza's clothes are in tatters after all she's been through."

Sorting through the outgrown dresses, Johanna came across her favorite blue gingham. Her mother had used the leftovers from it to dress Clara, her china doll. The thought of Clara in the stranger's arms irritated her all over again, and now her mother wanted her to be nice to Eliza. She needs someone to talk to, her mother had said. About what? Johanna wondered, folding the blue gingham away carefully. What could we possibly have to talk about? She pulled out an old brown linsey-woolsey and held it up. This will do, she thought.

Eliza was sitting on a chair in the sewing room, her hands folded tightly in her lap, when Johanna came in with the dress. Clara sat primly on the table, her skirts and petticoats spread in a neat circle.

Johanna cast about for something to say. "Mother doesn't think you'll have to stay cooped up in this tiny room for long."

Eliza darted a glance at the dress Johanna had laid on the bed, then looked down at her tightly folded hands. "Place Mist' Fuller fetched me from was lots smaller'n this." Her voice was no more than a whisper.

"Whatever do you mean?"

Eliza sighed, then put out a hand to stroke the dress. "We was headed for our last stop on the Underground Railroad." Her voice was so low, Johanna had to strain to hear. "Freedom's just a step away, they said. Look for the lantern in the upstairs window and we'd be safe." She paused and glanced up at Johanna. Then she looked down at her hands again.

"So we walked all night. I was near to droppin' by the time we saw the light. Just afore dawn it was, but the missus, she took us into the kitchen, nice as anything. 'Just set there a minute,' she says. 'I'll stir up this

fire and make you some breakfast.' Pan fries, it was. My mouth could just about taste 'em." A smile flickered across Eliza's face, then died. "Heard a great fuss out in the yard. Shoutin' and I don't know what. The missus, she grabs me and stuffs me into a hidey-hole in the wall. 'Stay quiet,' she says, and slides a little door across."

Johanna heard a catch in Eliza's voice. The girl folded her thin arms around her body and started to rock back and forth. She's going to cry again, Johanna thought. As she turned to shout for her mother, she glimpsed the doll. Catching it up from the table, she held it out. Eliza reached for the doll and buried her face in its silky brown hair. After a moment the whispery voice continued.

"Just like being in a coffin, it was. No room to stretch or turn. But I could hear, clear as day. Shoutin' and boots stompin' down the stairs and then — shriekin' an' cryin'. And me clawin' at the door because that was my momma. But try as I might, I couldn't shift that door. Nothin' I could do. Just laid my face on that dusty floor an' cried and cried."

Eliza's voice trailed off. She dashed tears from her cheeks. "Musta fell asleep. Next thing I know, there's hands pullin' at me and me fightin' them. Then I see it's the missus. She sets me on my feet. Nearly fell over, I was so stiff. And then she tells me. Slave catcher has my momma."

Eliza stopped again and squeezed her eyes shut to hold back the tears. She drew a ragged breath, then she set her jaw and said through clenched teeth, "But she promised they'd find her. And Mist' Fuller, he promised they'd find her an' . . . an' I know my momma will fight them." Then the fierceness went out of her voice. Her shoulders sagged. "But I don't know." She nestled one cheek into the doll's hair. "Bad things happen."

All the rest of the day, Johanna thought about Eliza's story. As she ironed and folded, peeled and chopped, washed and dried, pictures flashed through her mind — the tiny, dark hiding place in the wall, the booted men on the stairs, the screaming woman. Was the same slave catcher still after Eliza?

"What I don't understand," Johanna said late that afternoon as she sat helping her mother peel potatoes, "is why a slave catcher would bother with Eliza. She's just a girl, not even as old as me."

Mrs. Reid pursed her lips. "Everything to do with slavery is hard to understand." She put down her knife and sighed. "According to Abram Fuller, Eliza and her mother are good household servants. That makes them valuable."

"Even so, to come all the way to Canada . . . "

"Mr. Fuller says their owner has offered a very large reward. Enough to make it worthwhile for a slave catcher to cross the border. It's happened before, Johanna. People who thought they were safe . . . No one must know she's here. You understand, don't you?"

Johanna nodded. But what if he *does* show up here? The thought made her hand tremble so that the paring knife slipped and drew a bead of blood. What would we do? What *could* we do?

THE UNDERGROUND RAILROAD

The Reids' house in St. Catharines, Canada West (now Ontario), was the end of a long, dangerous and frightening journey for Eliza. When she and her family ran away from a small plantation in Virginia, they knew only that freedom lay far to the north. They had also heard the rumor, whispered at night in the slave quarters, that somewhere there was a road, an underground railroad, that would carry them to freedom.

There was not, of course, an actual road running underground. But there was a network of farmers and townsfolk who worked in secret to pass the runaways from one safe house to another. They were angry about the treatment of the slaves, who were often whipped the moment they were caught. So they began watching out for fugitives and hiding them in their homes and barns until the pursuers gave up and left. Then they gave the runaways food for their journey and information to help them find their way north.

How did this pathway to freedom get such a strange name? In 1831, a plantation owner chasing a fugitive slave named Tice Davids reported that he'd almost caught the runaway, practically had him in his hands, when he seemed to disappear into thin air. No matter how hard he searched, the owner never set eyes on Davids again. "It was almost," the baffled plantation owner said, "as though he'd disappeared onto an underground road." Later the name was changed to Underground Railroad because the fugitives seemed to move as fast as the new steam trains that crisscrossed the country.

Before 1850, slaves were free once they reached a northern state that had outlawed slavery. But the Fugitive Slave law of 1850 forced all Americans, even those in free states, to help slave owners capture escaped slaves. As a result, fugitives had to travel farther north to Canada to find freedom. Even then they needed help to stay out of the clutches of slave catchers.

Some "stations" had hidden rooms and tunnels leading to secret forest paths.

KEEPING THE SECRET

"Parcel arrives on the evening train." This sounds like a straightforward message, but to a person who recognized the code, it carried a hidden meaning. When Mrs. Reid heard it, she knew a fugitive would arrive that evening.

Code words were essential to keep the activities of the Underground Railroad secret. The runaways were called "parcels" or "freight." The person showing them the way was a "conductor." The safe houses were "stations" and the people running them "station agents." Using these code words, a message was sent to alert the next station to prepare for the arrival of a fugitive. If the message fell into the wrong hands, it would be taken for news about a shipment arriving by train.

Codes were used by slaves long before they made contact with the Underground Railroad. Many used music to send messages from plantation to plantation. Someone singing about "crossing the river" was passing on information about how to escape by crossing the Ohio River into a free state. "Canaan" and the "Promised Land" were often used as code words for Canada. A slave singing "Steal away, steal away, steal away to Jesus" was alerting other slaves that an escape attempt was coming up. When the punishment for doing or saying anything that angered the owners was a flogging, slaves needed secret ways to communicate just to survive.

THE ROAD TO FREEDOM

The Underground Railroad had many routes. All led as directly as possible from the slave-holding states of the southern United States to the closest free territory. After 1850, escaping slaves had to go all the way to Canada. That meant weeks, sometimes months, of walking.

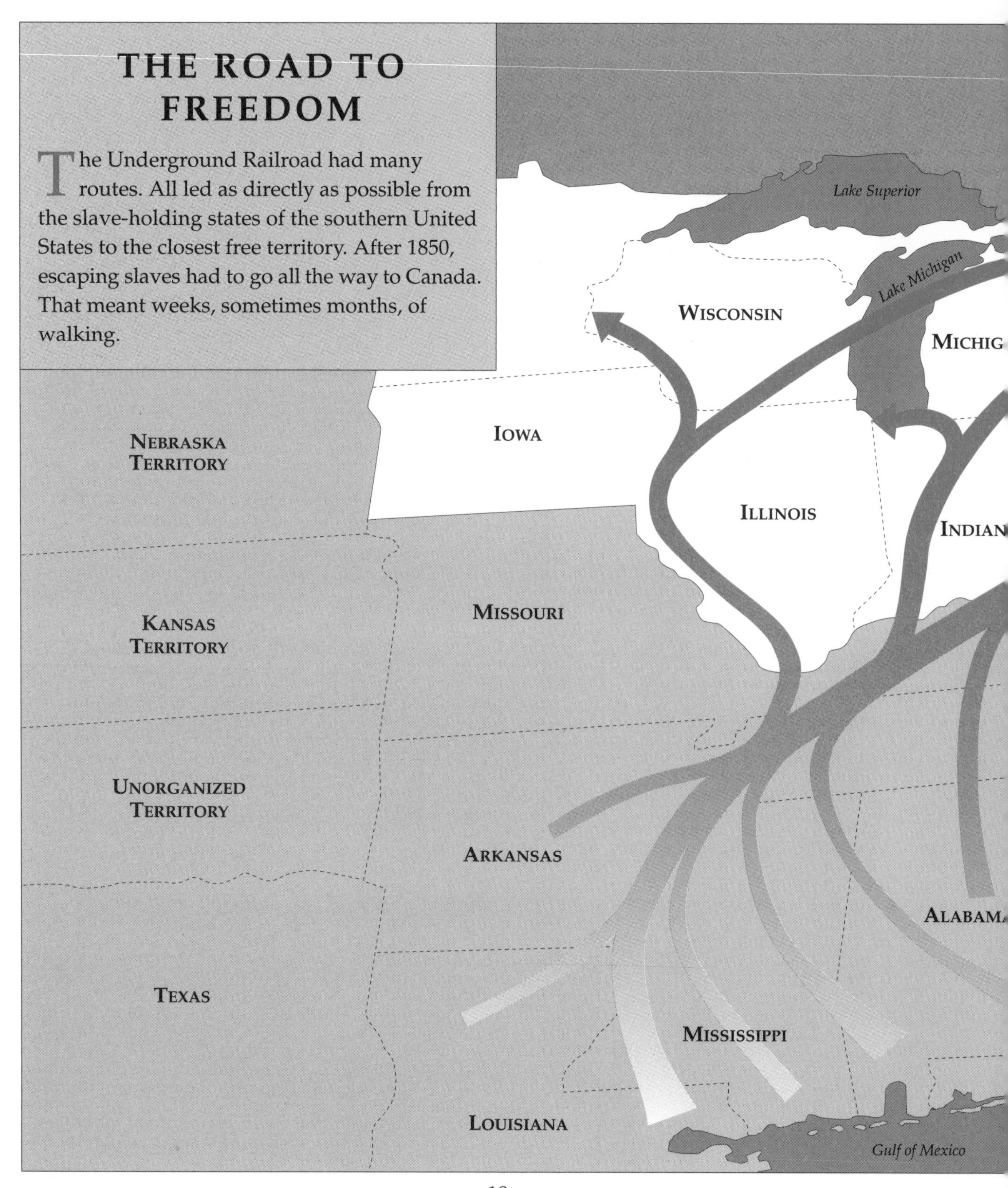

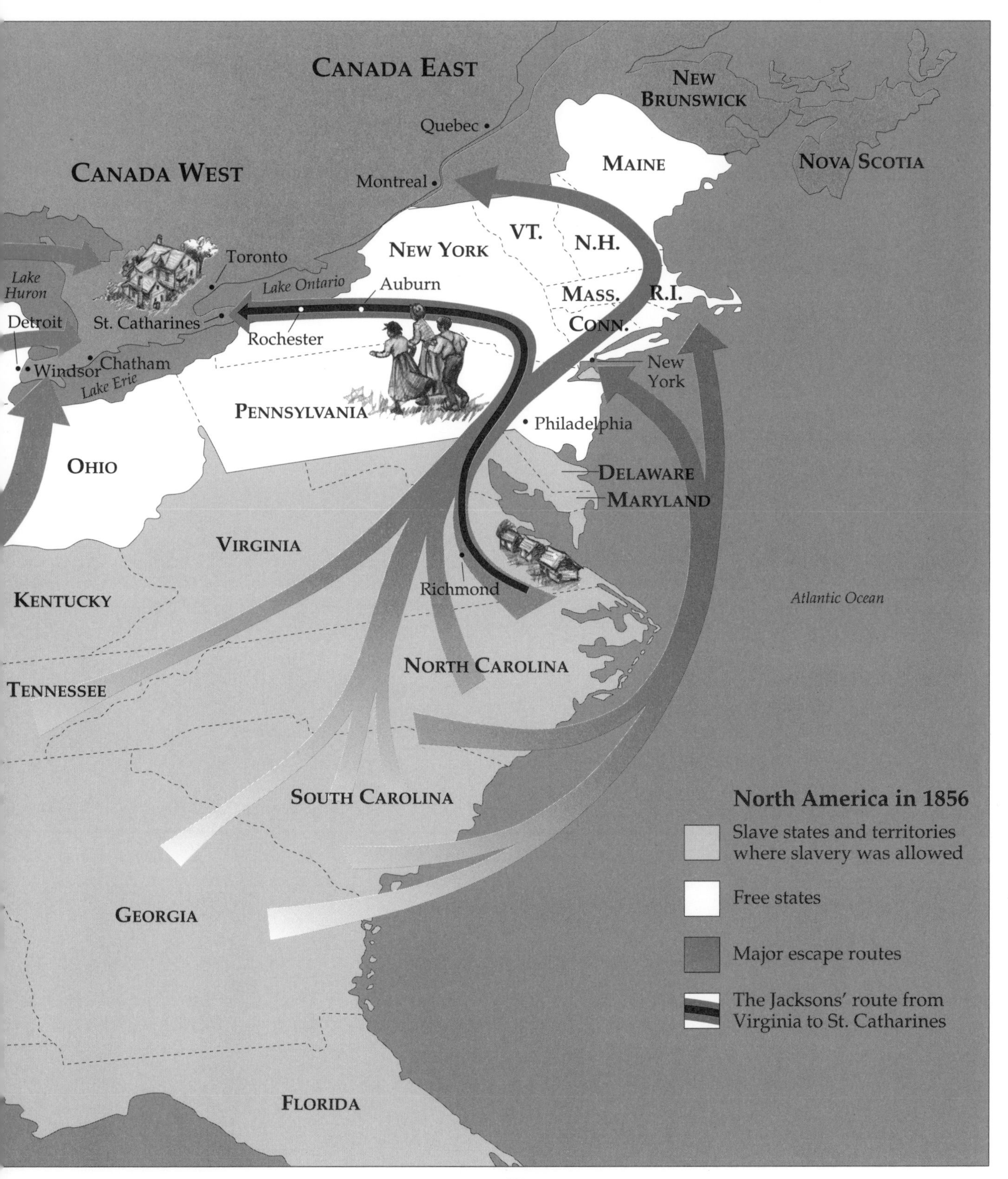
Canada East
New Brunswick
Quebec
Maine
Nova Scotia
Canada West
Montreal
VT.
N.H.
New York
Toronto
Lake Huron
Lake Ontario
Auburn
Mass.
R.I.
Detroit
St. Catharines
Rochester
Conn.
Windsor
Chatham
New York
Lake Erie
Pennsylvania
Philadelphia
Ohio
Delaware
Maryland
Virginia
Kentucky
Richmond
Atlantic Ocean
North Carolina
Tennessee
South Carolina
North America in 1856
Slave states and territories where slavery was allowed
Free states
Major escape routes
The Jacksons' route from Virginia to St. Catharines
Georgia
Florida

A WOMAN CALLED MOSES

The most famous code name on the Underground Railroad was "Moses." In the Bible, Moses led the Israelites out of slavery in Egypt to freedom in the Promised Land. On southern plantations, when the whisper came floating on the night breeze, "Moses is here," slaves suddenly felt hope. Moses had led many to freedom. Perhaps this time it would be their turn.

The conductor code-named Moses made 19 trips into the southern states and led more than 300 fugitives to freedom in Canada. Even though slave owners posted a reward of the incredibly large sum of $40 000, Moses was never captured. Few people at the time knew that this courageous freedom fighter was an escaped slave named Harriet Tubman.

Harriet was born in Maryland about 1820. Although she and her ten brothers and sisters worked hard for their owner, they were often whipped. Once Harriet was struck by a chunk of wood that had been thrown at another slave. Badly treated though she was, Harriet never considered running away until she heard that two of her brothers were to be sold.

The prospect of her family being torn apart made Harriet think about her life. "I will have freedom or I will have death," she decided.

Harriet could neither read nor write, but her father, an expert woodsman, had taught her to move silently through the forest, to tell her direction from the stars and to find edible plants in the woods. Using these skills, she fled to safety in Philadelphia, Pennsylvania. Although she was free, Harriet could not forget her family. If she could find her own way north, surely she could lead her family to freedom, too. Back she went to the dangerous south. Over several trips, she led not only her sisters and brothers, but also her elderly parents to safety. Then she went back for others.

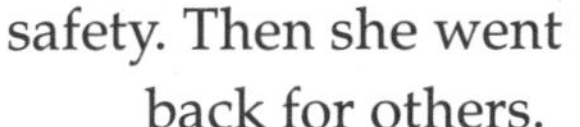

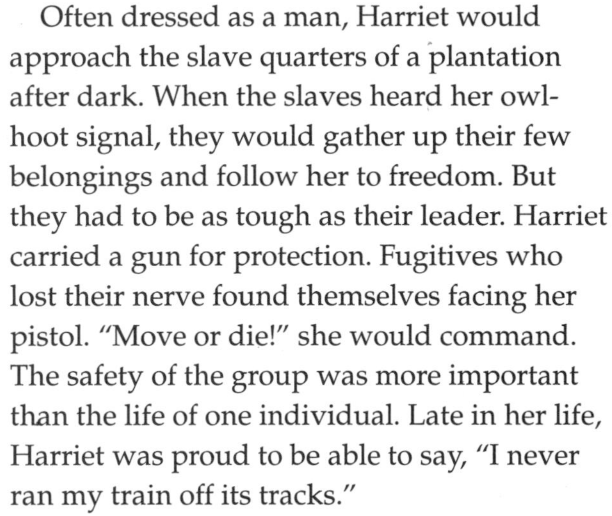

Often dressed as a man, Harriet would approach the slave quarters of a plantation after dark. When the slaves heard her owl-hoot signal, they would gather up their few belongings and follow her to freedom. But they had to be as tough as their leader. Harriet carried a gun for protection. Fugitives who lost their nerve found themselves facing her pistol. "Move or die!" she would command. The safety of the group was more important than the life of one individual. Late in her life, Harriet was proud to be able to say, "I never ran my train off its tracks."

Harriet Tubman used St. Catharines as her headquarters until 1858. During the Civil War (1861–65), she became a nurse and an army scout. By 1863, when President Abraham Lincoln passed the Emancipation Proclamation that freed all slaves, she was living in the small house she had bought for her parents in Auburn, New York. When they died, she invited other needy elderly people to share it with her. That house is now a museum to honor the courageous woman who was called the Moses of her people.

Often dressed as a man, Harriet Tubman would approach the slave quarters of a plantation after dark. When the slaves heard her owl-hoot signal, they would gather up their few belongings and follow her to freedom.

SOLD INTO SLAVERY

Eliza was born a slave, just as her mother and grandmother had been. But Eliza's great-grandmother was born free, on the west coast of Africa. She grew up in a village where she was loved and happy. One day, while she was walking through the jungle with a group of other young people, men jumped across the trail in front of them. The group turned to flee, only to find more men behind them. Some of the strongest young men escaped, but Eliza's great-grandmother and six of her friends were knocked to the ground. Chained to one another, they were forced to walk out of the jungle, away from their village, toward the sea and waiting ships.

The kidnapped young people were herded onto a ship and forced down into the hold with many other prisoners. There, they were packed in like cargo and chained together so closely they could barely move. Fed poorly and in despair because they had been stolen from their homes, many of these young men and women did not survive the six-week voyage across the Atlantic Ocean.

For those who did survive, worse was to come in the new land. They were sold to plantation owners in the southern United States who used whips to force them to work from sunup to sundown. Under the blistering sun, they planted, hoed and harvested sugar cane, tobacco, rice and cotton. Some rebelled and ran off into the swamps and forests, but often starvation drove them back to the plantation. The brutal floggings they received as punishment were used to warn others against running away. Most slaves simply worked until they died under the lash or from disease or exhaustion.

In the 250 years that slavery lasted in the United States, millions of people were sold into bondage so that plantation owners could grow rich selling the sugar, tobacco, rice and cotton grown by their captive laborers.

The misery, fear and longing for home the slaves felt came out in the songs they sang and the stories they told. Later generations of slaves often used stories from the Bible to express their longing for freedom. In one famous song they sang:

Go down, Moses, way down in Egypt land
Tell old Pharaoh to "let my people go."

ELIZA'S STORY

"How did you know where to go?" Johanna asked, as the two girls rolled out cookie dough on the kitchen table.

"Followed the North Star. That's all we knew. Follow the North Star to Canada, the Promised Land."

"The Promised Land? You mean like in the Bible?"

"The very one!" Eliza's face lit up. "A land flowin' with milk and honey, my momma says."

Johanna gave the dough a last roll. Milk and honey! She thought about her arms aching after milking their Daisy and the stings she'd got while gathering honey. Milk and honey don't flow around here without a lot of hard work, she thought.

Not that Eliza shirked hard work. For three days she'd been hidden upstairs while the Reids went about their business, alert for news of strangers. "Can't just sit idle," she'd said, stitching away at the brown linsey-woolsey dress. Rolled carefully on the table beside her was the thread she'd unpicked. "Dress is enough," she'd said. "No need to trouble you for thread."

And this morning, the first day she'd been allowed downstairs, Eliza had immediately pitched in to help with the bread making, then offered to make gingerbread cookies "just like my momma's."

Now, with the dough rolled thin on the table, the girls were stamping out cookies. Johanna slid the last of the circles off the spatula onto the cookie tray. "All done," she sighed, wiping floury hands down her apron.

Eliza was hunched over a triangle of dough, tracing something with the point of a knife. Johanna leaned across to have a look, and Eliza glanced up shyly.

"That's me," she said, flicking the extra dough away from a striding figure. "Runnin' away from the fox. You know that story? I ran away from the little old woman and the little old man — " Johanna chimed in, "And I can run away from you, I can." Eliza clapped her hands and laughed. That's the first time she's laughed since she got here, Johanna realized. Must be the message from Mr. Fuller. "May have located lost parcel," it had read. "Will forward when verified."

"Reckon that story saved my life," Eliza said as she opened the oven door for Johanna.

"How was that?" Day by day they'd heard more of Eliza's story. Just snippets at first, told in a shy whisper, but they'd soon realized that Eliza was a born storyteller. Even Tom was spellbound. Last evening Johanna had caught him sitting on the stairs outside the sewing room, listening to Eliza spin stories as she stitched.

"Goodness, girls, aren't you done yet?" Mrs. Reid bustled in from the parlor where she'd been filling the oil lamps. "We'll have to get started at the noon meal soon."

Eliza muttered, "Sorry, missus," but Johanna just raised an eyebrow at her mother's retreating back. It wouldn't take a minute to wash up, for goodness' sake.

Eliza started scrubbing down the table, using a knife to scrape the leftover flour and bits of dough into the mixing bowl.

"Oh, that can wait," Johanna said, sitting down. "The washing-up water hasn't even boiled yet. First I want to know how that story saved your life." She waved at a chair and Eliza flopped down, arms leaning on the kitchen table. Her eyes glazed with a faraway look.

"It was right after Ben went missin'," she started, and for a second her eyes clouded. "Man helpin' us says we gotta move along fast. So we come into a little town flat out on the bottom of a wagon, under a load of hay. Nothing so prickly as hay when you have to keep still. And the bouncin'! Near shook us to pieces. Drove right into the barn so's no one would see us. We'd just crawled out of that scratchy old hay pile when the missus come runnin'.

"'Get them out of here,' she says, all panicky. 'Two men just rode into town with a marshal.' She was real scared. Big trouble for them if they was caught helping us. The man tells us to get back in the wagon and he'll take us to the next safe house. But my momma, she's looking out the barn door and she says, 'Scuse me, missus. Notice you got laundry all bundled up. How's if we carry it on down the street like we's taking it for washin'?' The man, he thinks that's a mighty fine idea. 'Watch for a house with two sycamores out front,' he says."

Just then the kettle started to burble.

"Don't stop! Don't stop!" Johanna jumped up to pour hot water over the dishes in the washing-up bowl. But nothing could stop Eliza now. On she went as they washed and dried and put away.

"My heart was near poundin' out of my chest. Walk down the middle of the street, right under the noses of those slave catchers? Laws! But my momma says, 'Liza, you remember that gingerbread boy? Well, *we* run away from the little old man and the little old woman. No reason on God's green earth why we can't run away from the fox.'"

Eliza's eyes danced. "And she was right. We marched down that street with laundry on our heads like we belonged. My heart near jumped into my mouth when those men come clip-cloppin' up the street. Momma, she says, 'Keep your eyes down and your back straight.' Then she sails right on past them, with me comin' along behind. In no time, we were at the safe house, creepin' like moles through a tunnel into the woods. And my momma squeezin' my hand and whisperin', 'Fooled you, Mr. Fox.'"

And Eliza was up, whirling about the room. "Fooled you, Mr. Fox. Fooled you!"

"Look out!" Johanna cried, just too late. The mixing bowl Eliza had been clutching sailed out of her arms and smashed against the stove.

Mrs. Reid whisked back into the kitchen. "Really, girls," she said crossly.

Eliza's face went blank. Then suddenly she was shrinking into the corner, covering her head with her arms. "Sorry, missus, sorry . . . didn't mean . . . sorry." With each "sorry" she cowered farther into the corner.

Mrs. Reid's frown softened. "My dear, it's all right," she said quietly. "It's just a bowl."

Eliza nodded and crept out of the corner. She scooped the pieces into her apron and backed away, flinching as Mrs. Reid reached to take them from her.

Why, she's terrified, Johanna thought, terrified of my mother, who wouldn't harm a soul.

Even when her gingerbread girl came out of the oven, Eliza was quiet. After she'd helped peel potatoes she said in a subdued voice, "Better go back upstairs."

Johanna and her mother worked on in silence. Finally Johanna burst out, "Why all that over a broken bowl?"

Mrs. Reid gave the gravy a few more stirs, then she sighed. "You know what your father says — you can always tell if a dog's been mistreated. I imagine it's the same with a person."

"But a broken bowl? You wouldn't . . . "

"No, but where Eliza's been, from the stories I've heard . . ."

"You mean she's been beaten for breaking something?"

"Or for a lot less, I'll wager. You know what Orrin Brown told us — a lot of the owners treat their slaves like animals. Beat them for any little thing. Eliza doesn't understand that things are different here." Then, in her usual brisk tone, "Now go and bring her down for dinner. It's just ready to go on the table."

Johanna turned slowly toward the stairs. What could she possibly say to reassure Eliza? Then she saw, cooling on the window ledge, Eliza's gingerbread girl. Carefully she picked it up and started upstairs.

Eliza was rocking as she sat on the bed, the china doll in her arms. She seemed to be murmuring into its ear. When she saw Johanna she sat up straight and thrust the doll away.

"It's all right," Johanna said. "You can play . . . you can hold her."

"I had a doll. My momma made it for me." Eliza smoothed the china doll's blue gingham skirt lovingly. "She was carryin' it for me in her apron pocket when those men snatched her."

Johanna struggled for words to comfort Eliza. Should she remind her about Mr. Fuller's note? But what if he hadn't found Ben? Then she remembered the gingerbread girl. "Look!" She held it out to Eliza. "It's you — running free."

Eliza looked at the little figure for a long minute. "No." She shook her head. "Not free. Just runnin'. Til they find my momma and Ben — just runnin'."

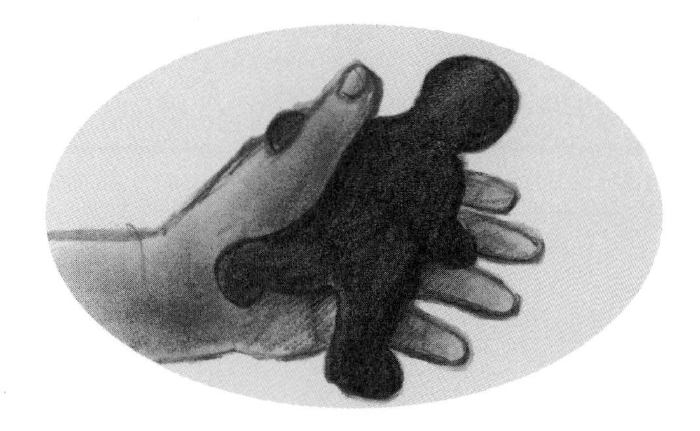

A COTTON PLANTATION

The Jacksons' run for freedom started on a plantation in Virginia. A plantation is a large farm on which one main crop is grown. In some areas of the southern States the crop was tobacco. Sugar or rice was grown in hot, moist areas. But the most important crop was cotton.

Plantations were far from towns, so each one had to produce all the food, clothing and goods that the owner and the slaves needed.

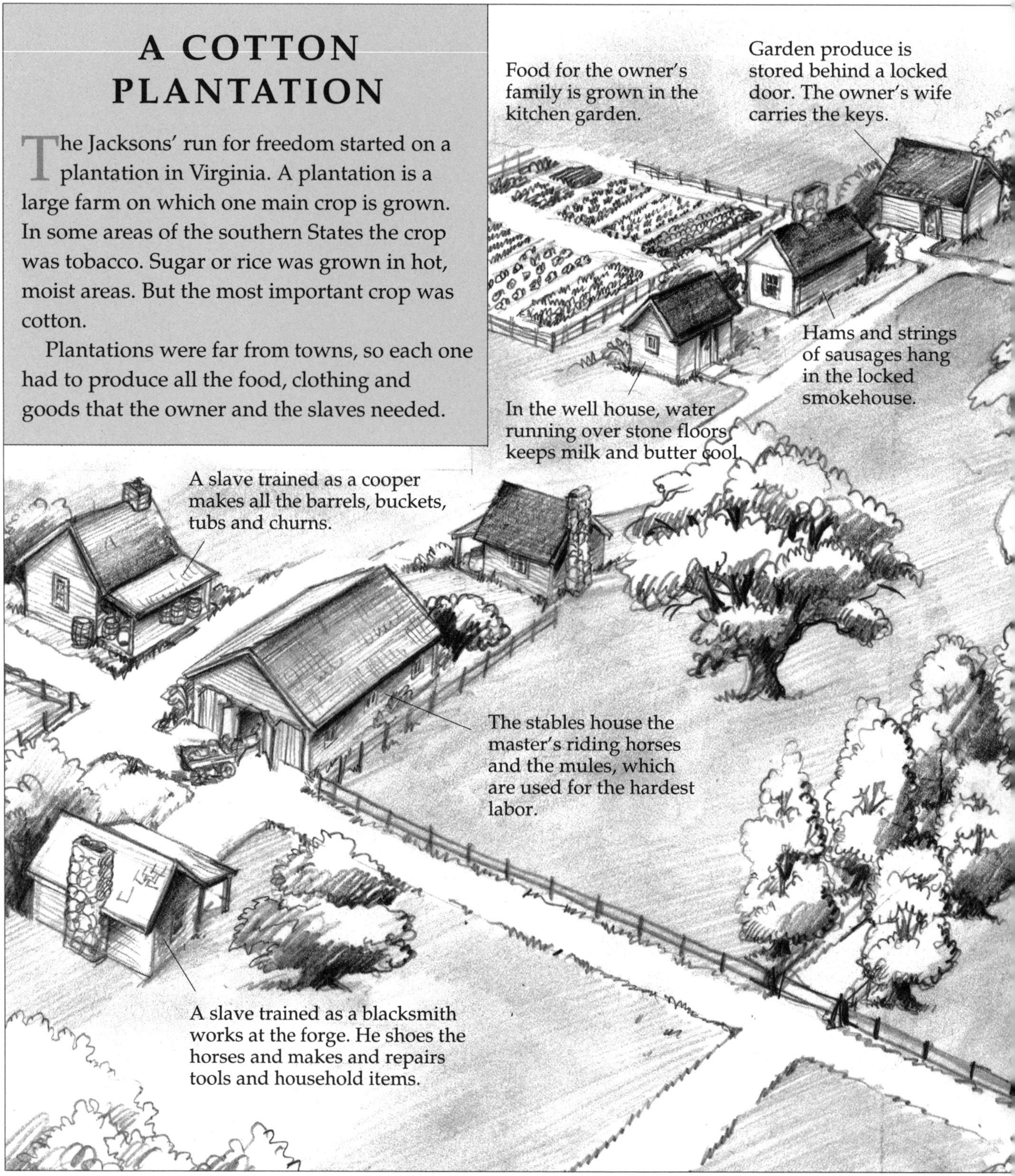

Food for the owner's family is grown in the kitchen garden.

Garden produce is stored behind a locked door. The owner's wife carries the keys.

Hams and strings of sausages hang in the locked smokehouse.

In the well house, water running over stone floors keeps milk and butter cool.

A slave trained as a cooper makes all the barrels, buckets, tubs and churns.

The stables house the master's riding horses and the mules, which are used for the hardest labor.

A slave trained as a blacksmith works at the forge. He shoes the horses and makes and repairs tools and household items.

The owner, or master, and his family live in the Big House.
In the laundry, slaves wash and iron clothes for the owner's family.
In several small buildings, slaves make soap and candles or weave, dye and sew cloth.
The kitchen, with its large fireplace, is in a separate building, to keep the Big House cool.
Rows of cabins make up the slave quarters. Often a family of six or eight lives in one cabin.

WORKING IN THE BIG HOUSE

When Eliza was born, her mother prayed that her daughter would be trained to work in the Big House, where the master and his family lived. Household work was hard but it was not as backbreaking as working in the fields from sunup to sundown. So Leah Jackson was delighted when her mistress decided that Eliza, at six years old, would begin to learn how to cook, sew and help with the laundry.

COOKING

In the kitchen building, the mistress supervised one or two slaves in the work of preserving the garden produce and cooking the meals for the family. There was no stove, only a large fireplace where geese, chickens, pork and even opossum were cooked. Sweet potatoes and collard greens boiled with peas were favorite vegetables. Eliza helped by shelling peas and turning geese roasting on the spit.

Every morning Leah Jackson got up early to make spoon bread or corn bread for the master's breakfast. Once a week she baked yeast bread. Then, while the oven was still hot, she put in cakes, pies and cookies. As Eliza pitted cherries or cut out molasses cookies with a cup, she watched her mother and learned how to cook and bake for the family in the Big House.

SEWING

Every year the mistress bought bolts of cotton cloth and linsey-woolsey, a combination of wool and linen or cotton, to make summer and winter clothes for the slaves. Eliza learned to sew by helping her mother and the other slave women make dozens of simple shirts, pants and skirts. She also helped piece together the scraps for quilts.

All the sewing was done by hand, even after sewing machines became available in 1845. In the south there were always enough hands to do the work the old-fashioned way. Because Leah was a fine seamstress, she often made frilled petticoats and drawers for the master's children. Once she was allowed to use leftover scraps of blue calico to dress a doll for Eliza.

LAUNDRY

On washing day, Leah started by boiling all the white things in a big copper boiler. She put the dyed clothes in a tub of warm water so they wouldn't fade. Then she scrubbed soiled spots on a wooden washboard. With a large pronged stick she lifted the soapy clothes into tubs of cool rinse water. She used a wooden wringer to squeeze water out of the heavy sheets. Small things were wrung out by hand.

Eliza helped by spreading handkerchiefs and collars on the grass to dry and bleach in the sun. She stretched damp stockings over foot-shaped boards to keep them from shrinking. By the time the laundry was hung out to dry everyone was exhausted. But the work was far from over. It took most of the next day to do the ironing.

Making Gingerbread Cookies

One of the specialties Leah made for the master's children was gingerbread. At Christmas she cut out little gingerbread people for the children to string with dried cranberries.

You can make gingerbread cookies or a running gingerbread figure like the one Eliza cut out.

You'll need:

- 75 mL (1/3 c.) butter
- 75 mL (1/3 c.) brown sugar
- 1 egg, well beaten
- 15 mL (1 tbsp.) baking powder
- pinch of salt
- 5 mL (1 tsp.) ground ginger
- pinch of ground allspice or cloves
- 10 mL (2 tsp.) ground cinnamon
- 750 mL (3 c.) flour
- 150 mL (2/3 c.) molasses
- currants or raisins for decoration

1. Ask an adult to turn the oven to 200°C (400°F).

2. In a large bowl, mix together the butter and brown sugar until creamy. Stir in the beaten egg.

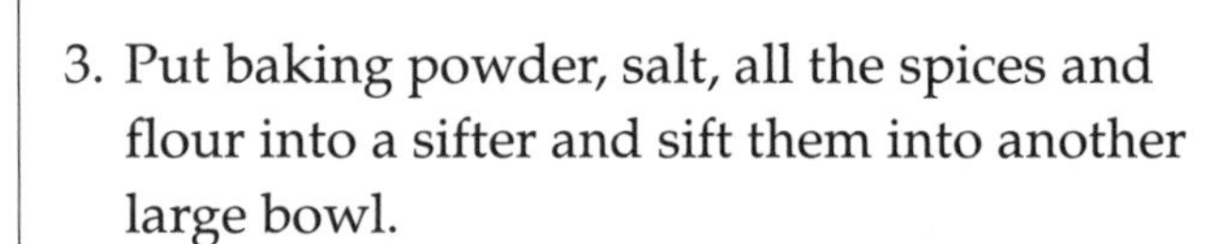

3. Put baking powder, salt, all the spices and flour into a sifter and sift them into another large bowl.

4. To the first mixture add a spoonful of the dry ingredients and mix well. Then add a spoonful of molasses and mix well. Continue until all the dry ingredients and molasses are used up. The dough will be stiff.

5. Turn the dough onto a square of wax paper. Roll it up and refrigerate for two hours.

6. Sprinkle some flour onto the counter and roll out the dough to a thickness of 0.5 cm (1/4 in.).

7. Cut out gingerbread figures or other shapes. Make faces and buttons from currants or raisins. Use a spatula to transfer the cookies to a baking tray that has been greased with butter.

8. Ask an adult to put the tray into the oven. Bake for ten minutes.

9. Use a spatula to transfer the cookies to a rack. Let them cool.

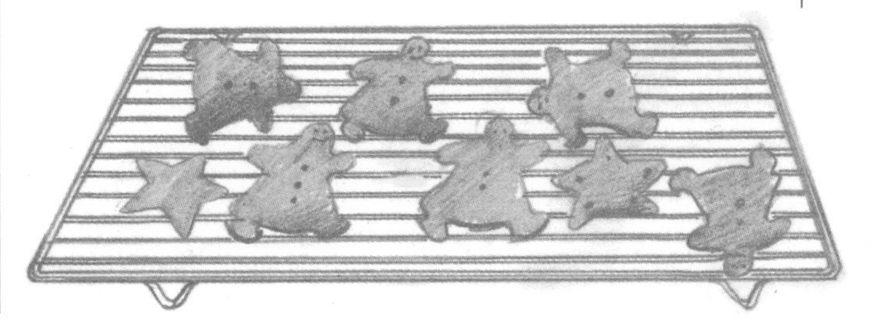

DECIDING TO RUN

"That girl's coming up 11. Bright, well trained and biddable. And the boy's good and strong. They'd fetch a fine price at auction. And we could sure do with the money."

Those words struck terror into Leah Jackson's heart. She'd worked hard for her owners and made her children behave well in the hope that this would be their home forever. But now the master was talking about putting Eliza and Ben on the auction block.

Selling slaves was not unusual. Owners had complete control over their slaves' lives. They decided where slaves lived, what they worked at, and how many hours a day they worked. They also had the right to sell their slaves, even if it meant breaking up families.

Slaves were sold at auction in the town marketplace. Here the slaves stood up on platforms, called auction blocks, so that customers could look them over and bid for them.

Leah herself had gone to the auction block once. Back when she was a young mother she had worked on a large plantation as a laundress and cook. Her husband, Sam, was the plantation blacksmith. They were useful and well-thought-of by the master's family. Then one day Sam learned that his brother and three other slaves were to be sold to pay the master's gambling debts. He knew what that meant. The best way to make money was to sell slaves "down the river," to a cotton plantation on the southern Mississippi River. There, brutal overseers worked the field hands almost to death. Sam's strong, young brother would fetch more than $1000 from a cotton grower.

After midnight, reckless with grief and rage, Sam slipped out to the shed where his brother and the others were manacled to a post. Using his blacksmith's tools he snapped their chains, then he watched them run off into the night. Somehow the master found out. As punishment, Sam himself was sold south. Leah, with her baby and toddler, was also sent to the auction block. The master didn't want any rebellious slaves on his plantation.

Leah never forgot the humiliation of standing up on the auction block while buyers looked her up and down as though she were a prize mare. She was determined that her children would never suffer that fate, even if it meant running away.

Like many other slaves who had decided to run, Leah sang in her heart what she didn't dare breathe out loud until she reached freedom:

No more auction block for me,
No more, no more.
No more auction block for me.
Many thousand gone.

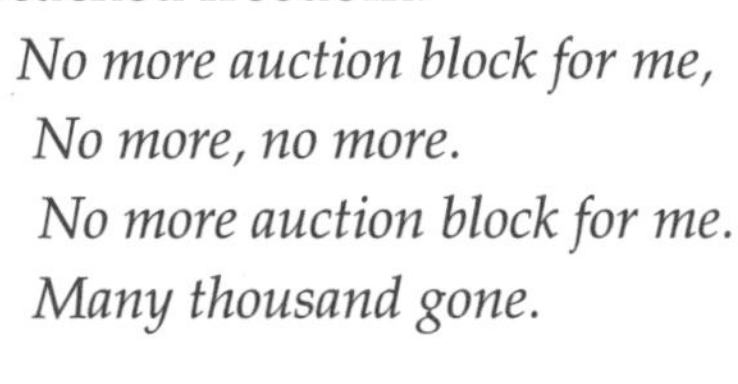

Follow the North Star

When Eliza and her family started out for Canada, they had no maps, only a saying to guide them: "Follow the North Star."

Sailors and explorers have always used the stars to help them find their way. To sight the stars, they had instruments called astrolabes. Fugitive slaves had no such instruments. Instead, they used a constellation called the Big Dipper to help them find the North Star.

You too can find the North Star.

Look for the Big Dipper. Find the two stars that form the side of the dipper farthest from the handle. Imagine a line joining these stars and continuing out into the sky. Look for a bright star all by itself along this line. This is Polaris, or the North Star. When you are facing Polaris you are facing north.

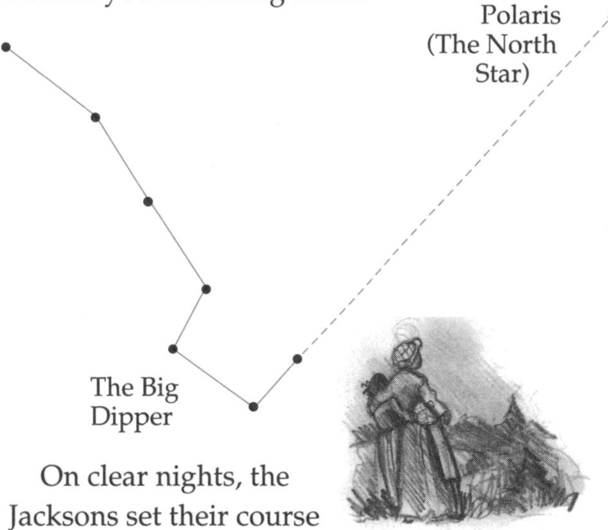

On clear nights, the Jacksons set their course by the North Star. One night when clouds blocked their view, Ben remembered a hint he'd been given at the start of their journey: moss is always thickest on the north side of a tree. Look for moss growing up the trunks of trees. See if you can find north this way.

SLAVERY IN CANADA

Slaves who had heard that freedom lay to the north thought of Canada as the Promised Land. But Canada had not always been a land of freedom.

Early settlers needed laborers to help clear the land. Some bought slaves from the American colonies to the south. Others enslaved Native people. More slaves arrived when the American Revolution broke out in 1775. Many fleeing American colonists brought their black slaves to Nova Scotia and Quebec.

John Graves Simcoe, Lieutenant Governor of Upper Canada (now Ontario), tried to abolish slavery in 1793, but too many influential families were slaveholders. He *did* pass a law saying that no more slaves could be brought into Upper Canada and that children born to slaves already in the colony would automatically become free at age 25. The law also made owners accountable if they mistreated their slaves. By 1834, when the British government abolished slavery in all its colonies, Canada was already slave free.

After the United States passed the Fugitive Slave law in 1850, forcing all Americans to return runaways to their owners, Canada became the slaves' only safe haven. Many Canadians were strongly anti-slavery. In 1851 the Anti-Slavery Society of Canada was formed in Toronto to help abolish slavery and house and clothe black fugitives. Other cities and towns had similar organizations.

By 1863, when the Emancipation Proclamation finally freed all slaves in the United States, as many as 60 000 fugitive slaves had found freedom, safety and a new life in Canada.

THE ABOLITIONISTS

People who fought to have slavery made illegal called themselves abolitionists because they wanted to abolish, or completely do away with, a practice they felt was wrong.

Among the earliest abolitionists was the Society of Friends, a religious group often called Quakers. They believed that all people were equal in the sight of God. The Quakers not only refused to own slaves, they believed it was their duty to help slaves escape to freedom. Often they were fined or jailed for their actions.

Abolitionists tried many different ways to change public opinion about slavery. Harriet Beecher Stowe used the power of a story to make people think. In her novel, *Uncle Tom's Cabin*, she told the story of a kindly old slave beaten by a cruel master named Simon Legree. It convinced many people in the northern states that slavery had to be abolished. When war was declared between the northern and southern states, the story of Uncle Tom was one of the reasons northerners were so willing to fight.

LEVI COFFIN

The most famous Quaker abolitionist was Levi Coffin. He and his wife, Catherine, lived in Newport (now Fountain City), Indiana, on a route of the Underground Railroad. By building hidden rooms and cellars in their home, they were able to hide many runaways. Later they continued their work in Cincinnati. For over 35 years they helped more than 2000 slaves on their way to freedom.

Although he and his wife gave much practical help to runaways, Levi Coffin is best known for influencing others to get involved. He was a successful storekeeper and business people trusted him. When he needed money to help the conductors and station agents on the Underground Railroad buy food and clothing, he was able to raise it quickly from these contacts. He traveled up and down the Underground Railroad encouraging workers and seeing for himself that runaways were being treated well. He even visited Canada to see how runaways were settling into their new communities. Coffin's work for fugitive slaves earned him the honorary title of president of the Underground Railroad.

BEN ON THE RUN

"Am I truly here? Safe and free?" Ben could hardly see Eliza through the sudden rush of tears to his eyes. He swallowed hard. Don't let me cry, he thought.

"Free! And safe at last." Eliza's words echoed his. "Now if only Momma was here."

Ben blinked back tears. He hadn't allowed himself to think of Eliza or Momma for a long time. He brushed a hand across his eyes and looked down at his little sister who was hugging him tightly around the waist.

The Reids had left brother and sister alone in the kitchen after the first excitement of Ben's arrival had died down. "There's soup in the pot on the back burner," Mrs. Reid had said as she shooed her family out the door. "Your brother will need something warm in his stomach after what he's been through."

"Set down and eat," Eliza said, placing a bowl of soup on the table.

She took up a knife and started slicing the new loaf of bread Mrs. Reid had put out beside a large wedge of cheese. "Couldn't believe my eyes when you come through that door," she chattered on. "Heard a wagon pull into the yard and the missus, she says to hustle upstairs, just in case. Next thing, the door opens and there you are."

Ben sat at the table silently spooning up his soup. It was almost too much to take in. First the ride across the bridge crammed inside one of Mr. Fuller's cider barrels, then Mr. Fuller telling him about the surprise waiting in St. Catharines.

The kitchen door opened, startling him. Would he ever stop jumping at little noises? Mr. Reid came in shaking rain off his hat. "Thunderstorm," he said. "Abram'll be caught halfway home, I shouldn't wonder." Tom followed him in, his arms full of kindling. And then Mrs. Reid and Johanna were back in the kitchen, pulling chairs up to the table.

"Tell what happened since we lost you," Eliza said, taking away his empty bowl.

"Wouldn't mind hearing about that myself," Mr. Reid added, lighting his pipe with a rolled paper spill.

Ben didn't know what to do with his hands. He wasn't used to just sitting and talking. A pile of newspaper squares sat on the table. Almost without thinking, he picked one up and began rolling it into a spill. Eliza offered him the jar half full of spills she'd already rolled. He smiled at her and then looked shyly around the ring of faces.

Why were they so interested? His little sister, yes, she'd want to know. But these strangers? All the way north he'd wondered about that — why would so many strangers care what happened to him?

He cleared his throat. Where to start? "On the run five days, Eliza and Momma and me," he began hesitantly, feeling shy with all the eyes on him.

"Sixth night out there's a full moon. Near bright as day. Shoulda stayed put, but we kept goin' anyways. That's when they spotted us. A patrol with four dogs, huntin' hounds. 'Only chance,' Momma says, 'split up.' Closest cover's a big forest. I was lost in no time. Then come the swamp."

And suddenly he was back in that moment, with the muffled yelping of the hounds sounding behind him and a narrow trail twisting away into darkness before him. Had the dogs picked up his scent? As he pounded barefoot along the unfamiliar path he prayed for a creek he could run through to break his trail. Or should he climb a tree? Would that confuse the dogs? Or would he just be stuck up there waiting for them? Desperately he ran on, every bump and root on the path pummeling his feet until they went numb.

Something clutched at his ankle and he pitched headlong onto the hard-packed mud of the trail. Snake! He drew a sharp breath. No. Only a trailing vine tripping him up. He let out his breath slowly. Then he heard the dogs again, muffled but still following. Get up! Get up!

He put his palms flat on the ground and pushed. With a sickening squelch his right hand disappeared into slippery mud. His arm was buried past the elbow before he managed to wiggle backward, keeping his weight spread over the firm path behind. Slowly he pulled free of the mud's gluey grasp. One more step and he would have plunged right into those sucking sands and been swallowed alive. As his pounding heart slowed, he heard again, faint but following, the baying of hounds.

Despair washed over him. How could he find a way out? Crouching on the pathway staring into the dark, he imagined the tree limbs twisting and twining into an impenetrable wall ahead of him. But the urgency that had driven him this far kept prodding him. There must be a way. There must!

Wait. What was that? A flicker of light! Fireflies? No, more like a glowing ball bobbing slowly toward him. Fear raised cold prickles on his scalp. Swamp ghosts! He'd heard tell of them. Always moved in a ball of light, they did.

"Ah, there you are, brother. Praise be." The scratchy whisper came from behind the light. "We knew someone was runnin'," the voice continued. "We heard the dogs. Rise up, brother, and follow."

Ben scrambled to his feet. Behind the soft lantern glow he glimpsed a frizz of white hair and the flash of a smile. Not a ghost. A flesh and blood human being. "But the swamp . . ." And the dogs, he thought, now that he could see how frail and wizened this old man was.

"The path of the just is as a shining light. Take this, brother. Drag it behind you and follow close."

Out of the stench of rotting vegetation rose a more pungent smell that caught at Ben's throat and brought tears to his eyes. Dead skunk, he thought, feeling a weight swinging at the end of the rope he'd been handed. Goodbye, dogs. Towing the skunk behind him, he hurried after his guide, who was striding into the wall of darkness.

All around, Ben sensed the treachery of the swamp. But his feet, following closely behind the little man, felt the path firm and safe underneath. Where had he come from, this swamp angel?

"His voice is as the sound of many waters." The whisper drifted back from the bobbing lantern. And Ben glimpsed in front of them a black gleam of water and a small boat moored to a post.

"Climb aboard, brother."

When Ben was seated in the stern, the little man blew out the light, climbed in himself and untied the rope. The boat dipped and bobbed as he swung the oars out, then they were skimming over the water. They seemed to be heading toward a faint light in the distant darkness. Ben dared not ask questions — voices carried over water. His guide was silent now, and even the oars made no sound as they dipped in and out, in and out.

Soon they were gliding up to a dock. As he clambered out of the boat, Ben brushed against the rags that muffled the oarlocks. Halfway up the hill stood a small house with a lantern burning in an upper window. "Look for the lantern," his momma had said. "The lantern will keep you safe."

The little man disappeared through a dark doorway. Ben followed him into a room dimly lit by a dying fire, then froze in his tracks. Had his swamp angel betrayed him? A man sat rocking in a chair. His smile looked friendly, but his face was white.

"Have no fear," said the soft voice from beside him. "In this house, we are all brothers under the skin."

Ben took a deep breath. What choice did he have but to trust them? "Where am I?" he asked at last. "Who are you?"

"Henry's the name," said the man in the chair. "You've fetched up at a station on the Underground Railroad, brother. Your conductor there is Reuben, so I guess that makes me the station agent. You're welcome to hop on board. No guarantees, but we'll do our best to pass you safely along the line."

"What happened next?" Eliza's voice startled Ben out of his trance. The pictures in his head dissolved. What had he been saying? The swamp. He looked around the circle of eager faces and started in to tell the story of Reuben and Henry.

"You were safe from then on?" Mr. Reid asked.

"Safe?" Ben shook his head. "No not safe, just out of sight for a bit."

"How did they pass you along the line?" Tom wanted to know.

"Oh, wily as foxes, those two. Tinsmiths, they were. Next day they

set out in a wagon hung about with lanterns and dippers an' I don't know what all. Under the floorboards there's a hidden cupboard. I crawl in there and off we go. Peddlin' to farmers all up and down the country."

"You could have suffocated!" Johanna exclaimed.

"Downright strangulated most of the time," Ben agreed. "And all that janglin' from the tinware! Near drove me silly. Just when it was comin' on for dark, my little cupboard door opens and Henry, he tells me it's the end of the line. Pretty soon I'm down a cellar ready to move on again."

"So," Mrs. Reid said with a satisfied sigh, "you *did* meet up with good people."

Ben thought about that for a moment and then nodded. In the end, he'd met only with kindness, despite Reuben's parting words. "Be vigilant, brother," Reuben had said, and his usual gentle smile was gone. "Your adversary, the devil, as a roaring lion walketh about, seeking whom he may devour."

And he *had* been vigilant, ready to run at the first sign of trouble. Every time he'd knocked on a door late at night and whispered the password, "A friend of a friend," his stomach had knotted in fear. Could there be others as willing as Reuben and Henry to risk their own safety? But each time the miracle had happened. An opened door, a whispered "Welcome, friend," and he was safe for one more day.

"How long did it take you?" Tom asked.

Ben thought for a moment. "Lost track," he said finally. "Full moon six nights after we run. Another some nights ago."

"Say a month and a bit," Tom decided. "A month of walking." He sounded impressed.

Ben looked at Eliza. She was the only one who really knew what that meant. Not just walking all night, but lying still as death under a load of manure as searchers challenged the driver, or squeezing through a narrow dirt tunnel from a safe house out to the surrounding woods. It wasn't the running. It was the fear.

"And now you're here," Eliza said softly. "Safe at last in our Promised Land."

That brought back another memory — his old master, laughing. "Canada? The Promised Land?" They'd been standing by the plantation gate looking down the road to where a black man in chains shuffled beside a horse and rider. It was Joe from the next place over. There'd been rumors he'd run away.

"You see that, boy?" Massa had said. "That's what thinking about Canada gets you. Didn't even make it through the swamp, that one. And what'll running get you anyway? Canada? It's so cold your toes'll drop right off. You know that ice I got packed in the icehouse? That's Canada — like livin' in that icehouse."

As cold as the icehouse? Ben looked around at the ring of welcoming smiles. No. Old Massa had been clean wrong about a lot of things. And, for sure, this was one. Whatever Canada was, it wasn't cold.

LIFE ON A PLANTATION

As Ben sat and ate with Henry and Reuben that night, they exchanged stories. Reuben told how he had started out life on a southern Mississippi River plantation. From the time he was five until he escaped at fifteen, he had worked in the fields, tending the cotton crop.

Large cotton plantations needed huge gangs of up to 200 workers. An overseer hired by the owner ran the plantation. He handed out each slave's daily task and saw that it was done properly.

For Reuben and the other slaves, life on the plantations of the Deep South was short and brutish. The day started before dawn, when the overseer sounded the horn. In the slave quarters, men, women and children scrambled up from mounds of straw piled on the mud floors of their tiny huts. Hoes in hand, they headed to the fields to plant, cultivate or harvest the crops.

At ten o'clock they were allowed a short break to build fires and cook breakfast. Most made hoecakes by mixing a little cornmeal with water and baking it over the fire on the blades of their hoes. Then it was back to work.

All day the overseer rode up and down the fields. He snapped a long cowhide whip to keep them too scared to talk back or revolt. He flogged anyone who wasn't working hard enough.

After a short break in the afternoon, the slaves worked until dark. Finally, after about 15 hours of hot, backbreaking labor, they were allowed to return to their huts to cook their evening meal. Into a pot of boiling cornmeal they might throw some greens from the tiny gardens many cultivated. And once a week, they would be given a little salt pork or fish. Then they crawled under quilts pieced together from scraps of leftover fabric and slept until the overseer's horn woke them to another day of labor.

Sunday was the only day of rest, the only day to wash clothes, tend their small vegetable patches and enjoy family life. On some plantations, the owner or his wife might arrange a church service for the slaves. Here, the stories they heard and the songs they sang brought a little comfort into lives marked by hard work and abuse.

THE COTTON GIN

Southern plantation owners had been growing cotton for decades before they found an efficient way to remove seeds and dirt from the cotton fibers. In 1793, a Georgia plantation owner, Mrs. Greene, was impressed with the many useful devices a visitor named Eli Whitney had invented for her household. She wondered if he could find a fast way to clean the cotton.

Within days Whitney had developed a machine simple enough to be built by the local blacksmith. He strung wires across the bottom of a box to make a grate. Circular saw blades that fit into the openings between the wires bit into the thick mass of raw cotton in the box, pulling the fibers through the grate and leaving seeds and dirt behind. Using this cotton gin (short for engine), one slave could clean 200 times more cotton than before.

Later Whitney added a waterwheel that turned 80 saws at a time. One gin now cleaned 1000 times more cotton a day. With mills in England and the northern states buying cotton as quickly as it could be shipped, people saw the chance for huge profits. Sadly, the growing demand for cotton meant more slaves were needed, too. Even though importing slaves from Africa had been made illegal in 1808, traders found ways to smuggle them in. As slaves became more valuable, harsher laws were passed to stop them from running away.

The cotton plant is a low-growing shrub. In its seed pods, called bolls, white fibers surround large seeds. When the fibers are dried and fluffed up, they can be twisted together to form a strong thread. Woven into cloth, cotton produces one of the cheapest and most useful fabrics in the world.

A FREED SLAVE

When Reuben was 15, he was whipped for arguing with the overseer. It was one of many floggings, but this time, as his back healed, he made plans to run away.

Freeing a slave was called manumission. Owners sometimes freed slaves, usually house slaves, in their wills. Others were bought and freed by abolitionists. Some slaves, whose owners allowed them to work for others in their spare time, even managed to buy their own freedom. Freed slaves always carried their papers to prove that they were no longer slaves.

Reuben's experience made him want to become a conductor on the Underground Railroad. He patrolled the riverbank at night, listening for runaways. He also left a lantern burning in the upstairs window as a coded message of welcome.

Runaways felt safest when their contacts were black like themselves. Although many white people acted as conductors or ran safe houses, the majority of the workers on the Underground Railroad were freed slaves and fugitives who decided to go back and rescue family and friends.

One of the safe houses along his route was Henry's tinsmith shop. Henry gave him refuge and work, but they were both worried about the slave catchers. Finally Henry decided there was only one way to keep Reuben safe. He bought Reuben from his master and then set him free.

THE SWAMP GHOST

Many slaves had to make their way through treacherous swamps filled with snakes and, in some cases, alligators. Ben had heard stories about the swamps. By far the scariest stories were about the swamp ghosts, spirits that traveled in eerie balls of fire or in dancing flickers of light. The spirits were just a superstition, but the swamp lights really existed.

As the water level rises in swamps and marshes, grasses and other plants are submerged and begin to rot. This rotting releases gasses, including methane. A strong concentration of methane can burst into flames. This may happen spontaneously or during a lightning storm. The burning gas is usually seen as flickering lights darting through the trees — a spooky sight that led to stories about supernatural spirits. The spirit thought to live in the fire was called will-o'-the-wisp, ignis fatuus or jack-o'-lantern.

BOLD ESCAPES

Most slaves escaped from slavery the way the Jacksons did, by running away at night, then following the North Star. Even if they were lucky enough to meet up with a conductor to take them on the Underground Railroad, they still needed stamina, courage and determination to make the long, long walk to Canada. Some fugitives, however, found ways to make the trip shorter and safer — although not always more comfortable.

Henry Brown, a slave living in Richmond, Virginia, had white friends who helped him construct a cloth-padded wooden crate. He settled inside it with a store of biscuits and a water bottle made from an animal bladder (a common way to make watertight bottles in those days). Then his friends nailed down the lid and shipped him to abolitionist friends in the free city of Philadelphia, Pennsylvania. The train journey took 26 hours. From then on he was known as "Box" Brown.

Runaways were hidden in a variety of containers. One small child was smuggled across the Detroit River to Windsor, Canada West (now Ontario), in the domed lid of a trunk. Many slaves spent part of their journeys crouching inside barrels or lying flat out in coffins, arriving at their destinations nearly suffocated.

Disguises were often used. Slave catchers watching for ragged fugitives wouldn't look twice at a "Quaker lady." The deep brim on a Quaker bonnet could easily hide the face of a male or female runaway. A short man and a tall woman might exchange clothes to confuse pursuers. A much bolder disguise was adopted by Ellen Craft, who escaped with her husband from Georgia. She was tall and had a light complexion. Dressed in a top hat and elegant suit she could pass as a southern planter. Her husband, William, posed as her personal servant. Because Ellen Craft couldn't read or write, she bandaged her right hand and carried it in a sling to avoid having to sign the guest register in hotels.

One conductor on the Underground Railroad led a group of 28 fugitives north. To disguise the group as they moved through a city, he created a mock funeral procession. Some of the group rode in the coach while others walked behind as mourners. Slave hunters looking for a group of 28 saw not only the wrong number, but also the wrong clothing.

Quick, bold escapes were not easy to organize. They required money and sympathetic friends. The only hope for most slaves was the slow, dangerous walk north.

Put a Lantern in the Window

Ben hunkered down behind a bush watching the house beyond the picket fence. It was in darkness except for the light in one upstairs window. His stomach knotted. Should he knock on that door or not? Look for the lantern, Momma had said. But what if she was wrong?

Can't wait forever, Ben thought, as the sky began to lighten. Gathering all his courage, he crept up to the door and knocked. It opened a crack.

"Welcome, friend," said a soft voice.

With a thankful sigh, Ben slipped in.

Putting a lantern in an upstairs window was an Underground Railroad signal. It meant safety, food and help were available. You can make a lantern similar to the one Reuben and Henry shone in their window to welcome Ben.

You'll need:

- a clean, empty tin can with one end removed
- a felt-tip marker
- an old towel
- a hammer
- nails of different sizes
- wire
- a short candle
- matches

1. Fill the can with water and place it in the freezer. Leave it overnight or until the water is frozen solid. The ice will give you a hard surface against which to hammer your pattern.

2. Use the marker to draw a simple design on the can.

3. Lay the can on its side on a folded towel. Using various sizes of nails, hammer the design into the can.

4. For the handle, hammer a hole on either side of the can near the top.

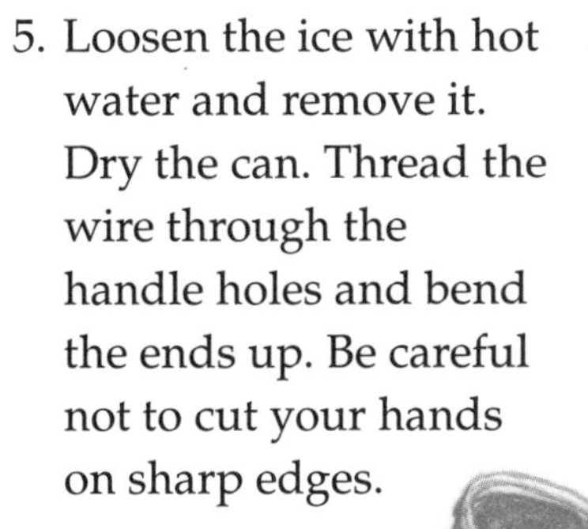

5. Loosen the ice with hot water and remove it. Dry the can. Thread the wire through the handle holes and bend the ends up. Be careful not to cut your hands on sharp edges.

6. Have an adult light the candle and drip a few drops of wax into the can. Blow out the candle and stand the candle upright in the wax. Let the wax harden.

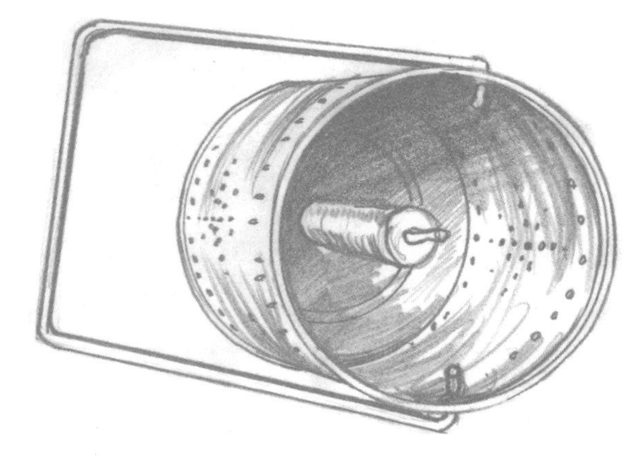

7. Ask an adult to light the candle, then watch the punched design throw a pattern onto the walls in a dark room.

OUTSIDERS

Johanna crumpled a sheet of newspaper and carefully stuffed it inside the glass chimney of the lamp. Soot smeared the back of her hand. Wiping it down the already smudged front of her pinafore, she sighed. No matter how careful she was, the black film got all over everything.

Across the table, four sparkling lamp chimneys sat in front of Eliza. She's as fussy as Mother, Johanna thought crossly. And if she doesn't stop that humming . . . Grinding her teeth, Johanna turned to look out the window. The rain had stopped at last. Two days they'd all been cooped up together. Two days of Eliza's irritating willingness. Can I help you with this, missus? Can I help you with that, missus? And those reproving looks from Mother. Why aren't you as helpful, Johanna, they seemed to say.

"Look!" Eliza said, and Johanna turned back from the window. Eliza ran one finger around the inside rim of a lamp chimney, gathering up the lampblack. On the sheet of newsprint she traced a sprawling *E* followed by a lopsided *l*. "I can write my name."

"Everyone can write," Johanna snapped.

Eliza's grin faded. "*We* can't." She dashed the palm of her hand across the paper, smudging the letters. "Asked how once. Missus said I'd better not ask again or she'd give me what for."

"Then how *did* you learn?"

"The littlest missy. She loved scratchin' away at her slate. Doin' her alphabets, she called it." As she talked, Eliza traced her name again. Carefully she dotted the *i*, then sat back to look at it, smiling. "One day I says, 'Draw *my* name.' And she did. Then she made it on a piece of paper. Kept it in my pocket so's I could practice at it — way off from the house, in the sand down by the river. Tramped all over the marks after. So's no one would find 'em." She dipped her finger in the soot again.

Johanna thought about the hours hunched over her desk at school, her paper splotched with ink blots and tears as she made circles and sticks, circles and sticks. Mrs. Halley had been quick to smack her ruler across any hand that couldn't write neatly. Johanna had often gone home with red knuckles and redder eyes. "If it was so much trouble, why did you bother?"

Eliza stared at her in surprise, then looked back at the spidery letters that spelled her name. "I like the shape of it. I like the way it starts all curly. Then there's this shout," she retraced the *l*, "and it goes all whispery at the end. When I look at it scratched out like that, I can say — that's me. Eliza. A real person."

Later that day, when she was sweeping up the wood curls from the shop floor, Johanna complained to her father. "Yes, missus this, and yes, missus that, and, Papa, she can't even write — except for her name."

"That's not her fault, you know, Johanna," her father chided gently. "Owners keep their slaves ignorant to control them. I believe they even have a law forbidding anyone to teach slaves to read or write."

Johanna dumped a dustpanful of wood curls into the barrel used for tinder, then tried again. "Mother wants us to be friends but how can we be? We don't have anything in common."

"It's only for a few more days. Once we hear from Mr. Fuller, we'll know what to do." Johanna heard the impatience in his voice and swallowed her next complaint. Oh well, she thought, he's right. She won't be here forever.

But the truth was she felt all jangly — watching her tongue and being pleasant every minute of the day and never having time alone. So when her mother announced she needed a few things from the store, Johanna felt like a bird released from a cage. "Two spools of thread and some cotton tape," she sang as she skipped out the door. The dry goods store was in the center of town. She was sure to see some of her friends.

Johanna hadn't walked ten minutes before she spotted Suzanne and Rachel. "Wait up," she called as she ran to overtake them. Just what she'd been hoping for, a chance to catch up on the news, especially the plans for the garden party next Sunday. In the flurry about Eliza and Ben it had gone clear out of her mind. With a sudden pang, she thought, We will be able to go, won't we? Surely we won't have to stay home just because *they're* here.

The girls stopped to wait for Johanna, each swinging a small market basket. She arrived beside them, out of breath and with a stitch in her side.

"It's been such ages since I've seen you. I was just thinking about the garden party." She turned to Suzanne. "Is your father still going to drive us?" The whole town had been invited to a strawberry tea on the grounds of Rodman Hall. But the six girls who had just graduated from Mrs. Halley's School For Young Ladies had a special treat planned — a ride in Mr. Blakely's new carriage.

Rachel darted a look at Suzanne, then began searching earnestly through her basket. Suzanne's cheeks turned red. "Well, I . . . The truth of the matter is, Johanna — "

"He won't take us?"

"No. No, he's still taking us, but we thought . . . that is, Caroline suggested . . . "

Caroline! Not Caroline again! At school it was always Caroline who directed their games, ordering this one here and that one there.

"She suggested what?"

"Well, she pointed out — and I guess I have to agree with her — there isn't really room for six in the barouche, not without crushing our skirts, and since your family is sure to be going in your father's wagon, we decided . . . "

"Decided what?"

"Perhaps you should go with your family. After all," Suzanne rushed on, "it doesn't matter how we get there, as long as we all arrive." She stopped abruptly. "I . . . I have to go now. My mother said I was to bring this ribbon straight home to her."

Johanna clamped her teeth together to stop her chin from trembling. Not for the world would she let Suzanne and Rachel see how hurt she was. As they scuttled down the street, she took several deep breaths to calm herself.

She turned and slowly walked the last few blocks to Dunsmore's Dry Goods. As she entered, the door flew out of her hand and banged against the wall. Heads lifted and turned. One of them was Caroline's.

Caroline had been inspecting a bolt of pink calico. She pursed her lips as though considering buying it, then glanced sideways at Johanna.

"I hear you have guests." Her trick of emphasizing the last word in a sentence always sounded slightly sneering.

"Where did you hear that?"

"Who knows where these little snippets come from? But I'm sure everyone's heard. So hard to keep a secret in this town."

Johanna felt her face going red. She had never been good at deflecting Caroline's catty remarks. And what exactly did Caroline mean by "guests"? Was she just fishing, or did she know about Eliza and Ben?

"Of course, one must be charitable," the high, cool voice persisted. "Mama always contributes to the clothing drive for them. But to have such people right in your house, Johanna. Mama thinks it so peculiar. Just not done in our circle, she says."

So that was it. Indignation rose sourly in Johanna's throat. Before hot words could spill out, Caroline had turned and was walking away. Over her shoulder, as she swept toward the door, she added, "By the way, has Suzanne mentioned to you — about the barouche? Quite ridiculous really for all six of us to squeeze in. I'm sure you understand."

Johanna gritted her teeth. "I understand perfectly, Caroline. Perfectly."

As the door snapped shut, Johanna had to reach for the counter to steady herself. How dare Caroline! And Suzanne agreed with her! Had let Caroline talk her into excluding Johanna! Forget it. Forget it until you get home, she told herself, suddenly aware of inquiring looks from people she should be greeting politely.

Back out on the road, her mother's parcels tucked into her basket, Johanna let angry tears spill over. She had daydreamed about the ride to the garden party for weeks — the six of them all in new dresses, with parasols to match, leaning over the elegant sweep of the carriage sides, waving to their neighbors.

Caroline's smile floated before her, so tightly sweet, so poisonous. She's not our kind, really, she could almost hear Caroline murmuring to Suzanne. Her father's only a cooper. And now her family is taking in slaves.

Snobs, Johanna thought. Stuck-up snobs. Who cares? Then she thought of the garden party again. If only we hadn't . . . She stopped herself. If only we hadn't taken in Eliza and Ben? Did she really mean that?

Johanna thought about the stories Eliza had told. About fleeing from tracking dogs and walking down the street right under the noses of the slave catchers, yes, but those other stories, too. Like the day Eliza was told she couldn't play with the master's children anymore. She was six and old enough to work in the kitchen, the mistress had decided. Or the way she'd been forbidden to learn her letters because she was only a slave.

Nobody should be left out like that, Johanna thought, tears welling up again. Well, there's nothing I can do about it. She trudged along, not caring who saw her tear-stained cheeks. Then a thought struck her so forcibly that she stopped right in the middle of the road. I *can* do something. I can.

And then she was running pell-mell toward their gate. As she burst through the kitchen door, her mother and Eliza looked up from the beans they were cutting.

"What on earth is the matter?" her mother asked.

Johanna yanked open the drawer of the dish dresser. Scrabbling under neatly ironed tea towels, she pulled out her school slate, a speller and her First Reader.

"Eliza," she turned to the girl staring wide-eyed at her, "how would you like to learn to read?"

Eliza swallowed. "Read?" she whispered. She sat very still, her gaze grave and questioning. "If I could read," she started slowly, then suddenly her face lit up. "If I could read, I could do anything!"

FREEDOM TO READ AND WRITE

By the time Eliza was born, most southern states had passed laws forbidding anyone to teach a slave to read and write. Because of that, on her flight to freedom, Eliza couldn't consult a map, check the names of towns and streets on signs, read a train timetable or recognize her description on a wanted poster. Running away was difficult for slaves who couldn't read, and that was just what slave owners wanted. Slaves who couldn't read books or newspapers seldom came in contact with new ideas that might make them question their bondage or lead them to revolt against their owners.

People who disobeyed the law and educated their slaves were sent to jail. Despite the law, some slaves did learn to read and write. Most learned from overhearing the owners' children at their lessons or were taught by the children themselves. And education *did* make them discontented with their lives. Many educated slaves became preachers and teachers, passing on new ideas, encouraging their fellow slaves to think for themselves.

FREDERICK DOUGLASS

Frederick Douglass risked his life to speak out against the practice of not educating black people. As a child in Maryland, he was taught to read by his owner's wife. Since this was against the law, the woman's husband ordered her to stop. But even that little bit of education made Frederick question his life as a slave. For asking questions he was beaten regularly.

At 21, he managed to escape and took the last name of Douglass. He began speaking at antislavery meetings about his life. His speeches were powerful enough to sway people to the abolitionist cause. In Rochester, New York, he started a newspaper called the *North Star*, in which he promised black people that he would "fearlessly assert your rights" and "faithfully proclaim your wrongs." He also urged them to work hard for an education and the right to vote.

Frederick Douglass used his home as a station on the Underground Railroad. Many escaped slaves hid safely in its secret rooms until he was able to get them across Lake Ontario to Canada. Eventually his work attracted powerful enemies. When a warrant was issued for his arrest, he was forced to flee to Canada himself. Based in St. Catharines for a few months in 1859, he continued to write and speak against slavery. Many people who defended slavery claimed that black people were too childlike to educate. Frederick Douglass, through his life and work, proved that all they needed was the opportunity to learn.

STORYTELLING

Slaves who couldn't read or write handed on their history, hopes and fears through storytelling and song.

Even though African people spoke different languages, the stories they brought with them had many elements in common. Some tried to explain how things began: why the sun seemed to rise in the east and set in the west, how people first got fire. Some told of heroes and heroines who performed great deeds. Many were animal tales that used humor to help children remember important lessons.

As they told one another stories around the campfire at night or in the dark of their small cabins, the slaves gradually changed the stories to suit their new land. In Africa, animal stories were told about Elephant, Lion, Python and Spider. In America, the animals were changed to such local animals as Bear, Fox, Raccoon and Rabbit. To show respect, the storyteller called the animals Sister, Brother, Aunt or Uncle. In one well-known tale about Brer (Brother) Rabbit, a little animal outsmarts a bigger, stronger animal, a message of hope and comfort for people who had to use their wits to survive.

Brer Rabbit and Tar Baby

Brer Fox was hungry. Rabbit stew, he thought, and his mouth watered. I'll have me some rabbit stew. Now, Brer Fox had tried time and again to catch Brer Rabbit, but Brer Rabbit always tricked him and got away.

This time, thought Brer Fox, I'll get him for sure. He took some tar, mixed it with turpentine and formed it into the shape of a baby. He set a hat on Tar Baby and put her down beside the road. Pretty soon along came Brer Rabbit — lippity-clippity, clippity-lippity.

Brer Fox lay low.

Brer Rabbit spied Tar Baby. "Morning!" he said politely, but Tar Baby just sat there and Brer Fox lay low.

"Nice weather this morning." Brer Rabbit thought he'd give her one more chance, but Tar Baby said nothing and Brer Fox just lay low.

Now, Brer Rabbit had a temper and he didn't like to be ignored. "You deaf?" he said. "'Cause if you is, I can holler!"

But Tar Baby never moved and Brer Fox still lay low.

"You're stuck up, that's what," said Brer Rabbit. "Well, I'll cure you of that." And blip! he whacked her on the side of the head. His fist stuck firm and he couldn't pull loose.

Brer Fox chuckled to himself and Tar Baby just sat still.

"If you don't loose me, I'll biff you again!" hollered Brer Rabbit. And *blip*! he whacked her with the other hand. It stuck fast. Tar Baby said nothing but Brer Fox could hardly keep himself down.

"Let go!" hollered Brer Rabbit, kicking Tar Baby. Pretty soon both feet and his head were stuck fast.

Then out popped Brer Fox looking as innocent as a mockingbird. "Howdy, Brer Rabbit. You look all stuck up this morning." And he rolled on the ground and laughed and laughed. "I got you this time, Brer Rabbit. You been running around sassing me for a long time, but this time you's come to the end of the row. I'm going to build a brushfire and boil you up in a stew."

Now, Brer Rabbit knew he was in trouble, so he kept his voice soft and humble. "Boil me up all you want, Brer Fox, but please, don't fling me into that briar patch."

Brer Fox looked at the briar patch and then at Brer Rabbit. "Too much trouble to boil you up," he said. "I'll just roast you over the fire."

"Roast me all you want, Brer Fox, but please, please, don't fling me into that briar patch."

Brer Fox thought about gathering up all that wood. "Too much trouble to roast you," he said. "I'll just stomp on you."

"Stomp on me all you want, Brer Fox, but please, please, please, don't fling me into that briar patch."

Brer Fox thought back to all the times Brer Rabbit had tricked him. He looked at Brer Rabbit crouched shivering on the ground, then he looked at the briar patch.

"Hee, hee, Brer Rabbit," he said, "I'll fix you." And he grabbed him by one leg and flung him as hard as he could right into the middle of that prickly, spiny briar patch. Then Brer Fox sat down to see what would happen.

By and by he heard someone calling. Way up the hill sat Brer Rabbit, combing tar out of his fur. "Hee, hee, Brer Fox," he called out. "I was born and bred in a briar patch. Born and bred!"

Share a Story

Eliza's favorite time on the plantation came when the day's work was done. Often, after supper was cooked and eaten, the slaves gathered around a fire or in the dark of a cabin to share stories. One person might turn a personal adventure into a tale, another might retell a story heard from a grandmother. In this way they passed on the history and wisdom of the tribe.

We all belong to tribes — our families, our schoolmates, our camp friends. With each group we have a shared history, shared stories. You can turn something you have experienced into a story to tell aloud, or you can look in collections of folktales and fairy-tales for old stories to retell. Here are some tips to make your story come alive:

1. Read or say the story out loud at least twice to practice. As you read, try to visualize what is happening in the story.

2. Organize the story in your mind by listing five or six important steps that move the story forward. This makes a framework for remembering the story. The framework for Brer Rabbit looks like this:
   - Fox wants Rabbit for dinner.
   - Fox makes Tar Baby and waits.
   - Rabbit comes along and talks to Tar Baby.
   - Rabbit gets mad and hits Tar Baby.
   - Fox appears and decides to cook Rabbit.
   - Rabbit tricks Fox and gets away.

3. Think of action words to brighten up the story. For example, instead of "throw" you could use "fling" or "pitch."

4. Look for places to add sound effects, such as different voices for the main characters or words that imitate sounds and feelings. For example, a snake might use words that start with *s*. Drag them out to imitate hissing.

5. Rehearse. Practice telling the story but don't memorize it. Be chatty. Try to sound as though you're talking to friends. It's all right if the story changes a little with each telling.

6. Watch yourself in a mirror as you practice. Experiment with hand gestures and facial expressions that emphasize the mood of the story.

7. Use your voice to add interest to your story. Speak much more slowly than usual. Change your tone from loud to soft and from high to low at appropriate times in the story. Pause just before an exciting moment.

8. Create a special setting for your story. Choose a quiet place with few distractions. Your audience should be sitting comfortably, either on chairs or on the ground. To create a dreamlike place, turn the lights down (or off for a ghost story). Some storytellers start by lighting a candle.

9. Pay attention to how you begin and end. Gather your listeners' attention with phrases such as "Once upon a time," "Long ago and far away" or "In the far-off days when animals could talk." At the end, release your audience from the story with such phrases as "And that's how . . . came to be," or "Snip, snap, snout, my tale's told out."

SLAVE CATCHER!

Johanna opened the back door to the cooperage and breathed in deeply. She liked to stand for a minute and let the smells surround her. The scent of fresh wood told her that her father and Tom were planing. As she stepped into the room, Tom's head came up, and the zip, zip of his plane stopped. No need to tell *him* it was dinnertime. He was already brushing the wood shavings from his leather apron.

At the front of the shop her father was smoothing the rim of a half-finished barrel, one eye on a thin-faced man whose elbows were planted on the display counter. Something about him made Johanna duck back into the shadows.

"Nice work y'do here," the stranger drawled. "See ya got a wagonload a' barrels out there 'bout ready to go." The only answer was the vroop, vroop of the palm-sized plane.

"Been havin' a good look 'round yer town," the man continued. "Reckon on stayin' awhile." As he spoke, his sharp eyes searched the room, stopping for a moment at the door to the house, then moving on to the wall piled high with barrels. "Fact is," he persisted, "gonna be needing some hired help. Pay a good wage to a young girl fer a bit a' cookin' and cleanin'. Some sewin' maybe. You know of any might be lookin' fer work?"

Mr. Reid eased the tilted barrel upright until it rested flat on the floor, then looked the man square in the eyes. "This is a cooper's shop. You want a hired girl, you'll have to look elsewhere."

Johanna felt her chest tighten. Her father never spoke to customers in that terse voice. Why was he being so rude to this one?

"No offense, friend. Just thought I'd ask." The stranger peered intently around the shop again. "Y'never know where yer likely to find exactly what yer looking fer. Y'hear of any interested party . . . " He paused with his hand on the doorknob. "I'd be obliged." And he sidled out.

Johanna felt a sick thud in her stomach as the door clicked shut. "Papa, what if he's — "

"Now, Johanna, no sense speculating," her father interrupted. "We'll just wait and see. Meanwhile, it's dinnertime, is it?" He glanced toward the back of the shop. Tom had already left. "And don't go worrying your mother about this, my girl. No need to borrow trouble."

Later, as they were finishing dinner, Mr. Reid said, "Tom and I are away to Queenston this afternoon with that load of barrels for Abram Fuller. So I want you to stay clear of the windows, Eliza, and scoot upstairs if anyone comes to call. We've no reason to think anything's amiss but we'd best keep on the safe side a few days longer."

"Better safe than sorry," Mrs. Reid agreed, then added, "After the dishes are done, you girls can finish making up those berry boxes. We'll be needing them soon."

Strawberry time, Johanna thought with a pang. She'd been looking forward to the strawberry tea for months and now the thought of seeing those stuck-up girls made her feel sick.

Eliza was singing softly as she set out the thin sheets of wood Tom had planed for them in the cooper's shop. "Freedom train's a-comin'. I see it close at hand. I hear the wheels a-rumblin' . . . " Eliza made her voice deep and grumbly and Johanna laughed.

"Get on board, little children, get on board . . . " Johanna joined in. Eliza had been singing nonstop since Ben had arrived. Even though he'd been sent off to Johanna's uncle so there wouldn't seem to be too much unusual activity at the Reids', Eliza was happy as a cricket. "There's room for many a-more," she sang out.

The girls had berry baskets stacked so high they were wobbling when a sharp rap came at the kitchen door. Scooping up the last of the unfolded strips, they darted into the small bedroom off the kitchen. Johanna listened at the door for a moment, then whispered, "That's my sister Jane's hired girl. What on earth can she be wanting?"

Mrs. Reid came bustling in. "I must go! Jane's baby has come down with spotted fever. I don't like leaving you two alone but Jane's frantic."

"We'll be fine," Johanna said. "You go along. We'll just sit in here and finish the boxes."

Reassured, Mrs. Reid set out for her older daughter's house.

The girls folded the boxes in silence. "I've got a splinter," Johanna said finally. She sucked at her index finger. "Let's have tea. You stay in here. I'll get it."

"Get on board . . . get on board . . . ," she hummed, clattering mugs and muffin tins onto the kitchen table. As she turned to lift the kettle off the stove, a movement outside the window caught her eye. Was it just a shadow, that tall, weedy shape? Suddenly a face peered in at her. Johanna's heart lurched into her mouth as the face grinned, then disappeared. The man from the shop!

She flew toward the door. Before she could bolt it shut, the handle turned and the door swung open. Without so much as a "by your leave," the man stepped into the kitchen.

"Yes?" she asked sharply. "What do you want?"

"Afternoon, missy." A thin-lipped smile stretched his stubbly cheeks. "Got some real good news fer yer little guest."

Johanna's quick glance toward the bedroom brought a glint of triumph to the man's eyes. His smile broadened to show crooked, yellow teeth. "Got a message from her ma." He raised his voice. "She's safe here in Canada and wants her little girl to come right away."

Standing firmly in his way, Johanna frowned. "You didn't say anything to my father about that this morning."

He raised his eyebrows and shrugged. "Didn't know the little lady existed this morning. Just met my good friend Abram Fuller on the road. Soon's I heard what he was about, I said, 'Don't you trouble yerself. I'll be right in that neighborhood. Be pleased to pass on the joyful news and bring ya the little girl myself.'" He grinned at her again. "Now just fetch out yer little friend and we'll be on our way."

"You're mistaken. There's no one else here."

The stranger's face flushed red. "You fetch me that girl — now!"

Terrified, Johanna turned to run. He caught her by the wrist but she twisted wildly and bit down hard on the hand that held her.

"Thunderation!" he spat, and let go just as Eliza swept out of the bedroom. Head down, she charged full tilt into the stranger, butting him so hard that he staggered backward, tripped on the doorstep and sprawled full-length on the porch. Johanna jumped for the door, slammed it shut and shot both bolts.

Weak with relief, the girls stared at each other.

"A slave catcher?"

Eliza nodded.

"How do you know?"

Eliza shrugged. "A feelin'. Just knows about folk like that. Anyways, what call's Mist' Fuller got to send him here? He knows your daddy's bringin' him barrels today."

Johanna sank limply onto a chair, but Eliza stood in the middle of the room, listening tensely. "What's he at now?"

Johanna tiptoed to the window. To her horror, the slave catcher was standing in the yard, staring at the roof.

"He's still out there. He's not going away," she said, half turning to Eliza. But when she looked again, he had vanished. She imagined him prowling around the house, searching, searching. There was no way in at the back. The shop would be locked and the lean-to had only one small window, though there was another window along the side of the shop. Surely he wouldn't dare try the front door. Anyway, it was locked — wasn't it? She raced into the parlor, Eliza at her heels.

Yes, it was locked. As an added precaution, Johanna shot the bolts, then checked the door that led from the parlor to the lean-to.

As she latched it firmly, she said, "Perhaps we should make a run for it. Mother's just down the road. The neighbors might hear us if we screamed." And then again they mightn't. The houses were far apart here on the outskirts of St. Catharines.

Eliza clutched at Johanna and pointed. A shadow passed in front of the window. The front door handle rattled briefly, then the shadow flitted across the next window.

"He's circling the house," Johanna whispered. "Listen, Eliza, as soon as he's around the back, head out the front door."

"How'll we know he's out back? Could be he's just ready n' waitin' to pounce. Better we wait right here. Long as he's outside, we're safe inside."

"*Shhh*!" Johanna said. "What was that?"

From somewhere came the crash of breaking glass. The girls stood rigid, straining to hear. The house was silent. A sudden thud made them start. Then a door hinge creaked.

"He's broken into the shop!" Johanna gasped. A loud bang and a sharp oath exploding into the silence told her the intruder had stumbled over something in the lean-to. Now only the flimsy parlor door with its hook-and-eye latch barred his way.

"We've *got* to run for it!" Johanna gasped, but Eliza was already tugging at the lower bolt on the front door. Johanna threw herself at the upper one, willing her mind to concentrate, to blot out the sounds of the blows that were shattering the parlor door. With a lurch, the bolt yielded. Now the key. Just as the big teeth tripped the lock, the back door splintered open.

"Run! Run!" Johanna screamed, pushing Eliza out in front of her. As they sped down the front steps, Johanna felt a hand on her shoulder, twisted out from under it and darted after Eliza. They turned into the road. Johanna raced ahead. Sprinting to catch up, Eliza stumbled in a wagon rut and fell.

"Gotcha!"

Johanna whirled around as the slave catcher dragged Eliza roughly to her feet. She ran at the man, pummeling him with her fists. "Let go. Let go. Let go!"

Her screams were drowned out by the thudding of horses' hooves and the clatter of wagon wheels. The slave catcher pushed Eliza away so suddenly that both girls fell onto the muddy road. As Johanna struggled to her knees, she saw her brother jump from the still-moving wagon right onto the fleeing slave catcher. Both crashed to the ground, rolling over and over. By the time Johanna was on her feet, her father had managed to halt the team. Neighbors came running. In no time a small knot of women huddled by the road, gawking as Tom pinned one arm behind the man's back and swung him around.

Mr. Reid seized the slave catcher by his lapels and glared into his face. "Listen, my friend." He was almost whispering with rage. "In this town we don't take kindly . . . to anyone terrorizing . . . our children. Neither do we like vermin . . . who traffic . . . in the slave trade. If you value your hide . . . you won't show your face . . . on this side of the river . . . again!"

After the last shake, he whirled the slave catcher around and, with a mighty shove between the shoulder blades, propelled him down the road. The man staggered for a few steps before he realized that he was free. Then he broke into a trot, stumbling from time to time as he glowered back over his shoulder at them.

Mr. Reid gathered both girls into his arms.

"You should have seen him go flying," Johanna said, "when Eliza butted him in the stomach."

Eliza smiled, but the sight of the slave catcher, shaking a defiant fist at them, made her say, "What if he comes back?"

"We'll set watchers, for him and any friends he's brought along." Mr. Reid sounded grim. "If he comes back, we'll be ready."

Yes, thought Johanna, whatever happens, Eliza and I will be ready, too.

SLAVE CATCHERS

"Why does she have to hide?" Johanna had asked the day she discovered Eliza in the sewing room.

Her mother looked troubled. "Things happen," she said. "More than we ever hear about."

Even in the safety of Canada, ex-slaves had to be constantly on the lookout. In 1830 Charles Baby hired Andrew, an escaped slave, to work on his farm near Windsor. Andrew's owner traced him to Canada and sent five men to kidnap him. They rowed across the Detroit River on a Sunday morning, hoping to catch Andrew working alone in a field. Charles saw them and called on his neighbors to help drive off the men. Andrew's near capture showed that he was not safe close to the border so Charles gave him money to go to Toronto.

In many other cases citizens, both black and white, rescued escaping slaves from pursuers. But the danger remained. In 1853, a young boy was grabbed by slave catchers on the streets of Chatham, Canada West (now Ontario). Black journalist Mary Ann Shadd heard his cries, snatched him from the kidnappers and ran with him to the courthouse, where she rang the bell to alert the townsfolk. When people realized what was happening, they chased the kidnappers out of town.

Because slavery was against the law in Canada, slave hunters who followed fugitives across the border often used guile rather than force. Some pretended to hire escaped slaves as servants. Using this trick, the slave catchers lured them back into the United States, where they were held in jail until their owners came for them.

Why did the slave catchers go to so much trouble? Money! Slaves were so valuable that owners offered large rewards for the return of their "property." As a skilled seamstress and cook, Leah Jackson could be sold for $1000 or hired out to earn money for her owner. Ben and Eliza were young and had many years of hard work in them. The owner might post rewards of $500 for each one — a strong temptation back when $400 was a year's salary for a teacher.

$500

REWARD

Hereby offered by the subscriber for the apprehension and security of a runaway negro man named

JOHN,

25 years, about 5 feet 10 inches high, of large build, with marks of the whip upon his back and neck.

june 14 -1843 A.L. Smith

The money attracted violent men. In the United States, slave catchers used dogs and guns to track down runaways. Because a dead fugitive was worth nothing, the slave catchers loaded their guns with bird shot, which would merely wound, not kill their quarry. One clever fugitive lined a vest with pouches stuffed with turkey feathers — an early version of the bulletproof vest.

Slave catchers were also unscrupulous. They didn't care if they found the actual slave described on a wanted poster as long as they were paid the money. As a result, free black people were often abducted and sold into slavery. In Canada, because the greatest danger lay near the border, many fugitives headed inland to such places as St. Catharines or Toronto, where an active abolitionist society kept watch. But the large rewards made slave catchers bold. Until 1863, when slavery was abolished in the United States, all black people, free or escaped slaves, had to be wary and vigilant every moment of the day.

THE REIDS' HOUSE

ALEXANDER ROSS

Escaping slaves must have wondered if any white person could be trusted, and yet many white people went to extraordinary lengths to help runaways. Alexander Ross, a doctor from Belleville, Canada West (now Ontario), spent much time and money helping slaves escape. He grew up in a family concerned with helping the downtrodden in society. When he read Harriet Beecher Stowe's *Uncle Tom's Cabin,* he saw it as "a command . . . to help the oppressed to freedom."

To see for himself the life that slaves led, Dr. Ross traveled through the southern States. He used his interest in bird-watching as an excuse to ask slave owners for permission to roam through their fields and woodlands. On these outings he made contact with slaves, inviting them to secret meetings where he gave detailed information about escape routes to Canada. Slaves who decided to escape were given money, a compass, a knife and some food. On occasion, Dr. Ross led the runaways all the way to Canada himself. One woman made the trip disguised as his valet.

Alexander Ross never stopped reaching out to the oppressed. Once he had helped the black community establish itself in Canada, he turned his attention to the problems of Native people.

SONGS

Momma, she sings all the time," Eliza said when Johanna asked how she knew so many songs. "Keeps you workin', keeps you happy, she says. But sometimes, at night, her singin's mighty sad."

Slaves hoeing in the fields under the blistering sun or hefting bales of cotton onto riverboats used music to lighten the burden of their work. They were forbidden to play the drums of their native Africa because these could be used to communicate with other groups of slaves. But they worked the old rhythms into their new songs. Taking words from the Bible stories they heard in the plantation chapels on Sundays, they sang about Jonah in the belly of the whale, Elijah and the great wheel of fire, and the hardships of Hebrew slaves in Egypt struggling to reach the Promised Land. These spirituals, as they were called, gave hope and comfort to a people who toiled in a hard and unrewarding life.

Get on Board

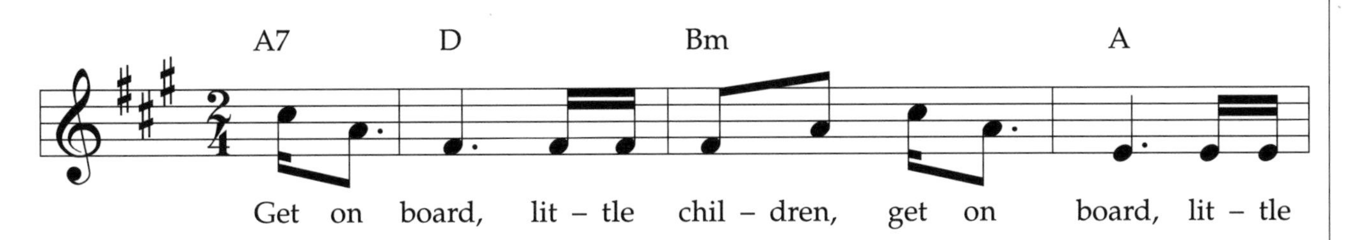

Auction Block

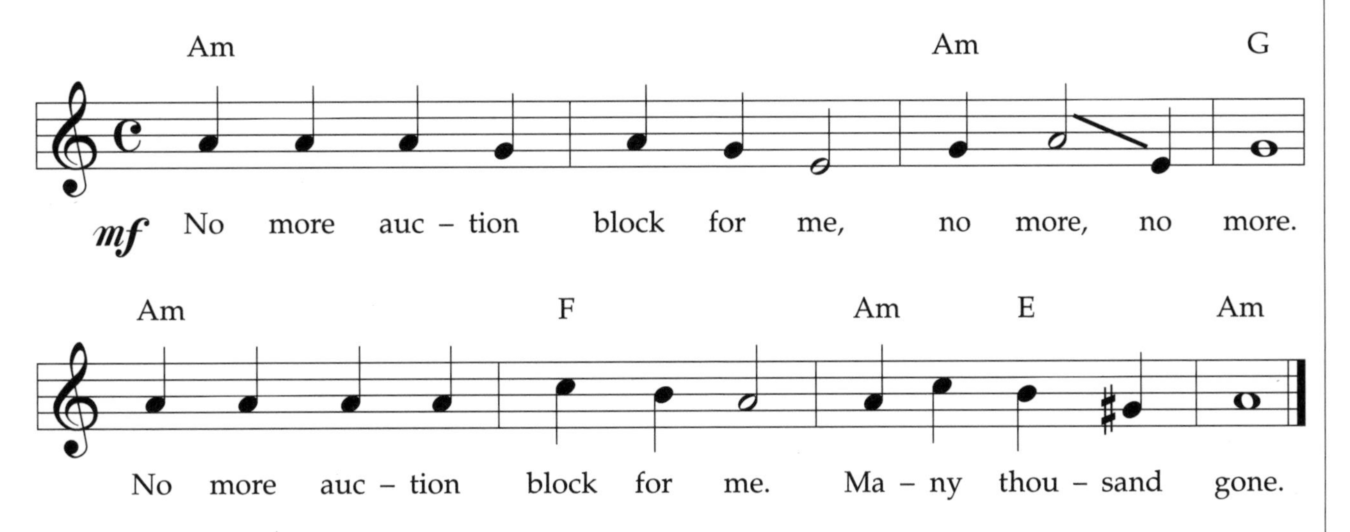

FRIENDS

J-O-H-A-N-N-A." Eliza's finger traced the letters running across a framed picture on the parlor wall. "It says Johanna! You sewed your name onto this."

"Yes. It's a sampler — a way to practice letters and sewing at the same time. Mine isn't very good. I got tired of doing it after I stitched the alphabet and my name and the date. Look at my mother's." Johanna pointed to a large framed sampler on the next wall. "She was only six and she did a Bible verse and everything. Here, I'll read it to you."

"Let me. Let *me*!" But the tiny cross-stitches and unusual words were too much for Eliza's shaky reading skills. She was practicing every spare minute, copying words onto the slate or reading from Johanna's First Reader. She had even stuck to her lessons now that Ben was back at the Reids'. He was learning to read, too. Ben was keen but Eliza was tireless.

"I used to watch the little missies do their letters and I knew, I just *knew,* if I could read, there'd be no difference between us."

Ben looked up from his slate. "Readin's good," he said slowly. "But folks'll still make a difference. Don't you go thinkin' otherwise."

Ben's warning bothered Johanna. She thought about the north end of St. Catharines. The neat, small houses crowded around the church where black people worshipped. Wasn't everyone supposed to be equal here? Most people were friendly, but once she'd seen Caroline and her mother pointedly cross the road and disappear into a shop rather than stop and talk to Orrin Brown. They were happy enough to have him mend their shoes, but to chat on the street . . .

After dinner the next day, Eliza asked to learn some everyday words. "Reader's fine," she said, "but I'd like to see what the words in my head look like." She scanned the list Johanna printed on a square of butcher's paper. Suddenly she went still, then copying carefully, scratched onto her slate, "My mother will come soon."

Johanna felt her heart contract. What if Mrs. Jackson never came? What would Eliza and Ben do? A large tear landed on the slate, blotting out "will," and Eliza's face crumpled. Then her shoulders were shaking and her head was buried in her arms on the table.

Johanna reached out and felt the thin body heave under great, gulping sobs. In a panic she shouted, "Mother! Mother!" She'd never seen anyone cry this hard.

Mrs. Reid came running. She took one look, scooped Eliza into her arms and began to rock her gently. "There, there," she said, stroking Eliza's head.

"Mist' Fuller promised . . . he promised," Eliza gasped. "But she's not comin', is she? I'll never see her again."

The door opened and Mr. Reid came into the room. He looked in alarm at Eliza and then at his wife.

"James, we must do something," she said. "Eliza and Ben can't live with this uncertainty any longer."

As they talked, Eliza crept out of Mrs. Reid's arms and sat erect on a kitchen chair, her hands folded tightly in her lap. "Sorry, missus," she said, scrubbing at a tear with one knuckle. "Didn't mean to be ungrateful."

Mrs. Reid reached out and clasped Eliza's hands. "You mustn't think that way, Eliza. We're glad to have you here. We just feel so helpless. We have no way of tracing your mother. We have to depend entirely on Mr. Fuller and his connections." She turned to her husband. "James . . . "

"I'll have Tom take a message to Abram Fuller. If there's any news at all about Mrs. Jackson, we must know. Then we can make plans about getting these children away to somewhere safer."

Johanna stared at her father. Eliza leave? Of course. The slave catcher had been run off, but who knew if he was gone for good. I don't want her to leave, Johanna thought, and was surprised at how strongly she felt.

Eliza had been listening carefully, too. "Oh thank you, missus," she said, jumping up to hug Mrs. Reid as the door closed behind Mr. Reid.

"Now, Eliza, please don't go getting your hopes up," Mrs. Reid warned. "There may well be no news." Or, Johanna thought, with a shiver, there may be bad news.

Eliza settled down to work again, reading out loud with a little prompting from Johanna. But after two pages, her voice faltered. She put down the reader. "Need to be up and doin'," she said. "Only thing stops me from thinkin' and worryin'."

"How about picking some strawberries?" Mrs. Reid suggested. "There should be enough for supper in the fence angles across the road. You're in view of the house from there. But take the dinner bell with you just in case."

Johanna opened her mouth to protest. They'd look ridiculous carrying a dinner bell. But the memory of the slave catcher made her think again. Silently she stowed the bell in the flat basket they used to cart the berry boxes.

"Three boxes will be plenty for supper," Mrs. Reid said. "Mind you put on your sunbonnets. It's hot today."

Eliza practically danced out the door. "Don't know if I should wear this pretty dress out in the fields," she said, smoothing down the blue gingham that Johanna had fetched for her from the blanket box that morning. Eliza's delight at the dress made Johanna feel doubly mean for keeping it back. Don't say it was my favorite dress, she thought when she saw her mother's look of surprise. "The apron will protect it," was all she said now.

They waved to Ben on the way out. He'd offered to load barrels onto the wagon. "Stay close by in the yard," Mr. Reid had warned him.

"Seems like forever since I was out," Eliza said as she followed Johanna across the road. "Smell that grass. Don't seem like anything bad could happen with the sun shinin' and the bees hummin'. Let's find them berries!"

"Should be lots along this fence. Let's try here." A cedar fence snaked between the road and a hayfield. The girls climbed the rails and dropped to the other side. "This field belongs to Suzanne's father, but he doesn't mind us picking his strawberries."

"Here's some!" Eliza crouched down and began picking.

"They always seem to hide themselves in the bends of the fence. Nice and sweet, these ones." Johanna worked one way along the fence and Eliza the other. In no time Johanna had a box full of the tiny berries. Some were so ripe they squashed as she touched them.

She was licking juice and berry pulp from her fingers when a voice called, "Hello! Can I come and pick with you?"

Johanna bobbed up to find Caroline peering over the fence.

"Oh!" Caroline's smile faded. "It's *you*." She looked down the fence line at the figure in blue gingham crouched some distance away. "I thought you were Suzanne. It *is* her father's field, after all."

Johanna glanced over her shoulder at Eliza. "You can come and pick if you like," she said. "Mr. Blakely won't mind, I'm sure."

Caroline hesitated, then clambered over the fence and started toward the stooping figure. "Suzanne?"

Eliza turned and lifted her sunbonneted face. Caroline stopped short. For one frozen moment, the two girls stared at each other, then Caroline whirled and marched away from the still crouching girl.

Johanna felt hot blood rush to her face. How dare she! Beckoning to Eliza to come closer, she stepped in front of Caroline, blocking her path. "Before you go, there's someone I'd like you to meet." She reached out to draw Eliza to her side and linked arms with her. "This is my friend, Eliza Jackson."

Caroline's eyes wavered. For once, she looked unsure of herself. Then her lips thinned into a hard line. Without a word, she turned and strode toward the fence, her bonnet flopping on its strings as she went.

Johanna turned to Eliza. "I'm so sorry . . . " But Eliza wasn't listening. She was smiling down at their linked arms.

Later, their boxes full, they wandered back to the house. "She gonna be mean to you 'cause of me?" Eliza asked.

Johanna thought of all the times she'd wanted so much to please Caroline. How often had she found herself swallowing arguments, giving in, doing things Caroline's way?

"Who cares?" Johanna was surprised to hear herself say.

They were sitting on the porch hulling strawberries when Tom rode into the yard.

Eliza's hands tightened on the bowl of berries. She looked at Johanna, then she smoothed down her pinafore and stood up. "No sense waitin' here, I reckon."

Ben appeared in the stable door. "Any news?" he called.

Without answering, Tom untied a cotton bag from the saddle and handed it to Eliza. She darted a quick look at Ben, then slowly pulled open the top.

Out of the bag she took a small figure made from twists and braids of cornhusking. It had been lovingly dressed in blue calico. "It's my doll! The very one my momma made for me." Pressing the doll to her chest, she turned to Tom.

He cleared his throat and then broke into a big grin. "Your mother's in Toronto," he said. "Safe and sound and waiting for you."

Over the next 24 hours they had hardly a moment to draw breath. Eliza and Ben were frantic to see their mother, and the Reids wanted them safely away from any slave catchers who might be lurking.

"Train's the fastest way," Mr. Reid said. "Besides, there might be watchers on the ferry at Port Dalhousie. Abram Fuller's sending his oldest son to ride with you, just to be on the safe side."

"Train?" Eliza's eyes were shining. "Never been on one of them before."

"Not the above-ground kind anyway," Johanna reminded her, and they both laughed.

Mrs. Reid found a small carpetbag in the attic and they packed the reader, speller and slate on the bottom, a change of clothes for Ben in the middle and, very carefully on top, the blue gingham dress. And all the while Eliza was singing, "Get on board, little children, get on board. There's room for many a-more."

I mustn't begrudge her this, Johanna thought. It's wonderful that she's going to be with her mother. But will she miss me as much as I'll miss her? All too soon, Johanna found herself standing on the railroad platform waving good-bye.

"Well, that's the end of that," she sighed, trailing upstairs a few hours later. The door of the sewing room stood ajar, just as it had the first time she'd seen Eliza. She gave it a small shove. The room was so tidy it was hard to believe anyone had lived there. Then she caught sight of the china doll and happiness swept through her. It sat, as prim as ever, in the middle of the neatly made cot. Resting against it, a calico arm tucked into the blue gingham one, was Eliza's cornhusk doll.

SIX MONTHS LATER

It was three days before Christmas when the parcel arrived. Johanna undid the string and opened one end. A letter was tucked underneath a square of linen. As she drew the linen out, it unfolded to reveal row on row of tiny, perfect cross-stitches. Around the edges, Eliza had worked a garland of the crimson hedge roses she would have seen the length of the Niagara Peninsula on her train ride to Toronto. The garland linked two names.

Johanna looked at the accompanying letter, her eyes almost too blurred by tears to read.

"My dearest friend," it began . . .

THE RESCUE

When slave catchers captured Eliza's mother, the Underground Railroad went into action. Coded messages alerted all agents in the area. Eyes and ears around the countryside soon located two men camping in the woods. They had tied Leah Jackson to a tree while they waited for her owner to arrive. Under cover of darkness, Underground Railroad agents snatched her away.

Once she was safely hidden, a coded message was sent by the new electric telegraph to Abram Fuller.

Stolen black portmanteau, now recovered.
Holding for return by first available boat.
Will advise.

Abram Fuller knew from this message that Leah had been found and rescued, but that it was too dangerous for her to travel the usual way, hidden among the cargo on one of his wagons. Instead she was to be rowed across the Niagara River. He waited for the message that told him which dark night had been chosen and where he should meet her on the Canadian side of the river.

Because the law in the United States was on the side of the slave owners, abolitionists depended on surprise or stealth to stage their daring rescues. Underground Railroad workers knew that once slave catchers captured a runaway, they usually telegraphed the owner, then looked for a safe place to keep their captive until the owner arrived. This gave abolitionists a few days to put their plans into action.

Just such a delay saved a fugitive slave named Patrick Snead. He had escaped to Canada but made the mistake of working in a hotel on the American side of Niagara Falls. One day a telegram arrived from his former owner ordering the local sheriff to arrest him. Even though the other waiters tried to defend him, Snead was dragged off to jail. But while the sheriff was waiting for the arrest warrant to be sworn out, Snead was spirited out of jail and across the river to Canada.

Patrick Snead was one of the lucky ones. Most captured slaves were returned to angry owners who made their lives much harsher than before.

Cornhusk Doll

The doll that Eliza left for Johanna was made from cornhusks, one of the few materials available to slave mothers like Leah Jackson. Slaves also made dolls from corn cobs, straw, twigs, nuts and dried apples, then dressed them in scraps of cloth. You can make your own cornhusk doll like Eliza's.

You'll need:

- 10 to 15 cornhusks (from the cob or a craft store)
- scissors
- newspapers
- 1 L (4 c.) warm water
- 10 mL (2 tsp.) glycerine
- a towel
- 2 pipe cleaners, each 10 cm (4 in.) long
- 2 cm (3/4 in.) plastic foam ball (or crumpled paper wrapped in tape)
- strong thread
- felt markers
- fabric
- a sewing pin

1. For husks straight from the cob, trim off the bottom ends so that the husks lie flat. Dry them between layers of newspapers for about a week. For husks from a craft store, start at Step 2.

2. Soak the husks overnight in warm water mixed with glycerine. Blot them on a towel to soak up the excess water.

3. Push a pipe cleaner into the foam ball. Fold a piece of cornhusk 13 cm (5 in.) long over the ball. Place a second husk at a right angle to the first one and fold it down. Shape the husks around the ball to form the head. Wind thread several times around the neck and tie tightly.

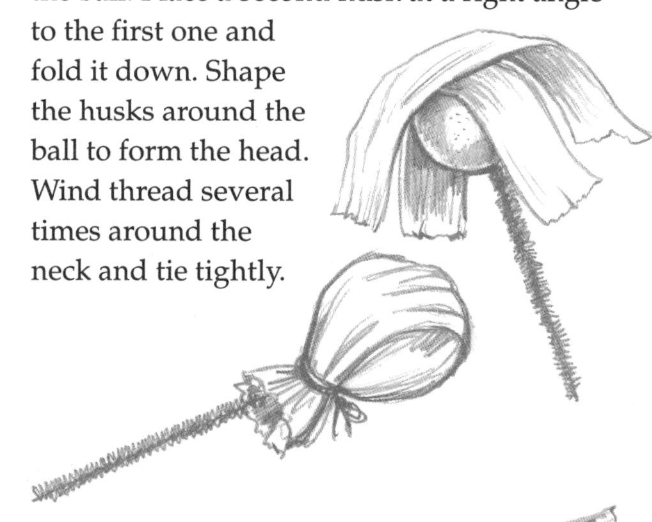

4. Cut a strip of husk 2.5 cm x 10 cm (1 in. x 4 in.). Lay the other pipe cleaner on it lengthwise and roll up as tightly as possible. Tie thread near each end to make the wrists.

5. Lay the arm piece across the body piece below the head. Wind thread over and under the arms several times in a figure-eight pattern, then tie tightly.

6. Cut two strips of husk 4 cm x 13 cm ($1\frac{1}{2}$ in. x 5 in.). Fold lengthwise to make strips. Crisscross the strips over the shoulders and down to the waist. Tie tightly around the waist with several turns of thread.

7. Bend the arms up beside the head. Overlap five or six husks around the waist with the wide ends pointing up. Wrap ten turns of thread tightly around the waist and tie. Fold the overlapping husks down one at a time to form a skirt. Trim it evenly at the bottom. Bend the arms down.

8. Use markers to make a face.

9. Cut a square of fabric 7.5 cm x 7.5 cm (3 in. x 3 in.). Fold it into a triangle to make a head scarf. Cross the ends under the chin and tie them behind the neck. To make an apron, cut a piece 2.5 cm x 4 cm (1 in. x $1\frac{1}{2}$ in.). Wrap it around the waist and use a pin to hold it in place at the back.

FINDING WORK

When Leah Jackson arrived in Toronto, she needed to find work to support her family. Leah had a number of skills that would help her. She was an expert seamstress, a good cook and a laundress. Even so, paid work was hard to come by in a country full of immigrants recently arrived from Britain and Europe. Many newcomers were scrambling for few jobs. But people who had the bravery to escape from cruel owners and the perseverance to find their way through unknown territory were not easily discouraged.

Unskilled women took in laundry, did mending, or became maids in large houses. Men who had few skills worked for the many hotels opening up. Others earned their first wages as laborers on the new steam railroad, laying track, or carrying luggage.

Railroad laborers

Shoemaker

Waiter

Washerwomen

Once they had saved enough money, some ex-slaves went into business for themselves. T.F. Cary and R.B. Richards opened the first icehouse in Toronto, cutting ice from the mill ponds in winter, storing it in sawdust, and delivering it daily by wagon in the warmer months to customers in and around the city. Another ex-slave, Thornton Blackburn, noting that Toronto was large and often muddy, bought a horse and carriage and started the city's first taxi service. Others opened shops and became barbers, seamstresses, shoemakers or bakers, using skills learned in their slave days.

Not all former slaves went to the cities. Some took up land north and west of Toronto. There they cleared the bush and established farms. Many descendants of former slaves still live in the Chatham area.

Seamstresses

Vendors

Taxi driver

LEARNING TO BE FREE

Ben had been a field hand on the plantation, so he had fewer skills than his mother and sister, but he was keen to learn. Like other escaped slaves, Ben knew that learning to read and write was an important step in finding work and settling down. He also wanted to learn practical skills, so he applied to the school at Dawn, near Chatham, Canada West (now Ontario).

Josiah Henson, an escaped slave, felt that ex-slaves needed schools not only to teach them how to read and write, but also how to buy and farm land. He joined with a group of Quakers and Unitarians concerned about the welfare of black refugees and built a school, sawmill and gristmill. By attending the school, working in the mills and farming the land, the students learned the skills they needed. The Dawn school lasted from 1844 to 1868.

A more successful school, The Elgin Settlement near Chatham, was started by William King, a Presbyterian minister. King felt that ex-slaves needed three things: land, schools and churches. He started by buying 3600 ha (8900 acres) of land, which he divided into farms of 20 ha (50 acres) each. Ex-slaves could buy land cheaply as long as they agreed to build a cabin and begin clearing the land and planting crops. Those who had no money were encouraged to work for the railroads until they had earned the $12.50 for the first payment.

King also oversaw the building of a combination church and school, which was open to everyone. Over the next 15 years, the school attracted an equal number of black and white students. By 1865, more than 700 students had attended the school, many of whom went on to university and became community leaders. Later, the school merged with other public schools to become the local district school.

MARY ANN SHADD

Some people felt that blacks and whites should have separate schools. Not teacher and journalist Mary Ann Shadd. She was against any form of segregation.

Mary Ann Shadd was born into a free black family in Delaware. Her family were strong abolitionists who helped many slaves on their flight north. In this atmosphere, she learned to care about the plight of the unfortunate and to speak her mind.

In 1850, Mary Ann went to Windsor, Canada West (now Ontario), to set up a school for escaped slaves. Unlike the school at Dawn, hers was integrated. She believed that only by educating black children and white children together would the two groups learn to treat each other as equals.

Some white people in the area disagreed. Many refused to let their children attend school with black students. In an attempt to change these attitudes, Mary Ann established a newspaper, *The Provincial Freeman*. But the double load of teaching and writing exhausted her, and after only two years she had to close the school. The newspaper survived and was moved to Toronto, where many people were strongly abolitionist and supported her ideas. *The Provincial Freeman* lasted for about six years and was a strong and influential voice for the black community.

In 1864, while the Civil War still raged, Mary Ann was asked to return to the United States to help recruit black soldiers for the Union army. After the war, she moved to Washington, D.C., where she taught school during the day and attended law school at Howard University at night. As a lawyer, she fought for many causes, including the right of women to vote. This remarkable woman achieved two notable firsts: she was the first black woman in North America to establish and run a newspaper, and the first woman to study for a law degree from an American university.

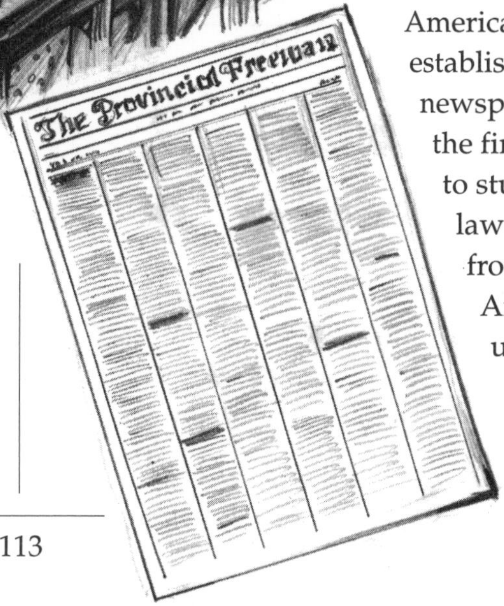

FREEDOM FOR ALL

On January 1, 1863, President Abraham Lincoln signed the Emancipation Proclamation, declaring all slaves free. At last escaped slaves in the northern States and Canada were safe from abduction by slave catchers.

The news of emancipation unsettled many of the refugees just learning to live in Canada. Most had left relatives and friends in the South. Although they had run from the whips of their owners and the tracking dogs of the slave hunters, they were still attached to the places where they had been born. Once the Civil War ended, hundreds decided to return to their birthplaces. Sadly, some faced harsh treatment and violence there.

But others stayed in Canada. They had built houses, established businesses and started families. They had put down roots. Difficult though it was to adjust to the colder climate and disappointing as it was to find that prejudice still existed, their new country was now home. Today, nearly a century and a half later, the descendants of ex-slaves are fifth and sixth generation Canadians with a long history of helping to build the country.

GLOSSARY

abolitionist — a person who believed in, and worked toward, the freeing of the slaves

American Civil War — a war (1861-65) between the northern and southern states that brought about the abolition of slavery

auction block — a platform on which slaves stood to be offered for sale

bondage — the institution of slavery

code — a system of words, sounds or symbols used to communicate secretly

emancipation — freedom from bondage

flog — to beat with a stick or a whip

free states — states that had proclaimed slavery illegal. (See pages 18-19.)

fugitive slave — a runaway slave

manacles — heavy iron bands that fastened around the wrists and were joined by a short iron chain to restrict movement

manumission — a legal release from slavery. Some owners left instructions in their wills that their slaves were to be freed or manumitted.

massa — the pronunciation some southerners gave to the word "master"

overseer — a person who directed the work of the field slaves

patrollers — men mounted on horseback who guarded southern roads against escaping slaves

plantation — a very large farm

Promised Land — a code name for Canada taken from the story of the Israelites' escape from Egypt in the Bible

safe house — a hiding place for escaped slaves

slave — a person held in servitude as the property of another

slave auction — a place where slaves were offered for sale

slave catcher — a person who earned his living by tracking escaped slaves, capturing them and returning them to their owners for the reward money

spirituals — deeply emotional songs based on Bible stories. They were created by slaves to give them comfort and hope.

BIBLIOGRAPHY

Every escaped slave had a unique story to tell. Here are more stories of the Underground Railroad.

Novels and Biographies

Lasky, Kathryn. *True North: A Novel of the Underground Railroad*. The Blue Sky Press/Scholastic, 1996

Lyons, Mary E. *Letters from a Slave Girl: The Story of Harriet Jacobs*. Charles Scribner's Sons, 1992

McCurdy, Michael. *Escape From Slavery: The Boyhood of Frederick Douglass in His Own Words*. Alfred A. Knopf, 1994

Paterson, Katherine. *Jip: His Story*. Lodestar Books, 1996

Petry, Ann. *Harriet Tubman: Conductor on the Underground Railroad*. Harper Trophy, 1955, 1983

Smucker, Barbara. *Underground to Canada*. Puffin, 1978

Picture Books for All Ages

Bryan, Ashley. *All Day, All Night: A Child's First Book of African-American Spirituals*. Atheneum, 1991

Edwards, Pamela Duncan (illus. Henry Cole). *Barefoot: Escape on the Underground Railroad*. HarperCollins, 1997

Johnston, Tony. *The Wagon*. Tambourine Books, 1996

McKissock, Patricia. *Christmas in the Big House, Christmas in the Quarters*. Scholastic, 1994

Winter, Jeanette. *Follow the Drinking Gourd*. Alfred A. Knopf, 1988

Histories

Gorrell, Gena K. *North Star to Freedom: The Story of the Underground Railroad*. Stoddart, 1996

Hamilton, Virginia. *Many Thousand Gone*. Knopf/Random House, 1993

INDEX

A LITTLE ANTHROPOLOGY

Dennison Nash
The University of Connecticut

Prentice Hall
Englewood Cliffs, New Jersey 07632

Library of Congress Cataloging-in-Publication Data

Nash, Dennison.
A little anthropology / Dennison Nash.
p. cm.
Bibliography: end of chapter.
Includes index.
ISBN 0-13-537689-0
1. Anthropology. I. Title.
GN25.N37 1989
306—dc19 8-2421
CIP

Editorial/production supervision and
interior design: Pam Price
Cover design: Photo Plus Art
Manufacturing buyer: Ray Keating/Peter Havens

A Division of Simon & Schuster
Englewood Cliffs, New Jersey 07632

Printed in the United States of America

10 9 8 7 6 5 4 3 2 1

ISBN 0-13-537689-0

Prentice-Hall International (UK) Limited, *London*
Prentice-Hall of Australia Pty. Limited, *Sydney*
Prentice-Hall Canada Inc., *Toronto*
Prentice-Hall Hispanoamericana, S.A., *Mexico*
Prentice-Hall of India Private Limited, *New Delhi*
Prentice-Hall of Japan, Inc., *Tokyo*
Simon & Schuster Asia Pte. Ltd., *Singapore*
Editora Prentice-Hall do Brasil, Ltda., *Rio de Janeiro*

CONTENTS

PREFACE

This book is my own attempt to interest a new generation of American college students, and others, in what the subject of anthropology has to offer them. When it was written, anthropologists in many American colleges and universities were struggling with the realization that theirs, like other "impractical" disciplines, was a subject of declining demand. Enrollments were down. Anthropology majors and graduate students had drifted away to more vocationally viable disciplines. The job market for anthropologists was tough and money for field research was hard to find. Finally, in their classrooms, anthropologists were having to come to terms with an indifference and even aversion to what they had thought was an intrinsically fascinating subject.

There had been a time in the 1960s and earlier when student interest in anthropology was strong; at that time our courses were full and at times even overcrowded. Except in the more privileged corners of academia, that time was obviously past. This came as a shock to old hands who remembered the earlier Golden Age, when even mediocre teachers had no difficulty in finding a respectable audience. Some of those old hands were unaware of what was going on in their classrooms or, if aware, preferred to concentrate on their research interests. Others recognized a decline in anthropology's fortunes, but did little more than curse the students, wring their hands, and hope for better days. Still others considered the drift of anthropology towards the academic periphery as something that might be addressed in a variety of adaptive ways. The production of new, more interesting reading matter about the subject was one of them.

A Little Anthropology is my own response to the challenge of dealing with the new, tough audiences that we anthropologists are faced with—audiences that must be engaged as well as instructed in the essentials of our discipline and its subject matter. These essentials, it seems to me, revolve around a number of general pedagogical questions: What do anthropologists study? How do they go about it? What perspective do they bring to their work? What have they found out about the subject? And finally, what is the relevance of all of this for them and for those whose interest they are trying to stimulate and satisfy? In my view, one of the reasons for the decline in anthropological fortunes was that many of us, for whatever reasons, had lost track of these essential pedagogical questions and the need to communicate what we knew about them to the *general* reader. That is what I have attempted to do here.

Most of the writing of this book took place during a sabbatical leave from the University of Connecticut, where I have passed most of my professional career. It would be hard to imagine more auspicious circumstances. Supportive and stimulating environments included a study made available by the Graduate School of my university; a lovely apartment in the center of Beaune (Burgundy), France, where I also engaged in some research; and an office in the Department of Anthropology at Vassar College, where I was a Visiting Professor during a part of my leave.

A number of individuals helped by reading and criticizing portions of the manuscript. I am indebted for this to Arthur Abrahmson, James Barnett, Robert Bee, Carole Berman, Scott Cook, James Faris, Jean Fuschillo, Bernard Magubane, Ronald Rohner, and Benjamin Wiesel. A special burden of critical assistance was taken on by E.J.R. Booth and Seth Leacock. Finally, many students in my large 1986 introductory course (Anthropology 106) at the University of Connecticut kindly offered their comments on three chapters that they had read in class. To all of these people, and to Rita Govern and Deborah Crary of the University of Connecticut Research Foundation, who typed the manuscript, I would like to express my appreciation.

The challenge provided by the new, tough generation of college students and the best possible outside assistance and support contributed greatly to the writing of this book, certainly, but it never could have been made without a deep and lively acquaintance with anthropology and its subject matter. It is a privilege for me now to share that acquaintance with students and others who would like to know what anthropology has to tell them about their world. If they find something of value in this work, it will add a bonus to the pleasure I've had in writing it.

Dennison Nash
Storrs, Connecticut

Chapter One

TO BEGIN

The ancient Chinese philosopher, Lao Tzu, said that a journey of a thousand miles begins with a single step. The reader of these words has just taken a few steps into the field of anthropology.

What is this thing called anthropology? Some people have never heard of it. Others have certain ideas that reflect what they've seen in newspapers or on television. Still others have read some of the anthropological literature. Some people think that anthropologists are scientists who are interested in ruins—that they dig up old things like foundations of dwellings, pieces of pottery, and stone tools and try to make sense out of them. Another view associates anthropologists with the theory of evolution, which leaves aside the work of a creator in accounting for the emergence and development of human beings. People who have a strict creationist viewpoint may want to protect their children from anthropologists and their doctrines. Still another view puts anthropologists in contact with strange or exotic people who may live on the edge of survival or carry on interesting sexual activities. All of these notions about anthropology contain a degree of truth; but like those views formed by blind men clustered around an elephant, each is only partially correct.

Anthropologists *are* interested in the past. They are concerned with human origins and evolution; and they do study primitive and exotic people. But they now also investigate the behavior of people in restaurants, in hospitals, and in modern businesses. They are concerned with modern nation-states as well as those of ancient times; and the behavior of the people next door can be just as interesting to them as that of an exotic people living far away. In truth, the subjects of anthropological investigations include all the human beings that have ever lived in all times and places. As far as we know, these creatures have only been found on the planet earth for a comparatively brief period of time. They represent one of the thousands of life forms that began to emerge on this planet more than four billion years ago. Humans have certain physical qualities that set them apart from other animals, but these differences are comparatively slight and mostly a matter of degree. Humans and chimpanzees, for example, share more than 99 percent of the same genetic material.

Anthropologists are not the only scientists who are interested in human beings. Political scientists deal with humans' political life, economists with their economies, psychologists with their psyches, physiologists with their bodies, and so on. But these other scientists do not view humans in the comprehensive way that anthropologists do; moreover, they tend to confine themselves to certain kinds of human beings, such as the ones who live in modern, Western society, or as is sometimes the case with psychologists, the students in their classrooms. Anthropologists, on the other hand, have tried to look at all aspects of human beings in all times and places. What do humans have in common? In what ways are they different? Why are they the way they are? These are some of the grand anthropological questions that will be raised throughout this book.

Like other scientists, anthropologists have their specialties. In the United States, where I happen to be based and from the point of view of which this book is written, there are three major areas of specialization: physical anthropology, archeology, and sociocultural anthropology. Physical anthropologists are interested in the physical side of human beings, including the genes that determine their body structure. They see humans as evolving along different paths from the time they first emerged on earth. Some of these anthropologists have become famous in the course of discovering fossils that shed light on the emergence and development of early humans. Other physical anthropologists are well-known forensic specialists; they deliver their expert opinions in court and lend assistance in murder investigations.

Archeologists search for things that humans leave behind. They dig a lot and sometimes even go under water. The remains of tools and weapons are grist for their mills, as are objects of art found in caves. The aim of these scientists is to use such evidence in order to reconstruct the way people once lived. Sometimes, it seems that they strain very hard in their reconstructions, but it is surprising how many scientifically defensible conclusions are drawn from only a few material remains.

This book is based mostly on the work of sociocultural anthropologists, myself included. This branch of anthropology corresponds to what others may call ethnology, or in some societies, sociology. It deals primarily with the behavior of contemporary peoples who have been studied directly by these anthropologists. I use the word *behavior* here in its broadest possible sense; that is, to include not only observable actions, but also what goes on in the human body and mind. Such behavior can be viewed as a property of a group or of an individual; in humans, it is heavily dependent on learning. This is what anthropologists refer to as culture, and it is the cultures of different groups of humankind that are the special object of sociocultural investigations.

For those who like to pigeonhole, this little book is an introduction to sociocultural anthropology. It doesn't cover the whole of that field, however. People who have had the opportunity to look at one of the many introductory texts will see that they include subject areas that are not dealt with here. However, I don't think that it is necessary to be exhaustive to give people the feel for our subject matter and the way we approach it. Later on, readers will be able to peruse more exhaustive or specialized books. Furthermore, I believe that it would be a mistake to insist that what is included here pertains only to the field of sociocultural anthropology. Any anthropologist ought to have an overview that derives not only from a specialized area, but other areas as well. It is this overview that makes anthropology so valuable. The important thing is never to lose sight of the complete human being and always to be willing to entertain what others have to say about them. Nothing about humans should be considered foreign to any anthropological undertaking. Accordingly, in this book I refer not only to the work of sociocultural anthropologists, but other anthropological specialists, social scientists, writers, and even some proverbial "men in the street."

A Little Anthropology has not been written to be studied. There are definitions in it. There are summaries. And there are names. For some people, these all cry out for underlining and for later regurgitation to some teacher. So it may be. But I had no intention of activating this almost reflex student mechanism when I began to write this book.I had thought, rather, to produce something that might be bought at an airport bookstall and read on what otherwise might have been a long, boring flight to somewhere. What I wanted to do was acquaint—even engage—a reader with the subject matter of anthropology. Being human, I thought that they would be fascinated by a discussion of the human condition as we know it. And being fascinated, they would continue their inquiries on their own, not only as students, but as people who must make a life for themselves. "Who am I?" "Where do I fit in?" "How should I live my life?" These are grand questions that should come to the fore on reading this book.

Anthropology is, then, about all human beings, and it is the charge of the anthropologist to tell our story. It shouldn't present just the good side, but the bad. It should include not just one group of people, but others. It shouldn't illustrate just one aspect of human life, but all. As Miles Richardson has pointed out, anthropologists are modern myth tellers who try, as accurately and as sympathetically as they can, to tell of the human condition. Modern people are the first to be able to witness this condition in its entirety and to see themselves as a part of the vast sweep of it all. The anthropologist speaks directly to them.

The reader may ask, "What, then, is in it for me?" That, as they say, is a good question. Certainly, anthropology will not fulfill some narrow vocational interest. Though it does have a practical, or applied, side, it seems to offer little that is of practical value. (Indeed, a colleague of mine once said that he became an anthropologist because he liked to pursue useless knowledge.) However, appearances can be deceiving. As one delves more and more deeply into the study of other human beings, one begins to see oneself reflected in them. The reflection may be real, reversed, or distorted, and it may undercut some cherished notions about who we are and where we stand. In the end, though, it is possible to know something about the whole human enterprise and where one fits into it. In a society like that of the United States, in which any solid ground is very hard to find, this would seem to be rather precious knowledge.

The study of anthropology can turn out to be something like a conversion experience. Whether it is that or not, I hope that it will offer the reader something of real value. Enough said. It is time for the second, third, and later steps, which is to say that now we shall really begin.

REFERENCE

RICHARDSON, MILES, "Anthrolopogist—the Myth Teller," *American Ethnologist*, 2, no. 3 (August 1975), 517–33.

Chapter Two

CULTURE

The word *culture* is something that many people associate with anthropology. To be sure, anthropology does not have exclusive rights to this concept. Biologists deal with cultures in their laboratories. A government may have its department or ministry of culture. And sociologists and historians use the term in their work. But if use alone is any indication, a good case can be made for anthropological ownership. The concept is all-pervasive in anthropological work, and it has spilled over into the public domain, where people often use it when referring to the customs of a group of people. Common usage, however, does not necessarily mean a common—or full—understanding. Even anthropologists may be fuzzy in their comprehension of the term, and they may differ in their views about what it really means. But there does appear to be some basic agreement on the meaning of the term *culture* in anthropology. What is this meaning, and how is it used in anthropological work?

Like all scientific concepts, the concept of culture refers to some aspect of the world *out there* that scientists are committed to study. It helps anthropologists to single out from this reality certain things that help them in their work. One anthropological line of investigation concerns the general nature of human beings as compared with other animals, particularly nonhuman primates such as chimpanzees and gorillas, which are most like humans in their physical make-up. Anthropologists are also interested in the ways of life of particular human populations in comparison with others. Are humans everywhere basically the same or do they differ? If, as seems likely, the answer is "all of the above," what is the extent of their similarities and differences? The concept of culture helps to further both of these anthropological lines of investigation.

How does the concept of culture help in the comparison of humans with other animals? The crucial issue here concerns the learning capacity of different kinds of animals. Bees go on about their business day after day, year in and year out, in the same inflexible fashion. Each type of bee is specialized for a particular kind of activity, and it continues (or tries to continue) this activity regardless of changes around it. For example, a worker bee "works" to collect pollen, which contributes to the survival of the hive. This behavior is mostly programmed by genetic mechanisms that change comparatively slowly in a manner independent of changes in the environment. Behavioral change, then, tends to await a change in bee genes. As a result, the behavior of bees is comparatively inflexible. Among humans, on the other hand, behavior is much more flexible. This flexibility is the result of the great human capacity to learn from experience. True, humans are not unique among animals in their ability to learn, but so great is their learning capacity and so important is it for adaptation that some kind of special marker seems to be called for. That marker, as used by anthropologists, is culture. Sometimes, in order to keep things neat, they may use a term like protoculture to distinguish the comparatively small amount of learned behavior (when it exists) in other animals. But whether this distinction is made or not, the term is used to refer to what is considered to be an outstanding (if not unique) quality of humankind.

In addition to this comparison of humans and nonhumans, anthropologists have been interested in the differences and similarities between human groups or populations, each of which works out (through learning) its specific adaptation to conditions of life. The anthropologist, when concerned with the (learned) behavioral characteristics of a specific group, will refer to its "culture," thus, for example, the culture of the Zuni Indians of the American southwest. When used in this way, the term *culture* is localized in a group of human beings. Observations are made about common behavioral tendencies within the group, and accordingly, one often sees in anthropological texts some statement about culture being shared. This does not mean that all people in the group behave exactly alike, but rather that they refer to certain agreed-upon social norms or rules for behavior. While recognizing that each individual has his or her own way of interpreting these norms, anthropologists see in each group certain central tendencies that become a point of reference in describing its culture. Thus, Group X may be characterized as being aggressive, monotheistic nomads. This type of general description helps anthropologists to identify a culture and to make comparisons within the species.

THE REALITY OF CULTURE

Culture is a concept that refers to an aspect of the world *out there*, that is, the real world as we know it. A particularly good way to come to terms with this reality is to spend some time in a foreign country. For example, consider the case of an American who set out to conduct business in the Catalonian region of Spain during the early 1960s. This businessman gradually became aware that there was a human reality in this place and that he had to adapt to it in order to be successful. The Catalans that he dealt with on a day-to-day basis tended to have things in common; they seemed to have shared patterns of behavior that were unlike his own. The American wanted to be able to count on his host counterpart to fulfill his promises. For example, would the construction of a factory be completed by the date agreed upon? It became clear that this was unlikely. Delay tended to follow delay, and things that were promised for mañana might appear weeks later. As he gained experience, the American learned that this was not the exception, but the *rule*. The Catalans tended to function in a totally different way than was customary at home. For them, mañana usually did not mean the next day; a close fit between promises and deeds generally was not expected. It also became increasingly clear to the visitor that considerations of family and friendship often entered into business dealings. In this less machinelike atmosphere, the American sputtered and fumed until he finally began to learn, (usually the hard way), that the Catalans were not wrong or crazy, only different. They had their own ways.

Then, this American was forced to reflect on his own, that is, American ways. He began to recognize that these ways, too, were different. This led to the revelation that each people has its own norms for behavior that are considered natural and right and that individuals in each society share in these norms. From personal experience, then, the American had come to accept the reality of the thing that anthropologists call culture. Having understood, he could then use this comprehension to advantage in his business activities.

The anthropologist might say that the transformed American had acquired a cross-cultural or transcultural perspective and that he was beginning to think like an anthropologist who makes comparisons between cultures. At first the businessman would have criticized the Catalans by referring to their lack of reliability or even modernity. At that point, the "States" would have provided a benchmark for making judgments about other cultures. Such observations—as any anthropologist would be delighted to tell him—were *ethnocentric*, that is, based on the assumption that his own culture was the center of the universe and that everything should be measured against it. The American lacked the power to make this ethnocentric view prevail in Spain. Accordingly, he acquired, however reluctantly, something like the anthropological viewpoint that any culture (including one's own) is simply one of a number of ways in which people have worked out their adaptation to specific life conditions.

If he were particularly perceptive, the American might have had another revelation at this point: that, for better or worse, one is a creature of one's culture. Each culture's norms have a hold over its people, and it is just as difficult to change them as to change the kind of person we are. Our culture becomes an inextricable part of our lives and sets limits on who we can reasonably be. Such a revelation points up a paradox. The capacity to create culture has liberated humans from the crass dictates of their biological heritage. But in each culture the weight of social custom or opinion limits people's outlook and their ability to change. James Baldwin, the American black writer, said that he did not realize how much of an American he was until he went abroad. The fact that Baldwin was not exactly in the mainstream of American society suggests how powerful a hold a culture can have on its people.

THE STUDY OF A CULTURE

All anthropologists deal with culture, but it is the sociocultural anthropologist, attempting to enter into the lifeways of a contemporary people, for whom the reality of culture is most evident. In their role of ethnographer these anthropologists are bent on describing particular cultures and attempting to explain why they are as they are. In order to do this they usually live with a people for an extended period of time—the period of fieldwork. During this period, which has acquired a kind of sacred aura in anthropological circles, they seek to acquire an understanding of a people's behavior from their own point of view. Such an immersion into an alien life, which begins with learning a sometimes very difficult language, is absolutely indispensable for the proper study of a culture. Unlike the biologist or geologist who study their subjects from outside only, the anthropologist, like the psychiatrist, has to contend with the dimension of consciousness in human subjects.

There are special problems in living with, and getting to know, an alien people. Anthropologists are not immune to these problems. Culture shock, a kind of situational neurosis that comes about when one loses one's cultural bearings, can seriously upset them. There may be problems in establishing rapport or maintaining the interest of people. This is illustrated in E. E. Evans-Pritchard's humorous introduction to his book on the East African cattle-keeping Nuer. After detailing a particularly frustrating conversation with an informant, this anthropologist speaks of the "*Nuer*-osis" that can afflict anyone who has to deal with these people. Difficulties of this nature appear to have increased recently as native peoples have become more independent and assertive. Anthropologists may have to engage in long negotiations before they can begin their study.

Today, our world is changing rapidly; it is also filled with conflict. Anthropologists must be prepared to encounter revolutions, terrorism, and ambiguous political authority. With increasing frequency, they are being forced to take sides and make moral choices that can have wrenching consequences. Imagine trying to conduct a first-hand, politically oriented study in South Africa. In addition to such hazards, there is always the threat of one's own enthnocentrism, which can skew one's observations and interpretations.

A notorious example of fieldwork difficulties occurred during Colin Turnbull's sojourn with the Ik, which he wrote about in *The Mountain People*. Prevented from pursuing their traditional hunting and gathering way of life in east Africa, the Ik have disintegrated into a people for whom collective interests have practically disappeared. In this condition where each person is for himself, the stronger take from the weaker and even families fall apart. As Turnbull immersed himself in this culture, he found that he was treated in the same way the Ik treated each other. He was so repelled by this "war of each against all" that he was unable to continue his role of sympathetic and objective fieldworker. As a result, Turnbull's book is a better analysis of his own problems in the field than of Ik culture.

This is an extreme example, surely. It is increasingly common, though, for anthropologists to report on their personal experience in the field. No longer is the anthropologist considered to be some kind of superhuman, cross-cultural reporter. It is now widely recognized that he or she may have problems like any overseas venturer. For many years, the experiences of Bronislaw Malinowski during his fieldwork in the Trobriand Islands (reported in *Argonauts of the Western Pacific* and other works) were taken as a model for the fieldworker. It came as a sensation, therefore, when Malinowski's *A Diary in the Strict Sense of the Term* revealed his personal turmoil and hostility—even prejudice—towards the Trobrianders. Having read this diary, one is in a better position to see where Malinowski was coming from when he wrote about Trobriand culture. Two anthropologists who approach a culture from the same point of view, who have equal access, and who look at the same things should come away with similar descriptions. If not, it could be that some personal factors are distorting the picture they develop. By telling the reader about themselves and their work in the field they are helping that reader to evaluate their report.

Now that anthropologists are doing fieldwork closer to home, questions have been raised about special problems associated with this kind of investigation. Take, for example, a study of the doctor-patient relationship in an American hospital. To begin, the anthropologist would become familiar with medicine and with hospital procedures. Then he or she would make arrangements to settle into the hospital routine as a participant observer. Finally, informants would be sought out to talk about the relationship between doctors and patients from different points of view. There would be no problems with the language and probably no culture shock. Ethical and political problems might turn up, but these are routine in dealing with human subjects. All of this suggests that in contrast with the study of another culture this would be a comparatively easy investigation. And that is just the problem. In a foreign culture everything seems new and problematic. In studying the "barefoot doctor"-patient relationship in modern China, an American anthropologist would probably be struck by the egalitarian nature of this relationship and try to account for it. The authority of the American doctor would be something less problematic and more likely taken for granted. As a result, the American would raise fewer questions about it than would, say, a Chinese anthropologist. Here, as elsewhere, it is the hold of our own culture over us that has to be constantly monitored.

For the anthropological fieldworker (and for the sensitive traveler), therefore, the reality of the thing called culture is indisputable. One gets in touch with this reality by dealing with people who are controlled by cultural norms. Anything that tends to loosen our culture's hold over us (as, for example, traveling abroad) can bring about an awareness that it is not only others, but we, ourselves, who are controlled by cultural norms. None of us can escape the reality of culture, but some of us are more aware of it than others.

THE LOOK OF A CULTURE

Anthropologists have a variety of theoretical orientations that they bring to their studies, and their descriptions inevitably take on the look of their theory. Beyond theories, though, there is a common perspective that anthropologists tend to share. This perspective gives each ethnography or field report a distinctive anthropological look that distinguishes it from, say, the look given it by a political scientist or travel writer. One of the dimensions of this look has to do with individual or subcultural variability. It was pointed out earlier that each culture has norms and that people's behavior ranges around these norms. Such variation has limits. People who go beyond these limits in their behavior put themselves, in effect, outside of their culture. Normal people will mark those persons as being off limits, so to speak, and treat them accordingly. A consideration of cultural deviation has been an important line of anthropological inquiry and has contributed not only to an understanding of deviants, but also the ways in which cultures maintain themselves.

Consider the fact that where witchcraft exists, people marked as witches or victims of witches tend to be cultural deviants. For example, M. G. Marwick, in documenting more than one hundred cases of witchcraft accusation among the Cêwa, an east African agricultural people, found that approximately one-half of the witches and two-thirds of the victims were deviants of one sort or another. Examples of deviants included people who did not meet traditional obligations or who were jealous or greedy. The standard way of accounting for the fact that there is a tendency for victims or accused witches to be social deviants is to argue that witchcraft is, in Clyde Kluckhohn's words, *good* for society in that it restrains deviation. To be accused of being a witch or to be thought a victim is considered bad or unfortunate. Those who are marked as witches or victims tend to have certain socially undesirable qualities. Therefore, it would be better for one's personal welfare to avoid acquiring these qualities. In this way, witchcraft works through the feelings of guilt, shame, or fear that exist in people. It serves to shore up cultural norms and prevent a society from falling apart. More familiar, if less dramatic, social pressures of a similar kind are brought to bear on the people we deal with in our own everyday lives. All peoples act to limit behavioral variability and thus maintain the cultural norms on which an orderly social life depends. However, no people, however collectivized, has managed to eliminate behavioral variability. For this reason, a true picture of a culture ought to give us some idea of the nature and extent of this variability.

Another dimension of the look that anthropologists like to give to a culture is called holistic. Each culture is seen as an ordered system of more or less integrated parts. Whether these parts stand out or not, they are dealt with as separate entities and then related to each other in some way. Every culture, in order to survive, must handle certain tasks such as organizing its people, producing material goods, bringing up its young people, etc. In the anthropological look, behaviors associated with these tasks are seen to hang together in some way. They may reinforce or concur with one another as in the case of capitalism and individualism; or they may conflict or contradict as in the case of different social classes. There may be a tight or loose fit between the parts. In any case, all cultural elements are seen to be part of the same system and shaped by its essential nature. The quest for that essential nature is the sixty-four dollar question that continues to preoccupy many anthropologists, but the days of easy formulations such as those of Ruth Benedict in *Patterns of Culture* appear to be over. Benedict thought that one could find a single principle that underlay all areas of a culture. For example, the essential principle in Dobuan life was an extreme suspiciousness bordering on what we might call paranoia. This formulation, at once simple and comprehensive, exaggerated the idea of cultural integration. Today, most anthropologists would be more cautious in tying things together. Nevertheless, they continue to search for more essential elements on which other components of a culture depend. In his famous study of kinship, George Murdock argued that the rule of residence (where the newly married couple lives in relation to their relatives) tends to act as a shaping influence on other aspects of kinship. And Maurice Godelier, in a number of sophisticated works, has asserted the primacy of relations of production (that is, social relations involved in the production of material goods) over other facets of a culture.

Another dimension of the look that anthropologists give to a culture is contextual. They tend to see a culture as fitting into some natural or social context. A culture is seen to be the way it is, in part, because of the context in which it is embedded. This ecological perspective can be overworked as an explanatory device, but it has become an essential part of most ethnographies, which usually begin with a discussion of the natural habitat and surrounding peoples. The trick here is to get at the *relevant* context. Not all aspects of the surrounding world are equally important for understanding a culture. For example, to understand American culture today, Canada, which is close by, is less relevant than Soviet Russia, which is far away. And different aspects of a culture's context may be more or less relevant depending on the focus of the research.

The San (Bushmen) of the Kalihari Desert in southern Africa provide a good example of a culture that is finely adjusted to its natural context. Before they were settled on reservations and otherwise pushed around by the more powerful South African society, these people practiced a hunting and gathering way of life that involved wandering about and stopping for longer or shorter periods according to the availability of water, game, and vegetation. Possessing only a simple technology, they had to adapt to nature's requirements in order to survive. The size of their bands, the length of their stay in a given spot, and the need to keep moving around all were dictated by the availability of naturally occurring food and water. And because substantial accumulation of belongings was impossible, the San worked only long enough and hard enough to provide for present satisfaction. This culture, which Marshall Sahlins described as the "original affluent society," existed in what some might consider an inhospitable desert. Yet it was well enough adapted to produce levels of health and longevity that even a modern people might value. Other hunters and gatherers, living in harsher habitats, have not made out as well, but all have had to be attentive to the dictates of their natural context in order to survive.

The natural environment is not always the first thing to be considered in analyzing a culture. Sometimes the social context is more important, as in the case of the San today. Increasingly, they have been settled on reservations where they are dependent on government handouts and part- or full-time employment in an alien society. Hunting and gathering ways are disappearing as the San adapt to the culture of a more powerful outside world. Increasing rates of illness and signs of demoralization indicate that this adaptation has not been entirely successful; but whether successful or not, the present culture of the San cannot be comprehended without reference to the one in which it is engulfed.

The pattern of sociocultural change just described has turned up often in recent anthropological literature that deals with questions of development or acculturation. Change now is so obvious that many anthropologists have sought to capture and explain it. It reminds us that every culture has a history that needs to be depicted in one way or another. This adds a further dimension to the look that the anthropologist must give to a culture—the historical. By knowing the historic trend in a culture, one is better able to understand the present and, perhaps, the future. Sometimes the picture the anthropologist offers freezes change at a particular point in time. This would be particularly appropriate for tradition-bound societies such as the San around the turn of this century. In other cases, the picture emphasizes change and attempts to give some idea of motion through time as in studies of recent San "development." Obviously, what is happening out there dictates what kind of picture should be presented, but sometimes change and stability are so intertwined that theoretical concerns will dictate which perspective is dominant. The dimension of history must be dealt with in some way, however.

To recapitulate, although anthropologists approach cultures from different points of view, there are certain common anthropological dimensions in the pictures that these scientists offer of the cultures they have studied. A culture is seen as normative, that is, as having certain central tendencies for behavior. Its people's actions are seen to vary around, and be limited by, social norms. It is a more or less integrated whole, the parts of which are tied together in some way. It is embedded in some natural-social context to which it is more or less adapted. And finally, it has a history that can be frozen in time or captured from the point of view of change. Every ethnography has a particular point of view, but its goal should be a faithful reproduction of the life of a people from that perspective.

The degree of accuracy of an ethnography may not be easy to determine, as debates about some famous anthropological studies have demonstrated. Because it is not so easy to check up on the work of one's scientific colleagues, the integrity and ability of each ethnographer would seem to merit greater scrutiny. The more open they are about their work, the easier it will be for others to evaluate it.

WHAT'S THE POINT?

Thousands of anthropological monographs have been written about particular cultures. What is the point of it all? One goal has been simple description: To describe the immense variety of human ways even as the naturalist describes the variety of living things that have inhabited our globe. It is possible to look at the entire panorama of cultures and to begin to classify them in various ways. For example, the manner in which food is obtained or the system of political organization are readily classifiable. Then, the anthropologist can begin to define the limits on all human behavior and discover cultural universals; that is, the elements that all cultures have in common. Thus, it will be possible to sort out pan-human from culture-specific traits. As an example, take the concept of the Oedipus Complex that was developed by Sigmund Freud. This psychological condition is supposed to derive from the little boy's lust for his mother and associated hostility towards the competing father. But Freud formulated his idea in a culture in which the nuclear family, that is, an independent social group consisting of a married couple and their offspring, was the norm. What about other cultures with other kinship arrangements? The anthropological debate, which at first seemed to favor the notion that the Oedipus Complex was culturally specific, now seems to be leaning toward its universality. Without a number of specific ethnographies to rely on, this debate never could have taken place.

A second goal of all this study is explanatory. Why the variety and why the sameness in all these cultures? A simple answer that has been proposed repeatedly is that behavior is biologically based, or controlled, and that people behave the way they do because of the gene packages they inherit. Thus, common biology accounts for the sameness in behavior and biological differences (racial differences, for example) account for variety. Adolph Hitler sought to explain two types of behavior that he considered important; cultural creation and cultural destruction. He argued that some peoples tend to create cultures and others to destroy them. These races cannot help what they do; it is in their blood, so to speak. So, for Hitler, differences in peoples' behavior were a result of differences in their physical make-up. This kind of racism, and other more sophisticated attempts to account for variability in human behavior in terms of biology, have not been welcome in anthropology where the stress on humans' culture-making ability has tended to downgrade biological explanations. Where behavioral differences between human groups are concerned, some kind of learned adaptation has been the preferred explanation. The things that all cultures have in common are more likely to have a biological basis, but even here, one has to be careful. All humans are biological creatures. They have bodies, without which there can be no behavior, and they share a common biological heritage. But in the course of their evolution they have developed a capacity for culture and thus vastly increased the flexibility of their behavior. There are common problems that all peoples face. Humans could just as easily learn to handle these problems in common ways as to have them dictated by biology. In accounting for behavioral differences and similarities between peoples, it would seem perilous to ignore the cultural mode of adaptation.

Another goal of the science of culture is to find out how cultures are integrated. How do different elements of a culture hang together and why? Are there, for example, certain sociocultural conditions that regularly go together with warlike tendencies? Might such tendencies have something to do with population pressure? Is it possible to find the keys to the direction of sociocultural change? Are they to be found, for example, in certain "contradictions" that develop in a culture? These kinds of questions continue to concern anthropologists, and it is appropriate that they who are most familiar with the workings of cultures should try to answer them.

One could argue that it is enough to know about the myriad cultural worlds that humans have created and to have this story told by scientific storytellers. But some would like to hear of the more practical implications of all of this scientific activity. ("What's in it for the average householder?", I used to ask of a physicist colleague in a radio series we were doing together.) So far in this chapter the argument has been that all humans (including the writer and reader of this little book) are creatures of their cultures. These cultures are ways of life that groups of people have created to deal with particular life conditions. In creating these ways of life, humans are the least controlled of all animals by their biological make-up. But the culture that a group of humans has created acquires through time the weight of a social heritage that takes hold of the people in it. People who have grown up in a culture tend to take its ways for granted and think of them as natural or right. One who has acquired a transcultural perspective will know the limitations of this point of view. Such a person, on entering another culture, will begin with the advantage of knowing that its people consider its ways to be natural or right in the manner of people everywhere. If bent on doing business, transculturally sophisticated persons will have an advantage because they take their hosts and their ways seriously. This is what the astute American businessman working in the Catalonian region of Spain learned to do. In a world in which intercultural mobility is increasing dramatically and in which national, corporate, and personal interests can extend around the globe, the ability to transcend one's own culture appears to have become a necessity. Surprisingly, it is something that is still not taken seriously by many Americans. Some American firms, for example, continue to deal with overseas problems by dispatching technically specialized troubleshooters, who have little or no knowledge of the host culture. One wonders how such a disregard of the culture of "the other" can contribute to the competitive advantage these firms say they are seeking.

The study of cultures can also increase an individual's self-awareness and help solve problems of personal identity. This is a project that, for some Americans, may assume cosmic proportions! For example, consider an average American young woman who is reasonably sensitive, open-minded, and intelligent, and who is working out her own line of self-realization. By learning about the various cultures of the world she becomes aware of the greater possibilities in life. She learns that cultures are the creations of humans in response to the dictates of particular life circumstances. It becomes increasingly clear that there is no right or natural way to live or be—only different ways. This realization may add to her growing awareness that life is not something that has been pretty much laid out for one from the beginning. Now she sees that there are possibilities, and she must ask herself what she will make of them all. Questions such as this may have intrigued the many students who made *Patterns of Culture* one of the more popular anthropological works. Among the cultures that Ruth Benedict wrote about in this book were the Pueblo Indians of the American southwest. She portrayed them as living a measured, harmonious, cooperative existence. Benedict pictured them as not asserting themselves and not engaging in the excesses exhibited by the Indians of the northwest coast of America, for example. The variety of lifestyles presented in her book opened up additional alternatives for self-seekers and conveyed a sense of freedom beyond one's dreams.

However, further study of the cultures of the world may show that one does not have all that much freedom after all in working out a personal identity. Consider the average American who attends a State Department orientation for people about to travel abroad. The lecturer suddenly asks how many of her listeners are touching the people next to them. From the benefit of her experience and, perhaps, from having read some of the works of the anthropologist Edward T. Hall, she knows that even though the people in her audience are seated close together they will not be touching each other. She uses this understanding to begin a digression about the personal "bubble" that

Americans carry around with them. Each culture, she says, has a different notion of personal space. For Americans, that space is rather large, but for others, like the San who lived virtually on top of one another in their little bands, it may be hard to find any personal "bubble" at all.

What is the upshot of this lecture on cross-cultural differences in personal space and others like it? One effect may be a realization that if culture can exert such an influence on an almost unconscious area of our lives, it must be a powerful determining force indeed. At this stage of her cultural awareness our average American might be forgiven for taking the opposite tack, which leads her to believe that, even if there are many other possibilities in life, they may not actually be realizable. By some mysterious means, each culture acquires a powerful hold over its members, a hold that extends even into the unconscious domain. One is, in fact, a creature of one's culture.

But the realization that our own personal identity is inextricably tied up with our own culture is not the whole truth either. Culture can be a strong determinant of individual behavior, but it can never be an all-determining influence. Even in totalitarian societies where deviation is treated harshly, individual variability exists. No culture can eliminate those individual particularities that exist in every human being. What it does is set up desirable lines of behavior and put limits on social deviation. Beyond these limits one takes one's chances, but within them there can be a good deal of space for maneuver. For more timid individuals, the possibility of socially acceptable freedom exists. It merely requires knowledge of cultural norms and their limits for one to realize the available alternatives. For the more heroic or daring—the revolutionaries, the great innovators, the rejecters, and all other major deviators—cultural limitations are less of a problem. Driven by powerful individual needs, they may succeed eventually in changing their culture, as was the case with Jesus of Nazareth or Karl Marx. On the other hand, their deviations may satisfy no one but themselves and they will fall into oblivion.

In the course of her odyssey of cultural awareness, our average American has come to grips with the concept of culture and its implications for her own life. And because she is reasonable sensitive, intelligent, etc., it may have some consequence for her own self-realization. Instead of being merely a creature of culture, then, she will have become one who is culturally aware. She will be able to use this awareness to chart her own, and perhaps even some collective, destiny. In a rapidly changing, open society such as our own, where one's fate is not predetermined, but must be achieved—often painfully—this is quite a contribution.

SELECTED REFERENCES

AGAR, MICHAEL, *The Professional Stranger: An Informal Introduction to Ethnography*. New York: Academic Press, 1980.

BENEDICT, RUTH, *Patterns of Culture*. Boston: Houghton Mifflin Co., 1980.

EVANS-PRITCHARD, E. E., *The Nuer*. Oxford: The Clarendon Press, 1940.

GODELIER, MAURICE, *Perspectives in Marxist Anthropology*. Cambridge and New York: Cambridge University Press, 1977.

HALL, EDWARD T., *The Hidden Dimension*. Garden City, N. Y.: Doubleday and Co., 1966.

MALINOWSKI, BRONISLAW, *Argonauts of the Western Pacific*. New York: E. P. Dutton and Co., 1922.

———, *A Diary in the Strict Sense of the Term*. New York: Harcourt Brace and World, 1977.

MARWICK, M. G., *Sorcery in Its Social Setting*. Manchester, England: Manchester University Press, 1965.

MURDOCK, GEORGE P., *Social Structure*. New York: The Macmillan Co., 1949.

NASH, DENNISON, *A Community in Limbo: An Anthropological Study of an American Community Abroad*. Bloomington, Indiana: Indiana University Press, 1970.

SPIRO, MELFORD E., *Oedipus in the Trobriands*. Chicago: University of Chicago Press, 1982.

TURNBULL, COLIN M., *The Mountain People*. New York: Simon and Schuster, 1972.

Chapter Three

THE INDIVIDUAL IN CULTURE

"*Cogito ergo sum.*" (I think; therefore I am.)

Any American adolescent could have told René Descartes that he was wasting his time worrying about the existence of the self. That is something that Americans generally take for granted. Anthropologists, on the other hand, are suspicious of such assumptions. Too many things that are considered natural by a people turn out to be culturally specific. Is it possible that somewhere (possibly in some Buddhist society in the Far East) some people might not recognize the human individual? The answer is no. All peoples do recognize the individual among the objects they discriminate. The first, second, and third person singular exist in all languages, and some concept of the individual person or self is found in all cultures. But that concept is not necessarily like ours. The anthropologist wants to know how it varies from culture to culture and what, if any, regularities exist. How may such differences and similarities be explained? What is the nature of the relationship between individual and culture? These are the main questions that will be addressed in this chapter.

We in the West tend to think of the self as independent or autonomous. There are sharp boundaries between it and the rest of the world. This conception has developed in a culture where individualism has been on the march for centuries. Other cultures with different histories have different conceptions of the self. There is a problem, therefore, with applying western psychology, based on the western notion of the individual, cross-culturally. It does not need to be rejected totally, but it has to be tried on with a good deal of trial and error in other cultures. Also, it should not be forgotten that the individual may be a more or less important element in one society than another. Finally, it should be remembered that anthropologists may be more inclined to think of a culture as the life-ways of a group or simply of a bunch of individuals. Depending on their orientation, the individual will be a more or less important element in their description and analysis.

Keeping all of these cautions in mind, it nevertheless is possible to assert that something roughly equivalent to the adapting psychobiological entity that western psychologists call a personality exists in all cultures. Along with culture, this concept has evolved through the ages, but it is far removed from the prehuman condition. One aspect of personality is the self-image, which is derived from humans' advanced capacity for conceptual thought. In his various writings on the subject, A. I. Hallowell traced the evolution of the human personality, including the self, and laid out a number of its universal characteristics. Following George Herbert Mead, Hallowell thought that individuals everywhere are constantly looking at themselves from others' perspectives, as well as their own, and evaluating the resulting self-image. All human behavior is self-oriented in this fashion, which is to say that it attends to both individual and social requirements. It would seem that, in order to survive, every culture must make some provision for both of these requirements. It is apparent, though, that some peoples prefer selfs that lean more in one direction than another.

JAPANESE AND AMERICANS

Japanese and Americans obviously differ in many respects. Many Americans these days would like to better comprehend the differences they encounter in dealing with Japanese businesspeople in the international marketplace. An understanding of the typical Japanese citizen can help to explain not only the suicide-prone *Kamikaze* pilots of World War II, but also the remarkable productivity of Japanese industrial firms today. To know how the Japanese tend to think of themselves is to know something about what makes them "tick." There is no lack of literature on this subject. In going over this literature, one finds that there is an emphasis on the collective orientation of the Japanese as opposed to American individualism. For the Japanese, an enormous firm like Mitsubishi is a kind of giant family to which everyone contributes for the common good. The firm, in turn, is expected to take care of all of its people throughout their lives, in good times as well as bad. More individualistic Americans are inevitably struck by the way in which a typical Japanese employee subordinates strictly individual goals for the good of the whole. For example, there is usually no question of taking a job in another firm to further one's own career. However, the employee will move willingly from job to job within the firm, regardless of his or her own personal predilections, simply because the firm requires it. What kind of self is to be found in a culture with such a collective orientation?

Looking at the Japanese in terms of their self-image, one sees that they tend to be less willing than Americans to put themselves forward or stand out. They seem to be, in Takie Sugiyama Lebra's words, "exposure sensitive." Eye-to-eye contact, which is idealized in American business circles, is anathema in Japan. The Japanese seem bent on keeping as much of themselves as possible hidden. Such reticence suggests to Lebra that, compared with Americans, the Japanese keep a larger part of their total self hidden or unexpressed. In contrast, the typical American would like to "put all their cards on the table," "tell it like it is," or "let it all hang out."

What happens when, for some reason, a Japanese person stands out from others? He or she may then begin to experience *haji*, which is a kind of shame derived from self-exposure. It is not the shame that comes from doing something wrong, but only from being exposed. Because such shame can be a painful experience, it must be avoided. This results in a reticent individual who prefers to blend into a group. But not always. There are times when the Japanese let their hair down with intimates at a bar or hotspring bath. In this type of setting, it is possible to put aside their covering-up operations.

The intense shame-orientation of the Japanese indicates that they keep themselves under considerable scrutiny from what they take to be others' points of view; and because they are very concerned with what they believe to be others' views of them, the selfs of the Japanese appear to be rather other-oriented. A further indication of this is to be found in the Japanese tendency to blame themselves for their real or imagined transgressions against others. It is no empty gesture when the president of Japan Airlines apologizes publicly to the families of victims of an air crash. Japanese bear a heavy burden of guilt (*sumanai* or *mōshiwakenai*), which is strongly other-oriented. If people have done things for you it is not possible to rest until they are repaid, possibly many times over. One gladly shoulders the blame for others' misfortunes. One offers endless apologies for what an American would like to think is beyond one's area of responsibility. Americans suffer other-oriented guilt of course, but in America it has become something to be gotten rid of—in therapy, perhaps. In Japan, one form of therapy actually involves promoting guilt consciousness through self-reflection.

This little cross-cultural excursion was not designed to make an exhaustive comparison of Japanese and American selfs, but it does suggest certain dimensions in which these selfs differ. First, the public-private dimension: It has been suggested that the public part of the self is smaller for Japanese than for Americans. Second, other-orientation: The Japanese self appears to be more other-oriented than the American. In Japan the burden of collective concerns imposed on the individual through the self would appear to require some release. One such release is provided in culturally sanctioned get-togethers with intimates in certain locales. Here, the individual side of the Japanese self is given room for expression.

Though this analysis may have given the reader a deeper understanding of the Japanese orientation towards the group, it does contain some rather sweeping generalizations. Is it legitimate to describe whole nations of people as having a single personality? Obviously, there are many different kinds of Japanese and Americans. At one time, some psychologically oriented anthropologists spoke of the national character, or basic personality, of a society, which was said to exist—more or less—in all of the people in that nation. An analogy might be a picture of a group of individuals who had all been dipped in the same pot of paint. More careful investigations, though, have shown that such a view is difficult to sustain. There may be several "basic" personality types—more or less depending on the culture and the viewpoint of the analyst. Even in some supposedly primitive cultures, where people were expected to be more alike, it became apparent that it was inaccurate to say that most people in a culture come in the same basic colors.

Having given up their tendency for easy generalization, anthropologists these days usually present frequency distributions of personality types or traits. For example, Lebra, whose work has contributed importantly to this discussion of Japanese and Americans selfs, details the frequency of shame- and guilt-type responses on the psychological tests she administered in a Japanese city. Such distributions are, of course, entirely consistent with the notion of cultural variability discussed earlier. Some authors try to tie down their generalization to a specific social location or subculture. Thus, they might refer to young, male, urban, middle-class Japanese and similarly located Americans. Such specification is more and more the expected thing in a discipline where impressionistic observations are giving way to science. So, the above excursion into certain qualities of Japanese and American personalities should be considered only a preliminary operation.

THE FORMATION OF THE INDIVIDUAL

It is possible, then, to begin with the assumption that in every culture there are recognizable individuals, each of whom can be thought of as having a personality that includes a self. Every culture has norms for how these personalities ought to be—or are—constituted. Hallowell called them "culturally constituted" personalities, which means that they have been shaped in terms of the culture around them. How this process occurs has been a major consideration for psychological anthropologists. Research in this area has proceeded by fits and starts. Earlier, more confident assertions have given way before the enormity of the problems of cross-cultural psychological research. Western ethnocentrism is a constant impediment in such investigations. There have been false turns now and again, as in the promotion of the notion of basic personality or national character. Though acceptable answers are only beginning to emerge, there appears to be general consensus as to the important questions and what kind of answers are to be expected.

First, consider the individual at birth, not just in our culture, but in all cultures. This individual is an organism with the potential for becoming a full-fledged human being. One may think of this organism as a bundle of biologically dictated impulses to behavior. These impulses, which ultimately are genetically determined, are not inflexible. The human infant is not a "full organism" at birth or "hard-wired." On the contrary, it takes growth and experience to form a human individual. There has been a good deal of debate about how great a role experience plays in this process, but it would appear to be considerable.

Through birth, the organism appears in some human population somewhere—a population that has a culture. To the developing infant this culture is a kind of environment that, through the mediation of certain humans, shapes its experience world and thus the direction of its development. The child, of course, makes something of himself or herself on the basis of specific needs, but ultimately what it becomes is dictated by its experience with the representatives of a culture. To the extent that a person is formed by this experience, it may be said to be *socialized*. Anthropologically viewed, the formation of the human individual takes place through the process of socialization.

Take a typical anthropological problem. Are the individuals in culture *A* more intelligent on the average than those in culture *B*, and if so, how may the difference be explained? To take an example close to home, American blacks and whites have been tested repeatedly with results that indicate that blacks generally score lower than whites on intelligence tests. This difference, however, is narrowed, but not eliminated, if the individuals being tested come from similar cultural backgrounds. Is the remaining difference to be attributed to biology or culture? A "biologist" like Arthur Jensen says that, even though culture is a factor to be considered, a significant part of the difference must be attributed to the different biological make-ups of the two populations. "Environmentalists," on the other hand, point out that the tests, which have been standardized and constructed for white populations, are unfair to blacks. Moreover, they argue, the fact of racial discrimination still exists in American society. Until it is eliminated, blacks —even those with comparable socioeconomic status—will not have an equivalent cultural background. As a result, their scores will continue to be inferior to those of whites.

The issue is socially important because acceptance of one or the other position can justify doing something about racial inequality or doing nothing. The issue is so complex, and the claims and counterclaims so strident, that one might easily give up trying to come to a rational conclusion and instead go on gut feeling. Even a superficial glance through the literature reveals that there is a wide variety of opinions as to the value of the hereditary component of intelligence. The truth appears to be that heredity and environment interact in different ways in different populations. Thus, any attempt to fix a value of the component for making comparisons between populations is fraught with difficulty. The "biologists" have been banking on a comparatively high value derived from sometimes fraudulent twin studies in the same culture, but cross-cultural studies of American blacks and whites have suggested that environment plays a greater role in the intelligence test performance of blacks than whites. This leads me to believe that *all* of the differences between average black and white scores are attributable to environmental factors. Given a fair test, adequate nutrition before and after birth, enough psychic and emotional nurturance, education, and economic and social opportunities, the average American black probably would do as well as the average American white. In sum, it seems reasonable to conclude that biological differences between the populations or races are not responsible for the difference in measured intelligence.

Does this mean that biology can be discounted as a factor in explaining psychological differences between populations? Unfortunately, no cut-and-dried answer is possible. It would appear to depend not only on the populations being investigated, but also the psychological traits involved. For example, consider behavior that might indicate a quality such as temperament. Are some populations more volatile than others, as in the oft-noted comparison between northern and southern Europeans? If so, is this difference attributable to biological or racial differences? Daniel Freedman investigated the responses of infants from what he refers to as "ethnic" groups. He found that Caucasian (in this case, white, American) infants, tested shortly after birth, tended to respond more readily, excitedly, and over a longer duration to a series of provocations (for example, holding a cloth over the baby's nose) than infants of Oriental origin. His experiments, which appear to support the idea that the alleged Oriental "inscrutability" is to some extent inborn, can raise storms of protest from some readers of his work. Their first reaction is to attack the methodology of these experiments. But Freedman had anticipated most, if not all, of these objections by employing a fairly sophisticated series of controls. The fact that he has a Chinese wife who assisted him in his experiments also tends to counter any accusations of racism that may come his way. Some additional controls are needed, but it now seems to be a fair inference that Oriental and Caucasian newborns do indeed differ in their reactions to various stimuli and that this difference is biologically dictated.

Does this mean that Caucasian Americans and Japanese will

exhibit what amounts to racially determined differences in temperament? Yes and no. Freedman also analyzed studies of communication between Japanese mothers and their infants in the United States. First-generation mothers and their infants behaved as would be expected from the experiments; there was very little verbalization between them. However, the anthropologist involved in this particular investigation reported that third-generation Japanese-American mothers and their progeny were chattering away at a "super-American" rate. Since their biology had not changed (there was no gene flow with Caucasian Americans through intermarriage), some kind of environmental influence must have been responsible. That influence was probably the result of being raised and functioning in American culture. It would seem, therefore, that however they differ from Americans at birth in their level of ebullience, Japanese are capable of changing more than enough to wipe out the difference in a lifetime. Freedman recognizes this in his concept of "reaction range," which specifies the range of possibilities for development of a particular behavioral trait. Some traits have broad ranges, others narrow. The particular course of development a growing individual takes within a range will be determined by the special nature of his or her life experiences.

To illustrate how all of this would look on a broader canvas, consider aggression in human males and females. The evidence suggests that males tend to be born with a greater disposition to aggressive behavior than females. There are individual females who show more aggression than males in a society, but the general tendency is toward greater aggression in males. The difference has been noted in early childhood not only in American culture, but in many cultures for which there are adequate data. (There are few cultures in which there is no apparent difference, but none in which females, generally, are more aggressive than males.) Moreover, the same pattern is found in nonhuman primates. This suggests that the difference in aggressive disposition is likely to be evolutionarily based and biologically dictated. In humans, levels of aggressiveness may change considerably throughout life. In his cross-cultural study, Ronald Rohner has noted that the difference in aggressiveness between females and males tends to disappear as the child grows into adulthood. There are exceptions, notably in American culture, but in most cases socialization appears to diminish, if not eliminate, the differences that were noted in early childhood. From Freedman's perspective, this would mean that males and females in a society generally differ in aggressive disposition at birth. However, the reaction range for the trait appears to be broad enough to permit environmental influences, acting through the process of socialization, to eliminate the difference completely. There seem to be no grounds, therefore, for any argument that suggests that women are biologically incapable of generating the kind of aggression needed to function effectively in, for example, military combat. They may have other drawbacks in this regard but this is not one of them.

You can't make a silk purse out of a sow's ear; but possibly some leather object can be fashioned. A human individual cannot be turned into something that the reaction range will not allow. "Environmentalists" used to argue that if you took a child from another culture and raised it from infancy as an American, it would become an American. Putting aside the possibility of prejudice, discrimination, and their consequences, many anthropologists would be more cautious these days about the plasticity of human nature. Biology is something that cannot be entirely dismissed in accounting for differences and similarities in the psychologies of different peoples.

Now consider another way in which biology may affect personality development. Piaget and others have suggested that there are stages in modes of thinking through which individuals generally pass as they grow up. Culture may delay or advance the times of these changes, but each individual nevertheless tends to pass through the same sequence of stages. Attempts to validate this hypothesis cross-culturally have run into a number of problems familiar to the psychological anthropologist, but some encouraging results have been obtained—especially for the early stages proposed by Piaget. However, there are enough discrepancies to warrant caution about accepting the hypothesis in too specific a form. Another way in which biology may affect personality development is by making the individual more or less receptive to environmental influences at different stages of development. Rohner, for example, has found that parental acceptance or rejection can have greater consequences if it occurs earlier, rather than later, in life. The infantile stage excepted (because the data are unclear), early socializing experiences appear to be of paramount importance in personality development. However, no psychological anthropologist these days would exclude later experiences—even those of middle and old age—from consideration.

All of this suggests that biological nature helps to make the individual an active agent in the socializing process. At birth, environmental influences do not fall on some *tabula rasa* on which anything can be written. The organism is more sensitive to certain influences than others, and, with growth, new biologically based sensitivities appear. As the capacity for conceptual thought emerges, the child begins to put itself imaginatively in the place of others and respond to their views. In addition, the child has its own views on what line to take. Out of this process of give and take, the human individual is formed.

The give and take is not always easy. Cultures differ in the harshness of their socializing practices. For example, some early New England Calvinists seem to have had a very rough upbringing, but one present-day community in the same region appears to be much easier on their children. However, no people have managed to do away with the frustrations of socialization entirely. This is because individual and social needs or requirements never can be completely compatible. Inevitably, in order to get along with others, the growing child must do some things that it does not want to do. Here, it is important to keep in mind that there are more or less "individualized" cultures and that what a more individualistic American would regard as a humiliating submission to the group might be viewed otherwise by a more "collectivized" Japanese. But socialization always requires some self-sacrifice. When this is severe, some initiation ceremony involving group support may be developed to mark the transition into group membership. Thus, in Tikopia in the Southwestern Pacific, a little boy's kinsmen help him to pass through a painful circumcision ceremony that marks an important passage in life by exhorting him not to cry out, but to suffer in silence as becomes a man.

The inevitable frustrations of socialization leave a residue of conflict in the self between social and personal demands. What the clinical psychologist or psychiatrist calls psychodynamic mechanisms are means that the individual (often called ego) uses to resolve these and other conflicts. Conflict, and the means to resolve it, tend to be culturally patterned and are an inevitable part of growing up in any society. I recall vividly the group of young men who came each day to the slaughterhouse in a Cuban community where I was doing fieldwork. These fellows may have been there to witness the killing of the animals and thus express aggression—some of which must have derived from the frustrations of socialization—in a culturally approved way. The same psychological processes appear to have been operating at local cockfights. In America, sports or business activities may perform the same psychological function, that is, to release aggression in socially standardized ways.

HOW DOES IT ALL HAPPEN?

Human socialization always takes place in some group, a group that has a culture. The actions of the socializers of each group tend to shape growing individuals along certain lines. How does this shaping take place? Psychologists speak of such mechanisms as reinforcement, modeling, or identification. Sociologists talk about role taking. These are specific ways of comprehending the process whereby the growing individual acquires new behavior through experience. But the child's development is always culturally directed. The active agents of the society in this regard are members of the child's family of orientation. These people usually have the greatest access to the child when it is in its most malleable state, and they act as a shaping environment even before birth. Any action by the mother or other socializer has potential significance for the child's socialization. The action might not even be directed at the child, as in the case of the working mother whose absence may be experienced as a kind of rejection, the amorous mother whose lovemaking might be observed, or the mother having problems with someone else in or outside of the family. Psychological anthropologists are slowly acquiring a scientifically based, cross-cultural understanding of the consequences of socializers' actions. Rohner's work, mentioned earlier, is one example of careful, systematic research in this area. His enumeration of the universal consequences of parental acceptance or rejection illustrates the depth and breadth of study that is now expected of anthropologists.

Taking his cue from a variety of psychological investigations, Rohner argues that children everywhere have a need for acceptance. That is, they need warmth and affection from significant others. If this need is not satisfied (if they are rejected), they will respond with, among other things, lowered emotional responsiveness and stability; greater aggression, dependency, or defensive independence; and lowered self-esteem—more or less depending on the magnitude of the rejection. These dispositions should be expected to continue on into adulthood unless contravening socializing experiences of later life turn them around.

Rohner has drawn his data from over a hundred societies, and recently, from his own intensive investigations in several societies. One of the peoples in his cross-cultural sample were the Alorese of the Southwestern Pacific who were studied by the anthropologist Cora Dubois. Using her reports, Rohner predicts that the Alorese, who are portrayed as possessing weak self-esteem, having difficulty sustaining emotional relationships, and being often angry, suspicious, and fearful, will have been rejected in childhood. This prediction appears to be correct. Alorese mothers view children as a great burden. They leave them at home while they work the fields. Child nurses, who take care of the children during this time, do not take up the slack. They often become impatient with their charges and sometimes abandon them. They and other socializers frequently tease and frighten the children. Such rejecting socializing practices, not overcome by later acceptance, appear to turn the typical Alorese into the kind of personality that is to be expected from Rohner's theory.

Abraham Kardiner referred to a society's whole body of socializing and related behavior as primary institutions. Like other aspects of a culture, they are affected by the context in which they are embedded. American mothers who follow the advice in a popular book on child rearing are acting in what amount to institutionalized ways suggested by the author. But the author's views on child rearing and the mothers' acceptance of these views are conditioned by their cultural context. What are the immediate forces that shape socializers' actions? Anthropologists have identified a number of these: household arrangements, family forms, and economic activities, for example. Ultimately, though, it is the whole culture that influences the socializers and, consequently, the socialization of its children.

HOW DOES IT ALL WORK OUT?

A writer on socialization may say that its aim is to produce individuals who will carry on a culture. Thus, Erich Fromm, in a famous statement, said that children must be made to want to act in the way they have to act if the culture is to carry on. Any people probably do have the power to turn the next generation—most of them, anyway—into reasonable facsimiles of themselves. Thus, the culture will be (to use a little jargon) internalized or recapitulated. But this does not inevitably lead to adaptive success either for the individual or for the society. Every society has collective prerequisites (some system of authority, for example) that must be met. If it is to survive, it must socialize individuals who help to meet these prerequisites. But individuals, no matter how much they are shaped for collective tasks, have their own personal needs to satisfy and they require some leeway to accomplish this. If they do not get it, frustrations could pile up to an intolerable level and threaten the social order. This means that each culture must allow for some accommodation between the needs of the individual and collective requirements. In looking over the cultures of humankind, it is possible to see a great variety of more or less adaptive ways in which this accommodation has been accomplished. One example was envisaged by the American founding fathers who sought to create a political society for individuals with certain *inalienable* rights. Though recognizing the need for some system of authority in the society, they also sought to put limits on the sacrifices individuals would be expected to make in helping to satisfy this need.

It is important to remember, finally, that though there are norms for socialization in any culture, there is also variability around the norms. This variability, combining with the genetic variability of the upcoming generation, produces a range of socializing tracks and, hence, personalities. Each of these personalities are recognizable individuals who work out their destiny in a complex process of give and take between their notions of what others want of them and what they want for themselves. Every culture offers culturally constituted selfs as ideals to help people in this task.

SOCIALIZATION GONE AWRY: AN IRISH EXAMPLE

In order to bring this discussion of socialization down to earth, consider a specific anthropological study (*Saints, Scholars, and Schizophrenics*) conducted in contemporary Ireland by Nancy Scheper-Hughes. Carried out in Western Ireland in an area that has interested scholars and artists over the years, this study shows how culturally patterned socialization can lead in the direction of mental illness. Though the author deals with other matters, her principal concern is with variation in mental illness (or mental health) in a particular population, which variation is seen to result from different, but nevertheless culturally patterned, socializing procedures.

Scheper-Hughes, settling into the little village of Ballybran (together with her husband and children) for her fieldwork, was aware of the decline of the small family farm that had been the economic mainstay of the region. Becoming a more and more marginal economic operation, this farm is increasingly run by what might be called "leftovers," that is, aging parents and a son (often the last-born) who has not emigrated in search of a more promising career. It is among these sons that the greatest rate of diagnosed psychosis is to be found. What is it about the socialization of this son that makes him turn out psychotic more frequently than his siblings?

The author is aware that schizophrenia has a hereditary component, but that is unlikely to be the cause of the systematic *difference* in rates within a family. More likely responsible, she feels, is a difference in the ways different children are socialized. Is there something about the last-born male's socialization in this culture that would tend to push him along the road to mental illness? Scheper-Hughes notes that Irish children, generally, are raised by cold, rejecting mothers who manage to make their boys, especially, quite dependent on them. However, it is the custom in this culture to favor some children more than others. In particular, it is the "runt" of the family—the last-born son usually—who experiences the worst side of Irish socialization. Normally he becomes a scapegoat for family difficulties and is made to feel the most inadequate of all. "Desperate," "hopeless," and "the bottom of the barrel" are expressions that Scheper-Hughes heard parents using in public to refer to these boys who grow up (the word may not be the most appropriate one to use here) anxious about sex and all other forms of self-assertion and who are constantly reminded how inadequate they are.

The rural Irish family today is faced with the problem of who will remain on the farm to take care of the aging parents and run what is increasingly a failing proposition. This thankless task is likely to fall to the last-born son who, bound by ties of guilt to his mother and unable to assert himself enough to marry or emigrate, remains caught in a situation of trying to please others who are giving him a very hard time. At home and in the community he must accept his parents' denigrating views of him; and still he must try to please. But deep down some kernel of self-respect asserts itself. What to do? Overt rebellion and escape would seem to be almost out of the question. They are made very difficult by his feelings of inadequacy and guilt towards his parents. The remaining adaptive alternative would seem to be some kind of psychological withdrawal which, in a person with the appropriate genetic constitution, could lead towards schizophrenia or some other form of mental illness. The higher rate of mental illness in last-born sons, therefore, appears to be the result of one variant of the primary institutions of this developing culture, that is, the way the last-born sons are treated.

This brief summary has hardly done justice to a rich and sensitive, prize-winning ethnographic study. It has not been possible here to delve into the theoretical matters that Scheper-Hughes treats in such a sophisticated way. Nor has it said very much about the fascinating field of culture and mental disorder. But it does make the process of socialization come alive and illuminate the anthropological perspective that has been presented in this chapter. First, Scheper-Hughes assumes that people are born with certain hereditary tendencies (in this case, towards mental health or illness). Second, she emphasizes the importance of experience, particularly within the family, in shaping these tendencies. Third, this experience is seen to be culturally patterned, that is, there are common socializing procedures that derive from the overall culture and what is happening to it. Fourth, the individual is seen to acquire a residue of conflict from his socializing experiences. This is something that all humans share, but in this case it is exacerbated by culturally patterned circumstances. Finally, individuals are portrayed as actively adapting creatures who cope as best they can with (in this case) difficult socializing circumstances. One might say that their adaptation is not very successful; but neither is that of the culture at this point in its history.

This brief visit to rural Ireland points up once again the problematic nature of any cultural arrangement including socialization. Working out a path that meets individual needs and social requirements at the same time is no small accomplishment. The fact that so many cultures have attained at least a minimum successful accommodation in this regard can be attributed to human social proclivities as well as their considerable ability to profit from experience.

SOCIALIZATION IN AMERICA

How does all of the foregoing illuminate what is going on in our society as far as socialization is concerned? Like any other culture, American culture has its primary institutions, which shape developing individuals in a certain way. However, growing up in America poses special problems not encountered in most of the cultures that have been investigated by anthropologists. America is a complex, rapidly changing society in which a good deal of individual mobility is the rule. Here, socialization pressures come at the individual from a variety of directions. Thus, a child raised in a small-town family will be brought up in certain ways. If the family moves to another town in another region of the country, new (sub-) cultural norms will be encountered and new tracks of socialization will open up. Will the individual go to college or university? If so, still other paths appear. Upon graduation a job may be taken in which career mobility is the norm. Still further lines of socialization now become a possibility. All of this takes place in a society that is undergoing continuous change and that exists in the shadow of nuclear holocaust. As the playwright said, there is "no foundation all the way down the line."

How does all of this affect the socialization of a more or less typical American? As compared with growing individuals in less complex and more settled societies, Americans tend to find themselves in a more destructured socializing environment. American socializers are less certain about how to raise children, and even if certain, are more likely to be contradicted by others. As a result, adults lose authority over their children and this creates a lack of certainty for children that is extraordinary in the range of contemporary cultures. Not being able to rely so much on the external world for guidance, the individual is forced back on himself or herself for direction. This means that the growing American is faced with a greater responsibility for his own or her own socialization. Some people may flee from this responsibility, others welcome it. But it is the rare American who can escape the fact that what one makes of oneself is increasingly up to each individual.

This would appear to be one reason why Descartes' problem with the existence of the self would be considered a false problem by most Americans.

SELECTED REFERENCES

COLE, MICHAEL, "Ethnographic Psychology of Cognition—So Far," in *The Making of Psychological Anthropology*, pp. 614–31, ed. G. D. Spindler. Berkeley: University of California Press, 1978.

EYSENCK, H. J. versus LEON KAMIN, *The Intelligence Controversy*. New York: Wiley, 1981.

FREEDMAN, DANIEL, "Personality Development in Infancy: A Biological Approach," in *Perspectives on Human Evolution*, pp. 258–87, eds. S. L. Washburn and Phyllis Jap. New York: Holt, Rinehart, and Winston, 1968.

JENSEN, ARTHUR, "How Much Can We Boost IQ and Scholastic Achievement?," *Harvard Education Review* 39 (Winter), 1969, 1–123.

LEBRA, TAKIE S., "Shame and Guilt: A Psychocultural View of the Japanese Self," *Ethos 11*, 1983, 192–209.

LEVINE, ROBERT, *Culture, Behavior and Personality* (2nd ed.). New York: Aldine, 1982.

LEVY, ROBERT, *Tahitians: Mind and Experience in the Society Islands*. Chicago: University of Chicago Press, 1973.

ROHNER, RONALD, *They Love Me, They Love Me Not*. New Haven: HRAF Press, 1967.

———, "Sex Differences in Aggression," *Ethos 4*, 1976, 57–72.

SCHEPER-HUGHES, NANCY, *Saints, Scholars, and Schizophrenics: Mental Illness in Rural Ireland*. Berkeley: University of California press, 1979.

WALLACE, ANTHONY F. C., *Culture and Personality* (2nd ed.). New York: Random House, Inc., 1970.

Chapter Four

SOCIETIES

HOW IS SOCIETY POSSIBLE?

Some philosophers once believed that before humans became social they lived alone in a state of nature. Their life often was not very pleasant, and there were times when they fought each other. But they were rational creatures and eventually figured out that life might be better if they lived together. The society that resulted was thus a rational creation of individual human beings who wanted to get out of the state of nature.

Anyone who knows even a little anthropology will recognize that this is one of those just-so stories about human origins that cannot possibly be true. From what we know now, there was never a state of nature in which human beings or any other related creatures lived alone. If living apes can be taken as rough models for the prehuman way of life, it would seem that some form of association existed among the Australopithecines and other ancestors of the first humans. Indeed, the existence of loose social groupings among chimpanzees and other apes suggests that the essentials of human society were established before humans came on the scene.

A good deal of ape association seems to be due to inborn nature, and undoubtedly, there is some carry-over of this nature into humans. The particular form that an ape or monkey society takes also appears to vary with biological type. Different types of, say, chimpanzees behave differently. Different groups of the same type also may behave differently according to the nature of their environment, but these variations are relatively minor. Among humans, on the other hand, variation in the nature of societies is very great and seems to be independent of the comparatively insignificant biological differences between them. So, while some thrust to human association is given by biology, the specific ways in which peoples associate is largely, or wholly a cultural matter.

Looking at a human society, one sees people constantly adapting to each other on the basis of assessments they make of their situation, which includes not only real, live others, but possibly dead ones in the form of, say, ancestral spirits. Out of people's give and take come the cultural norms that were discussed in Chapter One. These norms, which individuals adopt, more or less, as their own, regulate humans' actions and interactions. They help determine the form of organized systems of social roles, groups, and categories. In a highly industrialized society such as the United States, this organization is extremely complex; among the hunting and gathering San it is a simpler matter.

Though it may look like an inanimate object when viewed on an organizational chart, social organization is actually an ordered arrangement of real, live human beings playing parts. How do people come to play their parts in some social system? In America, people like to think that choice and individual effort count a lot. Although there are positions in this society that are beyond a person's reach, choice and individual initiative do play a greater role in filling up the positions of the social structure of the United States than they do in the culture of a more traditionally oriented people. When the part that one plays has been attained by choice and individual effort, it is customary in anthropology and sociology to say that the position has been *achieved.* If, on the other hand, the position is determined by factors beyond one's control, such as being born with black skin in America, the part one plays is seen to be *ascribed.* Traditionally, anthropologists have worked in societies where ascription has played a greater role in sorting people out for the parts they play in social life.

The particular criteria for this social sorting vary from society to society. Thus, different universities may use different mixes of criteria for choosing a freshman class. One may weigh academic excellence more heavily while another places more emphasis on well-rounded types. Depending on the part one is to play in a society, the principal criteria for selection could be physical strength and aggressiveness, the ability to enter trance states, or having the "right" connections. There are certain criteria that all peoples use, however. These are age, gender, and kinship, which are matters that individuals can do relatively little about and are therefore ascribing factors. Two of these, gender and kinship, will be discussed in this chapter. Age is certainly an important ascribing factor in all societies. For some reason, though, anthropologists have not yet given it the attention it deserves. Possibly in a future edition of this book there will be enough available information to warrant a discussion of age ascription as a separate topic.

Americans who believe that "the world is their oyster" may be impatient with so much discussion of factors that are beyond their control. They may wonder about the attention that has been given to these factors by anthropologists. Once again they need to be reminded that the United States is not the world and that in many societies ascription plays a large role in sorting people out. Also, it may come as a surprise to these Americans that gender and kinship are significant ascribing factors even in the United States.

GENDER

Though the extent and nature of the difference varies, all peoples recognize that men and women are different and assign them different roles. For example, males rarely, if ever, have the primary responsibility for child care while females seldom, if ever, hunt, trap, or herd large animals. Though there may be some modern women who believe that eventually they will be able to do everything a man can do, and vice versa, the odds would seem to be seriously against it. Men in some societies may actively participate in the birth of their child, but they will never be able to bear children. No matter how much a man attempts to share in this process, he can never do it directly.

Even so, the variation in gender-type roles in the various cultures of humankind is enormous. Some anthropologists were once so carried away by the possibilities of cultural variability as to suggest that temperamental differences between the sexes in western culture could be completely reversed with the right upbringing. That is what Margaret Mead suggested in *Sex and Temperament in Three Primitive Societies* (in New Guinea). And the rapidly changing roles of men and women in America, as well as other countries such as Sweden, tended to support the notion of very great plasticity as far as the sexes were concerned.

A number of developments in the modern world tend to undermine ascription by gender, and they demonstrate that both men and women are capable of becoming far more alike than has been supposed. Such developments may rile male chauvinists, who seem to feel that the natural order of things is somehow upset if women try to be something other than a wife and mother. Divorce, abortion, and inadequate parenting are only some of the terrible things envisaged by the chauvinist when women try to go beyond their "true nature." In *Women of the Forest*, Robert and Yolanda Murphy report an origin story of the Mundurucú Indians of South America. According to this story, women once dominated men; but because they could not hunt nor make ritual offerings of meat to certain spirits, they lost their power. Men have dominated ever since. Therefore, any attempt to reverse the position of the sexes in this male-dominated society works against the natural order of things and is doomed to fail. Male chauvinism, it would seem, is not confined to the United States. The chauvinist is entitled to his opinion, but when he invokes nature in support of his view, he comes onto anthropological turf, where the subject of gender differences is well established.

In their work, anthropologists, themselves, have not been entirely free of bias where gender is concerned. It is true that early anthropological considerations of the subject were mostly undertaken by men, some of whom may have had a male-oriented axe to grind. The extremely popular books of Margaret Mead, though, would seem to have more than made up for any anthropological tilt in the male direction. The subject continues to be emotionally charged, and one has to pick one's way carefully through the claims and counterclaims. Is it possible to come to some conclusion now about gender differences that will stand the test of time? Maybe so, as summaries of two pathbreaking studies would seem to show. One of the studies, to be summarized here, concerns gender differences in a *kibbutz*, a collective settlement in Israel. The other is a cross-cultural study that deals with the status of women and its causes.

Spiro on the Counterrevolution in a Kibbutz

Kibbutzim are small collective settlements in Israel. Melford Spiro is one of the leading authorities on *kibbutz* life. He first studied Kiryat Yedidim, a utopian agricultural community, in the 1950s. He returned to this kibbutz from time to time afterward. The European-born founders of this little community dreamed of getting rid of many of the evils associated with industrial capitalism. They thought that by developing a certain collective, agricultural way of life and passing it on to their children they would eliminate, or at least minimize, such things as individualism and gender differences in work and other roles. Their plan involved the abolition of private property and setting up collective routines that included communal dining rooms and children's houses. Males and females would circulate through all of the community's jobs. Children would be raised in mixed nurseries and dormitories and would see their parents only a couple of hours each day. The essentials of this regime had been established when Spiro first studied this *kibbutz* in the 1950s. Some of the developments that the founders hoped for had yet to occur, but they believed that time would take care of that. They felt that a dramatic change in their culture would eventually bring about great changes in the character of the people in it. All of this was reported by Spiro in *Kibbutz: Venture in Utopia*.

Twenty-five years later, Spiro reports (in *Gender and Culture*) that though some of the founders' dreams had been realized, the attempt to minimize gender differences had been only partially successful. There continued to be marked differences in work roles. Women, who had been concentrated in certain service occupations—in the kitchen, nursery, and dormitories—at the time of the first study, continued to be concentrated there. Men, who had been the principal handlers of heavy farm machinery, continued to monopolize this kind of work. Not only were men and women still concentrated in certain occupations, but they had come to regard this as normal, not something that would change. Other differences between the sexes that the founders had attempted to down-play were also being accepted and even emphasized.

Spiro, in his later study, found women, who earlier had disdained such things, emphasizing their femininity by wearing jewelry, cosmetics, and feminine clothing. In the dormitories, adolescent girls, who had been raised in a gender-blind environment, had made good a rebellion against mixed showers and bedrooms. These now had been almost entirely abandoned.

The founders had thought that they could reduce the family to its bare essentials by collectivizing community life, but Spiro now found a renewed emphasis on family ties. People continued to follow the socialist design of the community, which reduced private concerns and promoted communal preoccupations, but now they were having increasingly elaborate family affairs in their collectively owned apartments. In the early days of the community, parents and children got together for an hour or two after work. Now children were spending more time at home with obviously devoted parents. So, instead of withering away, family relationships were flourishing.

Apologists for the utopian dreams of the founders have pointed out that their scheme never had a fair chance. Any *kibbutz*, they point out, has to contend with outside influences from a bourgeois, capitalist order. They maintain that these influences were responsible for the counterrevolutionary tendencies that Spiro noted. Spiro does not share this point of view. He feels, rather, that the founders' attempt to remake human nature by creating a new culture had collided with certain unchanging facts of that nature. For example, the attempt to minimize the special relationship between mother and child by reducing contact between parents and children and turning over child rearing to nurses and teachers failed because the connection between a mother and child has a deep-seated biological basis. And the counterrevolution by the adolescent girls against mixed showers and sleeping arrangements, Spiro explains, reflected a specifically female reaction against surging sexuality in a highly charged, emotional environment.

Though he does not completely do away with the notion that the counterrevolutionary tendencies he noted were due to diffusion from outside, Spiro's argument that the girls' rebellion was not due to culture influences is not easy to dismiss. He points out, for example, that the adolescent girls could not have taken their cues from outside because their rebellion occurred before they had had any significant contact with city people or their culture. Moreover, the adults and boys with whom they were in regular contact were in favor of continuing unisex arrangements in the dormitories. The stimulus for their rebellion, therefore, was not likely to have come from either outside or inside the community. The evolutionary basis for a strong mother-child tie has been noted earlier. Finally, the tendency of men and women to gravitate towards different kinds of work has been demonstrated in a variety of cross-cultural surveys. There appears to be no society, for example, in which men play much of a role in child care and no society in which women have much to do with armed combat.

Spiro is careful about specifying the factors that he believes to be responsible for the persistence of gender-related differences in a culture that had been created to minimize or stamp them out. He refers to these factors as precultural, which is to say that they reflect either biological nature or the way that that nature has been treated. Besides, he is at pains to point out that whatever pan-human differences between the sexes do exist, they are not of kind, but of degree only. Human beings, he argues, are born with bisexual tendencies and some females lean towards maleness in their natures and vice versa. A society may socialize its children in a variety of ways, but it must contend with an essential maleness and femaleness that cannot be ignored. Whether this is genetically determined, or acquired through the experience with different kinds of bodies, is not clear. The limits for shaping male and female children through socialization are also unclear.

So men and women everywhere differ in some ways. Vive la difference! But the existence of such differences does not imply that they must differ in social status. The founders of the *kibbutz* also hoped to create real equality between the sexes. Spiro points out that though they had not managed to eliminate gender differences in behavior, they had, in contrast to the world outside, created a society in which men and women were considered to be fairly equal. This would suggest that the status of men and women is dependent on culture.

Whyte on the Status of Women

In an extremely ambitious cross-cultural investigation, (*The Status of Women in Preindustrial Societies)* Martin Whyte considers women's status in relation to men's. According to him, one has to be careful about speaking of women's status in a general way because there are a number of dimensions involved. He identifies eighty-seven relevant variables that can be reduced to nine status scales measuring such things as control of property, domestic authority, the valuation of women's lives, their solidarity with other women, and their control of the sex act. In turn, these scales would seem to be reducible to the three dimensions of social status that are used in this book, that is: respect or prestige, control of economic resources, and power.

Whyte found evidence about women's status in ethnographic reports from nearly a hundred preindustrial societies around the world.

He developed measures and sought evidence of a statistical association between them and other measures of cultural conditions. For example, he sought to test the hypothesis that in societies where activities requiring the greater strength, mobility, and aggressiveness of males (for example, warfare or hunting large animals) are highly valued, women will tend to have lower status compared to men. After noting the statistical associations between women's status, as measured on his nine scales, and a range of valued activities requiring more or less strength, aggressiveness, and mobility, he came to the conclusion that this hypothesis could not possibly be true.

Some have argued that the status of women depends on their economic contribution to a society. Thus the equality, or near equality, of San men and women has been said to reflect the importance of women's gathering activities in that society. This hypothesis, too, receives little cross-cultural support from Whyte's statistical tests. Nor do his tests support the hypotheses that a shortage of women or an absence of men (during times of war, for example) tend to enhance women's status. Finally, on the basis of his cross-cultural measures, Whyte cannot subscribe to the argument that an emphasis on private property and its monopolization by men is responsible for lowering women's status. That men at one point in the history of humankind used their newly acquired control over property to subjugate women appears to be another one of those "just so" stories about early human development.

So much for the more important negative findings of Whyte's study. They are bound to make some people who hold strong views on this question unhappy. But the author also has something positive to offer. He observes that, as the complexity of societies increases, the status of women in relation to men tends to decline. Thus, among hunters and gatherers who tend to have the least complex societies, women's status is comparatively high, while in more complex societies with plow agriculture, cities, or states it tends to be lower. Whyte is not sure what specific factors are responsible for this trend. He speculates about differences in economic circumstances. Whatever the reason, the statistical association between women's status and social complexity is significant. This raises a question about the status of women in modern, industrialized societies, which are still more complex than the most intensive agricultural societies in his sample. Is it reasonable to infer that there will be a continuing decline in women's status with the advance of industrialization?

Because industrialized societies were not included in his cross-cultural sample, Whyte has to be tentative about the status of women in such societies. He believes, however, that most of the social conditions that down-grade women in preindustrial societies tend to disappear with the advance of industrialism. Advances will be uneven and will occur by fits and starts. Generally, though, women's status will increase with industrialization. He warns, however, that because the different dimensions of women's status are loosely associated, if at all, there is no simple key to increasing their status across the board. People are doomed to disappointment if they believe that everything will fall into place when women acquire the right to vote or gain equal pay for equal work. Those who are interested in improving the overall status of women in industrial societies will have to push forward on a number of fronts at the same time.

These summaries of the studies by Spiro and Whyte are greatly simplified. Both anthropologists use sophisticated theoretical arguments and, in the case of Whyte, complex statistical methodology. However, the main thrusts of the two works should be clear. Spiro conducted a crude experiment in nature. That is, he created a before-and-after experiment that enabled him to suggest a reason why his *kibbutz* failed in their efforts to minimize differences between men and women. As is usual with natural experiments, there was a problem of controls, in this case cultural influences. However, Spiro makes a persuasive case that precultural factors were responsible for the failure of the revolutionary attempt by the *kibbutz* founders to reduce the gap between men's and women's roles. In retrospect, it should not be surprising that they failed in their attempt to do what no other people has done. Some division of labor by gender exists in all human societies. For whatever reason, child care is pretty much the province of women. In the home, women are likely to be the fuel gatherers, fetchers of water, and clothes launderers. Outside of the home, women rarely engage in activities such as hunting, fishing, mining, metal working, and clearing land. Using machines and collective productive arrangements, the *kibbutz* founders tried to develop a society in which men or women could do most jobs with equal effectiveness. Though many changes took root in their little community, they were not able to eliminate some division of labor and other differences between men and women. After reviewing a work such as Carol Ember's "A Cross-Cultural Perspective on Sex Differences," it is not surprising that this aspect of their utopian experiment failed.

What Whyte's cross-cultural investigation has shown is that role differences between men and women need not imply status differences. By working out statistical associations between different marks of social status and other cultural conditions, he has shown that in hunting and gathering societies there tends to be little difference in the statuses of men and women. In horticultural, pastoral, and especially agricultural societies the difference increases in favor of men. If contemporary societies can be taken as models for the past, it would seem that the general historical trend in the preindustrial world was towards lower female status. But if Whyte's speculations are correct, this trend is being reversed with industrialization. The founders of the *kibbutz*, then, appear to have been somewhat ahead of their time in this regard.

Finally, it should be mentioned that, to date, no study has provided a scientific answer to the question of why, when all the indicators are added up, women have never attained a position of superiority over men. There has been a lot of speculation about this, some of it revolving around the relative physical strength of the two sexes. ("The average man can beat up the average women.") The truth is that we just don't know why this is the case. One thing is certain, however: Deeply entrenched male dominance such as exists in much of the Caribbean, for example, will not be given up easily.

KINSHIP

"God gave you your relatives, but thank God you can choose your friends."

This was a saying of my father, and I think he spoke for many Americans who are impatient with the bonds of kinship. In a society where achievement is the ideal, relatives can be a drag. They are supposed to offer love and security, but they also represent obligations that can interfere with the plans of career-minded individuals. They are an ascribing factor, which many Americans like to down-play. There are Americans who don't think like my father, or if they do, prefer to keep such thoughts to themselves. But even they will be surprised to find out how important kinship can be in some societies.

So it was with Christopher Newman, the hero of Henry James' book, *The American*. A success at home (in manufacturing some kind of gadget), he went to Europe looking for a wife. He wanted the best, and he seemed to have found her. James makes it clear that both individuals were admirable people in their own ways and that they complemented each other perfectly. Moreover, there was a mutual attraction. But the woman's family stood in the way. They were poor but proud aristocrats who felt that the American did not meet their standards. He was not of the right class. Nevertheless, being poor, they reluctantly came to an understanding with the rich, young American. He agreed to provide for his wife in a way that was agreeable to the French family. He promised to love her and take care of her. All was set for the marriage, but at the last minute the family backed out.

Their daughter, not being able to go against their wishes, entered a nunnery, and the American went home empty handed. It was a triumph of kinship and status obligations over love.

It sounds old-fashioned, but most of the world operates that way. Even in America today, parental wishes about marriage partners cannot be totally disregarded. Kinship and other obligations still play some role in sorting people out for marriage. Impressed by the importance of kinship in structuring many of the societies they have studied, anthropologists may go to great lengths in treating this subject. A glance through any introductory text in anthropology will suggest just how important they think kinship is.

Kinship may be an important organizing factor in some societies—agreed, but it may not be the same type of kinship that exists in the West. Not all people think of relatives in the same way that Americans do. As usual in anthropological matters, one has to guard against ethnocentrism. As David Schneider points out in *American Kinship: A Cultural Account*, Americans tend to regard kin as people related by blood and marriage. Of these, the blood relationship is considered to be the most important. For these people, it seems only "natural" (a nice way of suggesting ascription) that people who are related by blood should feel close. "Blood is thicker than water," they say. As for relatives-in-law, they are acquired and can be unacquired through divorce or separation.

Such a biogenetic view of kinship poses problems for cross-cultural analysis. What is one to do in a culture where the biological facts of paternity are not known? How does one trace the blood relationship between a father and his children in that case? Also, Americans tend to think of kin as sharing degrees of biological substance. Because of this, they feel more closely tied to primary relatives on both sides of the family than to secondary kin. But many peoples emphasize kin on one side of the family, say the father's. In that case, relatives on the mother's side, though still considered as relatives, are seen as farther removed. This means that it is possible for people who share an equal degree of biological substance to be thought of as closely or distantly related. Finally, different peoples draw the line far or near when tracing relatives, and the cutoff point may not be determined by biological distance. In such cases, people who are equally related biologically may be considered relatives or not.

Thus, to think of kin relations as a natural reflection of shared biological substance raises problems in the investigation of peoples who don't think that way. Not everyone knows the biological facts discovered by western scientists; and even if they know them, they may ignore them in counting kin. The notion of shared biological substance is only one of a number of *concepts* of kinship, none of which is naturally given. Rather, these concepts are culturally constituted, which means that one learns how to think of kin and kin relationships just as one learns other aspects of a culture. It is the anthropologist's task to find out what a people have learned.

THE BASICS ON KINSHIP

Consider marriage to be a relationship involving sexual, economic, and reproductive rights. Though some might quibble about its universality, it does seem to exist in all societies. Men and women come into this relationship in a number of ways. The partners may have a lot to say about whom they marry, as in the United States, or less, as in the French upper-class family described by Henry James. A number of kinds of marriage partnerships may be worked out. One type consists of one man and one woman (monogamy); another, of one man and several women (polygyny); another, one woman and several men (polyandry); and still another, two or more spouses of both sexes (group); the last two of which are rarely encountered. The most frequently occurring marital ideal in the societies of humankind is polygyny. However, granted the usual sex ratio and the desire of most adults to marry, it can never be the most frequent form in a given society. The Tiv of Central Nigeria provide a typical example of the way marriages are distributed in a polygynous society. Among these people, the more important men tend to have several wives, while the majority of married men have only one. Since wives are considered by the Tiv to be the ultimate form of wealth, a man who has many wives is thought to be not only wealthy, but a big success. Male economic activities among the Tiv, therefore, tend to be aimed at acquiring a number of wives.

The sorting out process whereby people acquire mates and, later, children, everywhere is subject to social controls. One is not free to marry just anyone, as the woman who was the object of Christopher Newman's quest well knew. There are, first of all, an array of tabued relatives that one is not supposed to marry or even fool around with. When people do have sexual relations with such relatives, they are violating a cultural rule. Unless they have been granted a special exemption (as with Hawaiian or Egyptian royalty), this puts them at social risk. The range of tabued relatives varies and can be extended on the father's side, the mother's, or both. It always includes the nuclear family; that is the group consisting of a biological father, mother, and their offspring. The universality of this tabu has been explained in a number of ways. It has been said to be derived from either a natural, that is, built-in, or learned aversion that prevents harmful biological inbreeding. It has also been said that it derives from a learned adaptation that promotes advantageous social relationships. The fairly widespread violation of the tabu, the demonstrated existence of lust and even sexual relations between close relatives and those who have been raised together, and the asymmetric extension of tabued relatives (on father's *or* mother's side) in many societies suggests to me that the incest tabu is largely or wholly learned, which is to say, a cultural matter.

The obverse of the incest tabu are the rules about the people one is expected to marry. Everywhere, a person is supposed to locate mates outside certain groups (exogamy) and sometimes within others (endogamy). There will be violations of these rules, in which case there will be social consequences to suffer. Consider the ideal of the Tiv as an example. Before the advent of British rule, a man was supposed to find wives outside of a group of people related to him through the male (patrilineal) line. This usually involved an exchange of wives between patrilineally organized groups. A sister or cousin provided by his marriage ward group (a group of male blood relatives) was exchanged for a wife. Later, after British rule became established, a man was more likely to purchase a wife using bridewealth that he and his ward group had accumulated. In both cases, a man took a wife from outside of a group of patrilineally related relatives. This established a social tie with the outside that was shored up by the exchange of a wife and/or property.

Endogamous kinship groups are not found very often in human societies, but other forms of endogamy are more frequent. They are likely to occur, for example, where there are sharp boundaries between status groups, as in the traditional Indian caste system. And the line between European aristocracies and commoners once was sharply drawn, as Christopher Newman found out in his romantic quest in France.

Newlyweds must live somewhere. One possibility is to live with, or near the husband's parents (patrilocality) or the wife's parents (matrilocality). Sometimes there is an option to practice either of these (bilocality). And sometimes, as in the United States, the ideal is to establish a residence apart from any relatives in some nice suburban community (neolocality). There are a few other very rare alternatives. The Tiv practice the most frequent option, patrilocality. It is customary for a Tiv wife to move into a compound that includes her husband's parents, his married and unmarried brothers, and his unmarried sisters. She has to get along with them all, including (because the Tiv are polygynous) any other wives her husband takes. Not getting along with her husband's parents is grounds for annulment of her marriage and can raise tricky questions about other marriages, where wife exchange is involved, or bridewealth payments. It has been suggested that the more there is at stake in a marriage, whether in the form of property or social obligations to others, the more difficult it will be for the married partners to break it up. This may have been why the traditional Tiv wife usually made a great effort to get along with others in her husband's compound. She was not totally helpless, though, since she could call on her original kin group for assistance under certain circumstances. She also had the right to leave her husband if he did not, for example, prepare some land for her to farm or if he beat her for frivolous reasons.

Everyone—even in the United States where between 40 and 50 percent of all marriages end in divorce—seems to want marriages to succeed. Though there are provisions for termination of marriages in all societies, it seems everywhere to be regarded as regrettable. Those who fall out of marriage may be subject to negative sanctions like legal rigamoroles and economic penalties. In rural Greece, it was once customary for a widow to be a target of abuse and social ostracism even though she was not responsible for the termination of her marriage. The societal cards seem to be stacked in favor of, if not this marriage, then the next, and also the family that results. The nucleus of familial arrangements is what Americans prefer, that is, a married couple and their offspring. This nuclear family appears to be a recognized social unit in most, if not all societies, but sometimes it is not the most important domestic unit. Consider the household of a Tiv man of some status. It consists of that man, several wives and their offspring, not to mention parents and unmarried brothers and sisters. It is a recognizable social unit, the demands of which often take precedence over those of the different nuclear families that comprise it. Anthropologists have used a variety of labels for larger domestic groupings like this, depending on whether kin connections are through blood or marital ties. It would seem possible to call all of them extended families and keep in mind that in many societies they are the most significant domestic unit. It is also important to remember that where they exist, these extended families do not completely swallow up their composite nuclear families; sometimes the interests of the two entities will conflict.

To an American, the family might seem to be the farthest reach of important kin ties, but in many societies it is only the beginning. Individuals can be intimately involved with relatives beyond their family who are tied together in what anthropologists call rules of descent. In the United States, where these relatively weak connections ramify through mothers' and fathers' relatives, bilateral descent is said to prevail. Where one is affiliated with kin of both sexes through men only, the rule is patrilineal. If the affiliation is through women only, it is matrilineal. In a society where the latter rule prevailed, I would feel closer to my mother's than my father's sister. There are two additional possibilities, ambilineal and double descent, which are mentioned in the literature, but rarely occur. The social groupings or categories larger than the family that are based on these rules of descent have been called (in order of inclusiveness): lineage segments, lineages, and clans, where their organization is unilineal; and kindreds where it is bilateral.

Among the Tiv, the patrilineally organized lineage segment or lineage can be extremely important to the individual. At birth, children automatically become members of patrilineally organized lineage segments and lineages of both their father and mother. Those connected through the father are said to constitute the individual's *ityɔ*, through the mother, *igba*. The members of a lineage or lineage segment, when speaking of their common ancestor, may say that they have "one father" or "one mother," and they have a special term for all patrilineally related individuals in a compound or related compounds. In contrast to what usually happens in patrilocal situations, a Tiv wife acquires membership in her husband's lineages. Her husband's lineage membership, given at birth, does not change. All members of a lineage have certain rights and obligations. Thus, Paul and Laura Bohannan, whose work on the Tiv (see, for example, *The Tiv of Central Nigeria*) has been used as a basis for describing Tiv culture, point out that a man's *ityɔ* *must* do things for him. They must provide him with fields, a wife (through the marriage ward group), a place to live (near patrilineally related relatives) and assistance when he is involved in certain kinds of conflict with others. His *igba*, on the other hand, *may* help him only if they feel so inclined. In the Bohannans' words, they do things for him "because they will or like." The fact that a man is more obligated to members of his *ityɔ* than *igba* seems to be consistent with the patrilineal emphasis of this culture. Americans may get some idea of the comparative importance of kinship in different societies by asking themselves how many of their bilaterally related relatives *must* respond when they are asked for assistance. Probably very few beyond the nuclear family would do so.

To understand how important kinship can be in organizing a society, think of modern, corporate Japan. It is composed of thousands of businesses, each of which lays a claim on the people in it. A large firm like Mitsubishi is supposed to take care of its people (in good times and bad) for life. In return, employees are supposed to give total allegiance to the firm, take on uninteresting jobs, work overtime without pay, spend some leisure hours with other employees, and not leave the firm for a more attractive job elsewhere. Many Japanese employees tend to think of themselves and their relation to their company in a way that can scare more individualistic Americans.

A large corporation like Mitsubishi is a subsociety in itself, with many specialized roles that are organized bureaucratically, that is, with very specific rules and lines of authority. Mitsubishi commands huge resources and has great economic and political power in Japan and elsewhere. It has a vast network of working relationships in and outside of Japan. To take Mitsubishi and all of the other corporate structures out of Japanese society would reduce it to a shambles.

Now, suppose that instead of being acquired, all the roles in corporate Japan were ascribed in terms of kinship. Of course, that would not be possible in a modern industrialized society, but suppose that Japan could—just for a moment—be transformed into a more intimate, preindustrial society like that of the Tiv. In this mental experiment, corporations would be transformed into kinship groupings larger than the family. Such a transformation would produce a fair approximation of a society such as the Tiv, in which much of its social organization is accomplished by kinship. On the father's side, a Tiv belongs to a series of lineage segments that are included in some maximal lineage. All of the members of these groupings are supposed to be descended from common ancestors. Each of the groupings has a claim on a person in certain circumstances. For example, a man's marriage ward group may require his resources for bridewealth, while his maximal lineage may require his services in war. All of these social units have systems of authority that are mainly in the hands of men. They defend members' rights while insisting on their obligations. They can own property, as, for example, land, which is distributed to members of families for farming. These and other kinship groupings that include one's mother's patrilineal relatives are involved in every aspect of Tiv life and constitute much of the social organization of Tiv society.

Though there are many differences in the ways Japanese corporations and Tiv kin groupings are structured and function, they both may be seen as networks of social roles. The Tiv counterpart of the president of a large Japanese corporation would be someone they refer to as "great father." To know this and other Tiv kin terms is to begin to understand the nature of Tiv social organization. In the American nuclear family, there are a number of prescribed roles and associated kinship terms. There is a mother, daughter, sister, and so on. To describe someone this way in America implies that certain behavior is expected of her. In prerevolutionary China, a daughter-in-law was supposed to be an obeying, deferring, and generally abused creature while her mother-in-law played a complementary role. The kinship terms used by a people tell how they sort each other out in their minds. Whether the terms are associated with special kinds of behavior has to be demonstrated.

In most societies, individual relatives are lumped together or classified in certain ways. Thus, I, an American, put relatives of my own generation into the categories of "brother," "sister," and "cousin." In my parents' generation there are "father," "uncle," and so on. Usually there is only one father and one mother, but there can be several aunts and uncles. The Tiv do it differently. They have terms that correspond to Americans' father (*ter*), mother (*ngɔ*), and child (*wan*), but they lump all the people whom Americans discriminate as brother, sister, aunt, uncle, and cousin together. Regardless of generation, the Tiv differentiate these family members only by sex and, sometimes, age. A separate term is sometimes used for people on the paternal side, but again, it ignores the generation of the person. Thus, the Tiv recognize the difference between relatives who are lineally connected (through the parent-child line), and collaterals (through siblings), as Americans do. However, they handle the designation of collaterals somewhat differently. By looking at any genealogical chart, it is possible to see that there are several possibilities for separating or combining relatives into categories. These possibilities, however, are limited, and as it turns out, even more limited in practice.

The different kinds of kinship typologies that anthropologists have found so fascinating, and which generations of anthropology students have had to learn, all involve splitting and lumping relatives according to criteria like kinship distance, generation, lineal and collateral relations, relative age, and so forth. Drawn from a particular person's point of view, the typologies lay out the ways in which relatives are classified in one's own and one's parents' generation. Affinal relatives, that is, relatives by marriage, are not included. According to one scheme, which is based on the way peoples treat relatives who are called siblings and cousins in the United States, Americans have an Eskimo terminological system (the Eskimo are one of the peoples with this form of kinship nomenclature) in which cousins are distinguished from siblings. They also may be said to have a lineal system because they distinguish between parents and their siblings (thus, for example, between mother and aunt) as well as between the generations (mother and daughter, for example). In the schemes just referred to, there are six ways of classifying relatives of one's own generation and four for the generation of one's parents.

Though typologies may be essential for scientific work, it is important to remember that they are ways of bringing order to a reality that is usually messy. Accordingly, the various typologies of kinship nomenclature as well as other aspects of kinship ought to be used with caution. Otherwise one could make such a mistake as assuming that because Americans and Eskimos share the same kind of terminological system they are alike in all essential ways. Or, having the typologies down pat, one might try, as I did with the Tiv, to force a people into a particular slot only to find that they don't readily fit into any category. There are certain cautions to keep in mind. First, a particular type of kinship nomenclature refers to a rule or norm in a particular society. There may be greater or lesser variation around it. Second, what one anthropologist has taken for the norm may not be the norm for another. Anthropologists are sometimes mistaken about the way in which behavior is distributed in a society. Third, the terminology may not be used very often. For example, the Bohannans say that the Tiv tend to resort to people's names rather than kin terms. And finally, there may or may not be some specific behavior or attitude such as avoidance, joking, nurturance, punishing, or deference that goes with the term. Making and serving chicken soup is supposed to preoccupy the legendary Jewish mother. What are Jewish fathers supposed to do?

CONNECTIONS

Kinship is a particularly interesting area for exploring the connections between different aspects of a culture. Consider American kinship terminology as a starting point. It does not distinguish paternal or maternal relatives. An aunt is an aunt regardless of whether maternal or paternal. The same applies to cousins. Gender has no bearing either. This suggests that Americans are not concerned with specifying relatives as maternal or paternal, and in the case of cousins, that they are uninterested in distinguishing one from another. Their apparent lack of concern with these relatives is to be expected in a society where the nuclear family stands out and other relatives are considered less important. Further, it seems that from the way they label kin they do not favor one side of their family over the other, which is to be expected in a system where bilateral descent prevails. Thus, different aspects of kinship fit together in this society in a way that can be readily understood.

Other systems may not be so simple, nor their connections so neat. Different aspects of a culture may change at different rates and cultures have a tendency to fall apart as well as hang together. Still, it is often possible to discover some coherence between kinship nomenclature and other features of kinship. Even among the Tiv, who pose many problems of analysis because they rarely use kinship terms, there are special labels for collateral relatives on the father's side, which suggest the importance of the patrilineally organized *ityɔ*.

Both Tiv and Americans distinguish between lineal and collateral relatives, but most people do not. In the parental generation, many lump together fathers and father's brothers under one term and mothers and mother's sisters under another. The peoples who use this kind of terminology do, indeed, distinguish their own mothers and fathers in practice; but the terminological merging suggests that, say, mothers and mother's sisters have more in common in these societies then they do in America. Indeed, this is often the case. Where such a system prevails, some kind of unilineal descent involving clumps of relatives based on male or female ties often exists. A further corollary of this arrangement is that the children of the mother's sister and father's brother (parallel cousins in anthropological terms) are usually given the same term as siblings and are sexually tabu. At the same time, it is open season on sexual dalliance with mother's brother's and father's sister's children (cross-cousins), who are given different terms. Thus, among the Ojibwa Indians of North America, a man must avoid not only his own sister, but also all parallel cousins who are also called sister; it is, however, possible for him to joke around sexually and pursue cross-cousins.

Cross-cultural studies have shown that certain kinds of kinship terminology tend to be associated with certain rules of descent. The Eskimo form, mentioned above, for example, is associated with bilateral descent. Also, rules of descent and residence are related. Patrilineality is associated with patrilocality, matrilineal descent with matrilocality, and bilateral descent with bilocality and neolocality. The reason for this would seem to be that feelings of kinship are promoted among people who live close together. According to George Murdock, an American anthropologist, whose cross-cultural investigations of kinship (see, for example, his *Social Structure*) have been particularly influential, the rule of residence is the key element of any kinship system. If it changes, other aspects of kinship will tend to follow until they line up with it.

However, there does not appear to be one key determinant of the rule of residence. Important activities that require the organized effort of either males or females do seem to be associated with patrilocal or matrilocal residence. Thus, big game hunting and warfare are often found together with patrilocal residence. Neolocality and the nuclear family that goes with it are found in a variety of circumstances. One of these is a niggardly environment. The Shoshone Indians, for example, inhabited a region of the western United States that supported only a few wild animals and edible plants. This environment could sustain groupings of these hunters and gatherers that were larger than nuclear families for a small part of the year only.

Such an explanation of neolocality and the nuclear family will not do for industrialized societies where such kinship arrangements predominate. In this kind of society, even if the environment is naturally niggardly, it is possible for high technology (disease-resistant crops and more efficient machines, for example) to make it productive. Higher technology and larger productive systems, as in the case of a modern factory, make kinship more and more redundant. In a Spanish factory I knew of, a relative of a high government official had been given an important post simply because of his kin connections. It turned out that he was an incompetent person. Gradually, he was transformed into a figurehead while more capable technicians took over. Emerging factory systems can tolerate—even use—kinship connections, as did the water-powered mills of the eastern United States during the nineteenth century. However, as the scale of operations increases and job requirements become more complicated, kinship connections can begin to interfere with industrial operations.

Similar things happen in an economy as trading begins to play a more important role. In the days when they produced most of the goods they needed, inhabitants of a typical Burgundian village exchanged produce between relatives in and outside of the family. The distribution of economic resources, therefore, could follow the lines of kinship. However, as more produce came to be sold abroad and a good deal of what was used came from outside, kinship came to play a much reduced role in the way in which goods were distributed. Impersonal market forces gradually took over.

The result of cultural changes in the modern world has been the creation of societies in which kinship and other ascribing factors play less and less of a role in sorting people out and helping them to accomplish certain tasks. Larger networks of relatives and other intimates dissolve until the nuclear family stands alone. Even this unit is hard pressed to survive in the face of forces that pull its members this way and that. Modern societies still have to be organized, however. Kinship networks cannot handle their large-scale organizational tasks. In their place, large, bureaucratically organized corporations or state agencies have become central facts of modern life. Within these structures, relationships are, ideally, impersonal, rule-oriented, and highly specific. Individual roles tend to be acquired. Some large Japanese corporations have attempted to create a kind of family relationship in their firms, but even in Japan, where people are collectively oriented, such a scheme can have only limited success.

CODA

Gender and kinship are only two of a number of ascriptive factors that people have used to organize themselves. Another universal ascribing factor, age, has not been considered here because anthropological work on this subject is still in an exploratory state. Nor have status groups or ethnic groups been mentioned here. Being born into such groups can determine one's position in life. For example, the black population of South Africa has, since the establishment of foreign domination in that region, been relegated to an inferior position that is symbolized by the word *apartheid*. People born black in that country have had their status in life pretty much determined for them. And in India, people born into a certain hereditarily defined caste will find opportunities that are available to members of other castes closed to them. But there are forces at work in the modern world that have been working to undermine these and other ascriptive factors and to promote sorting out by achievement.

Ascription was a good way to sort people out in societies that didn't change very rapidly and had narrow horizons. In such societies, a person's potential occupation and social connections were basically laid out for them early in life. People may not have been happy with what they were doing, with the people they were obligated to, or with various deprivations, but any discontent was minimized by a lack of alternatives. Even if they were doing menial labor such as cleaning latrines, which was the work of one Indian caste, they carried on. Some among them may have grumbled or tried to do things differently, but unless some major upheaval was in progress, their initiatives stood little chance of success. As many informants have told anthropologists in a resigned way, "That's the way things are." Even when living a hard life, though, people in such a closed society had a sense of intimacy and certainty that people everywhere seem to value.

As the world has opened up through industrialization, commercialization, and other forces, life's possibilities have increased. It is no longer necessary for a woman to be simply a domestic laborer. Often, she will add a job, say, in a factory, to her domestic chores. And although some jobs in the factory may be closed to her, her life has been opened up. As the American anthropologist, Helen Safa, points out in *The Urban Poor of Puerto Rico*, even the poor who gave up a rural existence for a life in a shantytown in San Juan, Puerto Rico could sense increased possibilities in life and gain hope from them. They would soon learn, however, that there is a negative side to an increasingly open existence. People often become uncomfortable when they lack solid social foundations. In his book, *Loss and Change*, the British sociologist, Peter Marris, notes that migrant people in African cities often show the same symptoms as bereaved persons. Cut off from a more secure, ascribed existence in the bush, they act like people who have just lost a loved one. They show the wild swings of feeling of the bereaved and look about desperately for something solid to hang onto. Some of them may find it in revolutionary movements, others in reconstituted tribal enclaves and kinship networks in the city, but all seem to be yearning for the kind of certainty and involvement they left behind.

In the enormous fluidity of modern life, people can be afflicted with what amounts to a permanent identity crisis. For better or worse, they get sorted out, but many of them have to work hard to find their niche. Even if they become a big success, they still may have doubts about where they stand and who they are. As I pointed out earlier in this chapter, my father wanted to be able to choose his friends and his position in society. He only gradually came to realize, I think, the full consequences of this.

SELECTED REFERENCES

BOHANNAN, LAURA, and PAUL BOHANNAN, *The Tiv of Central Nigeria*. London: International African Institute, 1953.

EMBER, CAROL, "A Cross-Cultural Perspective on Sex Differences," in *Handbook of Cross-Cultural Human Development*, eds. Robert L. Munroe and Beatrice B. Whiting. New York: Garland Press, 1981.

JAMES, HENRY, *The American*. New York: Holt, Rinehart, and Winston, 1964.

MARRIS, PETER, *Loss and Change*. Garden City, N.Y.: Anchor Books, 1975.

MEAD, MARGARET, *Sex and Temperament in Three Primitive Societies*. New York: William Morrow, 1963.

MURDOCK, GEORGE P., *Social Structure*. New York: The Macmillan Co., 1949.

MURPHY, ROBERT, and YOLANDA MURPHY, *Women of the Forest*. New York: Columbia University Press, 1974.

SAFA, HELEN, *The Urban Poor of Puerto Rico: A Study of Development and Inequality*. New York: Holt, Rinehart and Winston, 1974.

SCHNEIDER, DAVID, *American Kinship: A Cultural Account*. Englewood Cliffs, N.J.: Prentice Hall, 1968.

SPIRO, MELFORD, *Gender and Culture*. Durham, N.C.: Duke University Press, 1979.

———, *Kibbutz: Venture in Utopia* (Augmented Edition). Cambridge, Mass.: Harvard University Press, 1975.

WHYTE, MARTIN K., *The Status of Women in Preindustrial Societies*. Princeton, N.J.: Princeton University Press, 1978.

Chapter Five

GOVERNING SOCIETIES

The newspaper says that a state of emergency has been declared in a bit of French territory in the southwestern Pacific called Wallis-et-Futuna. These are two islands in the remainder of what was once a considerable colonial empire. They are governed by a French administrator who declared the state of emergency because the normal operation of the government had been threatened by a dispute between French and local authorities. It was pointed out in a communiqué that "certain Wallisiens" had threatened to remove the administrator's deputy by force; on the other hand, the two natives who had been elected to the French parliament had expressed support for the regime. Meanwhile, some thirty state police have been sent to reinforce the seven gendarmes who normally keep order on the two islands.

Such an event is not unusual in today's world, but not too long ago, when more than 80 percent of the globe was under the control of the western, white nations, it occurred only rarely. Then, western colonial empires were well established, and though native populations fretted and occasionally rebelled, the colonial regimes seemed to be there to stay. As some British colonists once said, "Whatever happens we have got/ The gatling gun which they have not."

After World War II, however, the great European-based empires came apart with astonishing rapidity, sometimes under the impetus of open revolution, as in French Indochina, and sometimes under less violent conditions, as with the British in Nigeria. Some parts of empire remained, but they were not free of the questioning and resistance of native peoples. The incident in Wallis-et-Futuna is a tiny manifestation of this.

It is at times when authority is questioned that its true nature is laid bare. Regarding Wallis-et-Futuna, a statement by a French official is revealing. He proclaims that, as always, the authority of the state and of local custom will be preserved. What is revealed by this statement is the existence of two domains of authority. The boundary between these two domains had come into dispute. Discussions with local leaders had been under way to resolve the problem. Ultimately, though, the authority of the French state, backed up by force, was to prevail. To answer the question posed by the title of this chapter, the French state, capable of using force if necessary, was ultimately in charge. However, this tells only a part of the story of how this or any other society is governed.

THE ANATOMY OF GOVERNANCE

Those philosophers who believed that people once sought to move out of a state of nature by banding together into groups also had ideas about how those groups should be governed. For Thomas Hobbes, they would be subject to the control of a king who could not be deposed, while John Locke favored a government that could be changed by the will of the people. These philosophers were thinking in terms of western political systems, which represent only some of the various ways in which human beings may govern their societies. Anthropologists, on the other hand, are concerned with all of the systems of governance humans have ever created.

Governance requires not only governors, that is, people with social power, but also people who are governable. Human beings usually respond to the threat, or use, of force. The French were counting on this in Wallis-et-Futuna. But a society in which everything is handled by force would be like a prison; it would not resemble the usual society of human beings. So much effort and so many resources would be used in controlling people that other necessary areas of life would be neglected. No established human society today uses force or the threat of force as the only means of social control. People have a variety of interests other than the avoidance of pain and destruction that can be manipulated by people in power. Do I, an American, want to be a success? Why not, then, follow the example of someone who has succeeded and who attributes personal achievement to following the rules? Am I, a poor Burmese Buddhist, impatient with my condition in life? Why not do the socially acceptable things that are supposed to guarantee a better existence in the next life? Thus, the reasons for following social prescriptions or norms are at least as various as human motivations.

In all human beings there are anarchic or revolutionary tendencies that put them in opposition to any social arrangement, but they also have a desire to associate with others, and if properly socialized, they will have an active disposition to adhere—more or less—to the norms of some culture. This disposition, whatever its motivational basis, constitutes the basis of morality. The American anthropologist, A. Irving Hallowell, pointed out that human societies are moral orders composed of individuals who are capable of assessing themselves in terms of some social standard and feeling good or bad about that assessment. They are not made up simply of mutually adjusting individuals as is, say, an ant society, but of self-reflective persons who constantly evaluate themselves and their actions. The trick, then, in managing a society is to socialize its members so that they evaluate themselves more or less in terms of the same, or at least compatible, standards. Each individual's moral sense is thus collectivized and the basis of social control established.

People want to feel good about themselves, and every society provides its members with rewards for adopting an appropriate social posture and sense of self. Rewards may range from a simple lack of abuse, through the positive regard of others, to more tangible things of value. It may not take a lot to get a person to go along. In Laurence Wylie's book, *A Village in the Vaucluse* (France), a boy says that he does what is expected of him so that *les autres* (the others) will let him alone. This suggests that his attitude of self-regard and actions are already linked to the opinion of others, albeit in a somewhat negative way.

Most people in a society try to do the right thing—at least a part of the time. In so doing, they feel good about themselves. But there is also a negative side of self-regard that motivates people. When it is activated by behavior—or the thought of behavior—that violates some norm, a person may feel shame or guilt. One way of avoiding these painful feelings is to change one's thinking and behavior in a more socially acceptable direction. Does one lust after one's mother? Think of her, rather, as pure and self-sacrificing. Does one hate one's neighbor? Better to think that we are put upon this earth to love one another. A carousing college student wakes up one morning with a terrible hangover, or worse. Maybe it would be better to hit the books in the library. All people do wrong at times by their own and society's standards, but most of them have the capacity to alleviate the painful feelings that result by acting in a socially appropriate way. All societies make use of people's capacity for guilt, and shame, as well as the fear and anxiety from which they are derived, in order to control them.

The concepts of guilt and shame both refer to negative feelings people have after assessing themselves in terms of social standards. For example, I may feel worthless today because I failed a test in engineering, a subject my father thinks is important. Or I may feel a vague disquiet on the day following a particularly luxurious sexual dream in the night. The concepts of guilt and shame differ in one significant way: they involve differing degrees of internalization of others' expectations. Guilt-ruled people are capable of experiencing negative feelings about themselves in a vacuum. Thus, I have thoughts of forbidden pleasure and immediately feel a twinge of conscience. That is the internalized "other" part of me that is doing the twinging. Shame-ridden people, on the other hand, need others to be present to confirm their failings to them. Without others' presence, the feeling of shame will not be activated. Guilt and shame have been defined here as polar opposites. The majority of people probably are capable of entertaining both feelings in different degrees. Some anthropologists have suggested that people in a particular society tend towards the shame type of personality while people in another lean towards guilt. Thus, Ruth Benedict, in *The Chrysanthemum and the Sword*, a wartime study of Japanese national character, argued that the Japanese were a shame-oriented people; but recent, more careful investigations have shown that they are capable of experiencing both shame and guilt and that both of these feelings are implicated in their control.

Sometimes it may be difficult to know whether shame or guilt is at work in the controlling process, but there are occasions when it is quite obvious. For example, Laurence Wylie was conversing with a teacher in France about a teaching problem. As an example, the teacher pointed to one of the children and, in her presence, began to list her faults. Other children, who hadn't measured up in some way, were forced by their teacher to carry little signs indicating the nature of their failings. In both cases, the aim obviously was to use shame to get the children to mend their ways. As for guilt, the legendary Jewish mother is supposed to be able to turn it on in her offspring with hardly any effort. And typical Japanese hardly need to be reminded of their failings in filial obligations. Their latent guilt feelings are readily activated at any time.

People's moral sense depends on a sensitivity to others' views. In every society, there are some individuals (the psychopaths) who have very little, if any, of this type of sensitivity. They make social control difficult. There are others who may have a profound moral sense that is incompatible with that of the group in which they live. Thus, terrorists may be acting on the basis of a morality that is not shared with the people they attack. Because of this, no amount of exhortation, shaming, or guilt-selling by these people will make them relent. The others, to whom they respond in moral terms, speak with a different voice. This recalls a conversation I had with an informant in Spain. We were talking about the custom of bribing local officials, and I raised the question of whether it was moral for an American expatriate to do this. He said, "What is moral? I'll tell you what it is. It's what everybody expects you to do." For the American expatriates, then, the moral problem had to do with a conflict between reference groups: Americans and Spaniards.

In some societies, the moral sense of people and the mechanisms that activate it may be able to handle a good deal of the task of social control. In a particular Society of Friends (Quakers), for example, periods of talk and meditation may be enough to arrive at some kind of moral consensus. There is a coming together about what is the right thing to do under the circumstances. But sometimes a moral consensus is not so easy to arrive at. Various factions may arise around a particular issue, and there will be a good deal of pulling and hauling before a collective decision is reached. The processes of developing and carrying out collective decisions are aspects of governance. Every society must practice them in order to survive, and every society must have both governors and governed.

Who are the governors and who are the governed? In a sense, they are (to paraphrase Pogo) all of us who have a stake in making a certain social arrangement work. All social relationships involve some element of controlling and being controlled, that is, of social power, and sometimes it is difficult to distinguish governors from governed. For example, a visitor to the Mbuti pygmies, a group of hunters and gatherers of the central African forest, would not be understood if he said the equivalent of "Take me to your leader." This is because these people have no single, permanent leader. One person may take the initiative one day and another the next. Sometimes, as the Mbuti people bicker back and forth, it may seem to a Western observer that they will never accomplish anything. Eventually, they do take collective actions, and they do eventually resolve their disputes, but in a society where differences in power and importance are not well established, collective decisions often do not come about cleanly and quickly.

CASES

The San

Among the San, hunters and gatherers of Southern Africa, a variety of social mechanisms exist to prevent power or importance from falling into the hands of one, or a few individuals. Some people do stand out from others in socially valued ways, but they rarely have the opportunity to cash in on these attributes. Thus, in *The !Kung San*, Richard Lee reports that a successful hunter will hear a number of belittling remarks about the prize he has killed. Lee, himself, received many disparaging remarks about the goat he had provided for a feast. By these and other leveling tactics, the San prevent any significant monopolies of power or importance from developing. Many people participate in the act of governing.

Since the San are not saints and since no one among them has much power over others, it might be thought that their little bands (numbering on the average around twenty) would constantly be teetering on the brink of anarchy. These people do pursue individual interests at the expense of others. There are some serious disputes. Lee thinks that they do have a high homicide rate. But there are social mechanisms that prevent their little communities from falling apart. Sometimes, one of the parties in a dispute will leave and join another band. Other times, public discussion and opinion work to resolve differences. But above all, it is the collective orientation of these people, which develops early in the socialization process, that prevents their little bands from falling apart.

The Tiv

The horticultural Tiv, who are mentioned from time to time in this book, reveal greater differences in social status. They are organized into opposing lineages and lineage segments, which, when conceived spatially and administratively, are called *tar*. A minimal *tar* consists of a number of adjacent compounds and farms and may number from a hundred to a thousand people. Members of nearby *tar* are usually more closely related genealogically (in this case, patrilineally) than those who are farther away. People who live nearby will ally themselves more readily on issues affecting their members. How broad or narrow an alliance is depends on the issue involved. Thus, several adjacent *tar*, which may be opposed on a number of other issues and may even fight from time to time, will band together to seek retribution if a member of one of them has been killed by someone from a distant *tar*.

As reported by Laura and Paul Bohannan (in *The Tiv of Central Nigeria*), the Tiv have leaders, but no political offices such as a chief or prime minister. These leaders, whose base of operations is a *tar*, can have considerable influence, but they cannot give orders. They act as arbitrators in disputes and represent their kin groups in dealing with others. Those with great influence have to be skilled in discussion because public opinion plays such a large role in this society. They have to be wise in the ways of the people around them. They are likely to be older, wealthier, and more lavish in their hospitality. But most important of all, as far as the Tiv are concerned, they are possessors of valuable drums and titles, and they are thought to have coveted magical powers (*swem*) that are associated with their *tar*.

Individual Tiv share in the prestige of their leaders, and they seek their help for protection from others, but such is the egalitarian streak in these people, that those who rise too far above their fellows have to watch their step. People of higher social rank are envied, feared, and hated, and they must be constantly on guard against those who would bring them down (by witchcraft, for example). In such a situation, it is difficult for any individual or group to gain great power or prestige. It is not surprising, therefore, that the British were frustrated when they assumed administrative control over the Tiv at the beginning of the twentieth century. There was simply no centralized political institution to latch onto.

Fiji

The British had less difficulty establishing a colonial regime in the Fiji islands in the southwestern Pacific, where a system of hereditary chieftainships was in place. In "The Role of a Fijian Chief," Clellan Ford describes how this system works. Power is so concentrated in the chief that no decision of importance in his district could be taken without his approval. He is responsible for all visitors (including anthropologists), for directing collective activities such as fishing, gardening, and house building, and he supervises ceremonies such as funerals. Disputes between people are brought before him and resolved. If there is a special community project that needs to be done, he can command the labor to do it. Finally, he collects and redistributes a significant amount of the community's surplus production.

A Fijian chief is expected to be even-handed and generous. He should be tactful and carry himself with dignity. Although he assumes no special privileges at feasts, there is no question that the chief is in charge. An informant tells the anthropologist that, without the chief, all would be lost. Clearly, in Fijian society, power is centralized and differences in social rank are well established. Early western visitors found similar systems of governance in many of the Pacific islands.

Buganda

A Fijian chief had the kind of power and social importance that no San would dream of acquiring. But his high status paled by comparison with that of the Bugandan king (*Kabaka*) described by the British anthropologist, Audrey Richards, in "Authority Patterns in Traditional Buganda." In the early nineteenth century, Buganda (located in a part of what is now the nation of Uganda) was an east African society at the height of its power. Blessed with abundant natural resources, its people subsisted on a combination of horticulture (plantain, bananas); fishing, hunting, and animal tending (sheep, goats, cattle, poultry and buffalo); and trade. This society was ruled through an elaborate system of public offices arranged in several kinship- and territorially based status hierarchies. At the apex of these was the

Kabaka, or king, whose power was enormous. Holders of public offices were dependent on him and struggled for his favor. An effective *Kabaka* would use these struggles as one means of maintaining social equilibrium.

Bugandan society was stratified into two main classes: lords or chiefs and commoners. Some commoners could rise to high status, as in the case of the prime minister or a special aide to the king, but all were subordinates owing immediate allegiance to a lord. Those living on a particular lord's estate provided him with labor, produce, military service, and, should their lord desire them, women to serve as his wife or concubine. Always, the commoners were supposed to demonstrate publicly their respect for him. They are said to have crept about in his vicinity, to do immediately whatever was asked of them, to flatter him, and to accept his decisions in arbitration without question. The same pattern of dominance and submission pervaded the entire society. Richards points out, for example, that it prevailed in Ganda households where the father was a kind of king.

At the top of Ganda society, the *Kabaka* commanded more deference than any of his subordinates. Great lords fell flat before him and rushed to do his bidding. They were expected to show their loyalty by being present at court for a part of every year. A lord who was absent might fall into disfavor and even be punished—something to be avoided in a society where the king could kill at will. He had complete rights over his subjects' persons and could mobilize them for grand projects, some of which might do little more than feed his ego. Whatever reservations people had about all of this, they seem to have taken pride in the splendor of their king's court, his accomplishments in war, and his ability to keep the peace. Richards points out that they combined attitudes of terrified submission with great tenderness towards him.

The different systems of governance summarized here will seem more or less familiar to the reader. For example, one may find the Buganda system with its *Kabaka* not unlike certain European monarchies that existed in the Middle Ages. An American, however, probably will feel a distinct lack of sympathy for such a form of governance. Much has been written in favor of different kinds of governing systems, and proponents have gone so far as to claim that a particular form is more "natural" than another. Thus, the founding fathers of the United States claimed that all men were created equal, among other things, and argued for a system of political control that would complement this aspect of human nature.

Any survey of the political systems of humankind makes it difficult to claim that any one is more in tune with human nature than any other. Those who would argue that there is a natural system of social control that is modeled after something in the mind of God, in a flock of chickens, in a contemporary group of hunters and gatherers, or whatever, must face the fact that a variety of systems have worked well for their human creators and that humans have expressed satisfaction with quite different political arrangements. For example, in *Culture's Consequences*, Geert Hofstede reports on the job-related attitudes revealed by employees of a large multinational firm. One attitude he refers to is the "power distance" between employees and their boss. Respondents were given a range of choices that varied from an extremely democratic relationship, in which employees had great input, to an extremely authoritarian system, in which they had no influence. A wide variety of preferences were revealed, with responses varying significantly by country (that is, culture). Employees from Denmark, for example, were among the more democratic respondents, while those from the Philippines were among the more authoritarian.

GOVERNING ARRANGEMENTS

The examples given in this section cover much of the gamut of human systems of governance. The range could be filled out and extended into industrial societies, but the four examples would seem to provide a basis for a preliminary analysis of human political arrangements. A number of aspects of such arrangements have been of interest to anthropologists. For example, these scientists have been concerned with techniques used to secure compliance with collective rules—techniques that can range from the use of brute force to gentle persuasion. Force is resorted to in all four of the societies. The San, for example, kill one another from time to time, and Tiv *tars* may fight. But in established societies force is never the predominant method for gaining compliance. A variety of human dispositions besides fear and anger may be tapped to get people to comply with the rules of a society.

Anthropologists have also been interested in the ways in which people organize themselves politically, that is, in the kinds of social organization people create to govern. One might speak here about the delegation of power or the allocation of the various tasks of governance, as in the various branches of the American government and their subdivisions; but a more basic issue concerns the distinction between governors and governed and the nature of the relationship between them. In some societies like the San, such a distinction hardly exists. People play both roles from time to time. In Fiji, on the other hand, the chief is clearly a governor, while very few others have anything to do with governing that society. Governors exist because they have taken, or have been granted, the power necessary to create, maintain, and enforce social activities. They may depend a lot on input from below, in which case, there is (to use Hofstede's term) low power distance between governors and governed; or they may be extreme autocrats who tend to ignore input from the governed, in which case there is high power distance between the two.

In the four cases just summarized, there is a general trend (from first to last) towards an increasing separation or distinction between governors and governed and an increasing power distance between them. In terms of the social contract metaphor, one might say that there is a greater tendency for peoples to "contract out" to one or more of their number the task of running their societies and give them the power to do so. Anthropologists, who are always looking for the ways in which different aspects of a culture are tied together, have noted that a number of other characteristics of culture are associated with this trend. First, the size of the group being governed (whether measured in terms of territory or numbers of people) tends to increase. The typical San band, where governors and governed are hardly distinguishable, is a small, strictly local unit while the Buganda kingdom, with its autocratic *Kabaka*, is large and embraces a number of communities. There is, therefore, a tendency towards higher, more inclusive levels of social integration. Second, there is a general increase in the level of technology. The Ganda have a more complex technology then the San or the Tiv. Third, from first to last, the societies become more productive. Hunters and gatherers like the San tend to produce less than the horticultural Tiv. Fourth, the capacity to mobilize resources, human and otherwise, increases. More power in the systems is potentially available to the governors. The scale of public activities, such as warfare or buildings, tends to increase as a result. Fifth, there is an increasing social differentiation or specialization (as between governors and governed and the governors themselves), which is to say that societies tend to become more complex. Finally, the societies become more hierarchical, that is, there are increasingly marked differences in social status. This trend is associated also with the emergence of status groupings or categories—classes or castes—and thus an increasing stratification of society. Differences in social status are usually measured in terms of three criteria: power, prestige, and control of economic resources. The Buganda *Kabaka* and his lords constitute a ruling class or aristocracy that dominates a great mass of commoners. This hierarchical system seems to have been generally accepted; it had become a fact of life. Among the Tiv, on the other hand, where status differences are not as pronounced, there is an ambivalence about those variations that do exist. The leveling tactics that are used against people who seem to have risen too far are a manifestation of this.

The trends just described are general tendencies only. There are societies where nonpolitical aspects of a culture are out of synch, so to speak, with the political. For example, the different components of social status may be out of alignment. In Yankee City, an old New England town, the people with the highest prestige (termed upper-upper class by the anthropologist-investigators) were usually not the wealthiest nor the most powerful. The anthropological literature contains many other examples of societies in which differences in prestige are not entirely consistent with differences in wealth or power. Thus, among the Yanomamo, a fierce group of South American horticulturalists, each village headman tends to be wealthier and have greater prestige than his fellows; but because he is expected to be more generous, he may end up temporarily impoverished. Besides this, he has very little power to get people to do what he wants. He can set an example or harangue them, but if they do not want to go along on a particular project, there is little he can do about it. If one takes a broad view, however, there does appear to be a tendency in the societies of humankind for the different aspects of social status to line up with each other.

If contemporary societies can be taken as rough models for ancient modes of existence, the general sociopolitical trends just laid out would seem to describe in a general way what happened in the course of human history. Thus, the San system represents a very early form of human governance, the Tiv system a somewhat later form, and so on up to the relatively complex political arrangement in which great power is concentrated in the hands of a comparative few, the model for which is the Bugandan kingdom. Using a well-known typology, which identifies discrete stages of this trend, it may be said that in human history the earliest type of sociopolitical arrangement was the band, a small, fairly egalitarian group of hunters and gatherers; the next, the tribe; then the chieftainship; and finally, the state, which is the largest, most complex, and most powerful sociopolitical form of all.

CONNECTIONS

Why did the state come into being? Why did some humans give up their small-scale, more egalitarian mode of existence for larger, more hierarchical social arrangements in which power was increasingly concentrated in the hands of governing specialists? Such questions have preoccupied anthropologists and others over the years, and a number of explanations have been offered. One famous hypothesis accounts for the origin of the state, the most centralized governmental system of all, in the social coordination necessary to carry out early irrigation projects. This hypothesis, while applicable to some cases, needs considerable revision to make it cross-culturally viable. Irrigation projects are one type of large, complex public task that cannot be handled by a small-scale, strictly local system of governance such as exists among the San. If such large-scale tasks are to be accomplished, more centralized, specialized leadership must emerge. The trend towards a more powerful, centralized public authority may be explained in terms of the need to accomplish larger or more complex public tasks of any kind. People may or may not have responded to this need by developing a more centralized system of governance, of course, but some did.

More complex building projects of any kind would seem to require more centralized authority. This would also be the case in larger societies or societies with an increasing variety of people in them. Their larger scale would render the type of governance practiced by the San, or in a New England town meeting, obsolete. Further, consider that a society has to deal with powerful outside forces. Some of its people may have begun to engage in large-scale trading. Or there may be enemies that have to be dealt with. In such a situation, a people may choose or accept leaders who have the power to supervise and coordinate these activities. In all such cases, there has to be some trade-off between the social requirements of a larger, more complex mode of existence and the interests of individuals that were shaped by smaller and simpler regimes. If grand social tasks are to be accomplished, people must, willingly or unwillingly, hand over power to increasingly powerful governors or administrators. Their adaptive fate may hinge on whether they do so or not.

Who are these leaders to be? They are those who come to monopolize the things that give one social power. A list of these qualities would be endless. They can range from a certain facial expression to the use of a weapon, but in each instance, someone possesses something that gives him or her the power to make decisions for others. The search for key factors that underlie a person's rise to power continues. An important factor, surely, is the ability to control the production and distribution of economic resources. In an agricultural society, people with more land tend to become more powerful. A horticultural chief who acts as the focal point for the distribution of goods will acquire some power as a result. A key middleman in a trading network between societies will gain prestige and power.

As with other adaptive social arrangements, new systems of governance, once started, engage new motivations and achieve a momentum of their own. People then begin to acquire a stake in the new system. It is important to keep in mind, though, that some people always have a greater stake in a particular social arrangement than others. The tendency for individuals' behavior to vary around cultural norms is an indication of this. There is something of the revolutionary or anarchist in all of us, but those who have risen to higher status are usually the least interested in bringing their social system down. In a state, the elite may have great power, prestige, and wealth, which is to say that they have the best their society has to offer. Even the Yanomomo headman who gives away a good deal of his wealth and who has very little power has greater prestige than his fellows. Governors may complain about the heavy burdens of governing, but it is instructive to see where they will stand in relation to their fellows in regard to proposed changes in the status quo.

FREDRIK BARTH ON THE BASSERI OF THE KHAMSEH CONFEDERACY

In order to bring the whole discussion of governance down to earth, consider the Basseri, a group of nomadic, pastoral Muslims from southern Iran. In *Nomads of South Persia*, Fredrik Barth, an anthropologist who also studied in the United States and England, describes and analyzes the culture of this group of approximately sixteen thousand people. That aspect of his report that deals with their system of governance will be stressed here. The time frame is the late 1950s and Barth's study represents one instance of his (then) broader concern with pastoral peoples of Asia.

The tent-dwelling Basseri migrate up and down a strip of land approximately three hundred miles long and twenty-to-fifty miles wide in the Fars province of southern Iran. They subsist largely by herding sheep and goats who eat their way along a "tribal road" (*il-rah*) through a series of seasonally maturing pastures. The road passes over mountains, through valleys, and across rivers. Sometimes the Basseri are in desolate regions, other times close to towns and villages. The schedule and route of migration is set in a general way by the Basseri chief (*khan*). It tends to take on a traditional pattern, but from time to time he will institute changes.

During the course of their annual migration, the Basseri encounter various other Arab and Quashqai nomads whose routes of migration cross or run parallel to theirs. They also meet sedentary agricultural villagers and people from towns, the largest of which is Shiraz. Sometimes they encounter Basseri who have drifted away into a sedentary life or who have formed other nomadic groups. Thus, they have considerable contact with other people, both sedentary and nomadic. In addition, they deal occasionally with representatives of the Iranian government.

The minimal Basseri social unit is the tent (*khune*) in which there usually dwells a nuclear family. (A few of the wealthier families are polygynous.) These households cluster together into camps that vary in size (depending on the season of the year) from a few to forty or more tents. Each household owns movable property consisting of household items, riding and carrying animals (horses, donkeys, camels), and most important, a flock of sheep and goats that typically numbers about a hundred. This flock is the principal economic resource of the household. It provides meat, lambskin, wool, clarified butter, and milk for the consumption of the family and for sale outside. According to Barth, a typical Basseri household with its flock will move from one place to another about 120 days of each year.

The people in each camp, who have various kinship ties with each other, migrate together as a unit. They tend to settle disputes and correct deviation through public opinion. Each camp has a headman who may or may not have been appointed by the *khan*. Whether appointed or not, a headman does not acquire any power from the *khan*. If, for example, a dispute cannot be resolved through public opinion in a camp, it is not taken to the headman, but to the chief, who deals with the matter directly. Headmen do tend to be wealthier and have greater prestige, but they have little power to direct or coerce. Barth offers an intriguing analysis of the headman's role in working through what may be the most important thing a camp must do to maintain itself, that is, decide unanimously whether to migrate or not, by what specific route, and where to set up camp again.

As mentioned before, the *general* route and schedule of migration is set by the chief. His word is passed down through the heads of patrilineal descent groupings called *oulads*. Each *oulad*, which is comprised of a number of camps, is assigned certain pasture lands and a general migratory route and schedule. Within this framework that is set and passed down by the chief, each camp works out its own decision whether to move or not. The headman promotes his ideas through his kin, who then communicate them throughout the camp. The headman has his own opinions, but he has to be careful about asserting them. He cannot give orders nor step in to close out the meandering discussion that was so exasperating to the anthropologist, Fredrik Barth, who wanted to prepare himself to move or not. The headman, himself, may not actually know whose ideas have won the day until he looks out of his tent in the morning and notes the direction and nature of movement of the early risers.

In contrast to camp headmen, who are little more than discussion leaders, and *oulad* headmen, who are little more than channels of communication, the Basseri *khan* has a virtual monopoly on the right to command. His high status allows him enormous power as well as great prestige and wealth. He is expected to be endlessly hospitable and publicly generous. He should carry himself in a large and imperial manner. Much of his wealth is inherited, but he also has the power to impose taxes on his subjects from time to time. He and his immediate relatives constitute a real ruling class that mingles with the elite of towns and villages.

According to Barth, the Basseri chief exercises his authority in three main areas: tribal migration, dealings with outside authorities, and resolving disputes. The manner in which he settles disputes between subjects is an indication of the enormous power he wields. There is little formality on such occasions, but intimations of the *khan's* power are everywhere evident. For example, he may take up a dispute while engaged in other matters, such as eating a meal or chatting with visitors. His decision, which might take the form of a comment on the side, may follow precedent and custom or not. However it is rendered, the *khan's* decision is, according to Barth, a definite order that must be obeyed. There are very few areas in which the chief is unwilling to act. One of them involves disputes over inheritance, which are often handed over to judges in towns along the Basseri *il-rah*.

Barth takes pains to emphasize the enormous power of the Basseri *khan* over his subjects. One is a little uneasy, however, about accepting all of Barth's assertions on face value. He provides very little concrete evidence, and particular examples where the *khan* is disobeyed, or his decisions subverted, are missing. The overall picture he presents, though, suggests that this system of governance resembles the polar type of centralized authority discussed earlier in this chapter.

A particularly intriguing part of Barth's analysis involves an attempt to explain why the Basseri system of governance is the way it is. In developing his explanation, he makes comparisons with other nomadic tribes in the same area that live in somewhat different circumstances. For example, tribes to the east inhabit a bleaker environment than the Basseri. As a result, the density of their populations is lower and the movement of camps more erratic. There is no regularized migration such as exists among the Basseri. Since large-scale coordination cannot work under these circumstances, no centralized authority has emerged. The Basseri, in contrast, have a need for such coordination, and there is an incentive for the appearance of a strong, autocratic leader. To the west of the Basseri is the Qashqai tribe, which inhabits an even richer environment. Barth points out that because it is possible for an individual and his family to flourish under these conditions, the wealthier among them are not so tempted as their Basseri counterparts to drift away into an attractive sedentary life. As a result, they remain as power centers in the Qashqai political system. This leads to a much more complex hierarchical arrangement than among the Basseri, who have a single ruling class with greater power and a comparatively weak mass of subordinates who provide hardly any challenge to the chief and his relatives. Among the Qashqai, on the other hand, there are always potential challengers, and force must be resorted to more frequently by the chief.

Barth uses certain aspects of the social context of Basseri culture to account for the emergence of their strong, centralized system of authority. There are sometimes powerful outsiders who must be dealt with along their migratory path. Suppose that an individual Basseri has problems with a farmer over damage done by his flock. The next day, the Basseri and his family may be on their way and incapable of handling the dispute effectively. But a powerful chief who has a house in Shiraz and who moves intimately among the sedentary elite can act for them in this matter. Such an authority is also able to supervise the development of long-term trading relationships. Barth sees large-scale trading with a variety of peoples as one reason for the rise of the *khan* and the Khamseh confederacy in which the Basseri and other tribes once came together in a loose coalition dominated by a single kinship group.

In a society where wealth appears to be an essential element of leadership, Fredrik Barth is strangely silent on the role of economic factors in the Basseri system of governance; but his analysis does illustrate the importance of paying attention to the natural and social context of a culture. These people pass through a region that has pastures rich enough to sustain a considerable pastoral population. Some centralized leadership is necessary to coordinate such a group. The region also contains a variety of other peoples, some of them rather powerful. A centralized leadership is also necessary to carry on relations with them. The creation or acceptance of a strong, centralized system of governance in the person of the *khan* and his family is the Basseri adaptive response to such necessities.

There are no guarantees that this or any other social arrangement devised by human beings will survive, however. Drought could dry up the pastures on which the system depends. Trade routes could change. Neighboring, imperialistic chiefs could gain the allegiance of some of the Basseri. And the powerful Iranian government could change its ways of handling these people. Indeed, Barth reports that at one point the Iranian army, which had been charged with dealing with the Basseri, instituted a new policy of administration through local headmen.

Needless to say, such a policy threatened the existence of the *khan* and the autocratic, centralized system of government he represented.

* * *

This brief summary does not do full justice to Fredrik Barth's sophisticated ethnographic report on the Basseri. Readers who are interested in the whole way of life of this interesting group of pastoral nomads will want to read his book and, perhaps, other works on migratory peoples, including gypsies, references for a few of which are included at the end of this chapter. However, enough information has been given here to lay out the essentials of the Basseri system of governance and make an attempt to explain it. This explanation, which makes use of other aspects of their culture, as well as its context, illustrates the hypothesis that more centralized, powerful systems of governance are associated with the accomplishment of larger and more complex public tasks. Evidence to support this explanation has been derived from comparisons between the Basseri society and other nomadic societies in the same region.

WHAT ABOUT US? GOVERNANCE IN INDUSTRIAL SOCIETIES

So far, little comment has been made about the forms of governance in those societies that loom so large in the world today, that is, industrial societies where the nation-state reigns supreme. This is partly due to the fact that there is not a great deal of information about these systems of political organization in the anthropological literature. Until recently, anthropologists have shown little concern for them. There are a number of reasons why this neglect is unfortunate, only one of which is that these governments are often linked to the fate of peoples that anthropologists have been accustomed to study. What happens in the United States Congress, for example, can have consequences for the Yuma Indians of the American Southwest who have depended on the government for some kinds of support. But the lack of anthropological work in this area is no reason not to pursue this important question. Studies by other social scientists can be put to good anthropological use.

In part because of the increasing specialization of roles associated with their operations, industrial societies tend to be more complex, and as a result, require more centralized forms of administration. Their systems of governance may not be more concentrated than some of those that have existed under preindustrial conditions, but clearly, forms of governance such as exist among the San or Tiv will not do for them. Nor will a centralized form such as that in Fiji, where a chief has responsibility for nearly everything, suffice. The work of governance is too much for one or a few persons to deal with. So arrays of specialists who handle the complex tasks of securing compliance and carrying out public decisions appear and proliferate. Bureaucratic forms of administration take over more and more areas of social life. In the Soviet Union, citizens have to contend everywhere with representatives of the state bureaucracy. In the United States, both public and private sectors are bureaucratically organized. True, bureaucracies have existed in nonindustrial societies (ancient Rome and China, to cite only two examples), but nowhere have they attained such significance as in modern industrial society.

In *The Power Elite*, the sociologist, C. Wright Mills, developed an image of the American system of governance that can be applied to industrial nations generally. This image consists of a series of pyramidlike bureaucracies, the top people in each of which share common interests. In the United States, the interests of the leaders of the government, big business, and the military mesh with one another. This view of concentrated power in the hands of a comparatively small group of elite may sound familiar to readers who have demonstrated against the "military-industrial complex" of the United States or to Soviet citizens who have become frustrated by omnipresent state-run bureaucracies. Though the degree of concentration of power obviously varies from one industrial society to another, as does the amount of control leaders have over bureaucrats and others, the essentials of Mills' image would seem to be generally applicable to all. The bureaucratic organizations in these countries, and the people who manage to control them, can shape the world in profound ways. The president of General Motors, a large industrial conglomerate, is able, by signing his name, to end employment for thousands of people in one of G.M.'s subsidiary plants. And the President of the United States, by picking up a telephone and speaking in a certain way, has the power to start a nuclear war that might end all life on earth.

It is important, however, to distinguish potential from actual power. Industrial chiefs are usually not like the Basseri *khan* whose every decision is supposed to be instantly obeyed. They must contend with people who won't go along or who want to be consulted before doing so. Their bureaucracies may acquire a momentum of their own. Under certain circumstances, these chiefs can be reduced to the position of the Yanomamo headman, who may have a clear idea of what he wants to do, but does not know whether people will follow him or not. One of the problems industrial chiefs have is with the legitimacy of their rule.

In all societies, the exercise of power or authority is legitimated in one way or another. Whatever the basis of the "contract" between governors and governed, there are reasons or justifications for governors' exercise of authority. These legitimations are often connected with the moral values of a people. But what happens when a people become skeptical of *any* values used to justify the exercise of power? This is the case in more industrialized societies, where the point of view of one sector of society can be contradicted by so many others. It is this vastly increased rate of disagreement that undermines the plausibility of the legitimations of industrial rulers. Kings who have claimed that they rule by divine right may find that others, who do not share their view of the supernatural and its relation to the natural order of human affairs, disagree with this justification. The domination of a traditional Chinese mother-in-law over her son's wife, once justified in agreed-upon moral terms, begins to give way in the face of views derived from female employment outside of the home. The older generation in a French village find that the young do not automatically accept the notion that the elders know best. The decline in the plausibility of the legitimations of those in power is associated with a decline in the power distance between them and subordinates, who now feel that they are entitled to a greater say in the governing process. It is not a return to the near egalitarian conditions of a small-scale society like the San. That would be impossible in an industrial society, where the scale and complexity of public tasks is so much greater; but it is obviously at some remove from the autocratic systems of governance noted earlier in Buganda and among the Basseri.

Many authors have pointed out this egalitarian trend. In *Democracy in America*, Alexis de Tocqueville, a French observer of the early American republic, suggested that this young nation was in the forefront of a growing egalitarianism in the societies of the western world. Significant status differences are still evident in the United States, but they are not now accepted as inevitable and right as they are in truly hierarchical societies. Writing in *Homo Hierarchicus*, Louis Dumont, a French anthropologist, notes that (more industrialized) westerners, who have become accustomed to relationships of greater equality, have trouble understanding a hierarchical society such as India. Even today, an hereditarily based Indian caste system is still in place.

The implications of this are important for overseas Americans, who must deal with host nationals of less industrialized countries where people in authority pay less attention to the views of subordinates. In such countries, American housewives often try to cultivate a relationship with maids they could not afford at home. Doing business in these countries, American managers have sought input from host subordinates. That these Americans often fail in these endeavors is to be expected in societies where those in authority are expected to assert themselves, not consult.

Concrete evidence for the equality-inducing effects of industrialism is provided in the cross-cultural study by Geert Hofstede, which was mentioned earlier. Hofstede, it will be recalled, asked employees of a large multinational corporation how much they expected to be consulted by their bosses. He found that, generally, the higher the level of industrialization of their countries the more employees expected to be consulted, which is to say that the power distance between bosses and subordinates tends to decline with industrialization. Though this study touches on the socialist world only lightly, the evidence suggests that though the basis of power may differ, the trend is evident there also.

In order to survive, therefore, industrial nation-states must develop complex, centralized systems of governance, but their leaders have to contend with factors that limit their power. Among these are the difficulties of legitimating any governing arrangement among increasingly distant and various people, a greater desire of the governed to have some say in the governing process, and the intractability of bureaucratic organizations that are supposed to help governors decide and administer. Industrial chiefs, though, still have formidable ways of asserting themselves. First, they have inside information and connections. Second, by controlling the flow of information, they can tap a variety of motivations and promote consensus for their policies. The propaganda organs of the Soviet state, for example, work diligently to do this. The depth of the consensus they manage to obtain can never be as great as in a small-scale, tradition-bound society, but it can be impressive nevertheless. Third, if they manage to control the omnipresent bureaucratic structures, industrial leaders may be able to get a large array of social activities running in their favor. In France, for example, it is sometimes said, only half facetiously, that those who control the *fonctionnaires* (governmental functionaries) control the nation. The bureaucratic machines run continuously, and their operations can have a great influence on human behavior. Finally, by controlling powerful police and military forces, industrial chiefs can coerce people into doing what they want them to do. This, according to the newspaper report I was reading, is what the French had had to resort to in their little colony of Wallis-et-Futuna.

SELECTED REFERENCES

BARTH, FREDRIK, "Political Leadership Among Swat Pathans," *London School of Economics Monographs on Social Anthropology*, 19, 1959.

———, *Nomads of South Persia*. Oslo: Oslo University Press, 1961.

BENEDICT, RUTH, *The Chrysanthemum and the Sword*. Boston: Houghton Mifflin Co., 1946.

BOHANNAN, LAURA, and PAUL BOHANNAN, *The Tiv of Central Nigeria*. London: International African Institute, 1953.

DE TOCQUEVILLE, ALEXIS, *Democracy in America*. New York: Anchor Books, 1969.

DEUTSCH, KARL, *Politics and Government: How People Decide Their Fate* (3rd ed.). Boston: Houghton Mifflin Co., 1980.

DUMONT, LOUIS, *Homo Hierarchicus*. Chicago: University of Chicago Press, 1970.

FOGELSON, RAYMOND, and RICHARD ADAMS, eds., *The Anthropology of Power*. New York: Academic Press, 1977.

FORD, CLELLAN, "The Role of the Fijian Chief," *American Sociological Review*, 3, 1938, pp. 542–50.

FOUCAULT, MICHEL, *Power/Knowledge! Selected Interviews and Other Writings*, ed. Colin Gordon. New York: Pantheon Books, 1980.

HOFSTEDE, GEERT, *Culture's Consequences*. Beverly Hills, Calif.: Sage Publications, 1980.

LEE, RICHARD, *The !Kung San*. Cambridge: Cambridge University Press, 1979.

MILLS, C. WRIGHT, *The Power Elite*. New York: Oxford University Press, 1956.

RICHARDS, AUDREY, "Authority Patterns in Traditional Buganda," in *The King's Men: Leadership and Status in Buganda on the Eve of Independence*, ed. L. A. Fallers. Oxford: Oxford University Press, 1964.

SEATON, S. LEE, and HENRI CLAESSEN, eds., *Political Anthropology: The State of the Art*. The Hague: Mouton Publishers, 1979.

WYLIE, LAURENCE, *Village in the Vaucluse*. New York: Harper Colophon Books, 1964.

Chapter Six

LANGUAGES

TO DISCOVER LANGUAGE

People going abroad often hear from experts on the subject that the key to adaptation will be their ability to learn and use the host language. These experts will tell you that if you do not know the language you will not be able to get what you want nor understand what your hosts are thinking. Sometimes, Americans will learn the language on their own, as I did when I first went to Cuba, but more often, they will take a course. There is controversy about the best way to learn a language, but we do know that children are apt to learn it more quickly than adults and that, at any age, as with other things, the more you use it the better it will go.

In one course I know of, language learning involves not only speaking and writing, but gesturing as well. The teacher's idea is that a good deal of meaning is communicated by physical signs such as (with speakers of French) pursing the lips or shrugging the shoulders. Using gestures, early Western explorers were able to communicate with natives. There is evidence that certain facial expressions tied to emotions are understood in many cultures, and certain mimic signs such as putting the hands to the mouth (to indicate wanting to drink) seem to be widely understood. But gestures, bodily movements, and postures that play a part in communication vary widely between cultures. For example, if a person gazes directly and constantly at another, it may be interpreted as threatening or insulting in one culture, but polite or appreciative in another. Or, a raised thumb can be taken as a sign of approval or an insult in one culture or another. The use of nonverbal signs is universal, but the frequency of their use varies. In no culture, however, do nonverbal signs rival speech-based forms as a means of communication. Among humans, spoken language, with or without its written counterpart, is the principal means by which communication is accomplished. Like other social animals, humans need to communicate in order to survive, and since at least the time of the earliest Homo sapiens they have relied on spoken language to do so. It is only this form of language, which is unique to modern humans, that will be considered in this chapter.

Let us suppose that the person heading overseas takes the advice of the language expert and begins to learn the appropriate language. Such learning will involve acquiring a vocabulary of words and their meanings, a task that is aided immeasurably by having a dictionary on hand. It is not enough to know just the words and their meanings, however. You must also learn how the words go together and how they change in form according to their uses—the grammar. In English, for example, one says "I go," not "I goes." In French, the corresponding expressions are "*Je vais*," not "*Je va*." Generally, students find the grammatical part the most boring and difficult part of learning a language, but for many linguists, the grammar of a language is its most interesting part.

As you gain experience with different languages, you begin to comprehend that some are easier to learn than others. Thus, Spanish is a comparatively simple language for Americans to learn while Chinese is difficult (and even harder to write). Traditionally, anthropologists have taken on some of the most difficult language learning tasks. Not only have they had to learn languages of cultures that were very different from their own, but these languages often have had no written counterpart. So unless they were willing to use a translator, or rely on someone else who already had worked out the language in phonetic terms, they had to do it on their own. An American anthropologist, Jules Henry, once told me about his beginning interviews with Pilaga Indian informants in southern Brazil. At that time, he was still trying to gain a minimal competence in that language and he wrote things down very slowly in phonetic terms. Because of this, his informants sometimes got bored and went away.

So, as you begin to learn a language, you begin to realize the enormity of this human creation. Until now, you probably have taken your language pretty much for granted. Like other aspects of your culture, it was something that you didn't think about very much. But now, as you learn a new way of communicating, it all becomes more problematical. If you are of a reflective nature, you may begin to raise questions and make comparisons between your own language and the new one. The nature of these languages and other languages may become interesting to you. Now you can begin to profit from the work of scholars who have made it their business to understand these languages, groups of related languages, or all of the languages of humankind, written or unwritten. From the anthropological point of view, the consideration of all languages is of the greatest interest. Anthropologists want to know something about the nature of human languages, how they are different and how similar, how they fit into the various cultures that humans have created, and why they are the way they are. In short, anthropologists raise the same kinds of questions about language as about other aspects of culture.

LANGUAGE: WHAT IS IT?

To point out that language is an aspect of culture should bring back all of the things about culture that were discussed in Chapter One. First of all, language is learned, and though the importance of precultural programming is increasingly being insisted on by linguists, one could never come to speak, say, the Tiv language, without learning it. Second, a language, like a culture, is associated with a group of people. Linguists use the term language community when speaking of such a group. Third, the language practiced by the people in the group varies, as does any other culture trait, around norms. Not everyone speaks it in the same way. People in northern Castile (Spain) speak differently than those in the south (Andalusia). Fourth, a language is related to other aspects of a culture and to its context. Consider only the specific terms that have to be learned in any vocation. Computerese goes with computers, not with hunting and gathering. And finally, a language has a history. An investigation will show, for example, that the language of the dominant group in the United States has changed over the course of three centuries, but the change has not been so great as to make it impossible for a typical Texan of today to communicate with (were they still living) an ordinary citizen of colonial Boston.

Different aspects of a culture are oriented towards different primary tasks that must be performed if a people are to survive. The job of language is to communicate. Without communication people could not adapt to each other and a society would fall apart. All of the projects that require some kind of collective enterprise would founder because the individuals involved could not let each other know very much about their intentions nor adjust their intentions in order to complete their projects. Something of the problem involved is experienced by people in an overseas training group who are given a task to complete without an agreed-upon language to work with. Or one can think of an immigrant who has been in an accident and has been transported to an emergency room of a hospital where the personnel speak a different language. Doctors usually depend on their patients to tell them something about what ails them, but in this case, that aid to diagnosis would be lacking. Other examples of communication failures could be added in endless succession, all of which would attest to the importance of adequate communication in carrying on social life.

Spoken language (with or without its written counterpart), which takes care of most human communication, has certain elements that anyone will recognize. A language is composed of words with meaning and these words go together to form phrases or sentences. You may even know something about the way the words change in form according to their usage and relation to other words, which is grammar. There are language instructors who make a living at this sort of thing and will be happy to fill you in on the details. Such knowledge gives only a partial understanding of the nature of languages. Further probing, with perhaps the aid of a linguist, will reveal that there is more to language than people are generally aware of.

At the minimum—the atomic level, so to speak—are meaningless sound bits which may or may not correspond with minimal written units such as the letters of the English language. These bits, which can be distinguished from each other, as, for example, a single vowel can be distinguished from a consonant, are phonemes. They can be described in terms of the features of sound production, for example, whether the lips are open or closed or how the tongue is used. French speakers are more likely to use the front of the mouth in speaking than are Americans. The total repertoire of sounds available to humans for speaking is vastly superior to that of any other animal, but it is limited. Each language of humankind is drawn from this total repertoire of possible sounds, with the smallest number of sounds in a language being about fifteen and the largest about sixty. In English, the number of written letters is twenty-six, while the number of phonemes (because some written letters represent a combination of phonemes) is about thirty-five.

Regarding phonemes, it is important to remember that they are meaningless, just as most letters are meaningless, and that there are certain acceptable ways for putting them together. Thus, in English, three phonemes make up the word "bat" or, in reverse, "tab," but in my dictionary there are no "tb" sequences. In the tonal language that the Tiv use, there are certain sequences of pitch and not others. Thus, every language, even as it has a certain repertoire of phonemes, has rules for how those phonemes go together. Though a language may have comparatively few phonemes, and though the possibilities for their combination are limited, the number of ways in which sounds are combined to generate meaningful sound units is very great. This means that language is very efficient as a way of communicating because it can produce a lot of meaning with only a limited array of sounds.

In American English, "bat" and "tab" have meaning, but "tba" does not. The minimal meaning units of a language are called morphemes, which may be whole words or not. The word "*fermier*" in French is similar to "farmer" in English in that it combines a first morpheme ("ferm"), which signifies the act of farming, with a second, "ier," the agent who does it. An "s" added at the end is a third morpheme, which forms the plural. Thus, the combination of meaningful units produces a further meaning: "*fermiers*," in this case. Beyond words, there are phrases and sentences that have meaning in themselves and that are stated according to certain rules governing the combination of words. A sentence that says, "Dell the in farmer the" does not communicate meaning in English, although someone who knows the old round might give you the benefit of the doubt and rearrange the words into a meaningful sequence.

Any language contains not only elements, but an organization of those elements. The way in which the elements change in form according to usage and the way in which they relate to each other is called a grammar, which, if we are lucky, someone has already written down before us. But before that, some people or peoples developed it over the years. The difficulties that people have in acquiring a new language illustrates the immensity of this creation, which, like a great work of art, becomes more fascinating as we enter more deeply into it.

Language, then, is a special form of communication that requires extremely complex operations by the people who use it. On the "sending" end, a person has some meaning, or meanings, that he or she wants to get across. This meaning has to be coded in linguistic terms, that is, in terms of the elements and grammar of a language. The coded message, containing strings of grammatically arranged, meaningless sound bits (phonemes), is sent by activating the proper articulatory muscles. On the "receiving" end, the coded message is perceived and decoded on the basis of a "codebook" that is shared with the person sending the message. All of this takes place very rapidly, under the control of something like a linguistic computer in the brain. How specialized this "computer" is in its operation, that is, to what extent its operations are language-oriented, is not yet clear.

DIFFERENCES AND SIMILARITIES

In order to chart the variability of human languages, or any other kind of variability, it is necessary to have some catchall framework that will apply to all cases. So, taking marriage to be a certain kind of socially recognized relationship between men and women, it is possible to chart its variation in terms of the number of men and women involved. In the case of language, it is fairly easy to note the variability within a language community. It is not terribly difficult to note the variability for a couple of related languages such as French and Spanish or the different Bantu languages of Africa. It becomes progressively more difficult as the differences between languages increase. Besides embracing all of the variability in question, any comparative framework ought to have a minimum of ethnocentric bias, that is, it should not favor the nature of one language over others. Because there are unwritten languages, a scheme based on something like written English will not do. Any system that uses words as a minimal basis of analysis will fail to do full justice to the subject matter. A too-particular form of grammatical analysis, such as the Western form that goes back to the Greeks and Romans, would also generate problems. It would turn out to be rather inadequate when applied to, say, Chinese. But if the essentials of all languages are kept in mind, it is possible to develop a scheme that will enable us to chart the differences and similarities of the thousands of versions of this uniquely human form of communication.

To venture into these very deep waters only a little way, I have chosen a little exercise worked out by Joseph Greenberg, a linguist and anthropologist, in his fascinating little book, *A New Invitation to Linguistics*. He looks at one sentence as rendered in a small number of languages of the world: English, Russian, Turkish, Classical Arabic, Hausa (a West African language), Thai, and Quechua (from western South America). The sentence in English is "The boy drank the water." The point of the exercise is a grammatical analysis of the three components of the sentence: noun subject (in English, "boy"), verb ("drank"), and noun object ("water"). The question is to what extent do these three components vary in form in the seven languages in terms of traditional grammatical categories: case, gender, number, definiteness, and word order for nouns; tense, completion, agreement with the subject, and word order for the verb. Beginning with the subject word, he asks if it varies in form according to whether it is subject or object of the sentence. This is what the grammarians refer to as case. In English, Hausa, and Thai it does not, but in the other languages it does. Gender concerns the variation in form of the nouns of a language, as in the masculine, feminine, and neuter forms in German. English and Thai are the only languages in this group that do not have gendered nouns. Number refers to variation in form according to whether one or many are indicated. In all of the languages except Thai, there is such variation, and in one, Classical Arabic, there are two plural forms, one for two and another for more than two. Definiteness refers to whether a noun needs to be specified in every sentence. In English, despite what I find in some student papers, this is done by adding the word "the." In Arabic it is accomplished by putting an initial "1" before the noun. Variations for definiteness do not occur in the other languages. Word order refers to where in the sentence the word appears. In only one of the languages, Classical Arabic, does the subject word ("boy" in English) not appear first.

The analysis of the object noun ("water" in English) works out in almost exactly the same way as for the subject. The only exceptions are that the place of this word in the sentence is usually different and that definiteness in Turkish is indicated for the object, but not the subject of a sentence.

As to the verb ("drank" in English), Greenberg's first question is whether it varies in form to indicate the time or tense of the action. In all languages except Thai, this occurs. Is there a way of indicating whether the action is completed or not (in English, for example, "was drinking" versus "drank")? All of the languages do that. Is there grammatical agreement in gender, person, and number between verb and subject? In English and Thai there is none (although English in the *present tense* does have agreement for number). In the remainder of the languages there are one or more kinds of agreement. Finally, the place of the verb varies from beginning to end in these sentences, which reminds me of my attempts to find the verbs in an ethnography written by a German around the turn of the century. In those days, Germans wrote very long sentences—fifty words not being unusual. The fact that in German the principal part of the verb comes at the end of the sentence made this document very difficult to translate. I remember mumbling in my cubicle in the library, "Where's the verb?"

So much for the grammatical variations of this simple sentence. There appear to be a good many of them, so many, in fact, that there is only one grammatical category, that is, whether the verb form indicates completion or not, in which all of the languages are alike. But Greenberg points out that these and other languages do have a number of properties in common. First, all languages have a fundamental vocabulary that includes a word or words such as "boy," "drink," and "water," and that such words are intertranslatable. There is a common fund of things that people in all cultures seem to want to communicate, and, as has been pointed out elsewhere, the words that are used more frequently tend to be shorter. Second, all languages have words and sentences, as well as morphemes and phonemes. Third, all languages distinguish nouns and verbs in some way and specify the subjectness and objectness of nouns.

Moreover, as Greenberg indicates, the categories for far-ranging linguistic analysis that have been developed seem to embrace most of the significant variations in human languages. Take, for example, the category of word order. It is known that if a sentence contains subject, verb, and object, as does "The boy drank the water.," there are limits to the way in which they can be arranged. The SVO, VSO, and SOV orders are most frequently used, while VOS is rare, and OVS and OSV never occur. So, there appear to be not only language universals, but constraints on linguistic variability; and as the list of these continues to grow, one begins to wonder about them. The question, "Why all these languages?" then begins to give way to "Why language?"

WHY LANGUAGE?

The explanation for the differences in human languages given by anthropologists has tended to be the same as for other cultural differences: They represent different learned adaptations to different life circumstances. To take a simple example, people in northern and southern regions of the world must learn a word for snow, while those in equatorial regions have little or no need for such a word. The way in which differences emerge becomes apparent in tracing the histories of related languages. Emerging from a common stem, they gradually diverge from each other in a way reminiscent of the formation of new species. Thus, the Romance languages of today are further radiations of what originally were merely dialects of Latin. No one has ever claimed that these radiations are due to biological changes in the peoples carrying these languages, however. The view is, rather, that they came about as the peoples involved learned new ways of expressing themselves in circumstances of increasing isolation from each other. So what were once simply dialects gradually diverged until they became different languages.

It is more difficult to argue, however, that the commonalities of languages are learned. Which of our common life circumstances generate through learning the universalities and constraints mentioned above? There may be common influences, such as mothering, that everywhere shape the developing individual's linguistic capacity very early in life. A more likely source, though, would seem to be certain pan-human biological dispositions towards linguistic or language-related cognitive capabilities. Whether built-in or acquired, it is important to know the exact nature of these factors. Are they language-specific, or do they involve broader cognitive capabilities? There has been a good deal of scientific work concerning such issues.

A number of authors, as, for example, Ignatius Mattingly, (in "Phonetic Prerequisites for First-Language Acquisition") have pointed out the ability of infants to discriminate sound patterns containing linguistic structures from others. Peter Eimas and his colleagues (in "Speech Perception in Infants") have shown that prelinguistic infants make the same phonetic distinctions as adults. The implication of all of this work is that human infants are set up early in life to zero in on whatever language happens to be used by their caretakers. If this capacity is, indeed, built into the organism before birth, it then constitutes an evolutionary specialization that has emerged in the same manner as other traits that provide an adaptive advantage for humans. The development of the large brain increased hominids' cultural capacity; and the development of a linguistic capability, by increasing the ability of these creatures to communicate, has added to that capacity. As a result, each generation has been able to communicate more and more of what they have learned, not only to each other, but to succeeding generations.

The physical basis of humans' evolving linguistic capacity is rather shadowy, but the emergence of upright posture undoubtedly was an important early development. It was associated with the emergence of a J-shaped vocal tract that had a vastly increased sound-producing capacity. Apes, who have been used as a loose kind of model for the earliest hominids, have a vocal tract that resembles a slightly curved tube. In it, sounds involving the tongue can only be produced in a one-dimensional way, that is, by moving the tongue up or down. But humans have, among other things, the back of the tongue to work with and they can also make sounds by moving that part back and forth. Evidence for a corresponding cerebral development is not so clear. For most humans, language is processed in the left hemisphere of the brain. Some anthropologists say that they can detect an increased lateralization in favor of this hemisphere from endocasts made of the inside of the skulls of early humans, such as Homo erectus. Scientists are always straining for more evidence about early human developments. It would be best to have some written observations, but unfortunately, writing goes back only a few thousand years, which is not very long as far as human evolution is concerned. Undoubtedly, more evidence about the evolution of human linguistic capacity will be forthcoming, but most of it will not be the kind that a laboratory scientist would accept.

However and whenever the human capacity for language evolved, it is apparent that it became a specialization that probably does more to set humans apart from other animals than any other trait they possess. Experiments with apes initially suggested that these animals had a significant capacity for language. They could not speak, of course, but contrary to what some believed ("The ape doesn't speak because it has nothing to say."), they seemed to be able to communicate a lot of meaning. Thus, one chimpanzee, who was trained to use the American Sign Language for the Deaf, acquired a vocabulary of several hundred words, which it used in communication with its trainer and even other chimpanzees. The apes clearly have some linguistic capacity and the brain development that goes with it, but later research has raised questions about how much. A particularly thorny issue concerns the apes' capacity for grammatical constructions, which is a crucial aspect of human linguistic ability. It appears that apes are fairly limited in this regard.

Another line of research pointing to pan-human linguistic capacities has been followed by scientists who have probed for the underlying grammatical structures of human languages. The work of the linguist, Noam Chomsky, and other "structuralists" involves getting at the "deep structure" of a language, which, through certain transforming processes, generates a number of "surface" grammatical structures. Investigations like this point to the existence of some basic grammatical principles that are common to all languages. These principles or preferences could be determined by the structure of the human brain, though very early pan-human socializing influences have also been suggested.

The way a child acquires a language is often cited in support of the motion of such universal principles. After an initial period of growth in which nothing of linguistic importance seems to occur, children appear to leap into linguistic competence. Of course, they have to learn the words, but they seem to be able to put them together correctly with only limited teaching or example. They appear to be active, rather than passive, learners who already have some "idea" of what their language-to-be is all about. They do not acquire a language bit by bit as adults, who have surpassed the critical period for language acquisition (up to about fifteen years of age), must do. People who insist that all aspects of a language have to be learned, and that the human organism is, at birth or shortly after, an empty vessel that must be filled up entirely through socializing procedures, are in for a hard time when confronted with such facts.

A CROSS-CULTURAL STUDY OF LANGUAGE ACQUISITION

In order to get a handle on the actual process of language development, it would seem best to observe closely the acquisition of language in young children. Elinor Ochs and Bambi Schieffelin do this in their cross-cultural study, "Language Acquisition and Socialization," the main points of which will be summarized here. The authors start with the assumption that there are certain biological dispositions that shape the process of language acquisition anywhere, but the exact way in which a language is acquired and used reflects the influence of cultural expectations that are transmitted to the child in the socialization process. To demonstrate this, they analyze language-related socialization patterns in three cultures: that of the Euro-American middle class (which the authors take pains to distinguish from lower classes); the culture of the Kaluli of Papua, New Guinea; and the culture of the Samoans of the southwest Pacific. Their developmental stories for the first two of these cultures will be summarized here.

Ochs and Schieffelin take the ethnographic point of view, that is, they look at the socialization process as an ethnographer looks at any aspect of culture. They focus on what actually goes on between infants and their caretakers from birth until around three years of age. In two of the cultures, Kaluli and Samoa, one of the authors actually observed the transactions. As far as the Euro-American middle class was concerned, they sought out descriptions in the psychological and linguistic literature and used them as ethnographic reports. In their article, they construct typical developmental stories for each culture, show how they fit into a whole way of life, and make comparisons in terms of a scheme that emerges from their data. As far as this scheme is concerned, both the Kaluli and the Samoans contrast in the same way with the middle class.

The middle-class socialization pattern may sound familiar. The process usually involves two people, a mother and child, who share a great deal of eye contact. From the time of birth, the mother tends to regard her baby as a communicative partner. The mother has expectations that the child will begin to communicate through gesture, and later, through language. There is give-and-take between these partners; the child often initiates the transaction and the mother asks questions. ("What do you want mommy to do?") She then expands on the question. ("Open it up?") Finally, she interprets the response. ("Oh, what a nice smile.") During this process, the mother simplifies adult language into what is called baby talk, which is one aspect of her general accommodation to the child. As the infant develops linguistic capabilities, adjustments are made, but the general pattern continues. The infant is exposed to a regime in which gestures and vocalizations may not be immediately understood. It learns to deal with this ambiguity through a process of give-and-take that produces progressively more accurate meanings, which the infant can agree with or not. Finally, it comes to understand that communication and understanding involve a two-person transaction in which language plays an important role.

The Kaluli do not believe that newborn infants are capable of understanding and do not regard them as communicative partners. A Kaluli mother is responsive to her infant's needs, but in the first few months she rarely addresses the infant directly. Instead, she often faces the child away from her so that it can see and be seen by others who address it. Then, the mother, speaking through the child, responds in a high-pitched, nasal voice while moving the child up and down like a puppet. Except for the special tone, the language she uses is adult. Later, at six-to-twelve months of age, the child is given a few orders, but is still not regarded as a communicative partner. The infant may then be vocalizing and gesturing. It may even be saying a word or two in the Kaluli language. But until it says the words for "mother" and "breast," it is thought to be incapable of language. From this time until about three years of age, the infant is put through a routine that involves the mother and other participants. The child often becomes a third party in what amounts to a conversation between the mother and another child. The child is told to say things to that person in adult language. ("Whose is it?" "Is it yours?") If the child makes a mistake, it is corrected until it gets it right. Throughout this process, it is considered the child's responsibility to accommodate to the adult world, which frequently involves three or more people in communicative transactions. Since the Kaluli believe that one cannot know what another thinks, they do not explore for meanings as do middle-class adults. Rather, they specify a lot in order to make things perfectly clear. The child is socialized in a way that is compatible with such linguistic practices.

It is apparent from this cross-cultural investigation that children in different cultures acquire languages at different speeds and with different kinds of input. They may be drilled into it in a highly specific way; they may acquire it through verbal explorations with others; they may learn from listening to the conversations of others; or they may realize that some sound they have produced amounts to something significant. Their caretakers may accommodate or not accommodate to them. Regardless of the means of socialization, children ultimately acquire a linguistic competence that is more or less appropriate for their culture. Ochs and Scheiffelin argue that this could not be accomplished without a biological disposition for language that produces an active language learner; but neither could it come about without hearing a language. There must be some kind of appropriate input from outside.

There are also paralinguistic things that go on in the socialization process. Children not only acquire a language, but also an understanding of the way to use it. They are taught their language in certain ways that reflect other aspects of their culture. From the way in which they are socialized, they also learn what people are like as communicators, the social conditions in which certain expressions ought to be used, how expressions are to be communicated, and to whom. Ochs and Schieffelin argue that the child not only has to acquire a code for language, but a sociocultural code that goes with it.

THE USES OF LANGUAGE

"Talk is cheap." "Actions speak louder than words." "He is a man of his word."

All of these expressions used by Americans testify to their insistence that, compared to concrete actions, language is secondary. For them, the bottom line has tended to be that actions like money across the table or help given in time of need mean more than words. Perhaps the expressions are a throwback to an earlier era, when the exchange and processing of information had not yet moved to the center of the American stage. Even so, language has always been an important aspect of American culture, as well as other cultures. One way of measuring its importance is by examining its uses.

Earlier, the significance of language for communication was discussed. Without language, very few human social projects could get off the ground. Think, for example, of trying to coordinate a big-game hunt at night without language or of carrying out a complex heart operation in a modern hospital. When there are linguistic barriers in projects requiring cooperation, as when Americans and Japanese try to iron out a business contract, the value of language for communication becomes clear.

Language has other uses, one of which is for thinking. It obviously plays a huge role in helping people to classify their world. Thus, the word *agua* in Spanish embraces a variety of specific waters, "cousin" in English includes a number of specific relatives, and "incest" covers a range of specific sexual relationships between relatives. In addition, the existence of names for things promotes their manipulation in the extremely capable human mind. Thus, people who have mastered certain rules of logic can reason: All men are mortal; Socrates is a man; therefore, Socrates is mortal. Although humans are not alone in their ability to think, language obviously enhances their thinking abilities.

It has been suggested that the way different people think about things is dependent on the nature of their languages. Edward Sapir, an anthropologist and poet, and Benjamin Lee Whorf, an insurance man from Hartford, Connecticut, thought that such important concepts as time, space, matter, and color would vary according to the nature of a language. They developed this idea on the basis of observations they made of a number of different peoples, including the Hopi of the American Southwest, Americans, and Europeans. A good deal of additional research has followed, all of which has run into the difficulty of stating this exciting hypothesis in a precise, cross-culturally testable form. Considering the amount of interest in the hypothesis, it is surprising that researchers have come up with so little concrete evidence that is suitable for testing it. Moreover, where the evidence is adequate, it has not been too supportive. One famous study by Brent Berlin and Paul Kay (*Basic Color Terms: Their Universality and Evolution*), for example, explored basic color terms used by ninety-eight different peoples. They found that members of different societies classify colors into labeled classes ranging from a minimum of two (black and white) to a maximum of eleven. Although people from different societies have different numbers of color terms (the reasons for which are not yet understood), they all sort out their basic colors in the same way. Subsequent research has shown that this is done in terms of certain categories of hue and brightness, which operation appears to be governed by universally built-in psychophysical predispositions. Thus, some of the way in which humans classify and talk about their color world does not vary with language, but rather, seems to be everywhere given. This kind of evidence is not very encouraging to those experts who argue that knowledge of a language will give you the key to the way people think.

Languages also serve as social markers. People who speak one language, or a variant of a language, are marked off from others. People who speak the Basque or Catalan languages in Spain set themselves off from other Spaniards by using these languages. William Labov found that natives of Martha's Vineyard, an island off the coast of Massachusetts, distinguish themselves from summer residents and other visitors by, among other things, the way in which they use their tongues in pronouncing certain phonemes. There can be differences, also, between social classes, as Henry Higgins, the professor in *My Fair Lady*, knew when he took on the task of turning a lower-class Cockney girl into a creature of high society. There also appear to be differences between male and female speech patterns in all cultures, which help to establish the gender of the speaker.

The use of language to mark the degree of formality (and therefore, social distance) of a relationship is something that students of German learn very early. Like many other languages, German has a formal and informal way of indicating "you" (*sie* or *du*), and one learns that, on beginning a relationship, it is better to use the formal form. The distance between college professors and their students is also marked by different linguistic usages. American young people have their own argot, an example of which is their current word that means something like "great." As a college professor whose job it is to communicate with students, I have sometimes tried to break through into their world by using what I take to be the current word for expressing this meaning. There was "cool," then "tough," and so on to whatever it is today. Somehow, I have always been a little behind the times, and though the students have taken my efforts to establish greater intimacy with good humor, I think they have been pleased with my little failures. They seem to have preferred that a more formal relationship exist between us.

Language plays a role in the functioning of all aspects of the cultures of humankind, including their reproduction through the generations. The Tiv people who are mentioned from time to time in this book would be hard put to sort out their relatives and the nature of their obligations to these relatives without language. Tribal elders could not hear, discuss, nor pronounce judgment on a case involving a dispute between neighbors. Buying and selling in the marketplace could scarcely begin. Bride purchase, which involves discussion between men of different kinship groups and with their wards, could hardly exist. There would be no gossip about the latest elopement. People could not tell their children about the witches that fly at night. Songs could not be sung, and nights would be long for a lack of storytelling. There might be some dancing, but it would be harder to teach. Some rituals might be practiced, but there would be no accompanying language and belief. Finally, what part of the Tiv material world—their drums, dwellings, agricultural implements, weapons, cooking utensils, and all the rest—could they have been able to fashion without the aid of language?

Language has many uses in human life, and it vastly enriches our existence. Think, finally, of a group of chimpanzees living in the forest. The chimpanzees can think, though not as well as humans. They can learn and they have a form of social organization as well as systems of authority. Collective rituals have been noted among them. On the whole, though, whatever culture they have is only rudimentary. Why is this? An important reason would seem to be their lack of language, which is something that humans alone possess.

REFERENCES

BERLIN, BRENT, and PAUL KAY, *Basic Color Terms: Their Universality and Evolution*. Berkeley, Calif.: University of California Press, 1969.

BROWN, CECIL, "Folk Botanical Life-Forms: Their Universality and Growth," *American Anthropologist*, 79, 1971, 317–42.

CHOMSKY, NOAM, *Language and Mind* (2nd ed.). New York: Harcourt Brace Jovanovich, 1972.

———, *Reflections on Language*. New York: Pantheon Books, 1975.

COLLETT, PETER, "Meetings and Misunderstandings," in *Cultures in Contact*, ed. Stephen Bochner. Elmsford, N.Y.: Pergamon Press, 1982.

EIMAS, PETER, E.R. SIQUELAND, P. JUSCZYK, and J. VIGORITO, "Speech Perception in Infants," *Science* 171 (22 January), 1971, 303–06.

FODOR, J., *The Modularity of Mind*. Cambridge, Mass.: The M.I.T. Press, 1983.

GREENBERG, JOSEPH, *A New Invitation to Linguistics*. Garden City, N.Y.: Anchor Books, 1977.

LABOV, WILLIAM, *Sociolinguistic Patterns*. Philadelphia, Pa.: University of Pennsylvania Press, 1973.

MATTINGLY, IGNATIUS, "Phonetic Prerequisites for First-Language Acquisition," in *Baby Talk and Infant Speech*, eds. W. Von Raffler-Engel and Y. Lebrun. Lisse, The Netherlands: Swets and Zeitlinger, 1976.

OCHS, ELINOR, and BAMBI SCHIEFFELIN, "Language Acquisition and Socialization: Three Developmental Stories and Their Implications," in *Culture Theory: Essays on Mind, Self, and Emotion*, eds. Richard Shweder and Robert Levine. New York: Cambridge University Press, 1984.

WHORF, BENJAMIN LEE, "The Relation of Habitual Thought to Language," in *Language, Culture and Personality: Essays in Memory of Edward Sapir*, eds. Leslie Spier, A. Irving Hallowell, and Stanley S. Newman. Menasha, Wis.: Sapir Memorial Publication Fund.

Chapter Seven

IDEA WORLDS

All humans live not only in an objective world (the world *out there*), but also in a subjective world (the world of our conceptions); and even as our actions are related to the world *out there*, they reflect our *inner* world as well. We dream, plan, fantasize, speculate, calculate, and formulate all through our lives. Other animals have thoughts. Studies of chimpanzees, for example, have revealed some remarkable conceptual abilities. But no creature has a mental life that comes close to that of humans. So important is this aspect of human life that it must be routinely considered in any discussion of humanity. Because anthropology is the science that has humanity as its principal concern, the study of human idea worlds has always been a part of its work.

Through the use of participant observation and informants, anthropologists try to enter into the thought worlds of the people they study. It is essential to understand people on their own terms and to reconstruct what W. I. Thomas referred to as their "definition of the situation" or what A. I. Hallowell called their "behavioral environment." If you have ever tried to make sense of a stranger's apparently incomprehensible actions you will understand how difficult this can be.

The anthropologist is not totally at a loss, however, in trying to comprehend idea worlds. An informant can explain what he or she is thinking or meaning; and if the investigator is especially astute, it may be possible to dig up something that the informant is not consciously aware of. Also, people objectify their subjective worlds in language, art, philosophy, scientific treatises, folklore, myth, and religion. These "extrinsic symbols," which Hallowell thought to be uniquely human, can be a major entree into the idea worlds of a people.

Consider two sets of extrinsic symbols made famous by two American coaches. Leo Durocher, a baseball coach, said that "nice guys finish last." George Allen, a football coach, proposed that "when the going gets tough the tough get going." The publicity given to these slogans suggests that the ideas that lay behind them are shared by many Americans. What are these ideas? Students of American culture have often pointed out the importance of achievement and winning, competition (fair and unfair), and a general orientation to action (rather than contemplation). The slogans would appear to be related to these values, and Americans' actions tend to be informed by them. Are such ideas to be found in other cultures? Certainly, but not to the same degree and not, perhaps, with the same flavor. The anthropologist's concerns in all of this are, first, interpretive, that is, to discover the meaning of the slogans to the Americans themselves; second, holistic, that is to try to discover how these and other similar slogans fit together into some kind of system; third, comparative, that is, to compare these elements of American culture with those of other cultures. Something of the excitement of such operations, whether narrowly or broadly conceived, is conveyed in *The Interpretation of Cultures* by the American anthropologist Clifford Geertz. But, as mentioned earlier in Chapter Two, interpretive audacity sometimes may carry us beyond the realm of ethnographic fact, and we may have to make a conscious effort to keep our feet on the ground, so to speak.

THE CASE OF RELIGION

A religion provides a particularly interesting example of a world of ideas and its associated actions. Its practitioners are involved in using and generating ideas concerning the nature of the world and the place of humans in it. These ideas are expressed in oral or written beliefs and ritualistic behaviors by a group of people. For example, in the strictest of early Protestant sects God was seen to be a powerful father figure who had a plan for the world and the creatures in it. This plan, the exact nature of which was not revealed to humans, included the salvation of some humans in an afterlife. One's actions in this life could not affect salvation (which was up to God); they were only a way of honoring God, so to speak. Collective rituals in a place that we Westerners have come to call a church were to celebrate God and his works, not to help humans in this or the next world.

Though we may find this type of religion not our particular cup of tea, most of us will have little difficulty recognizing it as a religion. This may be because God is involved. The early Protestants' idea of God referred to a supraempirical being who possessed qualities going beyond the world of the senses. All Jews and Christians have an idea of some such being, as do Muslims, Hindus, and Buddhists. We shall have no trouble calling such people religious. We probably would not want to put the polytheists of the world beyond the pale. We would count them as religious too, although some of us might raise questions about the correctness of their religions. The idea of supraempirical powers as an essential element in religious ideas is an attractive one and has drawn many to a definition of religion as something that is concerned primarily with the *supernatural*.

There are problems with this definition as with any definition; but it has good cross-cultural utility, which is essential for the comparisons that anthropologists like to make. If we are going to compare a main-line American religion such as Catholicism with a sect such as the Hare Krishnas, or either of these with the religion of the Balinese or the ancient Aztecs, we will find common core ideas in all of them relating to a supernatural realm, which will permit us to make comparisons. If we employ this view of religion relentlessly, we will have to include not only gods, but angels, witches, fairies, demons, souls, giant talking birds, and animate rocks as elements of religion. We may feel a little uncomfortable about putting all of these together in the same category, but that feeling of uncomfortableness may come from our own ideas about the *reality* of these things. Our particular god, angels, and souls may be real, we might think, but other supernaturals are fantasy, or even superstition. Such concerns with the realness or rightness of ideas cannot preoccupy the anthropologist in his anthropological work. All believers have some kind of evidence to support the realness or rightness of their views. There is, however, no *scientific* evidence for or against the existence of supernaturals, so one has to put whatever faith one has about them in brackets, so to speak, while doing anthropological work. For the anthropologist it is enough to know that people *really* believe in the existence of supernatural powers and act in terms of their ideas of them. A group of such people, whatever the quality of the supernatural realm they believe in, can be said, then, to have a religion.

To sum up, for anthropological purposes a religion may be thought of as organized around some group's idea of the supernatural. Accompanying this idea is a set of beliefs and behaviors (ritualistic and other) that reflect the idea. The really religious are supernaturally guided, that is, by their ideas of supernaturals. The scientist cannot make any judgment about whether these ideas refer ultimately to something real, and so, *as a scientist*, the anthropologist is not concerned with wagers such as Pascal's concerning the existence of God.

WHY RELIGION?

Paul Radin said that religion comes from life and is directed to life. By this he was suggesting that religion could be explained in terms of (empirical) life circumstances. Many such explanations have been offered. Intellectualists have found the cause of religion in the human mind, as, for example, in the need to explain extraordinary events. Emotionalists have argued that feelings such as awe, excitement, fear, or anxiety give rise to religious ideas. The sociologically oriented have emphasized social conditions or needs such as legitimation or integration. It will not be particularly useful to go over grand explanations like these in detail since each has been found wanting in one way or another. A principal criticism concerns the evidence on which they are based.

Often, the grand theorists of religion have sought its cause in some archtypical condition of human life, especially primitive life. Freud, for example, thought that religion arose from a guilt complex derived from conflict between father and sons in the "primal horde." Direct evidence for such a horde does not exist; nor is there direct evidence for most of the life circumstances of the earliest humans such as Homo habilis or Homo erectus. Some material evidence for religion among Upper Paleolithic hunters and gatherers (art, burials, and possible ceremonial arrangements) has been found, but it is not extensive and its religious significance is open to question. When the grand theorist of religion refers to primitive religion, he is usually referring to the practices of contemporary primitives, which are supposed to be the same as those of the ancients. Emile Durkheim, for example, thought that he had found evidence of the earliest religion in the totemism of the Australian aborigines. He considered their societies to be primitive because they were small and undifferentiated. But totemism, a kinship-based religion involving plants or animals with supernatural qualities, is not always associated with such societies, and there is no direct evidence to indicate that it existed among the earliest humans.

Modern anthropologists have largely given up the search for the origin of this or that sociocultural trait. It is just too speculative. But some things can be said about the origin of religion. Almost certainly it arose among a people whose brains had evolved enough to permit a mental life that included ideas of supernatural powers, that is, of unseen things. If the sense of reality of these things was great enough, humans could have established relationships with them and acted in terms of these relationships. But what kinds of circumstances would have brought about the creation of supernatural beings in primitive minds? The question seems a little wrong-headed when one looks at people in our society who have not been dominated by the scientific frame of reference. For them, a subjective world that includes supra-empirical beings is nothing extraordinary. With them, the question of "Why supernaturals?" might be more profitably turned around to "Why not?"

Some of us have supernaturals on our minds more than others, however. Even as some societies appear to be more religiously involved than others, degree of religiosity seems to vary from person to person. Paul Radin said that only a small percentage of any society are truly religious. People like Bernadette Soubirous of Lourdes; the modern Indian mystic, Sri Ramakrishna; Jesus of Nazareth; or Handsome Lake, the Iroquois prophet; all appear to have had an extraordinary capacity for supernatural involvement. They are the "religiously musical" people (to use Weber's felicitous expression) who practically live in a supernatural world. We know about them because they have acquired significant followings. No doubt there are others, equally gifted, who have not acquired followings and who are not known to us. Whether successful or not, these "formulators" (to use Radin's term) would seem to possess special qualities. It has been suggested that they have specific personality attributes such as intense psychic conflict, and they have been branded as "neurotic epileptoid" or "paranoid schizophrenic." Some have argued that their religiosity comes from ingesting certain substances such as mescaline or ayahuasca. Certain "altered" states of consciousness have been related to bodily deprivations such as a lack of sleep or food. Possibly some of these people might be religious frauds. If so, their alleged religious involvement would be found in qualities associated with con-artistry. There is little solid scientific evidence about factors associated with religiosity, but at least one study has produced encouraging results. Richard Shweder, comparing Zincatecan (Mexican) shamans (that is, people who divine and solve problems with supernatural assistance) with non-shamans found a difference in mind-sets. Responding to unstructured stimuli, the shamans were quicker to impose their own order. They showed greater mental productivity and more "inner-directedness." In other words, they are the kind of people who tend to impose their richer subjective world on the objective world *out there*. This conclusion, which is consistent with some earlier speculations, has to be treated with caution as a cross-cultural generalization, but it does suggest lines of fruitful research. The reasons for variation in religiosity between individuals and societies are only beginning to be discovered.

Variation in the *quality* of religion is a question that has always been of interest to anthropologists. Early grand theorists often saw religion varying through time in some evolutionary way. Culture evolved from some primitive state, and religion, as a part of culture, was seen to evolve as well. Some saw humanity gradually falling away from a "pure" primitive monotheism. Others saw religious evolution as a relentless march *towards* monotheism. These and other grand evolutionary designs have little basis in fact and are rarely encountered in the anthropological literature these days. Instead, one finds anthropologists searching cross-culturally for the causes of religious variability. Although there continue to be many impressionistic observations, some scientific evidence has begun to emerge in the form of statistical studies that demonstrate associations between forms of religion and personality or social factors. For example, Guy Swanson, taking his cue from Durkheim (one might also have suggested Marx), found that religion tends to act either positively or negatively to support the moral codes of socially stratified societies. It appears to provide supernatural sanctions that keep the socially deprived "in their place" and justify a situation of social dominance and subordination. In the same cross-cultural study, Swanson also found beliefs in monotheism, polytheism, active ancestral spirits, reincarnation, witchcraft, and immanence of the soul (that it is a part of the body and not transcendent) to be associated with specific kinds of social arrangements.

On the psychological side, a number of cross-cultural studies have found a significant statistical association between belief in benevolent or malevolent supernaturals (good guys or bad guys) and what amounts to acceptance or rejection by parents in childhood. When the father of Anthony Eden, a British Foreign Secretary, looked out the window on a typical dreary English day and shouted, "Oh God, how like you," he was not only saying something about his god, but also about his personality that had apparently been formed in hard circumstances.

This is only some of the evidence that has linked religion's quality with secular, this-worldly factors. It is not exhaustive, but is only designed to give some idea about how anthropologists are trying to explain religious variability. We are nowhere close to fully explaining that variability; nor is it likely that religion will ever be explained away in terms of secular facts of life. But recent anthropological work does suggest that religion, whatever its ultimate origins, is clearly constrained by such facts.

THE NATURE OF A RELIGION

Whatever the factors that bring it into existence and maintain it, a religion, sooner or later, acquires a life of its own. It becomes, in Clifford Geertz' terms, a cultural system that has to be understood and described. The way anthropologists look at a religion derives from the particular definition they employ as well as certain invariant properties that most anthropologists use. Following the line taken in this paper, any religion can be seen to revolve around certain ideas in the minds of its believers. These ideas, which refer to supernatural powers, are the focal point of an array of ideas that may be called a belief system. Any anthropological description of a religion will include a discussion of its belief system and how it is organized. For example, structuralists like Claude Levi-Strauss will attempt to decipher this organization in terms of supposed universal properties of the human mind. In addition, the rituals of the religion and related behaviors are routinely analyzed as, for example, in the work of Victor Turner. Some anthropologists assign primacy to ritual and others to belief, but all recognize both of these aspects of religion and the fact that they are intimately interrelated.

Because a religion is seen to be anchored in life circumstances, the anthropologist usually discusses the social and environmental context in which a religion exists and to which it must adapt. There is also a concern with the characteristics of its believers and the way in which they organize or arrange themselves. The usual anthropological description of a religion is not, therefore, some dry-as-bones discussion of doctrine and ritual, but rather of something that is being practiced by specific human beings who have organized themselves in a certain way at a specific time and place. Religion, thus, becomes a *human* social fact, and it is the anthropologist's task to understand this and to describe it with the utmost fidelity and sensitivity. Not all anthropologists are equal to this task. No matter how well trained, some of them are more religiously "musical" than others.

Finally, it should be noted that anthropologists are, by nature, comparers. By using invariant properties in their descriptions, they help others to make comparisons and to make general statements about what kinds of beliefs, rituals, contexts, and believers tend to go together.

In order to bring this discussion of the nature of a religion down to earth, it might be helpful to refer to some specific religions. Two anthropological reports will be summarized. One, by Seth and Ruth Leacock, is to be found in their book *Spirits of the Deep*. It deals with the Batuque, an Afro-Brazilian religious cult in Belém, Brazil. The other, by Melford Spiro, is offered in his book *Buddhism and Society*. It treats one of the great religious traditions as it is being practiced, especially, in a Burmese village setting. Although the theoretical approaches of these studies are different, they have both been carried out from the anthropological perspective that has just been discussed and that pervades this book. Based on intensive fieldwork and impeccable scholarship, these studies permit us to see contemporary, non-Western religions in action. The summaries that follow can only hint at the richness and sensitivity of the original reports.

The Batuque of Belém, Brazil

The Leacocks, who developed an intimate acquaintance with their subjects during two field trips covering a period of nine months, tell us that the Batuque is one of a large number of Afro-American religions that stress spirit possession. Their description of the historical context of the Belém Batuque includes a treatment of the importation and subsequent integration of African slaves into Brazil; a discussion of the region around the mouth of the Amazon (where Belém is located);

and a search for the Batuque's African, Christian, and American religious roots. Their Batuque, like all Batuques, has taken on the coloration of a particular locale, which in this case is the Brazilian, urban, lower class. The Leacocks emphasize the poverty of the neighborhoods from which the Batuque draws its members. These people are nominally Catholics, but they do not usually attend church. Elements of Catholicism are mixed into the Batuque religion, however.

Batuque members believe in *encantados*, or spirits, who are thought to be capable of taking possession of the bodies of individual humans. When this happens, people take on the character of the spirit, whatever it is. If the spirit is an important one, the person in trance acts in a very serious, even pompous, manner; if the spirit is a known carouser, the person may act giddy and even drink beer or rum. Excepting the important fact of the ability to possess people, the *encantados* are not unlike Catholic saints in that they have supernatural qualities that can be tapped by people who develop a personal relationship with them. They require things of these people and will punish them if offended, but they also give supernatural assistance in, for example, maintaining family harmony, curing illnesses, or providing information. For Batuque believers, the *encantados* are thought to have a more specific, day-to-day interest in a person's life than the Catholic saints or God.

The Leacocks emphasize that the rituals of the Batuque are more loosely structured than those of more conservative cults like Xangô or Candomblé. The central ritual takes place in a *terreiro* or cult center, which is headed by a *mãe de santo* (mother) or *pai de santo* (father). The public ceremonies (which are directed by the *mãe* or *pai de santo*) involve, first, a prayer to Catholic saints, then a series of drum-accompanied songs and dances that "call on" and honor various *encantados* who are thought to reside above or under the earth. These spirits are believed to make their appearance as members of the company become possessed by them and take on their characteristics. In many ways a spectacle, the ceremony attracts large crowds who press against the railing of the *terreiro*. The spectacle is enhanced by the ornate clothing of the participants, the burning of gunpowder in bare hands, and the drumming, dancing, and singing that goes on long into the night. Another important activity involves consultations concerning personal problems, which are given by mediums during the public ceremony or at other times at their homes.

In Belém there are a number of mostly independent *terreiros*, each headed by a *mãe* or *pai de santo* who have a somewhat competitive relationship with each other. They do not have a great deal of power over their members, who generally tend to be poor, over thirty, female, and native to the city. Some of the members of a *terreiro* are mediums who are capable of being possessed and some are not. Among the mediums there is a rank order leading up to the *mãe* or *pai de santo*. The Leacocks emphasize that trance-possession is learned, but that not everybody can learn it; and for those that do, some learn to "control" it better than others.

Buddhism in Yeighi, Burma

The focal point of Spiro's investigation is a small agricultural village located not far from Mandalay in the heart of the Burmese culture area. (The principal crop of the village of Yeighi is rice.) Additional inquiries were carried out in other agricultural villages, in Mandalay and some other cities, in other Buddhist countries such as Thailand, and through historic documents. Spiro generalizes widely from his Yeighi data because he found little variation in the essentials of the religion in space and time; but the people of Yeighi and their religion constitute the focus of his investigation.

The religion in question is Theravada Buddhism, which Spiro contrasts with the Mahayana Buddhism of northern and eastern Asia. Buddhist beliefs are reported to be variable, with one or another emphasized in a particular time and place. The history of Buddhism in Burma and recent historic developments that have affected it are considered. Spiro is careful to specify the sources of his data on current practices. In Yeighi, they come from questionnaires administered to almost every household, interviews with a "blue-ribbon panel" of fifteen religiously involved laymen and with monks in the local monasteries, and participant observation in and outside of the community.

In contrast to the Batuque, which does not stress this subject, Theravada Buddhism, like Christianity, is very much concerned with the matter of personal salvation, that is, the fate of the individual after death. In the Buddhist conception, such salvation is seen in a context of reincarnation, which involves a series of deaths and rebirths into different earthly existences until the individual ceases to exist. By following the teaching (*Dhamma*) of the Buddha, one of a number of supremely enlightened individuals who are thought to have released themselves from the "wheel of earthly existence," that is reincarnation, a person is believed to be able to alter his fate and ultimately attain deliverance. According to the Nibbanic version of Buddhism, the individual can attain this ultimately desireable state through the practice of morality, charity, and meditation, which if carried out with the correct intention, can lead to a condition of mind oblivious to worldly desires. In Kammatic Buddhism, a more popular form of the religion, the aid is more proximate, that is, to improve one's worldly existence in subsequent births through the accumulation of merit in this life. Thus, a woman can hope that by accumulating merit she can be reborn as a man in this male-dominated culture. She might therefore make contributions to the construction of a pagoda. Both of these religious traditions emphasize that personal salvation is to be attained by the *unaided* effort of the devotee, the Buddha acting only as a model and message-giver. The other forms of Theravada Buddhism tend to be more this-worldly in their orientation and prone to beliefs in supernatural powers, which include gods (*devas*) and spirits (*nats*)—powers that an individual can relate to directly for this-worldly ends.

Just as the Buddhist belief system is more complex than the Batuque, so is the ritual. Spiro goes over the rich array of Theravada Buddhist ritual practices. He deals with such rituals as the Confession of Faith, the various rites connected with events in the Buddha's life, and the extremely important (as far as gaining merit is concerned) initiation of a boy. He also speaks of cycles of rituals: the calendrical (daily, weekly, monthly, annual), the life cycle (initiation, death), and crises of natural or supernatural origin. Rituals are performed in private and in public. They focus on the Buddha, his teaching, and the Buddhist monastic order (*Sangha*). Monks teach and perform rituals that can help laymen, but more importantly, they conduct practices that will affect their own *karma*, a supernatural force for good or bad that is linked to one's present and past actions. A monk, in pursuing what appears to be a mostly selfish course, is conceived to be expressing the highest aspirations of his society, and it is by supporting and revering him that laymen can affect their own *karma* in a positive way. Monks at ordination take a vow of poverty, chastity, and homelessness, and they attempt to follow the monastic Rule, which stresses sexual abstinence, reverence for life, care about claiming the achievement of supernatural powers, and acceptance only of those things that are freely given. Violation of these and many other elements of the Rule require confession and either expulsion or an expiation ceremony.

Unlike the Batuque, which consists of largely independent cults, Theravada Buddhism has an elaborate organization that extends beyond the village. One can think of it, perhaps, as something like a loosely organized Catholic church. At its heart is the monastery, which has a structure not unlike Western monasteries. The head of the monastery is under the loose jurisdiction of the district and national organizations of a branch, which, in turn, is linked with other branches in the Burmese order. Lay devotees (both men and women) cluster around monasteries, whose members are all male. Spiro notes that women demonstrate the most ceremonial devotion. He also points out the qualities of the male initiates into the monastery. They are mostly boys of rural origin who have received a religious education in a monastery rather than a secular education. They have come under the influence of a monastic teacher and are on the way to becoming what Spiro refers to as "world rejectors." The author speculates that they have strong dependency and narcissistic needs and that they are emotionally timid. The Burmese recognize that, with or without the aid of monastery life, only a few become *arahants*—people who are supposed to be delivered from the fetters of worldly existence and placed on the immediate path to *nirvana*, that ultimate state in which the individual ceases to exist.

* * *

The summaries just given are inevitably inadequate. They attempt to distill only the descriptive parts of two anthropological studies of religion. (The authors' attempts at explanation and integration are barely touched on.) Readers will have to read the books in order to experience the religion in detail. But the summaries do give us some idea of the kind of picture that anthropologists "take" of a religion and of the possibilities of comparing these pictures. The religions are located in different parts of the world in different contexts. One is a "great" codified religion of considerable complexity. The other is comparatively simple. They offer vastly different views of the universe and how one should act in it. In Theravada Buddhism, the aim of most believers is to do better in one's next earthly existence. The ultimate goal, however, is to be done with all earthly existences altogether. Batuque members hope that their beliefs and practices will ameliorate a poverty-ridden existence in this life. What happens after that is not dwelt upon. Catholicism may serve as a kind of back-up where serious matters of the afterlife are concerned. As in the case of belief, the ritual system of the Batuque is much less complex than that of Theravada Buddhism.

The authors of these two studies are acutely sensitive to, and properly respectful of, the religions they have studied. They deal with these religions on their own terms, lacing their descriptions with quotations and observations that lend them a compelling personal immediacy not usually found in accounts by other scholars. They do not make any judgments about the "correctness" of the religions. That issue is beyond the scientific pale. Above all, they deal with religion as something that is lived: an aspect of human life practiced by flesh-and-blood people who arrange themselves in a certain way in a specific historic context. Through a consideration of its believers, religion is made to come alive.

What now is to be done with descriptions such as these? A natural step is to compare the religions with each other in a fashion intimated above. Next, one might want to make comparisons with one's own religion. The inevitable result of this would be to erode culture-bound conceptions of religion. We come to see our religion (if we have one) as being more like this or that other religion and as located somewhere in a range of variability exhibited by all the religions of humankind. A further, more analytic procedure might be to search for the causes of differences and similarities between religions in a manner discussed earlier in this chapter.

RELIGION'S CONSEQUENCES

A religion is shaped and maintained by the conditions of life in some group or society. This is something that has come to be taken for granted in anthropology. However, religion can acquire the power to act back on those conditions through the actions of its believers. In Iran today, it is easy to see the power that a religion can have in shaping a society. A modern Iranian religious zealot, waiting for the coming of the redeeming 12th Iman, believes that his Shiite version of Islam has the power to transform him, his society, and the world. Even the United States, which has been considered by such Iranians to represent the interests of Satan, can be transformed. Whether we believe these people or not, we can recognize that they are offering us a particular view of religion's this-worldly consequences. And indeed, the social transformations now taking place in Iran lend credence to their view.

What, then, does religion do for the individual and for society? Anthropologists have had their own views on this subject. Through their use of the concept of function, they have attempted to show that religion makes certain contributions to individual and social life. Thus, they have argued that the idea of an afterlife may make it easier for people to face death; the concept of the divine right of kings could contribute to a king's authority; a god-given value system, if shared by a community, could foster community solidarity; certain religiously based food taboos could promote adaptation to the environment; and malevolent supernaturals could serve as a safety valve for this-worldly hostilities. A particularly interesting, if tricky, illustration of religion's alleged functions is to be found in studies that explore the relationship between religion and physical well-being. In a famous article on the concept of "Voodoo Death," W. B. Cannon, a physiologist, proposed the exact psychosomatic mechanisms whereby magically inspired fear could cause a person to die. His views (which have been disputed) were not the same as those of Haitian believers, but he agreed with them that death, in fact, was the result of the application of certain religious practices. On the brighter side, the role of religion in restoring bodily health has been claimed by believers, who postulate the operation of supernatural forces, and scientists, who think in terms of psychosomatic processes.

We know now that too many of religion's consequences have, in the past, been assumed rather than demonstrated. Anthropologists should now realize that a religion may work in a variety of scientifically demonstratable ways for, or against, the adaptation of individuals and societies. The manner in which it works and the people whose adaptation is affected have to be carefully specified. An example of a more sophisticated type of functional analysis is to be found in Spiro's discussion of the worldly consequences of Theravada Buddhist beliefs and practices. Spiro considers both psychological and social functions. Among the social consequences, according to Spiro, are two of an economic nature: 1) Buddhism's effect on the distribution of wealth in Burmese society, and 2) its effect on Burmese economic development.

In Yeighi and the rest of Burma, Spiro encountered a socially stratified society—some people are wealthy and a lot of people are poor. In our society, this state of affairs is something that is to be, at least publicly, lamented. Not so in Burma, where Buddhism provides a moral justification for social inequality. A person believing in the Buddhist notion of *karma* would attribute his present economic situation to past actions in other lives. Spiro found that this view was especially prevalent among the poor, and he speculates (in the manner of Swanson, who was mentioned earlier) that this leads them to accept a condition of economic deprivation. Because the poor accept their situation and do not try to change it, and because the attitude that leads to this acceptance stems from its key beliefs, Buddhism, through its concept of *karma*, is seen by Spiro to function to conserve or maintain the system of social stratification in this society.

The Kammatic Buddhist variant, it will be recalled, stresses the concept of merit, which can be accumulated through such actions as religious giving. In Yeighi, Spiro says, approximately one-quarter of the income of a household is spent in religious giving, and the estimate is even higher for other villages in the area. The money is spent on such religious items as initiation ceremonies (a loose equivalent of the Jewish Bar Mitzvah), provisions for monks, pilgrimages, and construction and repair of pagodas. Because of this, a smaller proportion of the Burmese income is plowed back into productive economic operations such as agriculture or industry than in, say, modern China. This means that whatever efforts the Burmese government makes in the direction of economic development will be hampered by the Buddhist belief in the possibility of accumulating merit in this life for a better existence next time around. Spiro, contrasting this with the Protestant Ethic in early industrial Europe and America (which emphasized economic productivity as a sign or means of salvation), concludes that Buddhism is *dysfunctional* for Burmese economic development. Through its concept of merit (as well as *karma*), Buddhism is seen, rather, as functioning to maintain a less productive economic system.

Functional analysis is, at the moment, subject to a good deal of criticism by anthropologists. This is in part due to certain assumptions of early functionalists who often seemed to be oblivious to the forces of social change, conflict, and differentiation. The concept of dysfunction had to be coined to take into account the obvious fact that everything did not always work out for the best. But it is clearly evident that a religion does have consequences for the people who believe in and practice it, as well as for others. Whether functional analysis is the best way of getting at these consequences is, for the moment, undecided.

* * *

It may be possible now to recapitulate what has gone before. Religion, here, has been taken as one example of human idea worlds in action. It has been conceived as a social institution that is associated with ideas of supernatural powers. Anthropologists have been concerned with describing the religions of humankind, and their studies have made us aware of the enormous variety of these religions. Besides describing, comparing, and ordering religions, anthropologists have also been concerned with finding their causes and consequences. In their studies they have, knowingly or unknowingly, followed Paul Radin's dictum that religion comes from life and is directed to life, which is to say that it is part of some culture that guides one's actions.

WHAT TO BELIEVE?

Anthropologists, as scientists, cannot be advocates of a particular belief; nor can they provide the grounds for assessing the truthfulness or correctness of a belief. On the contrary, simply by describing the many religions of the world and their believers, the anthropologist may raise doubts about our own beliefs. In a course in anthropology, the student may find a heretofore unexamined world view put into question. Faith can be shaken by encounters with other ways of thinking.

The taken-for-granted quality of daily life in a stable society is something in which we have faith. When a famous religious formulator like Wovoka, the Paiute Indian, develops a new formula for life that responds to the developing needs of his people, that formula is tried on, adjusted, and reiterated until it becomes a faith. It will continue as a faith until other views, derived from other conditions, acquire currency.

The conditions that are necessary to sustain faith are suggested almost daily by young converts to certain American religious sects. Their parents, seeing strange things happening to their child, may begin to think that some kind of "brainwashing" is responsible, that is, that they are being transformed in an intense learning experience. As Wallace has pointed out, the acquisition and maintenance of belief in such situations is dependent on separation from nonbelievers, who carry information that is irrelevant or contradictory to the faith in question. Within the new "cocoon," an initiate, who goes through an intensive learning experience, begins not only to see the world in a different way, but also to take the new way for granted. The intensity of initiates' new religious convictions will depend on their personal needs and the nature of the life they lead in their new religion.

Always there is the possibility of a lapse or decline in faith, especially if outsiders (including, possibly, counter-brainwashers) are able to impose their views on the devotee. This kind of thing, of course, could never occur in the archtypical primitive society where a routinized existence is not jeopardized by many contacts with outsiders holding different beliefs. In the modern world, however, such an existence is not the norm. Social mobility and social differentiation encourage the development of multiple points of view. Even in modern totalitarian societies such as Russia, this trend exists, and the Russian government is having problems with its "heretics," too. The possibility of acquiring and holding a deep set of religious convictions is much more difficult in such a society. People who feel a vague disquiet when learning that others—real people—believe differently than they do are experiencing something that comes naturally in a modern society: the fruits of a way of life in which there is more freedom, but in which faith—especially religious faith—is difficult to maintain.

REFERENCES

CANNON, WALTER B., "Voodoo Death," *American Anthropologist*, 19, 1942, 169–81.

DURKHEIM, EMILE, *The Elementary Forms of the Religious Life*. London: Allen and Unwin, 1915.

FREUD, SIGMUND, *Totem and Taboo*. New York: Vintage Books, 1952.

GEERTZ, CLIFFORD, "Religion as a Cultural System," in *Anthropological Approaches to the Study of Religion*, ed. M. Banton. New York: Praeger, 1966.

———, *The Interpretation of Cultures*. New York: Basic Books, 1973.

HALLOWELL, A. IRVING, *Culture and Experience*. Philadelphia: University of Pennsylvania Press, 1955.

LEACOCK, SETH, and RUTH LEACOCK, *Spirits of the Deep*. Garden City, New York: Doubleday Natural History Press, 1972.

LEVI-STRAUSS, CLAUDE, *Totemism*. Boston: Beacon Press, 1963.

RADIN, PAUL, *Primitive Religion*. New York: Dover Publications, 1957.

SHWEDER, RICHARD, "Aspects of Cognition of Zincatecan Shamans: Experimental Results," in *Reader in Comparative Religion*, eds. W. Lessa and E. Vogt. New York: Harper and Row, 1972.

SPIRO, MELFORD, *Buddhism and Society* (2nd ed.). Berkeley: University of California Press, 1982.

SWANSON, GUY, *The Birth of the Gods*. Ann Arbor: University of Michigan Press, 1960.

TURNER, VICTOR, *The Ritual Process*. Chicago: Aldine, 1969.

WALLACE, ANTHONY F. C., *Religion: An Anthropological View*. New York: Random House, 1966.

WEBER, MAX, *The Protestant Ethic and the Spirit of Capitalism*. New York: Scribners, 1930.

Chapter Eight

ECONOMIES

OIKONOMOS

It has been said that the word economics is derived from the name of a steward of a noble household in ancient Athens. This man, a slave named Oikonomos, was responsible for provisioning the household. He decided what crops would be grown, what animals to raise, and what commodities to purchase. He made sure that equipment and labor was available to do all of this and he organized the work teams to do the various tasks. He was in charge of distributing what was bought and produced to household members. In discussions with the household head, it was decided how much to save and how much to sell. Every day he made adjustments to take advantage of current conditions. Those were his duties.

In effect, the steward (with or without consultation) was doing pretty much what an economy is supposed to do, that is, provide the goods and services needed to satisfy the wants of a people. Because the satisfaction of one want may involve the frustration of another, and because the means to satisfy a given want are various, a number of choices have to be made. Economics deals with the choices that people make in the course of providing for their wants.

IS THIS AN ECONOMY?

Anthropologists interested in economic life encounter the same kind of problem they face in studying any other aspect of culture. They begin with some notion of the subject, which is most likely derived from their own culture. Then, they find that some elements of that notion are not cross-culturally applicable. Then, with a lot of give and take, they work out a preliminary definition that will permit them to identify their subject in many, or all, cultures. The science of economics grew up in the capitalist, market-oriented cultures of Europe and America. To what extent do such views on economies, and how they operate, apply to other cultures? Anthropologists who have been interested in this aspect of culture are not in complete agreement. They have different approaches to the subject, and they are always revising their thinking in the light of new information. But it does seem possible to venture at least a rough, preliminary definition of the field of economic action that will be cross-culturally applicable.

Consider that an economy involves all those activities that relate to how people provision themselves with goods and services. Probably best thought of as a social process, it includes the production of goods and services, the transfer of the rights to these from one person to another, and their consumption or use. These activities constitute only a part of any culture, but they can be singled out for investigation. A person may be said to be acting economically (as opposed to religiously, for example) when playing one or more parts in the economic process. Most economists would insist that economic actions involve "economizing," which means that people are trying to maximize their benefits and minimize the costs to themselves in a given situation. In other words, they are trying to do the best they can with what they've got. The ways in which different peoples do this in working out the production, transfer, and utilization of goods and services are the stuff of anthropological investigations of this aspect of culture.

To test the usefulness of this preliminary definition and show some of the problems of applying it cross-culturally, take two cases from very different cultures, each involving only a single valued good (services will not be considered). The first involves a typical small producer of premium wines on the Côte d'Or of Burgundy, France. This *vigneron*, who has become a familiar figure to me during several exploratory field trips, lives with his family in one of those little villages along the "Golden Slope" that have names to conjure with. He inherited some of its immensely valuable land from his father and acquired a little more from relatives. Now he grows and attends to the famous *pinot noir* grape and a little of the equally famous *chardonnay* in a number of precious parcels of land in several different locations. Attention to the vines and the grapes is a year-round task, but there are surges of activity during certain periods, as at harvest time. The grape growing and wine-making work involves all of the members of his family and possibly a hired hand or two. Still more people (students, for example) are brought in for the harvest in September. A number of machines are used, such as a tractor or wine press, but on the whole, this tends to be a labor-intensive operation.

Throughout the year, this *vigneron* makes decisions, any one of which can have important consequences for him and his family. When and how to spray against insects and fungi? What to do about the possibility of hail, which can damage a crop irreparably? How many additional workers should he hire and when? Who among his neighbors should he cooperate with and how? Which vines to uproot and replant? When and how to prune, to thin, and weed? How and when to harvest his crop? Whether or not to buy a new machine that might help him to make better wine? And above all, what price to charge for the crop and the wine that comes out of it? Custom and social constraints guide him in making many of these decisions, but he must make choices almost on a daily basis throughout the year.

Suppose that this is a year when the harvest is especially good, as, say, in 1978. What is to be done with it? Should he sell his grapes, make them into wine and bottle it, or choose some combination of these? Suppose he decides to keep most of the crop to himself, make his own wine, and bottle it. This process requires decisions all along the line that can affect the price he can command for his product. Fermentation, racking, aging in barrels, clarification, filtering, all raise questions that each winemaker answers in his own way. By the time the wine is bottled many months after harvest, a series of pitfalls, any one of which can affect the saleability of the wine, have had to be negotiated.

Meanwhile, there are the buyers, who, if the *vigneron's* reputation is good, beat a path to his door. He sells his wine to them at a price that he has worked out after considering a number of factors. What are the others charging? What was last year's price? What price did this year's Burgundies command at an auction for charity? And if the buyers, for some reason, do not come, or come in reduced numbers, how long should he wait before lowering the price or keeping the wine back for better times?

The clients do come, however. The demand is so high that price is not the major concern. The principal problem is to decide who will get what and how much. Loyal clients expect preferential treatment. They want more than their share of the best of the vintage. So not everyone is completely satisfied at the time of the sale when the rights to the wine pass from producer to consumers who, themselves, must make a number of economic decisions about when to drink it, how much, in what circumstances, and so on.

The second case involves the San of southern Africa, who, before they were forcibly resettled, practiced a hunting and gathering way of life. Among the things that they gathered were mongongo nuts, which they valued second only to meat as a food. Mongongo trees are to be found in groves scattered over the territory in which the San live. In contrast to the situation on the Côte d'Or, where land is exclusively held by individuals or corporations, and where territorial disputes can be serious matters, mongongo groves are owned only in a loose way by people in a particular band. Everyone in a San band has the unquestioned right to gather nuts from their groves, but people from neighboring bands can usually gather there also if they ask permission. The anthropologist, Richard Lee, whose book on one of the San groups (*The !Kung San*) was used as a basis for this brief account, does not report any significant conflict over mongongo trees and their fruit.

Unlike the grapevines of the Côte d'Or, which require a great deal of human intervention, mongongo trees grow wild, and it is only in harvesting their fruit (and the gathering of firewood and sometimes water) that humans have anything to do with them. The harvest commences in April when the nuts begin to fall to the ground and continues throughout the year until the nuts are used up or next year's fall occurs. Both men and women gather (this is one of a very few male gathering activities). Sometimes, they eat part of their harvest on the spot before carrying the rest back to camp for eating and processing. The harvesters may fill several carrying bags or nets for their own and others' needs. Shortly after the fall, both the soft outside and the hard inside are used; later, as the soft part deteriorates, only the hard nuts inside are of interest.

In their mongongo and other gathering activities, the San operate in terms of an order of food preferences, and in a given location they eat their way down this scale, that is, they first gather the most valuable mongongos, then less and less valuable plant foods. They also can be said to eat their way out of a given location, which is to say that they tend to gather from the closest trees first, the more distant later, and finally, when the distance becomes too great, they move camp and start the process over again. In all of this, the men, who are primarily hunters, stand ready to drop their gathering activities at the first sign of more valuable animal food. From this and other evidence provided by Lee, it is apparent that the San make a number of calculations or choices in their food-getting quests.

In a San camp, the mongongos are shared, processed (cooked, cracked), and eaten. A woman keeps a two-to-three day supply of nuts by the fire for her household. Visitors may be given some of these to eat on the spot. Quantities of nuts, processed or unprocessed, also are passed back and forth between relatives and neighbors on the basis of need and obligation. This sharing appears to follow well-defined, but generally unspoken, rules. Few calculations appear to be involved in a particular exchange. In some cases, the exchange may be balanced, as when two women pass approximately equivalent quantities of nuts back and forth over a period of time. In others, it may be unbalanced, as when children gather for their household without any expectation of an equivalent return.

The two examples given above are very different. One involves what might be called a basic necessity (mongongo nuts), the other, a less essential item (wine). Some economists feel that only basic necessities like food, clothing, shelter, and tools should be the subject of economic analysis. Others favor including more and more goods and services until anything that a people use, or that satisfies their wants, is included. Again it should be recalled that a definition depends on the problem set and the theoretical approach used. Readers who are drawn into the field of economic anthropology will want to keep various definitional possibilities in mind, but in an exploratory chapter like this, it would seem best to adopt a more inclusive definition. From that point of view, which includes all goods and services produced for people's use, something like an economic process is identifiable in the San example, as well as the one from Burgundy.

However, some cherished Western notions about economies still have to be excluded because they do not apply cross-culturally. If we were to consider them essential, comparative studies of economies would not progress very far. Consider, first, the idea of property. On the Côte d'Or, the conception of rights to things tends to confirm our taken-for-granted notion of private property. The *vigneron* owns land, for example. But where mongongo groves and their fruit are concerned, the San can hardly be said to hold such a view. Second, while the Burgundians practice a familiar form of market exchange that involves an abstract, impersonal pricing mechanism, San exchanges, though they do involve shifting valuations of things, can hardly be described as price-dictated buying and selling. Their exchanges of mongongos and other foods are more like the practice of gift-giving between relatives in the United States. Uncle Joe gets a tie and will give something of approximately equivalent value in return. Cousin Florence receives something for her house and returns a gift that is in the same price range. No one quibbles and no one is left out. Unlike the Burgundians in their wine dealings, the San seem to do little calculation about how much should be offered and returned. Valuations may have been worked out over time in familiar economic terms, but they have become customary and are not governed by whims or profit seeking. Finally, while the Burgundians use money in most of their economic activities, the San, in their aboriginal state, have very little to do with money. They do not calculate value in such terms and are not preoccupied with "making" it.

Some other taken-for-granted capitalist notions of economies may also have to be set aside if state-controlled economic systems, such as the one that exists in Albania, are to be included within the scope of anthropological investigation. Enough has been considered here, I think, to show what has to be done conceptually in order to get started on comparative studies. Because some apparently ethnocentric notions about economies have failed an initial test of cross-cultural applicability, it seems wise to leave them out of a preliminary definition. What remains is to be found in both of the cases just presented. Among the San, and on the Côte d'Or, goods with exchange value (wine, mongongos) are created by human actions, that is, they are produced. Then, the rights to these goods are transferred near or far between individuals in acts of exchange that involve "payment" of some kind for goods rendered. Through the system of transfers in a society, goods are divided up and passed around. Finally, they are consumed (drunk or eaten). That both peoples "economize" in some way is evident, but how much and what kind of economizing occur requires investigation.

In the anthropological literature on economies, there is usually an unstated assumption that an economic process is some kind of integrated whole. What is produced, for example, is seen to be related to consumers' or users' wants; or the way in which goods and services are divided up among people is related to how production is organized. It should almost go without saying that anthropologists tend to see an economy as a part of a whole culture and its context. When investigating any aspect of the economic process, therefore, they usually have in the back of their minds some idea about the way in which it will fit into the larger whole. From an anthropological perspective, then, what do the different aspects of economies look like?

Production

Human wants may not be infinite but they certainly exceed a person's capacity to fully satisfy them. Because of this, every society must make decisions about which of their wants will be satisfied, to what extent, and how. In working out their solution to these problems, any people will be constrained by their natural and human resources (what they've got). You can't, for example, kill a tiger with your bare hands or grow crops in the arctic. Working with what they've got, a people will develop more or less effective solutions to their provisioning problems.

What is to be produced? With their labor, humans produce a tremendous variety of goods and services, with each society tending to concentrate on certain things. Something like this was drummed into me in school by teachers who spoke of cities producing furniture, cereals, textiles, and so on. Anthropologists follow a similar path when they classify societies in terms of the ways they make a living. For example, a particular people is said to practice hunting (or fishing) and gathering, as with the San; horticulture like the Tiv; animal husbandry like the Basseri; construction like the high-steel-working Mohawk Indians who do much of the steel work on American skyscrapers; manufacturing, as in the Ruhr area of Germany; mining, as in Wales; trading, such as the sixteenth-century Venetians; or service, as in the case of the twentieth-century insurance city of Hartford, Connecticut. Although any people will engage in a variety of productive activities, and though each usually has a considerable mix of products, it has been standard anthropological practice to refer to one kind of productive activity as the mode of subsistence. Among the earliest humans, the mode of subsistence was hunting and gathering. Now this has all but disappeared, and manufacturing and service activities are preoccupying more and more of humankind.

How much is to be produced? The significance of this question would not be lost on the peoples of the Sahel region of western Africa, who have experienced famine, nor on economic planners who are trying to raise their country's Gross National Product. For them, the answer to the question undoubtedly would be "more." On the other hand, the answer of some American farmers or Saudi Arabian oil producers, both of whom are sometimes threatened by surplus production, might well be "less." In both of these cases, the problem is to adjust production to wants or the prices that reflect the interactions of wants and goods available.

How are goods and services to be produced? The necessary elements of any productive system are the resources, human labor, and materials (tools, machines, etc.) that are used in the production process; the so-called factors of production; and the social arrangement of people involved in it. What will be the unit of, say, agricultural production? Will it be a family, or will it be a large, industrialized operation? Will it involve little division of labor or much? How will the labor be mobilized and applied to the task and with what material support? Will it be a labor-intensive operation with little material assistance or will it be capital-intensive with much? And who will control the production process? Will it be kinship groups, the state, or private firms? Any society's productive system may be thought of as having answered these kinds of questions in its own way.

The *vignerons* of the Côte d'Or, for example, still tend to favor the household as the unit of production. There is a growing, but still modest, mechanization of activities. Some division of labor by age and sex is evident (for example, women and children do not usually drive tractors). Extra workers are hired in anticipation of surges of productive activity, and other specialists (for example, bottlers, brandy makers, and helicopter and airplane pilots who spray vines and "seed" clouds) may be brought in on occasion. In deciding how to carry out his grape-growing and wine-making operations, the *vigneron* may have to share some jealously guarded personal control with others such as bankers (who lend money); government bureaucrats (who tax and regulate); and associations of fellow *vignerons*, merchants, and others who concern themselves with various aspects of the wine business.

In addition to their use of the mode of subsistence, anthropologists have classified productive operations in a number of ways. Sometimes the level of technology has been taken to be of critical importance, as with the tool and weapon "industries" of early human societies. Sometimes the tendency to rely on human labor (labor-intensive), as opposed to nonhuman factors such as machines or animals (capital-intensive), is singled out. The division of labor by sex, age, and other criteria has been a common method for differentiating economic systems and societies. Occasionally, the unit of production (whether household or factory, for example) comes to the fore. And finally, ownership and control of the means of production (for example, whether private or public) has been taken to be a distinguishing feature. Whatever the scheme used, it is a construct that derives not only from the qualities of the cultures being investigated, but also the interest and point of view of the analyst. For example, an anthropologist interested in the consequences for economic development of following a capitalist or a socialist road, would probably concentrate on ownership of the means of production (private in the case of capitalism and public with socialism), which is an important distinguishing feature of these two forms of economy.

Transfer

Anyone who has just bought a new car in the United States will appreciate the importance of this aspect of the economic process. They have figured out what kind of car they want and how much they are willing to pay. Then, they have engaged in a sort of ritualistic haggling with a series of more or less agreeable salespeople, during which the parties involved have tried to work out a price that is best for them. One tries to buy cheap and the other to sell dear. What the selling price will eventually be depends on a number of factors, including the cost to the dealer, the number of cars on hand, and the eagerness of the buyer to buy. In this case, the selling price is a value that comes about from a sometimes intricate interplay of supply and demand. This is the market form of economic transaction in action. In real life, other factors may come into play, but in its ideal-typical form, exchange values are responsive to economic forces only.

To an individual raised in a culture where economic individualism and the market mechanism of exchange are taken for granted, it may be intriguing to find in the anthropological literature so many accounts of transfer transactions that do not conform to this norm. Some of the transactions seem to be irrational. One example is the *kula* exchange of the Trobriand and neighboring islanders of the southwestern Pacific, in which valuables (necklaces and armshells) that were never really used or possessed passed between trading partners on the basis of strict reciprocity. Equally baffling were the potlatches of the Indians of the northwest coast of America, in which huge quantities of goods that had been acquired were given away, and even destroyed. Whatever it was, it was not like the buying and selling of automobiles in modern America.

A number of kinds of nonmarket transactions have been identified. All involve a transfer value that is fixed by decree, as in price fixing by the state, or by social convention, as with the rate of giving and return of commodities among the San. In such transactions, the parties are usually freed from economic decision making because others have done it for them. The transactions range from centric, that is, focused on some person or group, to noncentric, as in one-on-one exchanges. In the ideal-typical hunting and gathering society where exchanges are noncentric, a noncalculating, balanced reciprocity is supposed to prevail. The truth, however, is that there are numerous unbalanced transfers in such societies, as between parents and children and more and less mature adults. Moreover, as market economies penetrate the world of hunters and gatherers, their transfers—balanced and unbalanced—come to involve more calculations by the parties involved.

As the distance between producers and consumers increases, the transfer process tends to become more complex. Among the San, most transactions take place between close acquaintances. On the Côte d'Or, the *vigneron* and some of his clients deal with each other on the basis of familiarity. But many *vignerons* have a substantial foreign clientele and are deeply involved in international trade, where the gap between producer and consumer is filled with a series of intermediaries: brokers, merchants, exporters, transporters, and importers. Under such conditions, the complexities of the transfer process can be rather daunting.

What kind of distribution or allocation results from certain kinds of transfers? In a fairly egalitarian society such as that of the San, people's incomes will not vary greatly. On the other hand, in many contemporary societies, differences of income and wealth can be very great. In the U.S. in 1983, the top 20 percent of the population received 59 percent of the income, while in El Salvador in 1974, the same top category of people received 66 percent. Many people are concerned about such income inequities, and some are actively trying to do something about them. A socialist activist, concerned about the distribution of income in the world today, may get some inspiration from the socialist slogan "From each according to his ability to each according to his needs." Whatever the practicality of this ideal, it addresses the question of the distribution of income, which is routinely considered by economists.

Consumption or Use

In the end, the goods or services produced by a people are applied to their wants. As I pointed out earlier, these wants, or bundles of wants, can be ranked in a general order of priority. What kind of schemes do a people work out to satisfy their wants? When a homemaker goes to the supermarket with her shopping list and only so much money, she may have to choose in terms of her priorities. She may decide to spend more on high-priority items, or she may put off buying some things until later. All of these are well-known economic strategies. Sometimes goods or services may be used directly, as when the San eat mongongo nuts they have just gathered, when a handyman fixes some household appliance, or when a Tiv sacrifices a goat he has just received in exchange for something. Sometimes things are saved for later consumption or use, as when food is stored or a worker is "stockpiled" for a later job. And sometimes goods are saved for later use in the production or transfer process, as with money capital that is reinvested in companies represented in the New York Stock Exchange, or to start up a new store.

Households are usually important consumption units. Each works out some arrangement for scheduling and apportioning its income. Since not everyone in the household is thought to have the same needs, the portions going to one or another will vary. The very young and very old, for example, receive less food, and men tend to get more than women. But a particular scheme may not be properly adjusted to the needs of some household members. A Western nutritionist, finding that children are being undernourished and that adults are receiving more than is necessary for carrying on their daily activities, might want to make a recommendation to change the pattern of distribution. However, such a recommendation would have to contend with cultural practices in which some people (those responsible for distributing food) have a stake. There will be more or less acceptable courses of action to take under such circumstances, and an anthropologist might be able to suggest the most acceptable alternative.

What people want, and what others think they need, may be two different things. Do Americans need all of the hamburgers they eat and the big cars they drive? Do the Trobrianders need all of the yams that they store for all to see until many of the yams finally rot? Do the Burmese need all of the pagodas that they have helped to erect in order to do better in the next life? A number of lists of peoples' survival needs have been offered by anthropologists. But human life everywhere involves cultural elaborations on such needs, whatever they are. Even in the most extreme circumstances, people don't just survive. Basic needs are everywhere socialized into culturally constituted wants, and it is with such wants that any analysis of consumption or use must begin. Here, anthropologists' personal involvement in a culture stands them in good stead. Through such involvement, they come to accept a people's wants and the ways in which they are willing to change them as given, not something to be judged good or bad by outside standards.

WHY ECONOMIES?

For purposes of study, analysts divide up economies into parts. However, it is important to remember that, as with cultures, economies are whole systems, the parts of which hang together in some way. Thus, it would be reasonable to expect that the norms governing consumption in America are related in some way to the ways in which goods and services are produced and transferred. The nature of the relationships between the parts, and with the rest of a culture and its context, must, of course, be determined by investigation. By establishing the nature of one of the interconnections bearing on an economy or any aspect of it, one would be able to begin to explain it.

Why are there economies? The answer should come immediately to one who has had only a little anthropology. Economies exist because peoples have wants that they try to satisfy. They do this through a social process involving production, transfer, and consumption or use of goods and services. Viewed in this way, economies are not unique to human beings. Other animals produce, transfer, and consume. They also do some calculating in the process. Human economies, though, are overwhelmingly cultural in their nature. Whether or not they are the most important aspect of a culture, as some believe, seems to me to be still an open question. But an anthropologist would be seriously remiss not to give extended attention to this aspect of culture.

What are the forces responsible for the differences and similarities of the economies of different peoples? Why are the economies of the United States and of the Soviet Union different? As is the case with other aspects of culture, questions about the reasons for the cross-cultural variability of economies have proved to be scientifically fruitful. From the way economic actions have been treated in this chapter, it may seem that people are free to choose any economic arrangement they want. Putting economic questions in terms of choices or calculations is to some extent an artifact of the way economists think. From their perspective, there are never enough means to satisfy wants, so choices must be made. But such choices are always limited or constrained by a culture, its context, and its history. It is to such factors that anthropologists have tended to turn in attempting to explain why economies are the way they are.

An example of an historical explanation is to be found in Bernard Magubane's analysis (in *The Political Economy of the South African Revolution*) of the developing crisis in South Africa. He argues that, after Europeans conquered the area in the nineteenth century, foreign capital was employed to open up and maintain gold and diamond mining operations, which came to be crucial elements in the South African economy. The conquered black population provided a source of cheap labor in the mining operations. In the beginning, these and other South African black workers went along with what the Europeans expected of them; but gradually, they began to assert themselves against these expectations. Though employers did raise wages, improve working conditions, and grant some limited rights, it was difficult to keep up with the wants of their workers. This was so because the employers were interested in making a profit, and this depended to a considerable extent on cheap labor. Eventually, according to Magubane, the conflict between owners and workers, that is, in the social relations of production, came to pervade all of South African society. Thus, Magubane explains the growing conflict in the South African economy, and in South Africa generally, in terms of a historical process that began more than a century ago.

In referring to the ways in which South Africa came to be dominated from outside, that is, the processes of colonialism or imperialism, Magubane also shows how the social context of a culture can be used to explain its economy. Natural contexts have also been used to account for the character of economic systems, especially when they have only simple technologies. With their machines, Americans have made themselves rather independent of their natural environment; but hunters and gatherers, who do not have an elaborate machine technology to help them, are much more dependent on the conditions of nature. Their economies, therefore, are more likely to reflect the natural conditions in which they live. One indication of this is the tendency for the size of animal and human groupings to vary together. Where animals exist in large herds, as did the bison of the Great Plains of the United States in the nineteenth century, larger groups of hunters ensure greater success; but because animals that move about singly cannot be followed profitably by larger groups of hunters, smaller productive units were the human response to the absence of herds of animals. A similar principle appears to apply to gathering activities as well. The Shoshone Indians of the western United States tended to concentrate in larger groupings when and where piñon nuts were available. During the remainder of the year, they scattered into small bands, sometimes consisting only of single families.

Other aspects of culture (economic and noneconomic) may be used to explain why certain economic practices prevail. For example, the often-noted association between complexity of technology, division of labor, and size of productive units has been explained in terms of the technical requirements that a more or less complex technology requires. As technology becomes more complex, increasing numbers of specialists are needed to handle a productive operation. Thus, the Côte d'Or *vigneron* of today, confronted by more complex productive operations in all areas, begins to resort to laboratory specialists to analyze his wine, meteorologists to predict weather, soil analysts to check the quality of his soil, plant specialists to predict problems in vine development, helicopter pilots to spray, and accountants to go over his records. Some think that advancing technology will reduce labor time. As machines become more powerful and efficient, people will have to labor less. For example, by using a tractor and attachments, *vignerons* can now cover a vineyard in a fraction of the time it once took with a horse or by hand. However, this common-sense notion receives a rude jolt from recent information about the San, where the working day, according to Lee, is six hours on the average. The advance of machines in Europe and America, though it has indeed been associated with a reduced workload outside of the home, has nowhere produced such a reduced workday.

In the discussion of economic transfer earlier in this chapter, the issue of the distance between exchange partners was raised. Does the nature of exchange vary with the distance (geographic or social) of the partners involved? Marshall Sahlins (in "On the Sociology of Primitive Exchange") has arranged transfer transactions between parties on a continuum extending from a "solidary" extreme, in which people do not expect to gain at each others' expense, to an "unsociable" extreme, where each party seeks to maximize their own gain at the expense of the others. He goes on to show that the character of a transaction tends to be associated with kinship distance, social rank, and a number of other factors. Considering kinship distance, he argues that people who conceive of themselves as closely related will be less likely to take advantage of each other in an economic transaction (toward the solidary extreme).Parents and children who love each other unconditionally would most likely operate the same way.

Frederick Pryor (in *The Origins of the Economy*) pursues this same line of thought when he analyzes the conditions that lead to the emergence of market transactions and of money (practices that approach

Sahlins' "unsociable" extreme). He argues that such economic practices tend to come about as economic systems (and societies) become more complex. An agricultural people, with their generally more complex technology and division of labor, therefore, would be more likely to engage in market transactions involving money than would a hunting and gathering people. Using a cross-cultural sample confined to pre-industrial societies from around the world, Pryor shows that this is indeed so, and he goes on to demonstrate that market exchanges in goods, credit, land, and labor emerge at different levels of economic complexity. This impressive study, which also considers other factors, is particularly important because it puts to rest so much theoretical speculation about this aspect of economic life.

An Analysis of Production: Scott Cook on the Brickmakers of Santa Lucia del Camino

As part of his interest in small-scale, nonfactory forms of industry, Scott Cook, an economic anthropologist who is an expert on Central America, and developing countries generally, turns his attention (in *Peasant Capitalist Industry: Piecework and Enterprise in a Southern Mexican Brickyard*) to the brickyards of a small community on the fringes of the city of Oaxaca in Southern Mexico. Once primarily agricultural, the people of this community now lean towards nonagricultural pursuits that are increasingly dependent on an urban market. At the time of Cook's study, approximately one-half of the households in Santa Lucia had one or more members working in the brick industry.

Cook begins his analysis by laying out the context and history of the brick industry in the Oaxaca valley. He describes a landscape pitted with clay pits that produce the raw material for bricks. The proximity of Oaxaca, with its demand for bricks and other commodities produced in the hinterland, is emphasized. The outreach of a centralized government, which regulates, taxes, and plans the nature of Mexican development, and of large-scale private enterprise, such as the construction industry in Oaxaca and elsewhere, are seen to have a strong influence on the brickmakers and their work. Finally, the local brick industry, which has experienced a surge of development since the late 1930s (when people began to build with brick instead of adobe), is described. Cook locates this small-scale Mexican industry in a context of global, capitalist industrialization.

Brick producing in Santa Lucia is carried out in small enterprises headed by a man (a *patron* or *dueño*) who owns or rents a brickyard. Usually, he has not come into brick production by inheritance, but from some other line of work, such as agriculture. He employs members of his family, hired workers (*mileros*), or both. Hired workers are paid mostly on a piecework basis, that is, according to the number of bricks they produce. Most of these workers originate outside of the community. In his analysis of this productive system, Cook concentrates on the hired, pieceworking *mileros*, their employers, and the social relations between them, that is, on the social relations of production.

The brickmaking process, which begins with the digging of soil and ends with the delivery of finished, kiln-fired bricks, is described in detail. For example, the actual making of bricks, the most demanding and time-consuming phase of the production process, is done by individuals who mold clay into bricks for sun-drying and, eventually, kiln-firing. The description of this and other phases of the production process is enhanced by comments from worker informants and detailed observational studies similar to those carried out by American efficiency experts.

The calculations of the principal actors in this economic system, which, at the time of the study, had an output of several hundred thousand bricks per month, receive extended treatment. The typical *patron* has bought or inherited a piece of land and turned it into a brickyard. The heavy start-up costs for land, buildings, equipment, and possibly a truck, are paid for with capital acquired from patrilineally related relatives and on his own. There are operating costs (for example, fuel for the kiln, gasoline for the truck) and costs associated with the replacement of equipment (shovels, buckets, molds, etc.). But the greatest cost in this labor-intensive operation is for labor, much of which is done by *mileros*, who are in short supply. Employers, their families, and the families of *mileros* are also active in brickmaking operations. The employer tends to deal with those who work for him in a paternalistic way. He is viewed as a kind of father and his actions are usually consistent with such a role.

Mileros are paid by the piece (in this case, the brick) instead of by the hour or day. By this system, a worker's family can contribute to his output without, themselves, being compensated. Thus a *milero's* wage may reflect not only his own labor, but that of his family. What that wage will be depends on the demand for bricks, the employer's short- and long-range costs, and the number of workers in the area. The anthropologist shows how the piecework rate is adjusted by employers to meet current conditions, compares it with a rate based on time, and describes the sometimes intricate give-and-take between *patrons* and *mileros* in regard to wages. In this exchange, which follows the market form, each tries to do the best he can within the framework of an emerging capitalist system of production. Although each has his own interests, both the *patron* and the *milero* are committed to this system and to a paternalistic form of relationship. The kind of conflict that is found in larger enterprises in the city, where unions strike and people may talk of revolution, does not exist here.

Cook takes issue with those who see this small-scale, labor-intensive form of production as an inefficient and regressive way of satisfying the wants of a developing society. He argues that, given the conditions that exist in this part of the developing world, this form of production has a definite place, which economic planners would do well to recognize. Such planners, with their grand designs based on economic science, may at times lose track of the value of small-scale productive operations. They may also lose sight of the human beings that make any economic system work. Cook, though he is fully aware of the issues that preoccupy economic planners, and of the science of economic behavior that guides them, brings real human beings into the picture. These people are dealt with sympathetically and respectfully, and the job they are doing is taken seriously. That they come across mostly as economic creatures, without the other human dimensions traditionally treated in an ethnography, can be excused in light of the depths he has plumbed in order to explore one important aspect of culture.

This brief summary hardly does justice to Scott Cook's sensitive and sophisticated treatment of the brickmaking operations of Santa Lucia del Camino, but it provides something to build on. Having understood this particular culture and some of the reasons why it is as it is, an anthropologist might heed the call to compare. Cook has already done some of this by pointing to other kinds of small-scale production in the developing world. Perhaps readers of this chapter have already begun to make some comparisons of their own—with some small, family-based enterprise that they know of, or with the *vignerons* of the Côte d'Or mentioned earlier. The *vigneron* may also be considered a kind of peasant capitalist, but with a product and clientele that are quite different. What other similarities and differences exist between their system of production and that of the brickmakers, and why? The search for answers to such questions would seem to follow naturally from an interest generated by Cook's work.

Allen Johnson on Time Use Among the Machchiguenga

As Cook's study shows, assessment of the amount of time people use in their daily activities can be an important tool of economic analysis. In American society, where people sometimes say that "time is money," an efficient use of time can be crucial for the success of a business enterprise. In his study, "In Search of the Affluent Society," Allen Johnson, an anthropologist with extensive experience in Latin America, deals with the subject of time use among the Machchiguenga, an Indian people who live in small villages scattered around the Amazonian rain forest of Peru. They are hunters, fishers, and gatherers, and they also practice horticulture in gardens they have cleared in the forest. Every five to ten years, as these gardens give up their fertility, the people move to another part of the forest, where they cut and burn out a new section for planting their crops. Johnson points out that the Machchiguenga do not have much in the way of material goods, but they have many other qualities that people in industrialized societies might value. They are honest, peaceable, warm, of good humor, and relatively content with their existence. In short, like the San, these "primitives" have created a culture about which there is much to admire.

Allen Johnson and his wife studied these people during several field trips for eighteen months in all. One thing that especially interested them was how the Machchiguenga used their time. Johnson divided up the day into production time, which includes all forms of work; consumption time, which refers to the time spent in utilizing goods and services; and free time, which includes such things as sleeping, resting, playing, conversing, and visiting. He recorded the amount of time these people spent in each activity. An extremely interesting fact emerged from this investigation. The Machchiguenga spent more time in activities classified as free than in producing and consuming. On the average, they spent more than fourteen hours per day in this type of activity.

Next, referring to data gathered in France, Johnson compared Machchiguenga time use with that of a sample of urban, middle-class French adults. He broke these down by gender and whether a person was working inside or outside of the home. This is particularly important because productive activities in the home, often accomplished by women, are sometimes ignored in analyzing systems of production. Johnson's comparison of the two peoples produced intriguing results. He found that French men and women spend more time in producing and consuming than do the Machchiguenga, with the difference being particularly marked in the area of consumption. In both cultures, women tend to spend more time in production than men, while Johnson found that French housewives were noteworthy for the great amount of time they spend working around the home. In effect, they maintain produced goods by performing such tasks as cleaning house and doing laundry.

The study of another people may make people more critical of their home society. So it was with Allen Johnson. After spending time with the Machchiguenga, he and his wife became more critical of more industrialized cultures such as France and the United States. He notes that, when people produce a lot, they also devote a great deal of time to maintaining and consuming what they have produced. This is why industrialization does not necessarily result in more leisure time. The more people produce, the more they must maintain and consume, and the less time there is for leisure. Time then becomes scarce, and being scarcer, more valuable. Then some may begin to say that "time is money."

That the wants of a people shape their system of production is clear, but Johnson makes the important point that the relationship between production and consumption is a two-way street and that what people produce and the way they produce it can also shape their wants. In the United States, for example, producers, driven by a profit motive, are constantly pushing consumers to expand their wants. So, a glass of water is replaced by a can—or two cans—of soda pop; and one car is replaced by two or more. But can this kind of thing go on indefinitely? Obviously, there are limits to economic growth. Moreover, a growing economy is not necessarily a better one. Such observations, which undermine the cultural ground on which most of us stand, seem to flow naturally from this particular anthropological investigation.

THE BOTTOM LINE

Peoples in different societies create more or less successful ways to satisfy their wants. The cultural process by which they do this involves the production of goods and services, the transfer of the rights to these, and their utilization. This process constitutes their economy. Economic science, which was traditionally preoccupied with the market-oriented, capitalist economies of the West, has had to expand and adjust in order to take into account not only the command economies of socialism, but also the economies of the peoples traditionally studied by anthropologists. In this chapter, the minimum prerequisites for any economy have been discussed. Seen from the anthropological viewpoint, an economy is also an aspect of a whole way of life, that is, a culture and its context. Additionally, it involves flesh-and-blood human beings who create and maintain it, and who act in ways that add up to the graphs and charts that have become an intrinsic part of economic analysis.

Like all aspects of a culture, economic norms acquire a hold over a people and shape their lives. As a result, they tend to produce, transfer, and consume in patterned ways; and in turn, they are affected by economic arrangements. Vocationally oriented college students probably don't have to be convinced of this; nor would those Americans who went through the Great Depression. But the manner in which economic actions affect other actions, economic or noneconomic, needs to be explored. In anthropology, one encounters many statements about the collective or individual consequences of certain economic arrangements. Thus, wife exchange between different kinship groups has been seen to create a greater feeling of solidarity between them. Or, private property is viewed as cutting people off from one another. But if these are accurate statements of the facts, how do these things come about? How do economic arrangements actually shape people?

Consider only one aspect of an economy: the work that people do. How does their work shape a people's behavior? One can see this happening through the process of socialization. First, on the job, workers are socialized through direct participation in a particular form of work. Thus, as they perform their duties, American nurses learn to defer to higher-ranking doctors. Second, there is anticipatory socialization: a worker-to-be is socialized in a way that is consistent with certain jobs. Thus, in a school of nursing, a typical American nurse will have been schooled in the art of deference. In this respect, the economy can be seen to be shaping a person's behavior through its work roles.

In a well-known, cross-cultural study that has stood the test of time, Herbert Barry III, Irving Child, and Margaret Bacon (in "Relations of Child Training to Subsistence Economy") found that, in over one hundred preindustrial societies around the world, there was an association between mode of subsistence and the socialization of children. Specifically, agricultural and herding people, who had a longer-run investment in food production, tended to put an emphasis on compliance in their socialization practices. On the other hand, hunters, fishers, and gatherers, with shorter-term strategies for producing food, tended to put greater stress on self-assertion. Although there is a dispute about the exact mechanisms involved, it does seem that, for those people studied, the work orientation of adults is being carried through into the socialization of their children. This has been very apparent to me in my explorations on the Côte d'Or, where the work patterns of the *vigneron* have traditionally pervaded all aspects of family life, and where sons, in particular, have acquired the dispositions that go with them. Such an association is found also in the much more complex United States where, as Daniel Miller and Guy Swanson have demonstrated (in *The Changing American Parent*), children of bureaucrats who work in large organizations tend to be raised differently from those of entrepreneurs who work in small ones, and the different modes of socialization are consistent with the kind of work involved in each form of productive enterprise.

In simpler societies, there should be fewer problems in knowing what work to do and how to do it. That is what Krishna, the Indian charioteer (God in an earthly disguise) was trying to tell the warrior Arjuna just before a battle involving kinsmen (in *The Bhagavad Gita*). Krishna points out that personal inclinations are irrelevant in such a situation and that Arjuna should do what his caste position requires him to do. Arjuna is of the warrior caste. Therefore, he must fight. In more complex societies, where questioning is the order of the day, such advice would seem to be less appropriate. How is one to know what to do in life in a society where the winds of socialization blow from different directions? Though economic and other forces do act through socialization to ascribe their lives, people in complex societies have opportunities for personal choice that do not exist elsewhere. The kind of work one is to do and the person one is to become has to be achieved in confusing and sometimes difficult circumstances. People have to find jobs, which, if they exist, will be more or less compatible with their talents and interests. The fortunate ones will find a niche that suits them in the economy. Others will spend their lives looking for something more desirable. Still others may find few opportunities for employment and sink into despair. But if any of these people have read only a little anthropology, they will know that economies are human creations that are subject to change—even failure. At a time when dramatic culture changes are the order of the day, it may not be so impractical to ask how the great economic questions are to be answered:

What is to be produced?
How is it to be produced?
How are produced things to be divided up and passed around?
How should people consume or use these products?
Where do I fit into this scheme?

SELECTED REFERENCES

BARRY, HERBERT III, IRVING CHILD, and MARGARET BACON, "Relations of Child Training to Subsistence Economy," *American Anthropologist*, 61, no. 1, February, 1959, 51–63.

COOK, SCOTT, "Economic Anthropology: Problems in Theory, Method, and Analysis," in *Handbook of Social and Cultural Anthropology*, ed. John J. Honigman. New York: Rand McNally Inc., 1974.

———, *Peasant Capitalist Industry: Piecework and Enterprise in a Southern Mexican Brickyard*. New York: University Press of America, 1985.

HEILBRONER, ROBERT L., and LESTER C. THUROW, *The Economic Problem* (7th ed.). Englewood Cliffs, N.J.: Prentice-Hall, 1984.

JOHNSON, ALLEN, "In Search of the Affluent Society," *Human Nature*, 9, no. 1 (September 1978), 51–59.

LeClair, E. D., Jr., and Harold K. Schneider, eds., *Economic Anthropology*. New York: Holt, Rinehart and Winston, Inc., 1968.

Lee, Richard B., *The ! Kung San*. Cambridge: Cambridge University Press, 1979.

Magubane, Bernard, *The Political Economy of the South African Revolution*. Durham, N.H.: Center for International Perspectives, University of New Hampshire, 1986.

Miller, Daniel R., and Guy E. Swanson, *The Changing American Parent*. New York: John Wiley, 1958.

Pryor, Frederick, *The Origins of the Economy*. New York: Academic Press, 1977.

Sahlins, Marshall, "On the Sociology of Primitive Exchange," in *The Relevance of Models for Social Anthropology*, ed. M. Banton. London: Tavistock, 1965.

Chapter Nine

THE DEVELOPING WORLD

A PERSONAL TRAGEDY

In *Salvador Witness*, the writer Ana Carrigan describes Jean Donovan as a brash but vulnerable young woman. Donovan grew up in Connecticut, went to college, and found a respectable job in an advertising agency. She had good friends and marriage prospects. Somehow these were not enough, and she put them aside to become a Catholic lay missionary. Sent to El Salvador, she became involved in work with the poor and with the network of Basic Christian Communities there. Archbishop Oscar Romero, an outspoken critic of social injustice and the outrages of the Salvadoran army and its associated death squads, became her idol. The biographer reports that Jean Donovan was transformed by her experience in El Salvador. Originally a naive political conservative, she came to believe that the problems of the Salvadoran poor were somehow tied up with United States' policies towards that country. She and her mission associates began to be viewed as subversives by some members of the establishment and they lived in an atmosphere of danger. Despite this, and despite pleas by family and friends that she leave El Salvador, she remained. With her associates, she continued to help the victims of a growing civil war and to propagate the faith. Eventually, she and three woman associates were abducted, raped, and murdered. Their bodies were found shortly afterward in a hastily dug grave. Efforts to find and punish those responsible have been only partially successful.

THE SPECIFIC CONTEXT: EL SALVADOR AND THE UNITED STATES

The personal tragedy of Jean Donovan occurred at a significant point in the history of El Salvador and its relationship with the United States. At the time she entered the country, revolutionaries were beginning to have some success in their drive against the established powers. While countering the guerrillas with aid from the United States, the government had also, at the insistence of the North Americans, undertaken some social reforms. However, El Salvador's problems were so enormous, and entrenched interests so resistant, that doubts were raised about whether such reforms would proceed fast enough and far enough to mitigate the many dissatisfactions of most Salvadorans.

In the early 1980s, El Salvador was a poor country with an economy primarily based on agriculture (mainly coffee, cotton, and sugar cane). It also included significant manufacturing, commercial, and service sectors. Economic growth, which had been substantial for more than a quarter of a century, had at that time begun to stagnate and even decline. This made the condition of the country's vast mass of poor, who were mostly of Indian stock, even worse. In contrast, the small group of European-derived elite (the so-called "Fourteen Families"), who had accumulated huge fortunes in agriculture and other sectors over the years, suffered only slightly, if at all. A small, but growing, middle class also suffered, but not to the extent of the poor, who usually bore the brunt of any economic downturn.

El Salvador was ruled by what amounted to an oligarchy, an alliance of large landholders, business interests, and an army, which tended to control whatever government was in power. The Roman Catholic Church, which had until recently been a full-fledged partner in this alliance, had begun to split into factions, one of which became especially concerned with the plight of the poor. The most significant spokesman for this group was Archbishop Oscar Romero, who was later assassinated. Members of this faction spoke of "structural injustice," that is, the exploitation of the poor and weak by the rich and powerful, and they implicated outside powers such as the United States, which was seen to be supporting the rich and powerful, in this sin. This group sought to work through Basic Christian Communities, small groups with a great deal of lay participation, in opposing such injustice and achieving meaningful change.

The United States had been the dominant power in Central American affairs since early in the century, when it had supplanted Great Britain as the principal outside influence. With strategic interests centering on the Panama Canal, and business interests such as those of the United Fruit Company, the United States was concerned with keeping the area tranquil and secure. To that end, it tended to side with governments in power no matter how repressive or exploitive they were. It intervened, directly or indirectly, from time to time to maintain these governments and to prevent potentially hostile takeovers. It had toppled one regime in Guatemala, and at the time of the Jean Donovan tragedy, the U.S. government was seeking to bring down the socialist revolutionary government of Nicaragua. For El Salvador, the United States government had two goals: social reform (within a capitalist system) and pacification. The guerrillas were to be defeated and their support dried up. Without the accomplishment of these goals, according to one government advisor, it would be impossible for capitalist development to proceed normally and for all Salvadorans to benefit. This was the official American view. It was implemented through economic and military aid to the Salvadoran government and its armed forces. American capital was also directly or indirectly involved in various economic undertakings.

But a number of Americans, as well as many Salvadorans, were not happy with what was going on in El Salvador. The country seemed to be a long way from pacification, and the continuing campaign of assassinations and other repressions, as well as deteriorating economic conditions, seemed to be pushing more and more people into the revolutionary camp. The inability of the government to curb the activities of the death squads, those semimilitary groups seeking to terrorize or punish opponents of the regime, and the slow pace of social reforms, led to the departure of an outspokenly critical American ambassador. Other Catholic missionaries besides Jean Donovan began to share the views of Archbishop Romero that American economic and military intervention, no matter how well intended, was doing more harm than good and was, in fact, contributing to the sinful structural injustice in the country. In the United States there were increasing doubts not only about the morality, but also the wisdom, of U.S. policies in Central America.

THE BROADER CONTEXT: THE DEVELOPING WORLD

El Salvador, at the time of the Jean Donovan tragedy, could be considered a part of the Third, or Developing, World, a world very familiar to anthropologists, who have often "caught" (during their fieldwork) some tribal or peasant society in the grip of developmental change. There are cities in Third World countries, but the typical community is a small one in which direct, personal relationships tend to prevail. It is a world of low productivity, which is often inadequate to meet the needs of populations that are frequently in an alarming rate of expansion. The peoples here have a history of their own making, of contact with each other, and they also share a legacy of imperialist or colonialist domination by powerful industrial nations of Europe and America that goes back to the time of the Great Discoveries. Most of the countries of the Third World had attained political independence by the middle of the twentieth century, but they were still likely to be in a state of economic or other dependence (sometimes called "Neocolonialism") and retained the marks of years of Western domination. The governments of these countries had in mind a variety of developmental goals, but one thing that they all shared was a desire to increase economic productivity (indicated by, for example, the Gross National Product). There were, however, certain impediments or bottlenecks, among which were inadequate natural resources, low technological skills, deficient institutions, inadequate demand for their products, a lack of capital, and continued foreign exploitation.

A possible way of eliminating some of these bottlenecks was through some kind of outside input. For example, consider a country that lacked capital and technological know-how for an agricultural project. A country such as the U.S. had a surplus of these available, and under the right conditions (perhaps if it were offered tax incentives or military bases) it might be involved in this developmental project. Theoretically, such assistance would eliminate the bottlenecks that were impeding development. There were problems, however. Outside assistance often has strings attached.

The ideal scenario from the capitalist point of view would go something like this: The project, aided by outside capital and technical assistance, would not only increase output, but also provide jobs for workers, who tend to come cheap in the Third World. These workers would then have the wages to buy not only what they produce, but also what other workers produce. Thus, the economic benefits of the project would spread throughout the country by what some have called the "trickle-down effect." At the same time, new, more modern forms of behavior (perhaps even true democracy) appropriate for such projects would be acquired through formal and informal education. So, the general standard of living would be improved and a general modernization of behavior would occur.

This rosy, capitalist scenario often was not realized, however. There were notable successes in places like South Korea and Taiwan, but often economic conditions in a country were no better, and were sometimes even worse off after developmental efforts. For those who wanted the trickle-down effect to benefit all of the people, there was the annoying tendency for benefits to flow towards the rich and powerful in and outside of the country. Thus, the fruits of development have often been sour for the peoples of the Third World. In addition, countries frequently found themselves more dependent on the outside, and less in control of their destinies, after assistance than before.

All of this is dramatically apparent in tourism development under capitalist auspices in the Caribbean, as John Bryden has shown (in *Tourism and Development*). The typical Caribbean country has only limited natural resources, but it does have the plentiful "sun, sea, and sand" that northern tourists seek, especially in wintertime. Tourism development would therefore appear to be a bonanza for such a country. But the results rarely meet expectations. It is true that tourism does provide jobs, but for the natives these are mostly low-paying jobs such as chambermaids, waiters, janitors, guards, and gardeners. The few higher-level positions have tended to go to outsiders or the educated elite. In addition, tourists (and the natives who often attempt to follow their example) require amenities, which usually have to be imported. Frozen foods, modern toilets, automobiles, and television sets are only some of those amenities. So, in addition to the profit that outside tourism agencies such as hotel chains and airlines expect, additional tourist income is paid out to secure these items. Further, subsistence agriculture may languish as people take jobs in tourism or related areas and acquire tastes for foreign things. Still more income is now paid out for what amount to basic necessities. All of this shows how a country that becomes dependent on tourism can profit very little, if at all, from this form of development. It also shows how the benefits it derives can be unevenly distributed. Such considerations have caused Bryden to argue that a good case can be made *against* those who think that in "sun, sea, and sand" are to be found the source of overall economic benefits.

There are reasons for questioning such development on noneconomic grounds, as well. Among the "social" costs of tourism development are environmental degradation resulting from various forms of pollution, as well as social disintegration. Social stresses may be caused when some people profit from tourism while others do not. There may also be a decreasing quality of life, which one scholar has referred to as the "Las Vegasization" of the Caribbean. In addition, there can be an increasingly narrow dependency on tourists and the outside forces that control them. Finally, one may expect the development of a kind of surly commercialism that infuses not only relationships between tourists and hosts, but among the hosts as well. It is not inevitable that such negative social costs, as well as economic costs, will outweigh the positive benefits of tourism development, but there are enough "bad" examples to make a people proceed with caution in promoting a touristic scheme.

And what of the socialist road of development? This path has not been so well studied, but there is enough information to form some initial impressions. There are plenty of "bad" cases to cite here too. In Africa, for example, one can point to a number of socialist, as well as capitalist, failures. A notable exception to this generally negative assessment for the socialist side is China, which must be judged a developmental success if for no other reason than its ability to eliminate the great famines that once struck this nation periodically. Working with collective and state ownership, the Chinese have sought to increase both agricultural and manufacturing productivity and have succeeded to a remarkable degree. Still, faced with a stagnating economy, they turned recently to individual and family incentives that once were associated with "the capitalist road." These included bonuses for workers in collective and state enterprises and the opportunity for individuals and families to produce for their own benefit.

On the "social" side, the costs of socialist development in China are more disquieting. China is a one-party nation, the present benign face of which may cause one to forget the abuses of the Cultural Revolution, when Red Guards roamed the streets and countryside pointing out those who they thought were following the capitalist line. These people were publicly shamed or imprisoned, and millions of city-dwellers were forcibly relocated to the countryside. Earlier, at the outset of the Revolution (1949–55), punishment of deviators took a more extreme form. Not only was there harassment by organized mobs, forcible relocation, and imprisonment, but also executions of several million people.

The infrequent success of the economic side and the considerable costs on the social side for Third World peoples already embarked on the socialist road of redevelopment are not likely to deter convinced revolutionaries. Looking about them, they see too few instances of widespread benefits under capitalism. Too often, any benefits are concentrated among the rich and powerful. This was certainly true of those Cubans I knew who congregated at the Havana Yacht Club in prerevolutionary times. Besides this, if revolutionaries have some knowledge of the history of the world, they are sensitive to the conditions of colonialism or imperialism in which one country dominates others. As with Jean Donovan and her associates, they may come to feel that one must look outside in order to fully explain the plight of a Third World people. They believe that the interests of multinational corporations, and the governments of the industrialized world that are associated with them, are the ultimate sources of their developmental problems. From this point of view, anything would be better than continuing the status quo, and a socialist program, even if it leads to a new dependency on the Soviet Union, which, like the United States, is always interested in acquiring clients in the Third World, can be quite attractive. No matter the possible strings attached, and no matter the negative sides of the Russian, Chinese, Cuban, and Cambodian revolutions, among others, these revolutionaries think that somehow things can be worked out along some socialist road that will lead to a better life for all.

For those who reject both the capitalist and socialist roads to development, or some mixture of the two, another road has opened up in the Middle East. Centered in Iran, this movement would chart a country's development according to a fundamentalist variant of Islam. This religiously inspired movement has only recently come under scholarly scrutiny, and there is very little reliable information about it. However, the increasing numbers of adherents throughout the Middle East and Asia suggest that it is a movement of consequence. One observer, the writer V. S. Naipaul (in *Among the Believers: An Islamic Journey*), has raised the irreverent question of how a country can do the things that are necessary for development while following the original tenets of the Shiite religion, which regulate the most minute aspects of everyday life; however, considering the success rate of the other roads of development, perhaps it is premature to sneer at these utopian dreams.

Whichever road of development a country chooses, it must make certain economic changes that will increase its productivity. This usually involves some kind of industrialization and the things that go with it, matters that are dealt with in Chapter Ten. People from the Third World may say that they don't want to follow slavishly in the footsteps of the advanced industrial societies. Their countries have some room for maneuver, of course, in, say, increasing and distributing the fruits of productivity, but they will also be constrained by the requirements of industrialization. Development everywhere seems to involve some form of industrialization, a process in which western Europe and North America have been the pioneers. Even a Third World revolutionary will recognize that, as is indicated by a comment from a patron saint of the Cuban revolution, Che Guevara. Asked by an American correspondent whether there was anything about the United States he liked, Che responded, "Your technology. Period."

ANTHROPOLOGY AND DEVELOPMENT

Development is often narrowly conceived in an economic sense, but the term might also be used more broadly to refer to any form of cultural change leading to desirable goals. Thus, changing methods for increasing food production, decreasing infant death rates, killing more people in wars, extracting more energy from the earth, distributing wealth more evenly, or increasing the efficiency of any of a number of projects could all be called developmental trends. All such trends involve cultural change, which is a process that has fascinated anthropologists over the years.

As Robert Bee has argued in his comprehensive treatment of anthropological approaches to the study of this subject (*Patterns and Processes*), the actual conditions of human existence involve both change and persistence, with one prevailing over the other at any given time. There will always be some mixture of the two, however, as is demonstrated by the phenomenon of culture lag, in which one aspect of a culture changes and others lag behind. In zeroing in on change, therefore, an anthropologist tends to emphasize one side of cultural reality. The questions asked are the usual scientific ones: What is it like? (the question of description). Why is it like that? (the question of explanation).

Originally, there were social evolutionists who saw cultures evolving according to some grand design, as, for example, from savagery to civilization. With views derived from the theory of biological evolution, these scholars saw cultures changing, usually in a Western direction, under impetus provided by mechanisms like invention (locally spawned innovations) and diffusion (borrowings from other cultures), all of this taking place according to the requirements of adaptation. Though some grand designs of cultural change are still with us, there has been an increase in more modest schemes that apply only to short-term changes in one, or a series of, related cultures. An example of one such study is Margaret Mead's investigation of the emerging Cargo Cult among the people of Manus, an island in the southwest Pacific (in *New Lives for Old*). These people, who had been studied earlier by Mead, were among those in the region who had been in contact with American soldiers during World War II. They had come to believe that they would be visited by ships from the United States, or elsewhere, laden with cargoes of the Western things they had come to want.

The common perspective that anthropologists have tended to share in looking at a culture (recall Chapter Two), will serve as a framework for this brief excursion into the problems involved in describing and explaining change. First, any culture has a historical dimension that gives it a certain impetus and direction. It also has an internal order. Its various parts hang together in a certain way. Thus, like an organism, its growth or change is limited by its nature. One has to be careful with this analogy, however. Cultural limitations on change are less restrictive than biological ones. Finally, there is the context of a culture—its natural and social environment—that contains sources of innovation (as in diffusion) and imposes selective requirements (through adaptation) for change. All of these aspects must be considered in accounting for the way in which a culture changes.

The role that the context plays in culture change has been especially noticeable under Western colonialism or imperialism. Around 1930, more than 80 percent of the globe was under the control of the big, industrial, capitalist nations of the West. Anthropologists, who have done most of their studies in this colonized part of the world, could not help but be struck by the consequences of this domination for culture change among the people they studied. Sometimes the effect was simply shattering, as when native people were decimated by a disease introduced from the West. Sometimes a people would survive, but their traditional way of life would be destroyed by, say, an incautious logging program that led to deforestation. Sometimes the change would be subtler, as when a traditional ceremony was turned into a tourist commodity. True, there were changes for the better, as when modern medicine was brought to bear on some intractable native disease, or a colonial government managed to impose some order on native warring factions. In most cases involving imperial or colonial domination, however, the changes were imposed from without, with the native population having little say in the matter. People who led movements that opposed such domination were often better educated and more Westernized. Gandhi and Nehru in India are examples.

After World War II, Western colonial domination of the Third World all but disappeared, but other forms of domination continued. The most important continuing form has been economic, as when a country must follow economic guidelines set down by the International Monetary Fund in order to qualify for American or European loans. Increasingly sophisticated Third Worlders are aware of this and other kinds of domination, including that which has been practiced by Western anthropologists. In the old days, anthropologists tended to feel that they were entitled to study any exotic people that interested them and report on their culture in any way they saw fit. Nowadays, the anthropologist may have to discuss a project with the people involved and take their views into account in writing and publishing a report. The new assertiveness and increasingly critical attitude of native peoples towards anthropological work (most of which continues to be practiced by Westerners) seems to have played a role in raising anthropological consciousness and sensitizing investigators to the value stands that they take in studying change under conditions of colonial or postcolonial domination. Most anthropologists have, understandably, been opposed—more or less—to such domination. The opposition has varied from total rejection, as with those who side with revolutionary independence movements, to what one anthropologist has called "elegiac regret," as in the case of the French anthropologist-missionary, Maurice Leenhardt. Despite witnessing all of the cruelties and exploitation of French colonialism in New Caledonia in the southwest Pacific, Leenhardt remained convinced that the best long-term possibilities for New Caledonian development lay with the French.

The attitudes that anthropologists have taken towards colonial or neocolonial domination have influenced their theories about culture and culture change as well. Consider a well-known problem encountered in most developing situations: the fact that the people are "multiplying like rabbits" and that this "eats up" whatever increased productivity there is. A Western anthropologist might see the high birth rate in a developing country as maladaptive or dysfunctional. But a Third World anthropologist (of which there is a growing number) might see this birth rate as adaptive in a situation where the infantile death rate is high, where social security in old age is usually provided by kinship groups, and where more hands will increase the productivity and, therefore, the welfare of an extended family. The point here is not which view is correct. Depending on the point of view, both may be. What this shows is that the vantage point from which the developmental process is viewed may influence one's picture of social change and development. The Westerner sees the high birth rate as interfering with successful development in the Western direction. "Get rid of it," this anthropologist seems to be saying, "and the sooner the better." Third World people, on the other hand, may be concerned with the near-term benefits for their people. In either case, some ethnocentrism would seem to be involved.

Although anthropologists cannot legislate points of view (a variety of which usually are scientifically desirable), they do have to grapple with the problem of what ethical stance they ought to take in their work. This problem has become more acute as the state of the world in which anthropologists tend to work has increasingly become an ethical mine field. It has been especially the case with the developing field of applied anthropology, which provides services to sponsors who would use anthropologically derived information. The variety of projects that applied anthropologists have assisted range from systems of food delivery in American fast-food restaurants to health-care delivery in Sri Lanka. Considering anthropologists' extensive involvement in the Third World, it is not surprising that much of their applied work has been done in the area of development. In Vicos, Peru, for example, a project jointly sponsored by Cornell University and the Peruvian Institute of Indigenous Affairs, sought to identify the sociocultural consequences of introducing a form of participatory democracy into the developmental process. This project eventually ran into vested interests seeking to maintain the traditional authoritarian way of life (and system of privilege) in peasant areas, and the anthropologists involved were forced to take sides. They chose to side with what they took to be the commitment of the Vicosinos to the new participatory way of doing things.

A more sticky ethical problem arose in connection with an ill-fated U.S. Army study called Project Camelot. Originally designed to identify the conditions leading to revolution in the Third World, and the ways in which a government might act to defuse the potential for revolution, the study needed to enlist social scientists (including anthropologists) who would carry out on-the-spot investigations. This project, which focussed initially on Latin America, eventually died from public exposure, but it had significant repercussions in the anthropological community. Here was an instance where anthropologists were being enlisted to find out ways of promoting stability and order, a condition that might not (as in El Salvador) satisfy most native people. At the same time, rumors of other "counterinsurgency" projects were being heard, and the general public outcry undoubtedly had something to do with the adoption by the American Anthropological Association of a statement of the problems of anthropological research and ethics ("Principles of Professional Responsibility"). This statement declared, among other things, that regardless of sponsorship, anthropologists' primary responsibilities were to science and to those whom they studied.

Two Case Studies of the Developmental Process

Let me summarize two anthropologists' studies of the developmental process as it has been taking place in two locations in the Third World. In both of these places, a socialist revolution had overturned a capitalist regime and put development on a new course. These examples, therefore, may upset comfortable notions of gradual evolution of Third World societies along a capitalist road that was opened up by countries such as Great Britain, France, and the United States. Although in both places change has been considerable, there is also evidence for the persistence of, and even regression to, prerevolutionary ways. Thus, they provide wonderfully rich illustrations of the process of development and of cultural change.

One of these studies was done by Norman Chance, an anthropologist who has been interested in problems of development since early in his professional career and who has participated in a number of applied anthropological ventures. Chance became interested in the Chinese revolution as a particularly dramatic example of the developmental process. He was inspired by an emerging sympathy for socialist revolutionary change. Having made contact with scholars, representatives of the Chinese government, and a number of Chinese citizens previous to, and during, two preliminary visits to China, he sought and received permission to go to China for a period of fieldwork. Together with his wife, he settled into Half Moon Village, a small peasant village in the Red Star Commune (one of thousands of Agricultural Producers' Cooperatives) near Beijing, China's capital. His report on the research is to be found in the little book, *China's Urban Villagers*.

The other study was done by myself. I came to this study inadvertently and as a byproduct of an interest in the adaptation of overseas peoples. In the late 1950s, just before the Cuban revolution, I encountered a small group of Japanese on *Isla de Pinos*, an island off the Cuban mainland, and became intrigued with the psychological aspects of their adaptation in Cuba, a question that I investigated during several field trips. Recently, when an opportunity to revisit the scene turned up, I saw the developmental implications of a restudy and resolved to do the best I could, with the help of this brief visit, to chart the developments in the culture of these Japanese since prerevolutionary times (reported in "Japanese Accommodation in Cuba").

Nash on the Japanese of Isla de Pinos

Just before the revolution of 1959, the Japanese of *Isla de Pinos* numbered approximately 130. They were dispersed over the northern part of an island about sixy miles south of the Cuban mainland that is thirty-to-forty miles across. There was a prison on the island, a little tourism, and some fishing, but the principal occupation of the *Pineros* was in small agricultural enterprises. The Japanese had come to Cuba, beginning just after World War I, mostly as contract laborers. After fulfilling their contracts, these mostly single males found work in agriculture or some service occupation. If successful, they either returned to Japan or acquired a farm or business and a wife from home. A few *Issei* (first-generation overseas Japanese) married Cuban women.

Japanese immigration to *Isla de Pinos* reflected the general pattern of immigration to Cuba. Most of the colony's first generation (Issei) came directly to Cuba from Japan, worked briefly on the mainland, then immigrated to the island. There, they encountered a friendly reception, and many of them established family farming enterprises devoted to raising fruits and vegetables. Even in this economic backwater, and with an uncertain market in Havana and the U.S., their economic achievements were considerable.

Things took a turn for the worse, however, during World War II. All Japanese males were incarcerated in the island prison, while the women and children were left to fend for themselves. On being released, the men found that much of their property and wealth had been lost and some virtually had to start over again. At the time of my field studies in the late 1950s, these Japanese, who comprised the largest single concentration of Japanese in Cuba, had recovered somewhat, but not up to their prewar level of achievement.

The preferred way of making a living among these Japanese continued to be the small family farm (usually with added Cuban or Japanese laborers). They used animals, some fairly primitive machinery, and their renowned diligence to produce highly regarded crops for their own use, for selling in town, and for marketing abroad. The market abroad was difficult to judge, and they were usually unpleasantly surprised by the prices they got. Additionally, their relations with packing-house owners, with whom they collaborated in a variety of ways, produced some tensions. This way of living obviously had limitations as far as economic advancement was concerned. Perhaps recognizing this, a couple of families had begun to move towards a more urban, commercial existence by acquiring bars and *bodegas* (grocery stores) in town.

It can be seen from this brief recital of facts that, before the Cuban revolution, the Japanese on *Isla de Pinos* were pursuing a familiar course of adaptation in a capitalist context. This course involved a family-based adjustment, first to a Cuban rural agricultural life, and then, gradually, to a more urban, commercial existence. In the course of making these adjustments, the *Issei*, but especially the *Nisei* (second-generation immigrants), had acquired qualities that some said made them "just like Cubans." Indeed, they seemed to be completely at home on the island, and most had become Cuban citizens. But psychological tests showed that they were working out an identity somewhere between the collaborative mode of striving of Japanese at home and the more individualistic mode of Cubans and North Americans.

What has happened on the island since the revolution and what has been the line of Japanese adjustment in the quarter century since the Batista regime was overthrown and socialism established in Cuba? The island has changed in a most remarkable way, from an underdeveloped backwater into a thriving showplace. It seems to have been completely transformed. Evidence of development is everywhere: almost complete electrification, telephone service throughout, an extensive, well-maintained system of roads and public transportation, blocks of government housing, socialized medicine, and a complex of dams for impounding water from the rainy season. There are numerous state-run agricultural enterprises, some military installations, and a variety of tourist centers. More ominously, the prison remains and is well filled. The population for what is now *Isla de la Juventud* (referring to the forty or so schools for Third World youths that have been constructed here and there) has increased dramatically. To reduce all of this to personal terms, the village in which I had lived during one field trip was almost unrecognizable, and the home in which I had rented a room had been razed and replaced by a police station.

Where do the 130 Japanese who have remained on the island fit into this picture of development? First, and perhaps most important, they have been allowed to maintain productive family farms on land that they can inherit, but not sell. The state provides a good and reliable market for their produce. It also provides spray, fertilizer, seeds, and machinery at reduced cost. The Japanese who have remained on their farms are obviously flourishing. Second, many Nisei are working in, or training for, jobs with the state that run the gamut from agriculture to telecommunications. Third, several *Nisei* work at the Japanese embassy in Havana. There has clearly been an increase in the diversity of occupations, a general dispersion, and a modernization all along the line. Some of these trends were begun in prerevolutionary times and continue still. The differences are the elimination of private commercial operations (for example, bars and *bodegas*) as a line of development and the increased role played by the state.

Obviously, there is more to this developmental story than has been said here. The *Isla de la Juventud* Japanese seem to have made out even better in a socialist, than in a capitalist, Cuba. They have no major political problems and continue to be well regarded by all. (The colony even received a special greeting from Fidel Castro on a visit he made to the island.) Their remarkable industry, desire to achieve, and careful consideration of their neighbors appear to have stood them in good stead both before and after the revolution. But these are only surface facts. What is the nature of their personal adjustments to the new socialist line of development and how are they related to the big changes brought about by the Cuban revolution? These changes, which have involved familiar socialist efforts to increase productivity and spread benefits more evenly, as well as gaining real independence from the United States, acquiring a new dependence on the Soviet Union, and seeking to propagate revolution around the Third World, have affected all Cubans. Only when I find out how the Japanese actually experienced the big changes involved in the Cuban revolution, will I be able to complete the developmental story of this interesting little band to my satisfaction.

Chance on Half Moon Village

Half Moon Village was chosen as a research site for Norman Chance by the leadership of the Red Star Commune. Chance's wife, an American interpreter, and a number of Chinese students assisted the anthropologist with his fieldwork. The book that resulted from the research is sprinkled with personal anecdotes and commentaries that give one a feeling for village life. It begins with a fairly traditional description of village culture viewed from the perspective of revolutionary change. The prime mover of this change, which informs all areas of life, is seen to be the political economy, which functions within a framework of centrally planned directives of a government dominated by the Communist Party. The government's notion of development is to improve the well-being of all Chinese not only by increasing general productivity, but by distributing the benefits of that productivity more evenly. It has also imposed—sometimes harshly—programs of birth control so that there will not be as many new mouths to feed. Chance pictures the government as trying to work out the optimum course for achieving its revolutionary goals and the villagers as seeking to choose the solution that seems best for them within the limits of governmental policy. For example, he devotes considerable attention to their deliberations on the "work point system," a merit-based method for distributing income from collective work.

Chance's study was done during a relatively benign period of revolutionary development when it became customary to condemn excesses instituted in the first phases of the revolution. It was a period when socialist zeal (sometimes called "redness") was giving way to more pragmatic developmental efforts. It also was a time when the revolutionary Chinese, who had initially adopted a totally hostile, rejecting attitude towards Western capitalism (which they thought had done them in in the past), were opening doors to Western contacts. It should be pointed out, however, that in their revolution, the Chinese had gotten out from under the imperialist domination of the big, industrial nations—even the Soviet Union. Unlike South Africa, El Salvador, Cuba, and most other countries of the Third World, development in revolutionary China has been mostly self-directed. Accordingly, Chance's failure to mention such contacts as a part of the context are in keeping with reality. At the time of his study of Half Moon Village, foreign influence on its culture was negligible. If current trends continue, however, it will be more important in the future.

Half Moon is a village in which most of the people work in some collective agricultural enterprise. Here, they are usually paid in terms of their productivity. A few people work in state-owned operations, which tend to be thought of as offering easier work and better pay. Most participate in household economies on the side, which, in this community, are primarily devoted to gardening and raising domestic animals. People in all of these economic spheres are depicted as making choices that will maximize their benefits within the constraints provided by the socialist program of development.

Such a program is ideally supposed to move in the direction of greater ownership and control of economic activities by the state, but during Chance's fieldwork, a new course of development was opening up. This course, which was designed to revive a faltering economy by increasing work incentives, put an increasing emphasis on household economies, free markets, and how well an individual performed a job.

It was a move back towards private enterprise and the capitalist road that was associated with the slogan "It's all right to become rich." It carried with it the potential for increasing the differences in income between households and individuals. For the moment, at least, a socialist goal was giving way before the goal of increased productivity. Chance does not tell us how this new policy came about, but takes it as a given that the villagers attempt to implement in their own ways while, at the same time, keeping their eyes and ears open for signs of new changes in governmental policy.

Although China has changed greatly from what it was before the revolution, Chance points out many continuities with the past. The patriarchal, patrilocal extended family continues to be important, and people use family connections ("backdoorism") to make out in the public sphere, which, since the revolution, as before, has been dominated by bureaucracies. Wives continue to have problems with tyrannical mothers-in-law, and despite socialist goals designed to bring about equality of the sexes, women in the village remain subordinate to men. The Chinese still favor indirect modes in their personal encounters (eye-to-eye contact, for example, is avoided). Sexual intimacies continue to be tabu in public, yet the facts of the body and its functions appear to be fully acknowledged. The straightforward manner in which the Chinese deal with birth control attests to this. It should be mentioned that this program is resisted by many villagers, particularly members of the older generation, who see children as the best way of guaranteeing security in their old age.

In referring to such cultural carry-overs throughout his work, Chance also shows that different people have different interests in the various historical changes associated with the revolution. It is clear that they make choices and use whatever freedom they have to actively promote these interests. In fact, one gets the feeling that they are more politically involved—at least on the local level—than many Americans. But the state, the powerful source of the directives that people respond to, is a very shadowy presence in Chance's work, as it is in my own study. Whatever the reason for this omission, the perspective adopted is that of the villagers, and, as in my earlier work on the Japanese (in "Achievement and Acculturation: A Japanese Example"), we gain a feeling for flesh-and-blood individuals involved in the developmental process.

* * *

The summaries of the studies by myself and Norman Chance, which are only two of the thousands of development studies done by anthropologists, are inevitably inadequate. This is not only the case because they are summaries, however. They are inadequate also because no single study can embrace the entire developmental process, which, in reality, has as many aspects as culture. Considering this, and considering all of the developing societies of the world, it would seem to be very difficult to make generalizations about them. However, there are certain things that the cultures of the Developing World tend to share. First, they share a history of colonialist or imperialist domination by the capitalist, industrial nations of the West and they bear the marks of that domination today. Because of this, and because they also have had relations with each other, it is incorrect to see them as developing out of some traditional culture entirely of their own making. Second, though most of the countries of the Third World have taken steps towards independence, very few are in a position to call the tune in their transactions with the Developed or Industrialized World, a world that now includes nations such as the Soviet Union and Japan. They now face not only national powers, but international ones such as multinational corporations or political alliances that can be worldwide in scope. From the point of view of a Third Worlder, which can have a touch of paranoia, these powers might be conspiring against them. Even the dangerous rivalry of the superpowers, with its expensive arms build-ups, could be seen as some kind of gigantic First World conspiracy to exploit and impoverish them. This means that the threat of nuclear catastrophe associated with this rivalry may concern developing nations less than the useless waste involved. Finally, according to most indicators of economic development, just as in the United States, the gap between the rich and poor peoples of the world is widening. From a global perspective, this means that the Developing World is getting relatively less of the fruits of the world's increasing productivity.

THE SIN OF THE FIRST WORLD?

Jean Donovan came to believe that the social injustice that prevailed in El Salvador was sinful and that the United States, in particular, and the First World, generally, were implicated in that sin. From this brief overview of the issues of development, it is now possible to evaluate this belief, not only as it applies to El Salvador, but to the rest of the Developing World as well. Since the time of the Great Discoveries, Western Europe, and later the United States and the Soviet Union attained power over this part of the globe. The present condition of Third World peoples is not entirely their own doing, but is (at least in part) due to this dominance; and to the extent that power is associated with moral responsibility, the First World can be seen to be morally involved in their developing fate. Most anthropologists would share this view. But though they may be on the side of the underdogs of the world and interested in helping them, the primary mission of anthropology is to understand; and it is clear now that a proper understanding of the Developing World involves unraveling complex networks of give-and-take that can extend into boardrooms of multinational corporations and the highest councils of First World governments.

And how might all of this go down for someone who is just being introduced to anthropology? They may have been surprised, first of all, to learn that there is a world out there full of legitimate others who are not like them nor the people around them. Most of these others are a part of the Third or Developing World, which is largely a world of have-nots. The fact that twenty-nine countries in sub-Saharan Africa are poorer now than in 1960, that Middle-Eastern terrorism has become a cause of great concern, or that the United States or the Soviet Union are considered to be Public Enemies Number One in some Third World countries can no longer be attributed entirely to the inadequacies or irrationalities of distant strangers. Indeed, because of shared histories, these others are more like political neighbors, or even relatives. This knowledge would seem to be a necessary basis not only for practical actions in an increasingly internationalized world, but also for whatever moral outlook a person chooses to adopt where the Developing World is concerned. No longer can its peoples be viewed as simply interesting or exotic—those who have invented intriguing cultural variations on human themes. Rather, they come to appear as struggling human beings with whom the First World has been, and continues to be, involved in important ways. This knowledge, as it did with Jean Donovan, can change a person's life.

SELECTED REFERENCES

BEE, ROBERT L., *Patterns and Processes*. New York: The Free Press, 1974.

BERGER, PETER L., *Pyramids of Sacrifice*. Garden City, N.Y.: Anchor Books, 1976.

BRYDEN, JOHN, *Tourism and Development: A Case Study of the Commonwealth Caribbean*. Cambridge: Cambridge University Press, 1973.

CARRIGAN, ANA, *Salvador Witness*. New York: Simon and Schuster, 1984.

CHANCE, NORMAN A., *China's Urban Villagers*. New York: Holt, Rinehart and Winston, 1984.

MEAD, MARGARET, *New Lives for Old*. New York: Mentor Books, 1956.

NAIPAUL, V. S., *Among the Believers: An Islamic Journey*. New York: Knopf, 1981.

NASH, DENNISON, "Japanese Accommodation in Cuba." Chicago, Ill.: Paper presented at the meetings of the American Anthropological Association, 1983.

———, "Achievement and Acculturation: A Japanese Example," in *Context and Meaning in Cultural Anthropology*, ed. Melford Spiro. New York: The Free Press, 1965.

RUSSELL, PHILIP L., *El Salvador in Crisis*. Austin, Tex.: Colorado River Press, 1984.

WOLF, ERIC R., *Europe and the People Without History*. Berkeley, Calif.: University of California Press, 1982.

WORSLEY, PETER, *The Three Worlds*. Chicago, Ill.: The University of Chicago Press, 1984.

ZUNZ, OLIVIER, ed., *Reliving the Past*. Chapel Hill, N.C.: The University of North Carolina Press, 1985.

Chapter Ten

INDUSTRIALISM

A MORNING ROUTINE

Consider an average American homemaker getting up one winter morning. She gradually makes her way from bedroom to bathroom to kitchen. During this process, she turns on several lights, turns up the heat, switches on a radio, opens the refrigerator, and turns on the stove. Various gadgets are made to do their work. Water will have been flowing in toilets, washbasins, sinks, and a dishwasher by the time she and her family have finished breakfast.

You know how it is on a winter morning. People act in an almost automatic, unconscious state. It takes a while before they really begin to think about what they are doing. But an anthropologist, scribbling furiously, could have been following most of these early morning actions. Indeed, anthropologists have sometimes been participant observers of family life. What would they report in this instance? First, they probably would comment on the ritualistic, taken-for-granted quality of the early-morning actions. Next, they might emphasize the central role the body plays in these actions: cleaning it (washing, shaving), getting rid of its waste (defecation, urination), filling it up (eating), dressing it up. Finally, they would probably refer to the use of machines all along the way—machines that are activated by turning a knob or flicking a switch, usually in an unconscious manner.

If a machine is taken to be some kind of inanimate object that does work, then the average American family seems to be dependent on quite a few in its morning routine. The light bulbs, radio, stove, oil burner, hot water heater, and refrigerator all turn electricity into useful work. So, too, do the machines that pump water for this household. In turn, electricity is produced and distributed by an elaborate network of devices. Needless to say, a group of hunters and gatherers like the San have a morning routine that has little, if any, dependence on machines, and their way of life is quite different as a result. An anthropologist doing fieldwork among them would see them stirring up their fires and using only a few simple implements as they get into the day. If they were deprived of these implements for a few hours, there would be nothing like the consternation of the average American family when the power goes off.

THE INDUSTRIAL WAY OF LIFE

In an industrial society, machines play an important role in the way of life. Though they enter into all areas of activity, it is usually to the productive, more specifically the manufacturing, sector that one refers in thinking about an industrial society. Furthermore, it is the factory that constitutes the model for the industrial way of life. What is the nature of this model? Consider a modern automobile assembly plant as an example.

Such a plant is a large-scale enterprise that is organized around the various machines that do its work. Each apparatus is designed to do a specific task in a reliable and effective way. There may be computer-directed robots that weld body seams. They work in conjunction with other robots that smooth out the welds afterwards and numbers of people who handle the computers and do various specialized operations by hand. As new knowledge becomes available, the design of machines and their arrangement is changed in order to improve performance.

As for the workers themselves, the timing and sequence of their activities are regulated by the machines of the plant. Depending on the job, individuals may have more or less control, but the general tenor of the manufacturing operation is established by the machines themselves. It would be fair to say that, as far as the relationship between the machines and the employees of the plant is concerned, the burden of adaptation is on the employees. Though human factors are taken into account in a general way, the overall manufacturing plan of the plant does not include any provisions for how individual workers feel at a given time about the job they are doing or the people they are working with. Whatever feelings a person has should either be put aside or controlled in order to promote a machinelike way of acting.

Workers should be hired and promoted on the basis of merit. Personal connections, though they do operate on an informal level, are not supposed to play a role in personnel decisions. Workers are selected and trained for specific tasks or a limited variety of tasks. Unlike the small dairy farm on which I once worked, there are no jacks-of-all-trades here. The ideal is to maximize competence by limiting the range of activity. Each job involves specific requirements that the worker should be able to handle adequately. Changing jobs involves having or gaining the competence to perform another specific role. In contrast to the work of the small farmer who does everything, industrial work engages only a small part of the whole person. Relationships with other workers on the job and with the machines are supposed to be emotionally neutral and impersonal. The average worker is a long way from the finished product that he or she has helped to make. Whatever alienation people feel as a result of all of these formal requirements has to be made up by informal arrangements on and off the job. The American coffee break puts people into personal contact with others. The Japanese have company outings that accomplish the same thing.

Governance of the automobile assembly plant is accomplished through a series of pyramidlike systems of authority in which there may be more or less input from below. In a Swedish plant there will be quite a lot of input, in a Spanish plant less. Americans may be amazed at the numbers of Japanese factory members who must be consulted before a decision is made and the massiveness of their agreement afterwards, but both Americans and Japanese would agree that there must be a chain of command that functions on the basis of precise rules that apply to highly specific areas. The areas of responsibility of bosses and their range of authority is carefully specified. Directives are phrased in terms of rules that deal with categories or types. For example, installers of engines will be told that a new procedure is to be employed in tightening certain bolts. People with authority are not supposed to act on the basis of personal whim, but according to the rulebook. There are ways of getting around this, of course ("backdoorism" in China, for example), but that is not how the system is supposed to operate.

Besides power differences, there are differences of income and prestige based on the type of job done. These differences may be more muted in some cultures, but they exist in any industrial system. A worker can receive more pay through seniority or doing a job better, but also by taking a job higher up on the pay scale. It is possible to move up in this system, therefore, by learning different kinds of work. Or, as in the United States, individuals may join another firm that offers better opportunities. Thus, individual mobility through job changes is an intrinsic part of this, or any industrial operation.

The automobile assembly plant that has been the subject of this discussion uses resources that must come from outside. On the human side, it must attract a workforce from a surrounding hinterland and help to maintain that workforce close by. It also depends on finished or unfinished materials that have been produced elsewhere. For example, the steel that is fabricated into automobile body parts has been produced from ores and coal that are mined and then combined at a high temperature before being transported to the plant. So, this industrial operation uses large amounts of raw materials, including those for producing power for its own manufacturing operations, in transport, and (indirectly) in the extraction and production of the materials it employs. By drawing on resources from outside, the plant affects the context in which it is located. Compared with preindustrial operations, that effect is tremendous. In addition, there is an effect on the world outside through what it produces. Waste from its power and from its various material operations is disposed of, and the vehicles it produces are distributed to affect the environment in a variety of ways, good and bad.

From the anthropological point of view, the automobile assembly plant has a recognizable subculture that, because it is organized around the large-scale, concentrated use of machines, is clearly an industrial one. Though there may be variations from society to society (between capitalist and socialist societies, for example) and according to the nature and technological level of the operation, there are certain features that all industrial operations have in common. These features are clearly evident in the automobile assembly plant, which is a large-scale, concentrated productive arrangement of machines and the people associated with them. Because of the machines, it tends to be a capital-intensive, rather than labor-intensive, operation. Everything in it should, ideally, work in a machinelike way, that is, according to the logic of machinery and mechanical processes. That logic involves, first of all, great precision and reliability of operation. Second, it is acutely specialized, that is, everything that is not directly relevant to assembling automobiles, is, ideally, ruled out. Third, its parts and functions are clearly set off from one another. People have specific areas of responsibility or authority, which, depending on the scale and complexity of the overall operation, are more or less specialized. Fourth, it is hierarchically organized. Regardless of the amount of input from below, it can never be a totally egalitarian operation. Fifth, everything has, ideally, been calculated to work in a certain way. Nothing is left to chance, personal whim, or feeling. People and machines are designed or trained, selected, changed, and discarded on an entirely rational basis. Sixth, through what it uses and produces, directly and indirectly, the plant goes heavy on its environment. And finally, the entire operation involves a supreme commitment to technology, which becomes a god of the industrial way.

If there is an automobile assembly plant, of course, there have to be other manufacturing operations in the society. The culture of industry pervades them all. The agricultural and service sectors, as well as other areas of life, begin to exhibit many of the same features. The growth of larger-scale, complex social groupings (cities, for example) will reinforce these developments. Thus, it would not be inappropriate to say that the society has an industrial way of life.

Something like an industrial culture, though not always conceived of as centering on factories and their operation, has preoccupied social scientists over the years. Termed "modern" or "industrial," and contrasted with its polar opposite, "traditional" or "preindustrial" culture, it was thought to have been emerging all over the world. Modern peoples were said to be more rational than traditional peoples because they put a greater emphasis on calculating how to do things. Their societies had larger-scaled social units, such as large corporations or cities, and were more differentiated and complex as a result. They were also more impersonal, more open to outside influences and to change, more achievement oriented (with a greater possibility for individuals to change their station in life), as well as being increasingly committed to higher levels of technology. There are a number of aspects of this scheme that grate on some present-day anthropologists. First, the notion of "modern" or "industrial" has sometimes been ethnocentrically biased towards the culture of the capitalist, industrial powers of Europe and America. Second, there seems to lurk in the scheme the notion of some inevitable evolution all over the world towards the culture that characterizes these powers. Third, there is a curious omission of economic, political, and other developments, which, as the chapter on the Developing World makes clear, can often be crucial in sociocultural change. And fourth, there seems to be a mistaken view that all the hunters and gatherers, agrarian, and pastoral peoples of the world have had basically the same traditional, confined, unchanged way of life that extends back into antiquity.

Keeping these criticisms in mind, there nevertheless appears to be more than a germ of truth in this scheme. Looked at from the very general perspective that includes all of humankind over the entire course of its existence, there does indeed appear to be a general trend towards higher technological levels, larger and more complex social units, etc. At one time or another, different aspects of culture seem to have taken on the role of prime mover of change, but as peoples' lives were increasingly linked to more sophisticated machines, as Americans now are, machine technology came to exercise a greater influence on the character of cultures and the way in which they changed.

INDUSTRIALIZATION

That the world has been becoming more industrialized should be evident to everyone. Take the frightening development of military hardware as an example. The superpowers are caught up in an arms race that involves seemingly endless technological innovation and elaboration. At the same time, their clients in the Third World follow in their wake with hand-me-downs or less advanced arms, which advisors try to teach them to use. This recent line of technological development is only one instance of an industrialization that has spread around the world. It is the latest phase of an historical progression in which peoples' lives have been increasingly bound up with machines. That process began long ago.

The first human use of machines probably occurred in the food-getting quest. Carrying devices, tools, and weapons were material aids that enhanced human powers and so aided peoples' adaptation. The archaeological record shows the development of tool and weapon technologies. They became more specialized, refined, and efficient. This record also reveals the emergence and development of other machines that enhanced human powers: agricultural implements such as the plow, for example, or means of transport like boats or carts. The record shows that the rate of technological innovation was at first quite slow, but it began to pick up from the time people first began to practice agriculture near 10,000 B.P., and viewed from a general historical perspective, the rate has been increasing ever since. Sometimes one society led the way, sometimes another. Inventions diffused from one society to another. The emergence and spread of machine technology became a hallmark of human development.

Through the early historic period, the technological pace continued to quicken with the lead first taken by peoples in the Middle East and Asia who now seem to have been responsible for the invention of such important devices as the cart, the canal lock, the kiln, the loom, the ship, and gunpowder. Europe, the cradle of the so-called industrial revolution, which many people tend to identify with industrialization, appears to have been a relatively late starter in the technological race, and it was not until the fifteenth century that it began to surpass other regions of the world in its technological inventiveness.

The industrial revolution itself can be traced back to eighteenth-century, capitalist England when the factory, which had been in existence since at least Roman times in the West, was filled with clockwork-like machines powered by water and then steam. The first of these factories produced cotton, silk, and pottery, and it is with the factory-based production of cotton products that the industrial revolution usually is associated.

Why in this place at this time? Certain features of English culture appear to have been conducive. First, there was a whole array of relevant technology such as the dam, waterwheel, spinning and weaving machines, and the steam engine, as well as the engineering and scientific interests that would contribute to an ever-increasing productivity. Second, the various private companies that in this capitalist society would undertake this new form of production had available to them adequate capital to finance their endeavors. Third, an expanding market ensured the increased demand for more productive arrangements. Fourth, there were adequate resources (coal, cotton, running water, wood, iron, stone, etc.) to support a higher rate of production. Finally (and this is debatable), it may have been more profitable (for profit-seeking capitalists) to substitute machines for human labor in an area having fewer people. Surely, other reasons for the onset of the industrial revolution in England in the eighteenth century can be advanced, but whatever they are, they all would serve to reaffirm the anthropological view that any culture (and its context) is a system of interrelated parts and that technological or other innovations and elaborations do not occur in a vacuum.

If one uses the term revolution to mean drastic and widespread change, then the industrial revolution was aptly named. Not only was there a rapidly increasing commitment to the use of machines in the productive sector, but in other areas of English life as well. The development of the railroad is an example. It combined the use of new steam engines with the increasing demand for transport of goods and people. The advance of technology also affected other aspects of the culture, as, for example, through the urbanized living that came to be associated with large factory complexes. Such developments were not confined to England. One by one, other countries followed Britain's example, and the revolution spread. In the newly independent United States, for example, English ideas were adopted as a part of an increasing commitment to technological development and the machine way of life.

If one assumes that there is a rough equivalence between technological level and energy use, an overview of the general trend of industrialization described in this section can be offered. All peoples make use of energy that comes indirectly or directly from the sun, but hunters and gatherers use relatively little (from plants and animals, water, and firewood) while highly industrialized peoples use a great deal (from various natural resources including coal, petroleum, natural gas, and uranium). Now, if the entire history of humankind can be seen as falling in a rough chronological sequence from hunting and gathering through lower and higher levels of agriculture, and recently into various stages of industrialism, it is clear that there has generally been an increase in energy usage and technological level among the world's peoples from past to present. Of course, not all peoples have passed through these stages and in this sequence. There are still hunters and gatherers, and some are being drawn directly into modern, industrial ways of life. But the general trend in the world from past to present has been towards higher levels of technology and energy usage.

However, as Earl Cook points out, regarding the use of energy, this general trend has been exponential rather than linear. In other words, it involves an increasing rate of increase towards the present, and the rate has increased most dramatically since the industrial revolution. If England just prior to that revolution can be taken to be an example of an advanced agricultural society and the United States today as the most advanced industrial society, then in the three centuries or so since the industrial revolution, there has been a greater increase in energy usage per capita than in the previous twenty thousand or so centuries of human development.

The energy that humans have used in recent years has come mostly from nonrenewable sources such as coal, petroleum, natural gas, and uranium, which are of limited supply. So, unless there are changes in the pattern of energy usage, this latest spurt of industrialization cannot go on very much longer. The day when the nonrenewable fuels are used up is being pushed back by various energy conservation strategies, but ultimately, if humans are to continue to elaborate their modern industrial ways, renewable energy resources (direct sunlight, wind, water, plants, the earth) will have to be tapped. The best estimates now predict the *necessary* changeover for some time in the twenty-first century. However, critics of this strategy argue that it should be done as soon as possible not only because the nonrenewable sources will eventually run out, but also because of dangers associated with the use of nonrenewable fuels. These dangers include the so-called "greenhouse effect," in which the climate of the world warms up from the increase of carbon dioxide in the atmosphere; various maladies associated with the pollution of land, water, and air; environmental destruction, as in the case of acid rain; and the enormous threat of radiation and nuclear explosive damage that has become all too evident.

And this is not the whole story. Industrial operations require not only energy, but other natural resources that are also limited. Humans can use other resources (that produce plastic instead of metal for automobiles, for example) or reuse (recycle) the ones they now use, but it would seem that there is no way that the earth can sustain the rate of industrial growth that humans now seem to want. This means that, barring some unlikely breakthrough in space, future generations are going to have to learn how to live with a reduced level of industrial operations. It will not be easy for people who are committed to economic growth to do that.

From an anthropological perspective, it appears that humans are now at an important juncture in their existence. In order to survive, they are going to have to change industrial ways of doing things that have produced many benefits and on which they have come to rely. Will they have to be dragged towards some new, more adaptive arrangement and thus reconfirm the old saying that "necessity is the mother of invention," or will they use their famed foresight and flexibility to prepare for, and bring about, the necessary changes? There is always the possibility, of course, that some of the machines they have created will, by accident or intention, produce some catastrophic destruction. It has been estimated, for example, that there are now many more nuclear devices in the world than are necessary to bring about a "nuclear winter" that would threaten all life on this planet. In that event, there might not be a twenty-first century.

A Case of Industrialization: Rockdale, U.S.A.

As has been customary in this book, let me once again bring a discussion down to earth by referring to a specific case involving recognizable human beings. The broad sweep of industrialization has been viewed here as beginning with the earliest humans and continuing up to the present. Generally, it has involved an increasing commitment to, and development of, machine technology by the peoples of the world over a course of more than two million years. Whatever one thinks about industrialism today, it is evident that this way of doing things has brought many benefits to human beings from the time of the first tools and weapons. However, as with any other aspect of culture where the issue of adaptation is concerned, technology has its good and bad points.

This is the way industrialization looks to anthropologists when they are considering the entire history of humankind. That history is a kind of summing up of thousands of specific cultural histories. In each one of these, industrialism is a part of an entire way of life, which it is the job of the anthropologist to comprehend. What kind of picture emerges when an anthropologist puts on culture-specific glasses and looks at industrialization as a part of an entire way of life?

Consider the industrialization of the small community of Rockdale, Pennsylvania in the early nineteenth century. It was during this period that the two thousand or so people of this community became involved in the water-power-based factory system of cotton production. Because all potential informants had died, this community had to be studied through the use of personal documents and various other historical sources. The anthropologist, Anthony F.C. Wallace, whose name is associated with a long list of psychological and religious studies involving, among others, the Iroquois Indians of North America, happened to live near Rockdale and became fascinated with the past of this little community. He decided to bring his anthropological expertise to bear on it.

Wallace sees Rockdale as a symbol of the early phase of the industrial revolution in America where, in contrast to England with its huge, steam-powered, urban factories, manufacturing was more likely (but not exclusively) to take place in small towns and villages situated along watercourses. Rockdale, which always has had a rural character, consisted in the early nineteenth century of seven hamlets situated along a three-mile stretch of Chester Creek in the lower Delaware Valley of southeastern Pennsylvania. In the time of the study, each of these hamlets came to be organized around a water-powered cotton mill that owed its existence to the comparatively steep drop of the stream bed over the three-mile stretch. Wallace shows how the natural features of the land and the necessities of a specific form of manufacturing conspired to influence the layout of each hamlet. He points out that the roads had to run "just so" and that the housing for workers had to be situated as close to the mill as possible. Higher up and farther away were the homes of the managerial personnel and the manufacturer or owner-manufacturer.

The people responsible for the industrial development were the men who bought the various mill properties (usually leftovers from previous water-powered operations). Sometimes, the owner of the mill site was also the manufacturer, but the owner usually leased the plant site and associated structures to someone who had accumulated enough capital to pay the lease, purchase the necessary equipment, hire managers and workers, and pay for the raw materials and transport to and from the mill. Wallace's study centers on the manufacturers (in some cases owner-manufacturers) who were the owners of the means of production and the ruling spirits of the hamlets of Rockdale.

These men were capitalists of an entrepreneurial sort, that is, they were willing to take considerable risks in seeking a profit. Risks were considerable because of the ups and downs of the cotton market, an often weak capital base, and competition from other cotton manufacturers in Rockdale, the rest of the United States, and abroad. Besides an entrepreneurial spirit, the personal qualities that contributed to success in small-scale cotton manufacturing at that time were an ability to inspire trust and confidence in personal relations (with the kinsmen and friends who provided capital, business contacts, employees, and even competitors), the patience necessary to start small and grow slowly, good business sense, and the technical know-how needed to recognize and implement useful innovations that would keep a factory up-to-date and competitive. The men did not need to be machine technicians themselves, but they had to be capable of drawing on knowledge about cotton manufacturing, which in the early part of the nineteenth century was changing rapidly.

The manufacturer (or owner-manufacturer) played a major role in shaping the culture of his hamlet. People were dependent on him for jobs, and their way of life was influenced not only by the work he provided, but by his general authority in community affairs. This was a system of more-or-less benign paternalism, and though workers did band together and even strike, and though there were those who flirted with more socialistic, that is, more communally based forms, the authority of the manufacturer to run his hamlet as he saw fit was never seriously challenged.

The manufacturer, as well as all of the other people of a hamlet, were creatures of a culture that involved small-scale capitalist enterprise and a factory system of production that could only develop so far, that is, it was limited by the potential for water-powered operations in this area. Wallace devotes considerable attention to the nature of the machines involved and to the people who created and dealt with them (the machine technicians, managers, and especially the manufacturers). One gets from him an intimate sense of the workplace, which is filled with picking and drawing machines and with the throstle, mule, and loom, all of these turned by a complex series of belts, shafts, and gears, as well as the human routines involved in working with them. Workers (there were usually several from each family in the hamlet, including children) were subject to rules designed to promote a general orderliness and precision of operation. (Rules involved cleanliness, punctuality, no smoking, no drinking of alcohol, no fighting, and no fooling around between the sexes.) The division of labor is seen to be affected by the machines and their arrangement, which were constantly being upgraded and displacing workers associated with them.

What kind of meaning did the people of Rockdale attach to their work? What to them was the point of their productive activity? Max Weber argued that certain kinds of Protestants in Europe and the United States worked in their jobs (callings) in order to save themselves in the afterlife. This and other versions of the belief in "salvation by works," that is, saving oneself in the afterlife by one's earthly activities, were to be found among the people of Rockdale. Referred to as Evangelicals by Wallace, these Protestants believed that it was possible simultaneously to pursue economic gain, help one's fellow humans, and accomplish personal salvation. Indeed, they felt obliged to do all three and to try to get others to do the same. Wallace views the development of Rockdale in part as a struggle of these Evangelicals, most of whom seemed to be of higher status, to make their views prevail among the nonbelievers and weakly spiritual in the community and outside. In short, they were missionaries (hence "Evangelicals").

So, the idea world of this community—or at least of the dominant people in the community—had a religious component that supported its industrial way of life. It was thought that some divine plan enjoined individuals to work out their own salvation not only by hard work, saving, and felicitous investments, but also by honesty in public dealing, church activity, and public service. Wallace quotes from personal documents to show how strongly some people in the community believed in this form of salvation by works. And because the people of higher rank appear to have had a strong sense of responsibility to convert others to the gospel as they saw it, their views, besides justifying a developing capitalist-industrial way of life, also appear to have provided support for a growing American imperialism in the world.

What is there about Wallace's study of Rockdale that is specifically anthropological? Couldn't it be considered a historical work, for example? Of course it could. Anthropologists, like other social scientists, are increasingly "trespassing" on what were once the preserves of other disciplines. Regardless of method and subject matter, however, they have a special intellectual heritage that others have only recently discovered. That heritage involves the concept of culture and the necessity of comprehending it wherever it occurs. Using personal documents and other historical materials, this is what Wallace has done in his study of Rockdale. As a result, the reader gets a realistic picture of these people who are "just down the road," as he puts it. The emerging species of social historian would have accomplished the same thing.

The picture that Wallace presents does not involve huge factories spewing smoke and other forms of pollution and degrading human beings in and around them. Here, something like a balanced equilibrium prevailed. Families appear to have been for the most part intact; and though there were social abuses (child labor and sometimes difficult working conditions, for example), most people appear to have gone along with what usually was a fairly benevolent, paternalistic social arrangement.

One problem with Wallace's study is the slight attention he gives to the context of this industrializing community. Where does Rockdale fit into the overall picture of industrialization in the United States? Wallace makes only vague references to other communities similar to Rockdale and to larger communities, such as Lowell, Massachusetts, with big industrial establishments. Where does the comparatively simple industrialism of Rockdale stand in relation to later, more expansive developments that involved widespread abuse of people and environment and significant conflict between management and labor? And what of the shadowy market that determined the ups and downs of production, the industrial competitors in Europe and America, and the cotton producers who provided the raw materials? All of these presumably played some role in the industrialization of Rockdale and should be brought into the picture.

Wallace also encounters a frequent problem with historical sources. Often, they concern people of higher social rank. Here, they tend to favor what Wallace refers to as "the managerial class." The letters of the manufacturers and their wives give us the best impression of real people in the book. Such people were the ones who, in this paternalistic community, had the most to do with shaping its culture, but one wonders about the humbler people of Rockdale who came and went more frequently. What were they like, and how did they view things in and outside of the mill? How did they take, for example, the efforts of some managers' wives to convert them? Information about such people has been obtained from live informants in some historical studies of industry, but in this case, the time frame was beyond the reach of this method.

These criticisms aside, Wallace's study does what any study of a culture should do. It reveals a way of life "in the round," that is, industrialism is seen to be a part of a whole way of life lived by a group of people. By showing how industrialization occurred in a specific case, Wallace was able to get a grip on a more general theory of culture change, one that involves the notion of a series of revolutionary inventions, each of which is elaborated over a period of time.

INDUSTRIALIZATION AND THE INDIVIDUAL

What does industrialization do to the individual? Earlier, it was pointed out that social scientists have associated certain sociocultural trends with industrialization. I say "associated" because I do not want to get hung up on the question of causation here. What is mainly responsible for these trends? Is it technological development, urbanization, or an increase in the scale of a variety of social tasks? Obviously, these are interrelated, but in the contemporary world, technology has come to assume a position of paramount importance. So, regardless of the nature of a culture (whether it tends towards socialism or capitalism, for example), as the scale and complexity of the technological task increases, so, too, will the social organization that goes with it. Consider as an example the Soviet or American space programs with their gargantuan technological tasks. Both have spawned enormous, complex organizations to run them. In such instances, there will be a greater specialization of the functions necessary to accomplish the organization's goals, as well as a more complex, bureaucratic system of authority that is needed to coordinate them.

What are the consequences of this for the individual? It means that he or she must deal with a greater variety of specialists, each of whom has a different perspective. Confronted with a greater number of alternatives, people fall back on their heels, so to speak, and rely increasingly on themselves. That this is, in fact, the case for contemporary America is demonstrated in a nationwide investigation by Carmi Schooler ("Social Antecedents of Adult Psychological Functioning"), which shows that employed American men who were raised in a more "complex, multifaceted environment," as, for example, in the Pacific states or in a city, tend to be more individuated, if intolerance of external constraints, subjectivism, and the development of intellectual capacities are taken to indicate this. The hypothesis also receives support from Geert Hofstede's cross-cultural study (*Culture's Consequences*) of the work-related attitudes of employees of a large multinational corporation, which shows a significant correlation between the general level of industrialism of an employee's country and his or her individualism. Data are hard to come by for socialist countries, but there, too, impressionistic observations suggest that the advance of the technological order is associated with a growing individuation.

What about the specific qualities of the increasingly individuated people required by the advancing industrial order? A number of more or less scientifically based suggestions come to mind. One way of making coherent sense out of all of these issues is to continue with the machine analogy that has dominated this discussion. If a society is heavily committed to the machine way of life, then its people ought to be more machinelike in their natures. They would, for example, be expected to put a higher value on scientific rationality, planning, and punctuality, which are essential elements of the logic of machine design and operation. Alex Inkeles and David Smith, in their cross-cultural study of developing people (*Becoming Modern*) show that, among other things, factory experience does indeed tend to inculcate these qualities.

Paradoxically, even though industrialization tends to foster individuation, it would also seem to undercut individuality. For a factory to function effectively, everyone in a specific job must behave, *at a minimum*, in exactly the same way. People on the assembly line cannot, for example, stop work whenever they feel like it. Ideally, there is little room for personal idiosyncracy on the job. This means that bodily functions, which have some logic of their own and which can never be completely socialized into machinelike ways, will become increasingly subject to the psychological mechanisms of suppression or repression. This would seem to account for the fact that, in a series of preliminary investigations, I have found evidence indicating that more industrialized peoples tend to be more alienated from their bodies, that is, less accepting of their bodies and their natural functions.

The transformation of the individual by industrialization is, of course, never so clear-cut as these hypotheses suggest. In the first place, it is difficult to find adequate cross-cultural data on the subject. Imagine, for example, trying to construct a cross-cultural instrument that would get at individualism, as Hofstede did. Second, there is evidence to indicate countervailing tendencies or throw-backs to earlier epochs at any stage of industrialism. There may be, for example, a vigorous informal culture in a modern factory or bureaucracy that is based on individual feelings and personal relations. The American coffee breaks and the Japanese outings, referred to earlier, are examples of this. In addition, family ties and feelings that are not supposed to enter into full-scale industrial operations can persist, and even be incorporated into them, as Wallace's study of Rockdale, discussed earlier, and Tamara Haraven's study of the mills of Manchester, New Hampshire (*Family Time and Industrial Time*) have amply shown. It would seem, then, that although the effects of industrialization on the individual can be considerable, even as people can never be completely socialized, they can never be fully transformed into machines.

CODA

It is all well and good for a more individuated person from an advanced industrial society to say that people cannot be made into machines (or, for that matter, into creatures of the state or some other social institution). But this possibly comforting idea is not the conclusion that an anthropologically trained person should draw. Looked at in anthropological terms, the culture of a highly industrialized people has both good and bad points. At the moment, however, some of the bad points are pretty disturbing. When all life on earth becomes threatened by certain cultural developments, one has to be concerned. Yet people may not want to think about it, or if they do think about it, feel there is little that can be done.

A little anthropological reflection would show that this is the way a culture comes to imprison the people who have created it. But as soon as one begins to think about the machine way of life and how dependent people are on it, one begins to loosen the hold that an industrial culture has on its people. The anthropologically trained person would see, as a matter of course, how machines and their operation pervade all areas of the culture and how they are tied up with the environment. Trained to think in terms of adaptation, he or she would also be able to delineate the harmful and beneficial consequences of such practices.

Having loosened the hold of culture by some anthropological consciousness raising, people now have a greater opportunity to choose. Surely, an important choice is whether to rule or be ruled by machines. Cultures are created by humans and maintained by them. Cultural ways can therefore be given up or changed. If, as seems likely, people decide that machines and the things that go with them are too good to be given up completely, the question becomes how to control them in order to maximize human benefits now and in the future. Ventures in "appropriate technology," in which the scale and complexity of machines and their operation are adjusted to the ends that people want to achieve, are examples of this. Thus, simple, small, wind-driven pumps, instead of electrically driven machines that depend on some huge power complex, might be used in small irrigation projects. Or, household enterprises could function along with factories to accomplish certain forms of production.

Finally, there is the question of how to implement the choices one makes about machines and their use. In some cases, it will appear that little can be done. There is not enough money; or some people with heavy investments in certain ways of doing things are too powerful. Possibly the side-effects on other aspects of the culture will be too damaging. But in other cases, the resources and freedom to make progress in a more desirable direction may exist. And possibly there may be situations that are entirely ripe for some desirable change. Now, with an awareness of how a culture operates and of the principles of culture change, informed people can act more effectively to implement their choices.

It is not only machine technology, but all culture traits that can be questioned and acted on this way. People who have studied anthropology know that though everyone becomes to some extent a creature of their culture, they are also capable of shaping it to better fulfill their own and collective needs. If she had read a little anthropology, the average American homemaker mentioned at the outset of this chapter might be aware of this—even early on a winter morning.

SELECTED REFERENCES

ARON, RAYMOND, *The Industrial Society*. New York: Frederick A. Praeger, 1967.

ASHER, ROBERT, *Connecticut Workers and Technological Change*. Storrs, Conn.: Center for Oral History, The University of Connecticut, 1983.

COOK, EARL, "The Flow of Energy in an Industrial Society," *Scientific American*, 225, no. 3 (September 1971), 134–44.
HARAVEN, TAMARA, *Family Time and Industrial Time*. Cambridge, England: Cambridge University Press, 1982.
HOFSTEDE, GEERT, *Culture's Consequences*. Beverly Hills, Calif.: Sage Publications, 1980.
HOSELITZ, BERT, and WILBERT MOORE, *Industrialization and Society*. Unesco-Mouton, 1963.
INKELES, ALEX, and DAVID SMITH, *Becoming Modern*. Cambridge, Mass.: Harvard University Press, 1974.
MEAD, MARGARET, *New Lives for Old*. New York: Mentor Books, 1956.
SCHOOLER, CARMI, "Social Antecedents of Adult Psychological Functioning," *American Journal of Sociology*, 78, no. 2 (September 1972), 229–332.
WALLACE, ANTHONY F. C., *Rockdale*. New York: Alfred A. Knopf, 1978.
WHITE, LESLIE, *The Evolution of Culture*. New York: McGraw-Hill, 1959.

Chapter Eleven

AMERICAN CULTURE: INDIVIDUALISM RAMPANT

THE PROBLEM

It is a challenge to try to comprehend American culture in a single, brief chapter. Consider some of the obstacles. First, there are always problems with studying one's own society. In an earlier part of this book it was pointed out that one takes a good deal of one's own culture for granted. As a result, the questioning attitude so necessary in any anthropological investigation may be lacking. Second, the United States is a big, complex, highly differentiated country. There is not one "city on a hill," to quote a phrase used by Ronald Reagan, but many "cities" with different ways of life. There is considerable variation according to wealth, region, ethnic and racial background, and gender, to mention only some of the differentiating factors. General statements about American culture, therefore, are more difficult to make than about, say, a comparatively simple hunting and gathering group such as the San. Third, American culture, like any culture, is multifaceted. Many different kinds of behavior make up a way of life, and to put them all together in some coherent way is a difficult task. Finally, any American knows that the ways in which things are done in this society are changing rapidly. To get at something that abides for more than a generation is not easy.

Despite such problems, anthropologists have been looking into American culture for some time. This has involved, mostly, the study of fringe elements such as the poor, the downtrodden, or strange religious sects with which anthropologists seem to have a special affinity. But anthropologists are now joining sociologists and other scientists to investigate more central aspects of the society. This work has provided the basis for the present chapter, which is informed with the anthropological perspective that has been cultivated in this book. In it, Americans are considered as one more of all the peoples it is the anthropologist's privilege to investigate. Americans, like all of the others, have a culture that has a history and fits into a social and natural context. From what we already know about it, this particular culture appears to be a very complex system of highly differentiated parts, which will make it extremely difficult to propose rules or norms that apply to all of the people. Generalizations may soon begin to founder in the melange of subcultural variability that is clearly evident. Is there *anything* that these obviously various Americans have in common?

One thing that many Americans share is what might be referred to as their middle-classness, and it is in the ideals of the American middle class that I propose to look for key elements of American culture. Over and over again in public surveys, the vast majority of Americans assign themselves to an amorphous category that they call the middle class. This is no surprise, considering the stress on equality that many students of the American scene, beginning with Tocqueville, have found in American life, as well as the current facts at our disposal. It is the members of the middle class, many of whom have recently left their ethnic identities behind, who establish the dominant tone of the culture. This is not to say that American Indians, recently arrived immigrants, or the considerable number of more or less deprived black Americans are unimportant. But these individuals tend to be something of the nature of outsiders, whose lives revolve around the predominantly white middle class. There are also the various power-wielding elites—the board members of the big corporations, the owners of expensive homes in Palm Beach or Palm Springs, the big donors to presidential campaigns and charity balls, or the more muscular, newly rich of the southwest—who, while undoubtedly accepting the perquisites of elite status, are nevertheless cautious about putting themselves too far above the great middling category. For them, even, the pull of middle-class values remains strong. In America, it is difficult to escape the influence of the middle ground.

The principal representatives of any culture are the people who have fully acquired or internalized it. On the whole, this comprises the adult generation, which means that children (who are in the process of acquiring the culture) cannot be of central concern to our study. Nor can the very old, some of whom suffer from failing faculties and (in a culture where change is endemic) maintain old-fashioned ways, or the mentally deranged or retarded occupy the foreground of this investigation. Again, the study of such people and their ways is important, but not when one is trying to get at the focus of the culture. Consider, then, the more than one hundred million, mentally healthy, American middle-class adults. What is central to their way of life? Many views have been offered about this. Charles Wilson of General Motors said that the business of America (and of these adults) was business. Tocqueville and others have stressed the strain towards equality among Americans, while Gunnar Myrdahl pointed out the paradox of inequality (especially between blacks and whites) in a society that is professedly egalitarian. Americans have been seen as dominated by capitalism (a form of economic activity), industrialism (a form of production), or having a political organization that stresses the separation of church and state. Max Weber saw America as the secularized heir-apparent of the Protestant Ethic. The United States has been viewed as a nation of joiners and filled with people who are friendly, open, and relaxed. It has been pictured as a world power, but with people who don't know very much about the world. Americans have been said to pursue material accumulation and to look to the future rather than the past. And so on.

What can be made of this vast range of more or less apt generalizations about Americans and their culture? Is there some key element that can be found in this cornucopia of labels? Obviously, to some extent one finds what one is looking for. Those interested in the economic facts of life will tend to look in that direction. But interest alone does not determine what we see. Is there some central thing *out there* that constitutes the focus of American life? I think that there is such a focus.

American culture revolves around the *ideal of the autonomous self*. Americans are highly individualistic, and they would like to think of themselves as detached, self-governing people.

Something of the nature of this self was intimated in an earlier chapter when comparisons were made between Americans and Japanese. It is important to keep in mind that the self we are considering is a culturally structured or constituted self, which is a distillation of tendencies that can be observed not only in individuals, but in the various idea worlds of the culture. In the advertisements, the movies, the songs, the agendas of the educational and therapeutic establishments, and the slogans of businesspeople and politicians, it is possible to discern the ideal of personal autonomy that, in my opinion, is the focus of American culture.

Many observers, beginning perhaps with the Frenchman, Alexis de Tocqueville, have noted the highly individualistic strain among Americans. To cite one recent example, Geert Hofstede, in the cross-cultural study of job-related attitudes among employees of the multinational corporation, which has been referred to at various points in this book, found that American employees were the most individualistic of the forty different nationalities that were tested. American individualism has been conceived and evaluated in different ways, but it is the rare observer of the American scene who has not been struck by it.

Where does this individualism come from? What are its determinants? Here, I will mention only some of the causes that have been suggested. Certainly, American individualism is at least partially derived from English individualism. In *The Origins of English Individualism*, Alan Macfarlane has traced this trait back into the Middle Ages. Industrialism also would seem to have contributed to it. As was pointed out in the last chapter, individualism is everywhere associated with industrialization, and America is perhaps the most industrialized nation of the world. Many observers have referred to the American version of a competitive, private enterprise economy as a cause. Protestantism, with its emphasis on the individual's direct relation to God, has been implicated. Some authors have suggested that the European-derived current of political ideas that flowed through the pens of the American founding fathers was responsible. Others have pointed to the wide-open spaces, especially on the frontier. Whatever the reasons, they have conspired to make Americans one of the most individualistic of peoples in the world today. In the United States, the self has come to be separated out from the context in which it must function. It stands increasingly alone, and despite rising collective pressures from the big bureaucracies and mass media, which Americans have created to organize their social life, it still persists. What is its specific nature?

THE AUTONOMOUS IDEAL

"I've Gotta Be Me" is the lyric of a popular song. Frank Sinatra, the singer who made it popular, seems to have taken the song writer's advice. The heroes played by the movie actor, John Wayne, or the various private eyes that fill American television screens, are people who manage to be true to themselves in an often uncooperative world. Many Americans would like to be like them. What is the nature of the self that goes with such a character? First, it is separate or distinct from others. There are clear boundaries between it and what belongs to it and the rest of the world. Second, it is thought to be located within the individual and not, for example, in his or her relationships with others. Third, this self is supposed to be the result of one's own choosing. Though responsive to social considerations, the individual makes up his or her mind about who to be and how to act. And finally, even though socially aware and involved, this self (when push comes to shove) is considered to be more important than any other. This is the American ideal, which, as it turns out, many Americans fall short of realizing. The struggle to come to terms with this ideal, which is the main theme of the modern existential novel, is in fact the story of a typical American's life. Born into a society where who one is to be is not laid out early in life, and faced with the difficult task of making sense out of the definitional input from a complex society in flux, Americans tend to be in a position of weakness when it comes to making up their mind about who they are. Is it any wonder that they may relapse into a reliance on outside elements in making their decisions? Such a reliance has its problems, however. In contrast to the people in simpler, more tradition-bound societies, Americans have difficulty identifying with such forces. The ideal of personal autonomy and the nature of American society prevent it.

That Americans have a tendency to think of themselves as separate and distinct from others is revealed in a study by Richard Shweder and Edmund Bourne ("Does the Concept of Person Vary Cross-Culturally?"). They asked people from Chicago, Illinois, and the state of Orissa in India to describe close acquaintances. Responses were categorized and compared statistically. Shweder and Bourne found that Americans were more likely to use abstract, context-independent terms in their descriptions. For example, an American might say that an acquaintance was "stubborn," "friendly," or "difficult." Though the Indians used terms like these, they were more likely to say something such as, "He shouts curses at his neighbors," or, "He jokes with his friends." This indicates that the Indian notion of person is more concrete and context-dependent. Indians are less likely to distinguish or separate the individual from specific others or situations. If the self is considered to be the subjective aspect of a person, this comparative study suggests that Americans are indeed more likely to think of themselves as separate and distinct from others.

Such a self obviously has its uses in a society where individual mobility is high. Americans tend to define themselves as detached individuals, which permits them to cut ties to specific people or situations more readily and move on (or up?). Indeed, part of the self-realization project of a typical American involves breaking free from ascribing influences such as the family, relatives, or community. College students who go away from home are involved in this process, and they may experience some of its difficulties, one of which is trying to make sense of a shifting, ambiguous world. In contrast to other peoples, Americans encounter greater confusion in their life courses. They find fewer tried-and-true recipes for defining themselves in a way that enables them to act with assurance. Ultimately, Americans are supposed to make up their minds about this, but many find this hard to do. For assistance, they may look to culturally emphasized areas that, depending on how one uses them, can provide either support or fulfillment. Among the more important of these areas are the worlds of work, material objects, and other selves.

Work is the area *par excellence* of what Robert Bellah and his associates refer to, in *Habits of the Heart*, as utilitarian individualism. To know what an American does—more specifically, the kind of work he or she does—is to get a preliminary idea about who that person is. At the beginning of the usual public opinion survey is a question about the respondent's occupation. Americans answer the question with "salesman," "machinist," "engineer," "housewife," and so on, and in so doing, they begin to define themselves. The importance of the job for many Americans is dramatically apparent at times of layoffs or retirement. In addition to sometimes severe economic pressure and associated anxiety there can also be a loss of identity; at such times an American may begin to creep about in an apologetic way until the job is restored and the self is once again secured. The job that the American has should also have prospects for the future. These people like to think of themselves as being on their way up to higher levels of income, power, or prestige. Women of a previous generation were more likely to depend on their husbands for their identity, and accordingly, referred to their spouse's achievements in the world when defining themselves. Now, they are more apt to pursue self-realization on their own, and they also entertain American visions of success, which, like happiness, is a goal with a quicksilver quality about it.

A job involves work, and to be involved in work is still important to Americans. A part of the *doing* orientation that many observers have attributed to these people, work seems somewhat less important than it once was in America. College students, for example, may be told by parents or professors that they don't know the meaning of work. There is probably some truth in this. They no longer feel the same pull of work the way the older generation did. Instead, there has been a rise in importance of institutions that cater to what Bellah and his associates refer to as expressive individualism. The vacation is increasingly an end in itself rather than a time to renew oneself for work. Leisure industry stocks are good bets for growth on the New York Stock Exchange. Retirement villages are springing up, especially in southern regions. In these villages, older Americans are exploring activities that open up new, more expressive areas of themselves. And for Americans who have trouble finding satisfaction with such things as games, hobbies, and pure sociability, there are any number of therapists or counselors who will try to help them express their feelings and gain satisfaction from *being* rather than *doing*. Though this trend is well under way, it would be a mistake to say that expressivity has supplanted the utilitarian attitude as the dominant orientation of American individualism. Work continues to be a cornerstone of American culture.

A second area in which Americans can gain self-support or fulfillment is in the realm of the material. The pursuit of wealth (a material symbol) is an overriding concern. If not making money, an American tends to feel some sense of inadequacy. All of the things that Americans identify with can be partially or wholly reduced (in their minds) to money. Consider their world of material objects. In an earlier era, things that one produced, such as a bridge, a railroad locomotive, or a loaf of bread probably played a more important part in Americans' conception of self than they do now. As alienation of the worker from the finished product has advanced, and as the service sector has expanded, it has become more difficult to think of oneself as a producer of some product. Instead, there is the realm of consumer goods. People buy houses and begin to think of them as their own. Or one believes the diet faddist who claims that "you are what you eat." People accumulate material possessions that become more or less tied up with themselves. Take, for example, the car, that archtypical prop for the American male identity. A young fellow may believe that he should have a high-powered machine that gives him a head start at the stoplight. Later on in life, he may move towards more sedate and opulent models. The purchase of a new car adds something to the self, but that something has to be renewed periodically. So, the American, urged on by a crescendo of advertising, is in the market for a new car more and more frequently. He may even purchase more than one to express different aspects of himself or provide for different members of his family. On the female side, clothes function in the same way. American women (more than men) think of themselves in terms of the clothes they are wearing. One must have on the correct dress for the occasion or time. Women renew themselves through the endless cycles of fashion, which are watched with radarlike sensitivity. In the workplace, they must worry about wearing the correct "uniform" and thus presenting themselves properly. On a night out they may want to exhibit a greater uniqueness, which David Riesman has called "marginal differentiation." American women, of course, are not alone in such preoccupations. Clothes are important to women in other cultures (for example, in France). How important clothes are, and what role they play in peoples' identities, can only be determined by cross-cultural investigations that have yet to be done.

Material accumulation is considered important in American society. Unlike the San, wandering hunters and gatherers for whom the accumulation of possessions amounts to excess baggage, Americans live in a culture where the desire for material things is supposed to continually expand. In *Culture Against Man*, Jules Henry traces the connections between an ever-expanding productivity and the characters of different kinds of Americans. He points out that, in contrast to a primitive society where (if all goes well) production rises to meet wants, American wants *must* rise to meet production. So, there have to be homemakers who feel a threat to their identity if they do not have the latest kitchen utensil and generals who experience fear if they do not have the latest missile in order to keep America ahead of the Russians. In their fascinating study of material possessions in contemporary American life (*The Meaning of Things*), Mihaly Csikszentmihalyi and Eugene Rochberg-Hilton point out the Americans have carried material accumulation so far that they have entered a phase of "terminal materialism," that is, a period when material possessions begin to be acquired for their own sake.

I have saved for last what may be the most interesting area for American identity work, that is, the world of other selves. The weakly autonomous will depend on others to tell them who they are, while the strong find in others a path to fulfillment. Whether they begin from strength or weakness, most Americans are enthusiastic participants in social life. It would seem that they need others almost as much as they need to stand alone. Many Americans are constantly "on the make," with their renowned openness and friendliness, to get others to respond to them in a way that tells them they are accepted—even loved—and that therefore they are *somebody*. How important this is for their self-conceptions is quickly apparent when strategies that have proven routinely effective at home do not work, as in a Vietnamese prisoner-of-war camp or with Frenchmen for whom friendships tend to be long-standing affairs and not easy to acquire.

How do Americans think of the other selves in their world? There are two general classes of such beings: those who play by the same rules and who are therefore entitled to a fair shake and those who do not. Ideally, every American is considered to have an equal right to exercise his or her self-interest provided that others' self-interest is not violated. Competition can be fierce in America and many competitors fall by the wayside, but the competition ought to be carried on according to the principle of fair play. This is why Joe Paterno, the highly successful Penn State football coach, has so much contempt for cheaters. They are not living up to the American ideal. Those who fail should not do so because others cheat, but because of some fault of their own (perhaps they haven't worked hard enough). This is at least part fiction because not all Americans are prepared to compete on equal terms. Paterno, for example, has all those sons of coal miners and steel workers living nearby who can be turned into linebackers. An American may be aware of the fiction involved here, but usually not enough to give it up as a guiding principle. A visit to a Third World country where people who get an advantage over others are expected to use it, and where life is a continual round of dominance and submission, would show a skeptical American how important this principle is for him or her.

Let us resort to an American metaphor: the ballpark. Outside of this ballpark are others who play by different or opposing rules. These people, who vary according to current American preoccupations, can be used as negative points of reference in defining the self. For a former generation, it was the Fascists, especially Nazi Germans. Since World War II, there has been the Communist threat, which continues unabated under what is believed to be the direction of Soviet Russia. There are terrorists spilling out of the Middle East and revolutionaries and hardened criminals spawned in big city ghettoes. "People who won't work" and who collect welfare checks for a living have always been targets of American strivers. For fundamentalists, that great abstraction of all evils, Satan, provides the supreme negative point of reference. And finally, there are members of current out-groups, racially, economically, or politically defined, against whom Americans define themselves.

On the positive side, that is, in one's own ballpark, there is considerable room for maneuver. Here are one's equals of the moment or better-than-equals whom one would like to emulate. They include advertising models who are manipulated to generate more desire (and therefore consumption), the people in one's own profession, the so-called Joneses whom Americans try to keep up with, and so on. In contrast to peoples living in simpler, more tradition-bound societies, Americans have more of a choice about whom they are going to "play" with. Jules Henry's acute analysis of American adolescents is an appropriate way of introducing the problems they face. American adolescents, he points out, are confronted with the challenge of leaving their families' orbit and getting involved in new personal communities. In order to do this they must make themselves appealing. Henry, using the adolescents' discussions of their own problems, demonstrates how unsure of themselves these young people are and how much anxiety they feel in their social life. This anxiety would seem to be, in essence, a matter of self-definition. American adolescents are bent on finding themselves through the responses of others, and they spend a good deal of their time presenting themselves in ways they hope will give them the kind of response they need.

One of Arthur Miller's characters, Willie Loman (in *The Death of a Salesman*), is an overgrown adolescent who, permanently unsure of himself, failing in his job, and past middle age, has dreams of being loved in Scarsdale, Providence, and other cities on his round. This, for him, is the primary measure of success. Loman, is, of course, a fictitious character, but Miller seems to have put his finger on a principal preoccupation of many Americans for whom achievement and the self-realization that goes with it are measured in terms of the acceptance, recognition, and even love they manage to wring from others.

The tragedy of Willie Loman illustrates the dangers of a context-dependent self in this society. Here is a man whom the world has passed by, and because he was dependent on that world for a sense of self, he succumbed. Whether it is through work or leisure, the material realm, or others that one finds self-definition, the context-dependent option can have only limited success in America. This is so because, in contrast to Orissa, India, where a more stable social world provides the long-term, consistent feedback that is necessary for a firm sense of self,

Americans live in a world of flux that offers conflicting and confusing signals about who they should be. For this reason, it would seem that a context-independent strategy of self-realization would be the more adaptive course in this society. That this course is being followed by Americans (how many?) has been suggested by the study of Shweder and Bourne mentioned earlier. That this option has also been accompanied by steps toward true autonomy has been confirmed by a nationwide investigation by Carmi Schooler, which was mentioned in the last chapter. And, in a rebuttal to those critics who argue that this development spells trouble for individual Americans, Schooler found that people with a more autonomous self had a greater feeling of self-worth. What was earlier regarded as a utopian goal for Americans and other advanced industrialized peoples by David Riesman and his associates (in *The Lonely Crowd*), that is, the development of individuals with more assured, autonomous selfs who carry out their lives on the basis of personal choice rather than external dictation, may be on the way to realization, in which case the American cultural ideal will be fulfilled. Considering the vast social forces that are arrayed against individuals in this society, however, this realization can never be accomplished easily.

THE CULTURE OF THERAPY: AMERICAN STYLE

In a Woody Allen movie, almost everyone seems to have a shrink. This is an exaggeration—even for Manhattan—but there are certainly many Americans who, struggling with problems of self-definition, are resorting to psychotherapy. In Hollywood I once asked a psychiatrist how business was. His response: "Are you kidding?" The American therapeutic establishment is flourishing as more and more clients, dissatisfied with the way their lives are turning out, beat a path to its doors.

This establishment consists of psychiatrists, counselors, psychologists, social workers, religious practitioners, and the like who adhere to a variety of therapeutic systems. Some of these people deal with psychotics and use drugs and hospitalization as principal methods of treatment, but even these are likely to treat neuroses and behavior disorders for which some kind of psychotherapy is indicated. It is these kinds of disorders and their treatment that I will consider here. The treatment is carried out by an establishment that turns out to have a subculture of its own. Using the information gathered by Robert Bellah and his associates as a principal source, I want to lay out some of the essential elements of this subculture and show how it is connected to the key fact of American culture, which is the self.

These days it is considered more and more acceptable for a troubled American to seek professional help from a therapist. This therapist may work one-on-one, with a couple, or with a small group. Medication may be prescribed, but ideally the form of treatment involves people talking to each other. In orthodox psychoanalytic therapy the patient does almost all of the talking, and other therapies try to keep the interventions of the therapist to a minimum.

The asymmetrical relationship between patient and therapist is contractual, that is, the patient is paying for the service of listening and intervention now and then; it is segmental, that is, it represents only a part of the participant's current life; it is ideally profound on the part of the patient, that is, strong feelings and significant changes can result; and finally, it is (hopefully) of short duration. The patient usually follows a fixed routine: regular sessions with the therapist and routinized procedures. Eventually, he or she is expected to leave the relationship and go it alone. Experts are uncertain about how much improvement is accomplished by this "talking cure," as one of Freud's patients called it, but its effectiveness is not at issue here. One might also raise questions about the prevailing custom in upper-class Britain a century or more ago of going to the French Riviera to cure bronchial ailments. A criticism of the effectiveness of a system of therapy need not invalidate its influence over peoples' behavior.

What are the reigning beliefs of the American therapeutic establishment? Bellah and his colleagues got at some of these by interviewing practitioners, clients, and bystanders who share (more or less) the views of the first two. Indeed, they found that the beliefs of the establishment permeate the society. They have been selectively adopted in the workplace, the political arena, and the church, for example. The first of these beliefs (which Bellah and his coworkers seem to have assumed) is that if conditions are right, some form of healing will take place. The establishment tends to be upbeat about its effectiveness. The prevailing view seems to be that if experience made the problem, other experience can unmake it. They, like the American educational establishment, may recognize that the possibilities for change are not limitless, but they certainly feel that they are considerable. Second, they believe that a large part of therapeutic progress is up to the patient. The patient must take an active role in the treatment. Third, they believe that during the course of therapy the patient must gain greater insight into, and acceptance of, the forces that move him or her. If there has been, for example, repression or selective forgetting of anger towards the opposite sex, it must be recognized and accepted, which enables the patient to gain a degree of control over the once-hidden force. Fourth, it is desirable for the patient to give up a sense of unreasonable obligation to others, as in neurotic guilt, for example. Ideally, you should come to realize that you do not owe others anything and that you should take responsibility only for your own actions. Others may be important to you, but you should act not for their sake, but for what they mean to (do for?) you. This means that a person stops running after others to define himself or herself. The American therapeutic ideal (in contrast to that of the Japanese mentioned in an earlier chapter) promotes an individual who knows who he or she is without a lot of feedback from outside and who accepts this knowledge, whatever it amounts to. The individual, thus, becomes the source of his or her own standards and is truly autonomous.

Bellah and his associates were worried about the social consequences of this radical individualism and they vigorously questioned some of their respondents to see how far they would take it. Asked if she would ever accept responsibility for another, one respondent said no. Was she responsible for her husband? No. And what about her children? Were they responsible for their own acts? Though hedging a bit, she nevertheless answered in the affirmative. So, in the end one is responsbile only to oneself. People should know themselves and know how others fit into their life. In their relationship with others they do have a responsibility to be open and aboveboard, but that is all. They should act in terms of enlightened self-interest, and if a relationship no longer satisfies that self-interest it should end.

All of this illustrates how different elements of a culture go together. In this case a therapeutic institution has arisen to deal with problems of the key element of a culture, the self. In America the process of individuation is far advanced, which means that people are very much on their own when it comes to establishing an identity. They have their problems, however. Attempts to define oneself by reference to the external world (the context-dependent option) do not work as well in America as in a simpler and more stable preindustrial setting such as Orissa. But the alternative strategy of developing a more context-independent self that will permit one to move with assurance in a shifting, impersonal world is not so easy in this society. Many people need help. Some of this is provided by a burgeoning institution of psychotherapy that aims to produce the truly autonomous selves that are the American ideal.

However effective American therapists are in solving people's personal problems, they cannot solve all of them. Intrapsychic conflict can never be eliminated, and problems of the individual with others and in society will continue. American psychotherapists, for example, cannot guarantee that a successfully treated person will find the long-term, intimate relationship he or she has been encouraged to look for.

And it would be difficult to give most Americans the feeling that their own affairs and those of the dominant institutions of their society are closely intertwined. American society itself also has its problems, which would appear to be beyond the reach of individual-oriented therapies. What, for example, can the American practice of psychotherapy do about the growing gap between rich and poor in America and the world? What is the answer to the many problems of an environmental nature, booms and busts in the economy, or the threat of nuclear holocaust that now threatens all life on earth? It is clear that even if all Americans do realize themselves perfectly, this realization cannot be a panacea for them or for other peoples. Freud, of course, was aware of all of this, but many American psychotherapists, who have taken on the effort-optimism orientation of this culture, tend to forget.

THE AMERICAN SELF IN ACTION

Despite problems with a world that seems to be getting more and more out of control and despite personal problems, most Americans remain optimistic about their life and the possibility of making it better. Constantly on the move towards some future goal or other, they tend to be impatient with past practices and with history. There is routine, of course, but in this culture routines are made to be broken. Americans seem to feel best when they are on their way somewhere or planning something new. In their various projects they like to take the most efficient course. "Time is money," they say, and it always seems to be "a-wasting." Speedy accomplishment is desirable, and the resulting frenetic pace of American life has been remarked upon by many observers. But Americans' speed is highly controlled and focussed. They set goals for themselves and move forward step by step to reach them. If there is a particularly large job to be done, such as trying to put someone on the moon, it is divided up into a series of rationally organized, manageable problems. In working on a problem they find it desirable to rule out all extraneous matters, which contrasts with the less task-specific behavior of people in less industrialized countries. Americans would find the behavior of a group of pot-making gypsies I once encountered rather bizarre. There they sat, those gypsies, chatting with each other and enjoying the give-and-take. Every now and again one or another would give a few whacks to a pot they were making. Their production moved forward slowly and unsystematically, it seemed to me, and I, being an American, was acutely frustrated by the irrationality of it all. I thought of my father's saying ("When you work, work, and when you play, play.") and my mother's ("Get a move on.")

and wondered why these people could not see the self-evident truth of such propositions. Other overseas Americans such as Peace Corps representatives and medical technicians who are trying to get their less industrialized hosts to adopt more efficient procedures have been similarly frustrated.

In going about their various projects in life, Americans like to think that they have their destinies pretty much in their own hands. They are supposed to live in the "land of the free." This ticket to apparent anarchy, or what has been called the war of each against all, does not in fact produce such dire consequences because Americans' freedom is strictly limited. One has freedom, true, but one also must recognize that others are entitled to a similar freedom that has to be respected. In addition, there is the need to be liked that was discussed earlier. The result of this is not a high degree of individuality, but rather, considerable conformity. As Florence Kluckhohn once said, "In America one is free to be like everyone else."

Sometimes peoples' projects get tangled up with one another. Then, it is considered appropriate for the individual to confront the other directly and not beat about the bush. Nurses may have trouble doing this with doctors, but assertiveness training courses are now helping them to do what others are supposed to do when really pressed. Problems between individuals and groups are thought to have some rationally based solution if only everyone will declare themselves and give a little. This is the way their democratic society is supposed to operate. The fact that it does not always do so, and that legal and governmental remedies are necessary, does not invalidate the moving power of this point of view. Despite evident contradictions here, as indicated by the increasing numbers of people who resort to these remedies (America has been called a litigious society), there remains a strong belief that, through individual initiative, things will work out. There is a can-do attitude and an essential optimism that this, combined with American know-how and effort, can solve most problems. This is especially the case when it comes to huge technological accomplishments such as space flight or in the development of a mammouth organizational structure such as IBM. People everywhere marvel at these feats of engineering and social engineering.

Americans, themselves, take satisfaction in the grand scale of their accomplishments, but their identification with them is superficial. Consider how often Americans use "they" rather than "we" in referring to the powerful others like the Pentagon, or Union Carbide, which can have important influence on their lives. Instead, they tend to look to more intimate groups such as the family, the small community, a club, or small friendship groupings on and off the job for support and fulfillment. In these circles they will try to "really get to know" others. However, in contrast to smaller, more intimate societies, getting to know and understand others in America is not easy. The comings and goings of people, the numbers involved, and the existence of special interests prevent it. And there will always be the possibility that what the other one is trying—perhaps desperately—to reach will be, like oneself, little more than a series of lightly held social postures, and thus rather empty.

Americans now know that there are a lot of problems in this world that they cannot solve; yet they continue to have great faith in the self and its abilities to accomplish things. A visit to a gathering of salespeople, a real estate developer's presentation, a political convention, or a backyard cookout in suburbia will convince even the most hardened cynic about this. There seems to be no question that this is a nation of optimists. But there is another side of these Americans that comes out, say, on a visit to the Vietnam memorial in Washington, or at a time when someone has drunk too much, or possibly on awakening in the dark of night. Then there are the fears, the most important of which in this society so dedicated to achievement and success is the fear of failure. These people may fear that they won't amount to much, that others won't have a good opinion of them, that the results of their individual efforts may not measure up to someone's expectations, or that all of their efforts and the efforts of like-minded others will be defeated by some atheist in the Kremlin, some madman in the Middle East, or some so-far uncontrollable disease out of Africa. And finally, there is the ultimate fear of all. It is that the self they prize so highly and which they have struggled so hard to realize will, like all other living things, eventually die.

SELECTED REFERENCES

BELLAH, R. N., R. MADSEN, W. SULLIVAN, A. SWIDLER, and S. TIPTON, *Habits of the Heart: Individualism and Commitment in Family Life*. Berkeley, Calif.: University of California Press, 1985.

CSIKSZENTMIHALYI, MIHALI, and EUGENE ROCHBERG-HILTON, *The Meaning of Things*. Cambridge: Cambridge University Press, 1981.

HALLOWELL, A. IRVING, *Culture and Experience*. Philadelphia, Pa.: University of Pennsylvania Press, 1955.

HEISS, JEROLD, *The Social Psychology of Interaction*. Englewood Cliffs, N.J.: Prentice Hall, 1981.

HENRY, JULES, *Culture Against Man*. New York: Random House, 1965.

HOFSTEDE, GEERT, *Culture's Consequences*. San Francisco, Calif.: Sage Publications, 1980.

KLUCKHOHN, FLORENCE, and FRED STRODTBECK, *Variations in Value Orientations*. New York: Row, Peterson, 1961.

LUKES, STEPHEN, *Individualism*. New York: Harper and Row, 1973.

MACFARLANE, ALAN, *The Origins of English Individualism*. New York: Cambridge University Press, 1979.

MEAD, MARGARET, *And Keep Your Powder Dry*. New York: William Morrow, 1965.

RIESMAN, DAVID, with N. GLAZER and R. DENNEY, *The Lonely Crowd*. New Haven, Conn.: Yale University Press, 1965.

SCHOOLER, CARMI, "Social Antecedents of Adult Psychological Functioning," *American Journal of Sociology*, 78, September 1972, 299–322.

SHWEDER, RICHARD, and EDMUND BOURNE, "Does the Concept of Person Vary Cross-Culturally?," in *Culture Theory: Essays in Mind, Self, and Emotion*, eds. Richard Shweder and Robert Levine. New York: Cambridge University Press, 1984.

STEWART, EDWARD, *American Cultural Patterns: A Cross-Cultural Perspective*. Chicago, Ill.: Intercultural Network, 1972.

TOCQUEVILLE, ALEXIS DE, *Democracy in America*. New York: Shocken, 1961.

Chapter Twelve

THE END?

This little venture into the anthropological domain is now finished. In it, the reader has been introduced to cultural ways that peoples of the earth have created and according to which they live. Compared with other animals, humans have a great capacity to adapt to the circumstances in which they live; but the adaptations of groups of people, once created, tend to solidify into social heritages that take on a momentum of their own. Persistence and change in these heritages or cultures is limited by their history and the context in which they exist. People have to live in groups and participate in their cultures in order to survive. This means that a good deal of their behavior is culturally dictated. One of the benefits of anthropological study is to reveal the sometimes hidden nature of our culture's control over us and the possibilities for individual freedom.

A good deal of anthropological work aims to explore particular cultures in depth, to find out how different aspects of a way of life hang together, and to work out the manner in which individuals fit into them. But anthropologists are also inveterate comparers. They like to find out the ways in which cultures differ from one another as well as the things they have in common. The peoples of the earth have developed an immense cornucopia of cultural ways, and any good library is filled with reports on hundreds—even thousands—of them. In this little book, the reader has been exposed to a number of cultures from different parts of the world and has been given the opportunity to compare them. One comparison that people like to make is between their own and other cultures. So it was with Samantha Smith, a young American, who made a visit to Russia at the invitation of the Soviet government. After her little bit of "fieldwork," Samantha Smith said that "down deep, they are just like us." There are those who would disagree with this assessment, but whatever its validity, it illustrates a mental process that often follows exposure to another culture, a process that has been developed to a high art in anthropology. Needless to say, a lot may hinge on particular comparisons of cultures, and they sometimes had best not be left to initial impressions of amateurs.

Besides being exposed to different cultures and guided in making comparisons between them, readers of this book have been introduced to the ways in which anthropologists explain why cultures, or particular aspects of cultures, are as they are. Why do the Tiv often purchase wives? Why are they patrilineal? Why don't the head men of the little Basseri bands have power to make decisions on their own? Why are the Japanese more collectively oriented than the Americans? These are the kinds of questions that begin to nag at us even as we begin to explore other cultures. Anthropologists have created a number of explanatory schemes, but all of them must take into account the fact that any culture trait has been created, and is maintained, by peoples who are subject to certain biologically dictated constraints and that it is a part of a whole culture that has a history and that fits into a particular context. Some of the ways in which anthropologists have worked out explanations have been touched on in this book.

In the foregoing, I have tried to suggest that readers who have finished reading *A Little Anthropology* have only begun to explore the human condition or conditions. If the book is, in fact, a genuine introduction, many readers will not want to stop here, but will want to continue on their own or in formal coursework. Perhaps they will take a crash course on the eve of some overseas assignment or begin a little fieldwork after they get there. For them, then, the anthropological quest will have only begun. They will not want it to end here.

The study of anthropology is not always simply an intellectual exercise, however. It can also contribute to a person's definition of self. In our encounter with other peoples, we are drawn out of ourselves into the world of others. We try on these others' roles in the same way as we have tried on the roles of fathers, mothers, and other significant others in our lives. Like new clothes, we may reject them, covet them, or accept them with alterations, but we are always asking, "Is this me?" Ethnographic reports, persuasively presented, provide a fertile field for self-realization. They can add to the crisis of identity that affects people, especially young people in complex, rapidly changing societies like the United States, but they can also spark creative solutions to identity problems.

As with former university students who give up academic pursuits when they take a job and start a family, some individuals will close out their search for an identity early in life. For them, further exposure to new and different others will only firm up what they already are. On the other hand, there are people who remain open to new experience of the kind that can come from travel or further study of anthropology. When they have finished *A Little Anthropology*, therefore, they will not have closed the book on self-realization. It will not end here, but will continue throughout their lives.

Another kind of awareness that can be promoted by the study of anthropology has to do with the links we have with our fellow humans. However cut off from others we may be, anthropology makes us aware that we are part of larger wholes. First, we are a part of some society, and second, of humanity. In a world in which the give and take between peoples has become an unremarkable fact of life, the poet's observation that no man is an island is more relevant than ever. Anthropologists have taken the lead in publicizing the condition of Third World peoples whose welfare, and even survival, are dependent on forces emanating from the industrialized world. A new journal, *Cultural Survival Quarterly*, makes the point repeatedly that there are many peoples whose environment and way of life are threatened by outside forces beyond their control. What will happen to the Mbuti Pygmies when the forest on which they depend is cut down? And what is to be the fate of all the "little people" of the world who happen to live in areas where big power conflicts are being played out?

It is clear, though, that the problem of survival is not now confined to the little peoples of the world. It has become a problem for us all. Humankind in the latter stages of the twentieth century is faced with the distinct possibility that it will wipe itself out by its own hand. The morning paper warns of a new escalation in the arms race between the superpowers, a step that could result in eliminating us all a few times over. Buried on a back page are reports of further deaths from a nuclear accident in Russia. These are reminders of the unthinkable thought that the end of the human saga that has been documented by anthropologists may be drawing near.

In times of great troubles in the past, prophets have sometimes emerged to define the plight of their people and point the way to new adaptations. In the anthropological literature there are stories of prophets like Handsome Lake of the Iroquois and Wovoka of the Paiutes and the movements they have founded. In the current world crisis, there are people like Jonathan Schell (*The Fate of the Earth*) who speak of the nuclear threat to all humanity and perhaps to life itself. Their words ought to fall on fertile ground among the anthropologically trained, that is, those who have considered the entire human enterprise and formed some notion of its value. They, it would seem, bear a larger share of responsibility for the fate of humankind because they have a better idea of what is at stake. Is there, indeed, a future for the whole human enterprise that they have just begun to comprehend in *A Little Anthropology*, or is it to end?

REFERENCE

SCHELL, JONATHAN, *The Fate of the Earth*. New York: Alfred A. Knopf, Inc., 1982.

INDEX